PENGUIN BOOKS

The Haven

Fiona Neill is a *Sunday Times* bestselling author and journalist. She worked as a foreign correspondent in Central America for six years and returned to the UK as assistant editor at *Marie Claire* before joining *The Times Magazine* as assistant editor. She has written features for many publications, including *The Times*, *Sunday Times Style* and the *Telegraph Magazine*, as well as having written a screenplay of her first novel for the BFI. Fiona grew up in rural North Norfolk and lives in London with her husband and three children. *The Haven* is her seventh novel.

The Haven

FIONA NEILL

PENGUIN BOOKS

PENGUIN BOOKS

UK | USA | Canada | Ireland | Australia
India | New Zealand | South Africa

Penguin Books is part of the Penguin Random House group of companies
whose addresses can be found at global.penguinrandomhouse.com

First published by Penguin Michael Joseph 2024
Published by Penguin Books 2024

001

Copyright © Fiona Neill, 2024

The moral right of the author has been asserted

Typeset by Jouve (UK), Milton Keynes
Printed and bound in Great Britain by Clays Ltd, Elcograf S.p.A.

The authorized representative in the EEA is Penguin Random House Ireland,
Morrison Chambers, 32 Nassau Street, Dublin D02 YH68

A CIP catalogue record for this book is available from the British Library

ISBN: 978–1–405–93681–1

In memory of Dad and Rosita

'I went to the woods because I wished to live deliberately, to front only the essential facts of life, and see if I could not learn what it had to teach, and not, when I came to die, discover that I had not lived.'

Henry David Thoreau

'Experience is not what happens to a man. It is what a man does with what happens to him.'

Aldous Huxley, *Texts and Pretexts*

I

Now

When I open my eyes, all is red. The branches of the trees above; the almost sun; and the sky beyond. I touch my face, and when I hold up my hand I see my white glove is stained red. It takes a few seconds to figure out that it's blood. My body tenses. *Where is everyone?* I mouth the words as if they're the first I've ever spoken but my tongue is dry and fluffy, like candyfloss, and they stick in my throat.

I'm lying on my back. The earth beside me is frosted cold and hard but the ground under my body feels warm and soft. When I touch it, I discover I'm laid out on a tenderly constructed mattress of leaves nestling in the dip of a fallen oak tree. *I am loved.* It feels like the purest thought I've ever had. Big red tears pour down my face and my head pounds painfully in protest. I try to calm myself by watching the branches above me embrace and pull apart in a graceful dance choreographed by the breeze and then cautiously test my own limbs. Apart from one finger, everything works. I shift awkwardly and a branch beneath me snaps in half.

'Did you hear that?'

I'm not alone. My throat constricts and my breath goes ragged.

In the distance a man and woman talk. They communicate pinball-style, words ricocheting from one to the other.

Even though I must be fifty metres away I can hear everything. I lie as flat as possible and cover myself with leaves, my heart beating so hard that it feels as if it's trying to leap out of my chest. Luckily for me they're distracted by the screech of a siren, swiftly followed by the flurry of wheels spinning hopelessly in the mud.

'DCI Wass in orbit!' warns the man, as a car door slams.

My stomach pitches. What the fuck are the police doing here? Nothing makes any sense.

'So, what have we got, Kovac?' barks Wass. 'Just the headlines, please.'

'A woman called to report her sister's family missing,' explains Kovac. 'Says they went on holiday to some crazy off-grid eco-community for the summer and never came home. The directions she gave brought us halfway up Blood Mountain. She's been pretty insistent, hasn't she, Sergeant O'Hara?'

'Called every day since the beginning of the week,' confirms O'Hara.

'Do you have any names?' asks Wass.

'Eve Sawyer, forty-five, and her children, Joe, seventeen, Cass, sixteen, and Maud, eight,' says Kovac. 'Eve's sister, Cara Rigby, filed the report.'

They're talking about me and my family. The tightness in my throat spreads to my chest. I'm breathing way too shallow. I struggle to pull myself up into a sitting position, but I've gone all ragdoll and the effort makes my head bleed harder. I spot our cabin through the trees and frantically scan the forest for Mum, Joe and Maudie.

'What I don't understand is how this place has managed to stay under the radar for so long,' mutters Kovac. 'How come no one knew about them?'

'You can't find folk who don't want to be found,' replies Wass.

'Cara Rigby sent a photo,' says O'Hara, handing a phone to Wass. I can't even remember the last time I saw a phone, let alone used one.

Wass scrutinizes the image and taps the screen. 'Who's he?'

'The brother-in-law, I guess, but the sister didn't mention him, ma'am,' says O'Hara, apologetically.

'That's strange,' says Wass.

'Take a look at this!' yells Kovac. He's right outside our cabin, pointing at the animal skulls hanging across the boarded-up windows. Rabbit. Rat. Vole. Rat. Fox. Vole.

'What is this place?' asks O'Hara apprehensively.

'Looks like Center Parcs gone rogue,' jokes Kovac. There's the sound of nervous laughter. Restless memories shapeshift. We used to go to Center Parcs for our summer holiday. We used to have a family Netflix account and share music on Spotify. It used to be that ordinary. I open my mouth to call for help, but some inner voice silences me again. *Trust no one, Cass.*

I need to find out what's happened to my family. I anxiously lick my lips and they taste of blood. An image of the orange propane cylinder that we use to fire up the gas ring cuts through the brain fog. There's the smell of burning flesh, and my brother's face, gaunt and sallow. A new spasm of panic sucks the air from my lungs.

'Check there's no one inside the cabin,' instructs Wass.

An icy feeling courses through my body. And then I get it. *They've come for me. Because of what I've done.*

2

Then

It started with the bees. Dad was in the middle of his third attempt to make fire by striking a flint against a piece of steel during my little sister's eighth-birthday party when a bee landed on his hand and stung him in the fleshy part between his thumb and index finger. I say in the middle, because back then I shared Dad's optimism about effort being the guarantee of success. Maudie didn't and was already quivering with impatience over his failure to make fire to light the candles on her birthday cake.

'I'll be nine before he's finished,' she wailed, as Mum tried to convince her she could see real sparks. As usual, my older brother, Joe, had disappeared, even on Snap Maps.

'Oh, my God! What's up with him?' I groaned, when Dad abandoned his fire-making and started yelling and slapping at his arms. Fortunately, my little sister hadn't reached the age when parents become a total embarrassment, but part of me had died inside when I'd got back from my Saturday babysitting gig to find Dad sitting cross-legged in a circle alongside Maudie and her friends, with black lines painted across his cheeks.

'I think it's part of him finding his inner warrior,' said Mum, distractedly. She was putting the finishing touches to the surprise pink Barbie cake she'd made for Maudie. 'Mo seems big on that.'

'Who's Mo?' I was struggling to catch up with the drama unfolding in our garden.

'Some random survival expert with a side hustle doing children's parties,' said Mum, gesturing towards the end of the garden. 'Dad met him at that festival we went to a few months ago.'

I saw a tall, lean man drifting languidly around the circle of children towards Dad. He seemed to flow rather than walk, and despite all the ruckus, he exuded total calm. I knew right away that Mo was nothing like the usual squeaky-clean, eager-to-please party organizers, with their false cheer and shiny white teeth. He had long, thick, sun-bleached hair, an untamed beard and tattoos. He was dressed in a faded black T-shirt, slightly torn at the neck, leather boots with a history, and a worn pair of jeans. When his T-shirt billowed in the breeze, I noticed his body was tanned and muscular in a way that suggested time spent outdoors doing hard physical labour rather than hours at the gym. I give it to Dad. Mo was an original, gorgeous individual.

'Walk the path of your own truth, Rick,' encouraged Mo, as he got closer to Dad and tried to work out what was up. 'Tap into that primal energy.'

'What the hell? I'm gone for an hour and there's chaos?' Joe had reappeared as mysteriously as he'd disappeared. He always liked to think our family couldn't function without him. He shook his head in disbelief at Dad's wild moves and I noticed his dark curly hair was now so long that it framed his face like flouncy curtains. 'He's lost the plot big-time.' He filmed Dad and did a voiceover: 'His enthusiasm will be the death of us.' It was a riff on Dad's second-favourite saying about cynicism being the ninth deadly sin (the first being the one about effort being the guarantee of success).

Joe posted the clip on the family WhatsApp. 'WTF?!' Mum's sister, Cara, wrote back within seconds. Her reactions never disappointed us. Laughing, Joe and I watched the clip again. I froze it on Dad's face and noticed that his eyes looked different. His dark pupils were glazed like black beads, as if he was about to cry, but his expression was one of rapture.

Mum, who often acted as Dad's interpreter, explained that this boundless positivity was to make up for the fact that six weeks earlier he'd vetoed the Witches and Wizards party that Maudie had set her heart on. 'Do you remember?'

How could I forget? Usually, Maudie knew exactly how to play Dad to get her own way; it was no secret that she was his favourite child. He even referred to her as his beautiful mistake, as if Mum hadn't actually been involved in her conception. This never bothered Joe or me. I was eight when Maudie was born, and Joe was nine, and it had been a relief to escape into the shadows.

This time, however, Dad had stood his ground, arguing that a Witches and Wizards party had no sense of purpose and would involve a lot of single-use plastic. Instead, he told Maudie about the amazing guy he'd come across at the festival, who knew everything there was to know about how to survive in the wild. He talked about the lost art of using a compass, of making fire without matches, of the way human beings had forgotten how to be self-sufficient and lost their connection with nature. Even as he said this, I sensed he wasn't just arguing the case for a bushcraft party but was revealing a kind of truth about something missing from his own existence.

Maudie had threaded herself through Dad's legs, like a cat, but for once he didn't give in. The tantrum that followed was epic even by Maudie's standards. Her face turned red and her body contorted into a pretzel shape. Maudie had been demanding from the moment she was born. She never slept. She got colic and croup and coughed her way through her first five winters. Everything about her was extreme. She had best friends and worst enemies. Her red hair was so curly it got matted with grim knots that Mum had to cut out with kitchen scissors. But this time Dad hadn't relented.

'How come nothing comes up about him on Google?' Mum had challenged him, when she did a search on Mo later. 'And is he DBS checked?'

'Give him a chance. This guy is the real deal. It'll be a party like no other,' he declared.

And it was.

At the moment when the second angry bee appeared on the scene and stung Dad on the lower arm, I think even he was regretting his decision to force through the bushcraft party. By that stage Maudie and her friends had begun to lose focus. Freddie was wrestling on the ground with another boy and Hasna had formed a splinter group that wanted to play Animal Rescue with Maudie's rabbits.

'Shit!' Dad jumped to his feet and flung his arm around so violently that he knocked over the central pole of the shelter they'd all spent the best part of the previous hour building. It slowly slumped to one side, like my aunt Cara after a family lunch.

8

'What's wrong, Rick?' Mum dumped the cake on the garden table and rushed towards Dad.

'I've been stung again,' shouted Dad. 'This one's gone up my sleeve. Fucking fucker.'

'Fucking fucker,' chorused Maudie's friends, re-energized by this unexpected turn of events.

'We need to get that shirt off right now,' urged Mo, his calm authority a total contrast to Dad's hysteria. That was the first time I noticed how he routinely used 'we' rather than 'you' or 'I' when he spoke.

'Please keep still,' Mum pleaded with Dad. 'How can we help if you keep jumping around?'

'His arm is swelling up,' warned Joe.

'He had a bad reaction once before,' panicked Mum, as she frantically attempted to undo the buttons of Dad's shirt in a way that made Joe raise an eyebrow. He literally thought about sex the entire time.

'Keep still!' Mo ordered. 'We need to get the stinger out or the poison will spread and the swelling will get worse.'

'Poison?' said Maudie, in the same hallowed tone she used when she cut herself and announced, 'There's blood.' Her friends stood in an arc at a safe distance from Dad.

'Cassia! Fetch the first-aid kit from my pack! We need antihistamines!' Mo signalled towards a dirty backpack sitting on the garden table beside the cake. I didn't even realize he'd noticed me, let alone knew my name, and was filled with hot pride that he'd picked me out of the crowd to act as his assistant. This very much didn't usually happen to me. I liked the way he used my full name instead of shortening it to Cass, like everyone else did.

'Shall I get tweezers?' suggested Mum, who was always good in a crisis.

'No,' said Mo. 'The stinger is barbed, and if you pull it straight out, you'll release even more venom.'

The backpack had a strong earthy smell, more animal than human, that I would for ever associate with Mo. It was so tightly packed that in the end there was no choice but to tip it upside down and shake it. Everything tumbled onto the table. Water-purifying tablets, loo rolls, Ziploc bags, soap wrapped in cellophane, a sewing kit, compass, insect spray and a whistle.

'Top pocket, Cassia!' shouted Mo. 'Emergency provisions are always in the top pocket.'

It was the only place I hadn't looked. I found the first-aid kit and instantly located the antihistamines. I nervously glanced at Dad. He was frantic. His brown hair was damp with sweat and his hand had now swollen so big that I could see it had its own pulse. I half wondered if it might burst open and release a whole new swarm of bees. It made Mum's efforts to undo his shirt even more futile because the sleeve would never fit over his deformed limb.

Mo leant so close to Dad's arm that, for a split second, I wondered if he was going to lick it. And then I wondered what it would be like if he licked my arm and slid his tongue along my collar bone to my shoulder blade and sucked it like a boiled sweet. I felt my face flush red as Mo caught my eye.

'We have them,' I said, copying his use of the collective pronoun as I triumphantly waved the pills in the air.

'We need to remove the venom sac before it injects more poison,' declared Mo. 'It releases a pheromone that encourages other bees to come and attack. It's very unlike honeybees to be so aggressive.'

'I think a stray arrow might have disturbed the nest at

the end of the garden during the archery competition,' Mum nervously explained.

Dad howled in pain. I tried to comfort him but he shook me off.

'Try to stay calm, Rick,' urged Mum.

'Do the bees really die after they sting?' asked Hasna, holding her hand over her mouth in shock. 'That's so sad!'

'I can't believe there's been so much death at my party!' cried Maudie. 'Can we bury them? Can we make little coffins from matchboxes and do a service with a procession?'

'Worry about Dad, not the bloody bees,' I snapped at her.

'I'm fading,' moaned Dad.

'Look into my eyes, Dad. Breathe slow and deep.' Even my cool older brother was getting the jitters.

Mo crouched and pulled out a knife from a sheath tied round his ankle. It wasn't like any knife I'd ever seen before. It was about fifteen centimetres long with a semi-circular blade that curved into a sharp point and a hole where he hooked his index finger. He sliced a neat line down through Dad's favourite plaid shirt to expose his arm. The stinger was clearly visible. We watched as Mo pressed the tip of the knife just shy of the small black barb and pushed hard to tease it out. A small trickle of blood streamed from Dad's arm.

'Fucking fucker,' yelled Dad, again. I had never in my life heard him swear like that. It was sort of wondrous. Maudie's friends excitedly crowded closer. This would definitely be the bit of the party they would remember. There was a collective gasp as the stinger slid intact from Dad's arm. Mo handed it to Maudie for further examination.

'Antihistamines,' said Mo, without looking at me as he thrust his hand in my direction as if I was a magician's assistant. I proudly held out the packet to him and felt his finger trace an exquisite line across my palm as he took it from me. His hands were rough as sandpaper and his fingers were stained brown. As he eased the pills from the blister pack, I checked out the tattoo of three interlocking triangles on the back of his left hand. Dad grabbed the antihistamines, swallowed a couple without any water and stared at Mo, panting.

Then, just as suddenly as the whole drama had started, it was over.

'You saved my life,' gulped Dad.

'You need to watch out, Rick.' Mo wiped his knife with the sleeve of Dad's shirt. 'Bee allergy gets worse each time you're stung. Next time it could be fatal.'

'Would you mind putting that away now, please, Mo?' asked Mum. 'It's not the kind of accessory you normally see at a children's party.' She shot him one of her winning smiles.

'Of course.' Mo nonchalantly slipped the knife back into the sheath on his ankle.

'Where did you get that?' asked little Freddie, suspiciously.

'It was a present from a Danish friend,' said Mo.

'What do you use it for?' asked Maudie.

'It has multifarious uses,' said Mo. It turned out 'multifarious' was one of Mo's favourite words and although he used it correctly then, he also used it wrongly to describe Mum's patchwork skirt, my freckles and the different colours of Maudie's pet rabbits. He didn't use it in relation to Dad and Joe. I should have noticed that. If Cara had been there, she would have been whispering, 'Red flag,' in my ear. When it came to relationships, she was good at spotting red flags even if she never acted on them.

'It can be used for lifting hot grates off a fire or cutting fishing line.' Mo spoke in a soft, throaty rasp. His accent was difficult to place. 'Mostly I use it for field dressing.' We all looked at him blankly.

'Is that something you put on salads?' asked Maudie.

Mo threw back his head and roared with laughter. 'When you kill a deer, you need to get the entrails out as quickly as possible to stop the flesh rotting. You put the hook in the deer's belly and pull it open like a zip, so you access the abdomen without slicing the muscle or puncturing the gut.' He put his finger on Maudie's tummy and pretended to cut it open. She giggled. He knew how to handle her. I was impressed. Most people needed a manual to deal with my little sister.

'You kill deer?' asked Maudie's friend Ali. It was difficult to tell if he was horrified or impressed.

'Sometimes. I only kill what I can eat. I take no pleasure in killing for the sake of it, but I enjoy the chase. Tracking an animal and killing it involves mutual respect. You don't get that when you buy meat at the supermarket.'

'That's very interesting,' said Dad. I hadn't seen him so animated in ages. 'How do you learn to track?'

'By becoming a predator,' said Mo, casually. 'You need to know how many are in the herd, where they've come from, anticipate where they're heading and when they'll get there. You have to feel as if they know you're following them. The truly gifted hunter learns to see his surroundings through the eyes of his prey.'

He sat down on his haunches and pointed at some foot-prints through the long grass to the end of the garden.

'Look. You can see this is a long thin footprint and there's very little distance between each step. I would say it belongs to someone young, short and most likely female. Like Cassia.' His piercing green eyes seemed to look into me rather than at me. 'If the gait was longer and the print deeper at the front than the back, I'd know the person was running.'

'What about rabbits?' asked Maudie, stepping in front of the cage where Juniper and Jason were gnawing on some carrots. 'Do you kill rabbits?'

'Rabbit kebabs. My favourite.' Mo smacked his lips at Juni-per and Jason. 'Where I come from, we like to be self-reliant. Dependent on no one but ourselves. We grow our own food, create our own energy, heal our own wounds. Live authenti-cally. We hope for the best but prepare for the worst.'

'What is the worst?' Freddie blurted out. I babysat Fred-die and knew the worst thing that happened in his house was when someone left crumbs on the kitchen island.

'Depends on who you live with. In our house it's one of Maudie's tantrums,' joked Joe.

Unbelievably Maudie didn't react. She was too busy lis-tening to Mo.

'We're in the sixth period of extinction,' he said sol-emnly. 'We've been through five and the last one was sixty million years ago when we lost the dinosaurs.' I was struck by how he made it all sound so vivid and real. The dino-saurs. The cavemen. Killing animals with crossbows. 'Think about it. Everywhere there are floods, fires, natural disasters, epidemics, droughts. Everything is more extreme. We've reached the tipping point. One more thing and the environment will be overwhelmed. Anyone who is smart is retuning their life. Because if we live in harmony with the natural world we can survive any disaster. You'd be surprised how little it takes to get by.'

I saw Mum raise an eyebrow and waited for Dad to react. Nothing. He stared at Mo the way I wished Brodie Thomson would stare at me.

'Don't stick your head in the sand and pretend everything's going to be all right, Rick,' said Mo. 'Because it's not. We all need to learn to be radically self-reliant.'

'Radical self-reliance,' I heard Dad repeat under his breath several times until he'd made the words his own.

'Will we make it through?' Maudie asked fervently. 'Will we survive?'

'After the environmental catastrophe most of the people you love will be gone, Maudie. Most of your friends will no longer be here.' He waved an arm around her group of classmates. 'It will be like the beginning of mankind all over again. But I have a very strong sense you will be one of the survivors. And so will Cassia. It's the female bee who carries the sting.' He caught my eye again. 'You are one of us.'

I felt a shiver of excitement.

'What about me?' asked Joe. Mo shook his head and Joe tried to laugh it off, but I could tell he minded. Unlike me he wasn't used to rejection.

'Time for cake before the world ends,' Mum smoothly interrupted. If I could have picked one quality to inherit from Mum, it would be her ability to know the right thing to say at any given moment. She was wasted as a teacher. She should have been running the United Nations. Twenty-four pairs of eyes turned away from Mo towards the bright pink Barbie cake that Mum had retrieved from the garden

15

table. She would never usually have produced something so outlandishly girly, but it was designed to make Maudie feel better about missing out on her Witches and Wizards party. She'd somehow constructed a billowing sponge skirt covered with pink icing around a real Barbie doll. The skirt was decorated with hundreds of tiny silver balls and flowers made from different-coloured icing. Maudie shrieked with excitement as everyone steamed into the kitchen behind Mum.

Mo followed us. But at a distance. Inside, he was less at ease. He stood stiffly, his gaze darting restlessly from Mum's blender to the dishwasher, from the portable speaker to the breadmaker. I was embarrassed by our life of excess and relieved when he paced towards the fridge to examine an old photo on the door.

'Who's this, Cassia?' he called to me.

I threaded my way through the crowd of children to stand beside him, my face burning red with the certainty that he'd caught me staring at him. 'My parents.' We were so close I could feel the hairs on his arm brush my hand. 'Wow!' He exhaled.

'They met backpacking in Colombia and spent a year on the road together.' I was relieved he'd focused on this because it was the only interesting thing about my parents, and I hoped it might shine a better light on us.

'They look cool.' He shot me a quick smile.

'Cool' was not a word I associated with Mum and Dad, but I could see where Mo was coming from as he took in their long hair, the endless woven bracelets around their wrists and the cut-off denim shorts.

'Actually, what I mean is they look happy,' Mo corrected himself.

'That's because we were,' said Dad, who'd appeared beside us nursing his swollen arm. 'Difficult to believe, but we once lived a life of total freedom.'

'And now?'

'I work long hours for shit pay in a job that no longer has meaning. And when I'm not teaching, I'm either doing pointless paperwork or writing polite emails to abusive parents about their badly behaved kids.' He gave a hollow laugh. It was no secret that Dad was fed up with his job, but I was shocked by the depth of his disillusionment.

'Nothing is perfect, but if you believe in your infinite potential, there are no limits to the possibility of transformation,' beamed Mo. He leant towards the photo. 'Was that taken in Minca?'

'How on earth could you tell?' asked Dad in amazement. I didn't like to point out that Dad was wearing a T-shirt that said 'Minca' across the front.

'I lived there for a while too,' said Mo.

'What a coincidence!' `exclaimed Dad, taking Mo by the arm to show him more photos of the Sierra Nevada.

'Sorry,' Mo mouthed. I gave what I hoped was a casual shrug. None of us could compete with Dad's tales of travel in Latin America. It was as if this was the place where he'd been most alive.

Mum called me over to help light the candles on Maudie's cake. She pressed the matches into my hand. 'Quickly before Dad notices and decides he needs to find his inner caveman again,' she joked.

Maudie's eyes were on stalks when I put the cake on the table. The icing had melted in the humidity so it seemed to shimmer. There were gasps of approval from her friends. Mo lent Maudie his knife and she cut into the cake, screaming so loudly when she hit the base that I had to put my fingers in my ears.

'Make a wish! Make a wish!' clamoured Flora.

'I wish I could fly,' screeched Maudie.

'Don't say it out loud or it won't come true,' said Mum. She took the knife from Maudie's hand and cut perfectly even slices of cake for everyone. When she'd finished, she eased out the Barbie doll as effortlessly as Mo had removed the stinger.

'Someone has cut off Barbie's legs!' cried Hasna.

It was true. Mum had amputated Barbie from beneath the torso. Judging by the rough edges she'd used a serrated blade, possibly the bread knife.

'Like something from *Saw*,' muttered Joe. Even I had to agree it looked pretty creepy.

'She's been hacked to death.' Maudie pressed her face into Dad's thigh and started crying. Dad put his arm around her and cradled her head in his still grotesquely misshapen hand.

'Fucking fucker,' said Freddie, running his fingers around Barbie's mutilated torso before licking the icing. 'That's so cool.'

'This is the worst cake ever,' sobbed Maudie.

'Worst cake ever,' Flora and Hasna loyally chorused.

Then, just as everything was lost, Mo pulled something out of one of his many trouser pockets. 'Gorilla glue,' he declared. 'No one should ever be without it. We'll perform an operation, Maudie.' The mood lightened again. When he finished sticking Barbie back together, he handed the glue to me. 'Keep it, Cassia.' Our hands hovered in mid-air and the tips of our fingers touched.

'How come you're always so calm?' I asked. I wouldn't usually have been so intimate with someone I'd just met, but Mo was one of those people who made you feel like you didn't need to pretend anything.

'Because I breathe the air of inner freedom.' He grinned at me, and I smiled back.

3

Now

I peer through the undergrowth towards our cabin and see the perimeter is partly staked with yellow crime-scene tape. The young policewoman crawls through a gaping hole in the side of the wall. Within minutes she's back.

'It's a total mess inside. Filthy clothes. Broken furniture. Stuff everywhere,' O'Hara squalls. 'No sign of the woman or her children. I doubt anyone's been there for days, ma'am. Looks like they left in the middle of a meal.'

I should be relieved it's not worse news. But if Mum, Joe and Maudie aren't in the cabin, where are they? My body tenses into a state of tingling fear. And then come the tears. I shove my hand into my mouth to stifle a sob. And what about Dad? I panic. Why does no one ever mention him?

'Maybe they've gone on holiday. Or they got lost hiking one of the trails on the north side of the lake,' suggests O'Hara. She doesn't sound convinced by either explanation.

'They came to this shithole on holiday,' replies Kovac, running a hand through his short spiky hair. 'That's what the sister said in her statement.'

'What do you think caused that hole in the side of the cabin?' asks O'Hara.

'Looks like there was a fire or some kind of explosion. I'm not sure this place has a big health-and-safety culture,' says Wass, icily. 'Let's check that outhouse before it gets dark.' Their voices fade.

It's getting colder. You can freeze to death in a city in plain sight. Out here in the wild it's far deadlier. In 20 m.p.h. winds, frostbite can set in within half an hour. I hold the hand without a glove to my face and see traces of blood, skin and dark hairs that most definitely don't belong to me, compacted in the half-moon of my nails. My guts convulse in disgust and I retch. A trickle of yellow bile slides to the ground.

What have I done? I frantically rub my fingers against my thighs. When this doesn't work, I use a holly leaf to gouge out the filth from under my nails until they bleed. The wound on my head is no accident. A jagged memory slices through the brain fog. There's the sensation of someone pulling me down. Of being dragged along the ground. Of hands around my neck. And a man's face, screaming at me.

Fighting for breath, I tuck my hand inside the warmth of my jacket and try to soothe myself by running through what I'm wearing: pale green jacket with a hood tied so tightly under my chin that I have to turn my head from side to side like a periscope to see; jeans held up with a belt that cuts uncomfortably into my hips, the denim so stiff with dirt that it feels as if it's been shellacked. One glove, a couple of sizes too big to be useful for anything apart from insulation. Not that I'm complaining.

It hits me that none of these clothes are mine and I'm not wearing any underwear, which means someone else dressed my naked body in them. I retch again. I'd tear them off right now, except the cold would kill me. My chest tightens and my mouth dries as I try to figure it all out. The person who dressed me must be the same person who built the leaf mattress for me. It's the same loving attention to detail that gives it away. The hood tied in a neat bow; the gloveless hand pushed inside the coat sleeve, so no flesh was exposed; and the boots coated in a new layer of dubbin to keep them waterproof. *I am loved.* But isn't it a strange kind of love when you don't know who loves you? This time the words weigh more heavily, crushing the air out of my chest.

I rummage through the jacket pockets searching desperately for clues. There's nothing apart from a semi-rotten apple. I lift my arm to my nose and close my eyes to inhale the jacket. It smells musty and smoky, as if it's marinated in damp. There's another layer of scent, more animal than human that I recognize right away. It's Mo's smell. The jacket belongs to him. Mo is the one looking out for me. Mo looks after us all.

A police radio crackles into life in the distance and I guess they're in the outhouse. By this stage my head is thumping again. But the pain is welcome because it eclipses the fear. When I touch the hood of the jacket it feels wet. I've bled so much that it's soaked all the way through the thick stuffing. I force myself to inch my hand inside the hood to check the wound. It's difficult because my hair is stiff with dried blood. But judging from the pain as my fingers crawl over my forehead the cut is just above my left temple. I moan softly when I feel a deep V-shaped trench. I pull out my hand and see the tips of my fingers are red to the middle of the nail. A rush of panic and the blood flows faster. If I don't deal with this quickly, I'll bleed out all alone under this tree. I need a first-aid kit. I check out the cabin. The yellow and black crime-scene tape has already unravelled and flaps in the breeze, like a badly wrapped present. There's no part of me that wants to go back inside.

The voices talking on the radio get closer. I force myself to stay completely still.

'Right. Let's go, people,' Wass instructs. 'A man and a woman have been sighted north of the lake, likely growers from one of the cannabis farms. They need us there right now. Let's re-interview the sister and come back here tomorrow.'

I want to call out, to order them to keep searching for my family, to command them to work out what's happened, but I'm too scared they'll find out what I might have done. And I can't risk that. Because this is all on me, isn't it? Their voices drift away. Wass, Kovac, O'Hara. Going, going, gone. I wait to feel lonely and am surprised when I don't. Instead, I feel something close to relief as the comforting murmur of the trees reminds me that love doesn't always have to be human.

4

Then

The hot weather finally broke somewhere towards the end of lunch the weekend after Maudie's birthday. The heavy atmosphere outside matched the mood around the table because by that stage almost every parent from Maudie's class had called to complain about what had 'gone down' at the party. It was ironic, Mum remarked, as she brought out the final leftovers of the Barbie cake, that the same parents who used phrases like 'gone down' and wanted their children to have 'free-range childhoods' to build middle-class qualities like 'resilience and independence', were the first to complain when their children might actually have to put these into action. 'Fucking fuckers,' agreed Cara, scooping out ice from her glass of wine to wipe her sweaty forehead.

Dad ignored Cara mimicking him and Maudie giggling to agree with her. But this rare moment of harmony between them underlined the precariousness of the situation, especially when Freddie's mum, Alessia, who'd become a kind of unofficial spokesperson for the parents, called with an 'urgent update'. Alessia's involvement was bad news for Mum because, apart from being our family doctor and co-founder of their book club, she was also meant to be one of her closest friends. Mum put her phone on speaker in the middle of the table so Dad could listen in.

'I just wanted to give you the heads-up, Eve, that there's still a lot of chat among the parents about what went down.'

'Sounds ominous,' said Mum, attempting to downplay the disasters as nothing more than a series of unfortunate events.

'I don't think you get how serious this is,' interrupted Alessia. 'There's no place for a hunting knife at a kids' party or telling the children half their friends are going to die. I'm sorry, Eve, I don't think playdates at your house are going to work any more.'

'No!' cried Maudie, from the opposite side of the table. 'This can't be happening to me!'

Until this moment, we'd never been one of those families that attracted much attention. Our parents had been like wallpaper. Unchanging. Always in the background. Exquisitely boring, which is what you want in parents. Mum had a still, luminous quality that drew people to her and made them feel safe. She was a fixer and problem-solver. Dad was less reliable, but in a dad-dance middle-aged teacher kind of way. He wrote 'cum' instead of 'come' in text messages, referred to the garden shed as his safe place in front of my friends and sang the wrong lyrics to songs on purpose ('We built this city on sausage rolls' was his favourite.) To be honest, I was grateful he hadn't done anything truly embarrassing, like the dad of Joe's best friend, who'd been caught using webcam girls on the family iPad and matched on Tinder with a girl in our sixth form. Now suddenly we were notorious and, even more strangely, Dad almost seemed to be enjoying it.

I nudged Joe, who was lost in Snapchat. He held up his phone so I could have a scroll through his messages. There was a sea of memes, LOLS and jibes about Dad going loco after being stabbed by a rogue entertainer at a slasher party.

'Oh, God!' I hissed. 'You've got to tell them what really happened!'

In the distance there was a long, low grumble of thunder that, for the briefest moment, stalled Maudie's tears.

'The truth is even more ridiculous.' Joe laughed. I fumed. It would be fine for him. It always was. But my year group was more fragile and ruthless. Being uncool was social death. I was also hurt on Mo's behalf and felt I should defend him.

Feeling anxious and despondent, I took advantage of the distraction to reach for the final slice of cake. Ever since I could remember, food had been my best friend and worst enemy.

'Those kids learnt more useful life skills during the couple of hours they spent with Mo than they will during their entire education,' muttered Dad.

'My life is ruined,' sobbed Maudie.

'Everything passes,' Mum tried to console her.

I think it was at this point that Cara gave Maudie a late birthday present. It was called Dog Show and consisted of ten hideous plastic dogs of different shapes and sizes in gaudy pastel colours with furry coats that could be combed and plaited into different styles. 'Best present ever,' declared Maudie, her tears instantly evaporating as she tore open the packaging and lined up the dogs along the kitchen table. She was ruthlessly good at moving on when it suited her. Unlike Cara, who never knew when to stop.

'In my humble opinion,' Cara slurred, 'the only truly terrifying bit of the party was when you went all woo-woo and started beating your chest to find your inner warrior, Rick. It was sort of *Apocalypse Now* meets *Pocahontas*.'

'How do you know that when you weren't even there?' asked Dad, sharply, moving the water jug out of the way so he could eyeball her.

'It's on the family WhatsApp,' replied Cara, moving it back again.

We were back on familiar territory now. Cara and Dad bickering was a staple of almost every mealtime. Their skirmishes were strangely comforting. Even Maudie got that it was a sort of proxy war because what they were really arguing about was who was getting the most attention from Mum. The only thing they had in common was that they both loved Mum too much.

'And why are you part of our family WhatsApp, Cara, when you don't even bother to turn up for your niece's birthday party?'

'I've known Eve twice as long as you have,' retorted Cara, sounding hurt. My grandparents had died within a month of each other just before Maudie was born so we were Cara's only family. That was what Mum told us when she first moved in with us five months ago.

Dad's response was swallowed by a massive crack of thunder. The storm was now overhead. Maudie yelped, the kitchen lights flickered and the whole house seemed to tremble. Almost immediately the rain started beating down on the glass extension, sheeting in ever-changing directions, like it was unsure what mood it was in. Sensing no one would notice, I spooned the final crumbs of cake into my mouth. And as I ate, I stared at the hedge gyrating at the end of the garden and realized the rain was in thrall to the wind. All at once, I saw myself as the rain and Mo as the wind. I thought about his lean, muscular body and wondered about the weight of it on top of me, and whether he would find my ugly round tummy repellent.

'Cass! Are you listening? We need towels!' I suddenly realized Mum was firing instructions at me. She gesticulated at the double doors that opened into the garden. Water was pouring in through the glass roof and under the doorframe to form pools on the kitchen floor. I ran upstairs. But instead of heading to the linen cupboard, I swerved into my bedroom to check my phone for the hundredth time that day.

I'm not going to lie. I'd shamelessly googled Mo before his truck had even reached the corner of our street after he'd left Maudie's party. But Mum was right. There was nothing. It was like he'd vaporized. Then four days later, just as I reached my lowest ebb, a parcel arrived for me in the post. Inside was a necklace with a bee encased in amber resin and a card with a hand-drawn bird of prey on the front and a phone number on the back. *Keep in touch*. There was a note about bees bringing good luck for people about to embark on the great journey of life. *Like you, Cassia!* In a single second, my mood flipped from gloom to euphoria.

It took me a whole day to compose my first message to Mo. I spent hours lying on my bed, googling anything from how to tell if someone likes you to what to say to make someone like you. In the end I bottled it and simply asked how to help the bees in the hive that Dad had damaged with the arrow.

Given all Mo's chat about living off-grid in a forest, I was prepared for a long wait to hear back from him. Instead he wrote almost immediately. His first message didn't mention the bees. Neither did the second. In fact, we probably messaged for half an hour before he explained that the outcome for the bees was dependent on whether the queen had survived. If she had, she would lead the worker bees to a new hive, and if she hadn't, then most likely the entire colony would be wiped out.

Mo asked questions about what was going on in my life. He wanted to know about my school, my parents, especially Dad, even Joe and Maudie. I told him about the hysteria after the party and how everyone, including my friends, made buzzing noises when I went near them. He said that, unlike me, they were obviously the kind of people who always swam in the shallows. There were more texts. He distracted me with descriptions of the tree-house where he lived in the middle of an ancient forest and the wildlife he saw each day. He described how he'd been in the army for a while, studied shamanism in Mexico and yoga in India, and now wanted a quiet life living close to nature. He knew so much about so many things.

Last night he'd messaged for an update on the bees. I rushed to the end of the garden in the dark and found the hive dangling in the wind and all the bees gone. I told him this and added lots of sad-face emojis. He sent me back a clip of him playing my favourite Tame Impala song on guitar and a voice text: 'This is the past. Come to the future.'

A flash of lightning illuminated my bedroom and was swiftly followed by another deep barrage of thunder and more pelting rain. Leaning against my bedroom door I clicked messages. Mo had written back: *The queen has led them to a new and better life. You can do the same, Cassia.* Heart surging, I touched the necklace. But the spell was instantly broken by Mum calling upstairs.

'Cass, where are you? We need those towels right now!' I'd completely forgotten what I was meant to be doing. I grabbed a pile from the linen cupboard and rushed back down to the kitchen. Mum and Cara were stuffing tea towels along the bottom of the French windows while Dad frantically mopped the floor. Maudie was involved in a complex emergency mission to rescue her plastic dogs in a Tupperware container. Joe, of course, had disappeared.

'It wasn't raining when Noah built the ark,' Dad roared over the noise of the storm. In spite of the rain it was still really humid, so he'd taken off his T-shirt and his torso glistened as if it was wrapped in cellophane.

'What does that even mean?' Cara shouted, as she boomeranged round the kitchen rescuing books, rugs and school bags from the floor.

'When disaster strikes the time to prepare has passed!' That was the first time I clocked how Dad had stopped sounding like Dad and begun to talk in sound-bites, like a motivational speaker. My brother finally made an appearance and Dad ordered him to check the cellar, which often flooded in heavy rain. After another age, Joe came back to report that the water was already sloshing over his trainers.

'It stinks of shit too,' he added.

I braced for Dad's inevitable explosion. But it never came. His eyes glazed over. 'This is Nature's punishment for the way we have abused the environment,' he proclaimed, as if he'd just had some sort of epiphany. 'We should use this experience to re-prioritize the way we live.'

The rains continued over the next few days. I should have been relieved because the tyranny of vest tops and shorts was over, and I'd no longer be red and sweaty when I sat next to Brodie Thompson in English. But when I described our flooded cellar to Mo, he told me that his community regularly got cut off for weeks at a time after heavy rain, and all I could think about was how, if this happened, it could be months before I saw him again.

Dad obsessively monitored the water level in the cellar. The higher it rose, the more elated he seemed. He came across an interactive website that showed how rising sea levels would affect different parts of the world. He looked at it several times a day and screenshotted his findings to the family WhatsApp with terrifying captions. *At fifty centimetres the east coast will disappear . . . At one metre London will disappear.*

'Our house will be underwater if sea levels rise by just half a metre. We need to head for the hills,' he said, staring into the middle distance with the same glassy look I'd first noticed at Maudie's party. He decided to share a screenshot with the parents from Maudie's class showing our school underwater.

'Is that a good idea?' Joe asked. 'I'm not saying you're wrong to be worried but aren't you trying to dial it down with them?'

'I'm suffering from a terminal illness. I've got nothing to lose,' replied Dad.

'What do you mean?' I asked, in confusion.

'I'm terminally bored,' he announced, as he pressed send. 'I'm doing these parents a favour. People need to escape the boundaries of their limited existence and wake up to what's going on.'

'Are you crazy, Rick?' I heard Mum berate him when she got a phone call from Alessia about Dad's latest digital hand grenade.

'If you're not part of the solution, you're part of the problem, Eve.' He raged against the futility of his existence, struggling to keep down a job he hated, teaching a curriculum he didn't believe in, to pay a mortgage on a house in a city where he had no desire to live, and started talking about us going away together for an extended period. He was deliberately vague about what this long holiday might involve, which encouraged everyone other than me to wallow in fantastical possibilities. Joe envisaged a house swap with a family in the Los Angeles hills, where we could attend Calabasas High for a couple of terms and mingle with the children of Hollywood celebrities. Maudie wanted us to volunteer at an animal sanctuary in the Amazon where we could swim with pink dolphins. Mum imagined a house overlooking the sea in Cornwall. Cara, who clearly assumed she'd be coming with us, promoted Lisbon as the ideal compromise. 'It works for us all,' she kept saying, her gaze flitting anxiously between Mum and Dad. I didn't bother to dream because I never thought it would happen. Dad was a failed enthusiast, full of ideas he rarely saw through, usually because they were bigger than our family bank balance.

Besides, I was on my own trip with Mo. By this stage we were communicating whenever he could access 3G. He sent me photos of the new tree-house he'd built for himself halfway up a mountain and described how his closest neighbour was an enormous bird of prey. *Red Kite,* he said. When she hatched six chicks, he sent me a picture. *OMG. Wish I could meet them*, I wrote back. *Come and visit,* he replied. I couldn't believe he was inviting me to stay. I stared at his message for ages and counted to three hundred before replying to avoid looking too keen. *Would love to. Where do u live?* I asked. *The Haven* he responded. 'The Haven. The Haven. The Haven,' I muttered, as I searched for it on Google Maps. When that failed, I tried an internet search. Nothing came up.

Mo explained it was an off-grid environmental community in the middle of a forest and that no one knew of its existence apart from the people who lived there. *How do I find it?* I typed. *Will work something out,* he replied. After an agonizing two-day wait, he told me he might be coming my way in a couple of weeks, but that plan fell apart days before he was meant to leave. There was a friend who was almost certainly hitching to the Haven, but she never got in touch.

My parents were becoming more isolated too. Cara was the first to notice something was up with them. I guess she was more tuned into their habits than the rest of us because she stood to lose most from any change to their situation.

So, it was Cara who casually asked if we'd observed how Mum and Dad not only stayed in most evenings, but also slunk off to the sitting room after dinner to watch reality TV shows instead of staying with her to finish a second bottle of wine. Even Joe, who didn't notice anything, agreed this was out of character. My parents were the kind who turned off the Wi-Fi at night without realizing we could all access the internet through 4G and had a poster in the kitchen that said, 'The People will not revolt because they will not look up from their screens long enough to notice what's happening.' I couldn't recall them ever watching any reality TV. 'Not even Season One of *Big Brother*,' observed Cara. But it was the kind of shows they were watching that wound her up. '*Building Off the Grid*, *Alaskan Bush People*, *Ben Fogle Lives in the Wild*, *Secrets of the Hive*. I mean what the actual fuck? Your parents' idea of getting back to nature and being environmental is a waterside cabin at Center Parcs.'

'Maybe it's all an excuse to get away from Cara,' I suggested to Joe, when he asked me what I thought was going on. I could tell Dad was tired of her living with us.

In the dragging hours of the night, when I finally became bored of fantasizing that the hand between my legs was Brodie Thompson's, I started to think about my parents' relationship in a way I hadn't done before. I didn't have many points of reference. There was none of the warmth and banter I witnessed in Alessia's house when babysitting. Neither was it the war zone that Joe described in Eadie's house because although Dad had a temper he never got angry with Mum, and they didn't bicker about things like heating or leaving out the milk. It dawned on me that I couldn't describe what their relationship was. Only what it wasn't.

I thought it was kind of sweet how they'd started snuggling up together on the sofa, Dad using Mum's thigh as a table to rest an exercise book where he made endless drawings and notes when he watched these programmes. He even unearthed an old photo album of their travels.

'Wouldn't it be so cool to have one last adventure together?' he asked Mum, as he showed her a photo of them floating down the Amazon on a boat. 'To recapture that sense of freedom and show the children a different rhythm to life?'

'It would be wonderful,' Mum wistfully agreed. 'Joe and Cass are umbilically attached to their phones the entire time.'

On school nights, after I'd finished revising for exams, I

started settling in with my parents and Maudie on the sofa in the sitting room to watch those programmes. I liked them in part because of their uncynical enthusiasm but mostly because their interests brought me closer to Mo.

Joe never joined us. He told my parents he was revising upstairs and slipped out of the house to see Eadie or Dana. Joe was as slippery as an oyster when it came to relationships. He was always falling in with someone, unlike Maudie, who fell out with everyone, and me, who never fell in with anyone. Although I didn't realize it at the time, the common thread was that we were all falling.

Dad began talking about the people in these shows like they were friends. 'Sunray', 'Mykel', 'Ben'. Which was not surprising, given he was spending more time with them than with his actual friends. So, when Cara slumped on the sofa beside us one night and drunkenly asked why my parents wanted to watch a bunch of rednecks talking shit, I genuinely thought Dad was going to explode.

'They make *Love Island* contestants look like Fulbright scholars,' Cara bumbled on. She hadn't noticed the tips of Dad's ears going red and his leg doing the angry tremble. 'Just saying.'

'These people are good, honest people, who believe in hard work, discipline and living sustainably. Unlike you, Cara,' said Dad. His tone was plaintive, like the cry of a dog that has been kicked. 'When did you last do an honest day's work? Would you even begin to know how to grow your own vegetables? Could you build a shelter or make a fire?'

For once Cara remained silent. Dad took the bottle of wine from her hand and placed it firmly out of her reach on the table. Cara didn't resist. 'These are real people with real skills that we've lost. Your idea of being environmental is sobbing over *Blue Planet* while eating a Deliveroo.'

Ouch! Dad's voice sounded weirdly thick, as if his vocal cords had been insulated with the same wattle and daub the people in the TV shows used for the walls of their cabins. Maudie threw a protective arm around him and rested her head on his shoulder.

'You've lost the plot, Rick,' Cara countered. 'It's not like you can do any of that shit either.' She sounded uncharacteristically unsure of herself. Or maybe she was the wrong side of another bottle of wine.

'At least I had a plot to lose,' said Dad, tautly. 'When have you ever made a plan and stuck to it? If it wasn't for Eve, you'd have nothing. Nothing.'

'That's enough, Rick,' warned Mum. Not wanting to piss her off, Dad pulled himself back from the brink by turning his criticism of Cara into a wider point about his new life philosophy.

'We are all the same species on the same planet at the same time. We share the same problems. We need to think and act collectively to work it all out. We need to tune into the natural world.' He bowed his head in a humble fashion, like a Buddhist monk. 'Dependency is weakness. Self-sufficiency is freedom. In my opinion.'

Cara riled him by asking how a passionate believer in self-sufficiency had had to call out the AA the previous week to change a wheel on the car, and buy new shirts when Mum went away for a long weekend with her book-club girlfriends because he didn't know how to iron. Everyone laughed, apart from me. *Dependency is weakness. Self-sufficiency is freedom.* I frowned. Hadn't Mo used the exact same words in a message to me the previous day? Except he wasn't talking about food. He was talking about how I needed to find my own path in life, away from my parents. I was certain he hadn't said this at the party, which meant that Dad must be in touch with him too. I felt an acid burn deep inside my stomach that I initially put down to anxiety but quickly identified as jealousy. Mo had picked me out from the crowd. Not Dad.

'No, it's not,' I said fiercely. Dad looked surprised. He wasn't used to me contradicting him. That was Joe's role.

'What's not what?' he asked.

'It's not your opinion. It belongs to Mo.' I felt guilty for exposing Dad but also good that, although I'd just discovered he'd been communicating with Mo, he clearly had no idea that Mo was also in touch with me.

'Who's Mo?' asked Cara, sensing a new battlefront opening up. 'Is he another of those woo-woo people from a reality TV show?'

'Mo is Dad's new man crush,' declared Joe.

'The wack job?' asked Cara, in a shorthand that indicated the two of them had already discussed him. Joe nodded.

There was an easy intimacy between my brother and my aunt like there was between him and Mum. They all got on with each other on a molecular level. I immediately regretted mentioning Mo's name because it highlighted how much attention I'd been paying him, which in turn made me blush in a way that Joe was bound to exploit without mercy. Unfortunately for me I'd inherited Dad's very pale Scottish skin, so my emotions rose volcanically to the surface. I covered my face with my hand as I always did when I got embarrassed, even though it encouraged a crescent of spots across my left cheek. Luckily, Dad bristled instead.

'Mo is one of the few people I've met who lives according to his beliefs. We could all learn a lot from him.' Cara pretended to be sick behind Dad's back, which made me feel bad for him and Mo. Later, I told Mo that he'd been the catalyst for yet another row. He loved this and so did I because it felt like he was already part of the fabric of our family life.

Just three weeks after Maudie's party, when the storms had blown themselves out and the flooding in the cellar had subsided, Dad said he had an announcement to make.

'I've found an extraordinary place where a couple of families are chosen each summer to experience life in an off-grid environmental community in return for a couple of hours' work each day. It sounds like paradise on earth. They grow all their own food, generate their own energy, even make their own clothes. They're entirely self-sufficient.'

'How amazing!' said Mum.

'What's this got to do with us?' asked Joe, suspiciously.

'I thought maybe we could go there over the summer,' said Dad. He was literally brimming with excitement.

'For how long?' I asked.

'Two months,' said Dad. 'They don't let you come for less. It's too disruptive.'

'Two months!' I spluttered. If I went away for that long there was no way I'd get to see Mo over the summer.

'You're kidding me,' said Joe, indignantly. 'I'm not leaving town for the whole summer after my exams.'

'Can't we just go to Center Parcs like old times?' I suggested, even though I pretty much hated Center Parcs.

'Too many people live in the ruins of their habits,' pronounced Dad. 'This could be an amazing opportunity for us to experience a totally different way of life.' We all stared at him in a state of dazed confusion. 'I'm done with sleep-walking through life. Come on, guys. Let's live a little!'

'What kind of work would it involve?' asked Mum. I knew right away she was sold.

'Cooking, working in the fields, chopping wood, washing clothes . . . whatever needs doing, I guess,' explained Dad.

'Doesn't sound like much of a holiday,' I pointed out.

'You might learn some new skills.' Mum was big on up-skilling. 'A week ago you guys were all super-enthusiastic about going away together,' she added.

'But not to some hippie commune,' muttered Joe.

'What would we do when we're not chopping wood?' asked Maudie.

'There's lots of animals that need looking after,' said Dad. 'Goats, chickens, sheep –'

'Are there badgers?' Maudie interrupted. 'I'm only going if there are badgers.' Dad nodded. I think at that point if she'd asked if there were unicorns he would have said yes. 'And can my rabbits come with us?'

'Of course.' Dad nodded.

'We can be like one of those families on TV shows who live together in the wild,' said Maudie, excitedly.

'So, where is this earthly paradise?' Mum teased him.

'It's a place called the Haven,' said Dad. 'Funnily enough, I found it through Mo. He runs the whole thing.'

I sat perfectly motionless in case anyone noticed the way my intestines turned inside out.

'It's a great idea, Rick, but how on earth could we take two months out?' asked Mum.

'We've got six weeks' holiday over the summer and we

could tack on a couple of extra weeks at the beginning of September. I'll come up with a good excuse.'

'And can we afford to go away for so long?' Mum pressed him.

'We'll let the house. We'll end up making more money than we spend,' explained Dad. 'I've looked into it all already.'

'I'm not sure,' said Mum.

'Don't we deserve one last adventure, Eve?' said Dad, turning to Mum and taking her hands in his. He had that damp-eyed look again.

'Where would we stay?' I asked. My voice was squeaky with excitement. Joe elbowed me in the ribs. He was counting on me to hold the line.

'Well, here's the thing,' said Dad. 'Mo has just built himself a new home and he's agreed to lend us his old cabin. The timing couldn't be more perfect.'

'Please can we go! Please can we go!' Maudie tugged at Mum's arm.

'Maybe we could go back to Center Parcs next year,' I suggested.

'What about Cara?' Joe asked.

'Mo's cabin only sleeps five,' said Dad.

'She'll have to find somewhere else to live. Until we get home,' said Mum. 'It'll do her good to be more independent.'

I tried to work out how much I minded that Mo had invited our entire family. Of course I would have preferred to go alone. But given all the problems in getting to the Haven, perhaps this was the only solution. After two months together maybe our relationship could go public. Suddenly I was living in the same glorious world of possibility as everyone else my age. When I questioned Mo about why he'd invited my entire family, he wrote back straight away. *Couldn't think of a better way to get you here. I'm desperate to see you . . . desperate. This way u can stay for longer.* My doubts evaporated. Usually with boys I found it impossible to read their signals. With Mo it was different. 'Desperate' was one of those words that wasn't open to interpretation.

When Cara got wind that our plan was becoming reality, she took Mum aside and told her it was the most batshit crazy idea she'd heard since Dad's last batshit crazy idea.

'Rick's been having a tough time. He needs to find his equilibrium again. This could be a great opportunity for him,' said Mum.

'He's had plenty of opportunity,' countered Cara.

'This could be a game-changer.' It was as if Mum had found a solution to an enormous problem without fully articulating even to herself what the problem was.

'It's always the same with Rick. It's not the job. It's not Joe. It's him. Can't you see? And what about you? You need to think about yourself too.' I'd never heard Cara sound so frustrated with Mum.

'You're only angry because you're not going with us,' retorted Mum.

'It's because I care about you and the children,' said Cara, tautly.

'Maybe when his spirit is liberated, the old Rick will come back.' Mum gave Cara a hug. 'It's going to be an amazing experience. For us all.'

'I hope you're right,' said Cara, hugging her back.

Within a week, Dad had arranged for us to miss the first two weeks of term after the summer holidays. I was ecstatic. For the first time ever, I felt that my time had finally come.

5

Now

I wait until I'm certain both police cars have left before abandoning my hiding place, jangly-nerved that the person who brought me here has likely been watching and waiting for this exact moment too. Heart pounding, I roll onto the frosty ground and pause for a moment on all fours. Now I'm clear of the shelter I see how much it protected me from the elements. I'm shaking hard. But I don't know whether to pin it on the cold, the fear, the pain or the blood loss from the wound on my head.

I squint through the trees, studying the route to our cabin, trying to figure out where the hardest-packed soil lies so my boots don't leave tracks. I cock my head to listen for sounds that might signal I've got company: twigs breaking; spooked pheasants; growling badgers. But there's nothing apart from the bone-chilling shudderings blowing in from the north. The sight of the water butts at the front of the cabin reminds me how thirsty I am. Dehydration makes you careless and I can't afford any mistakes.

The thought of going back inside our cabin gives me the chills. I don't have to remember anything to know bad shit went down there. It's visceral. But the wound on my head is pumping blood again and I need to get my hands on the first-aid kit if I'm going to survive in the wild for the next few days. I'm good. But not that good.

A distant memory of how my family once spent an entire Saturday night bingeing on a Netflix series about surviving in the Arctic, only breaking to eat a Deliveroo, takes shape. It was the kind of evening that used to make us feel adventurous. The idea of someone delivering a cooked meal on a bicycle is so absurd that I find myself maniacally laughing. And then the laughter turns to tears. What if my family is all dead and I'm the only one left? I feel crushed by the weight of their absence. I long to hear Mum's voice reassuring me. 'Everything passes. The sun always rises.' But all I hear is my own voice telling me I'm finished. *For every life a death*. That's how Nature works.

I make sure I leave no trace in the shelter. My plan is to stay low to the ground and hug the fir trees for as long as possible before breaking cover through the brambles and withered bracken towards the cabin. I crouch and leopard-crawl along the forest floor, propelling myself forwards on my elbows and the tips of my toes. I feel more like a giant slug than a leopard as I squeeze through the brambles, cursing the way they hold me back and dig their thorns into my hands and knees.

Crawling is so much harder than I'd expected. My arms go numb, and my leg muscles rage with the strain. The hand without a glove has already turned a waxy blue-grey and burns with cold. Every ten feet or so I slump to the ground to catch my breath and check no one is following me.

I force myself onwards, trying to picture where Mum kept the first-aid kit. But the rooms blur in and out of focus, shape-shifting into other rooms in other houses where I must have once lived. I see a sitting room with walls painted sunflower yellow and a sofa covered with a blue floral fabric. This quickly fades into a different room with a single bed and sheets so clean I almost want to cry. Then I see a small outbuilding where the wind whistles through the gaps in the worn wooden walls and a bucket of sawdust in the corner, and I know I'm thinking about the composting toilet on the other side of our cabin. There was a game we used to play, Worst Death Possible. Wasn't freezing to death while having a shit one of Maudie's top five? I smile for a second, then beat myself up for the way I can remember something so trivial but nothing that counts.

The wind picks up. I peer at the grey shards of sky visible through the trees and see a flock of Canada geese overhead, fluttering like bunting in a V formation above me. Using their guttural honk as cover I crawl pretty much non-stop to the edge of the undergrowth and lie flat on the ground for as long as I can bear the cold until I'm certain I'm alone. The fire in my lungs matches the fire in my head. I'm sweating but at the same time it's so cold I can't feel my fingers on the hand without the glove.

Now I'm close to the cabin I can see the damage. There's a large hole at ground-level, big enough for an adult man to crawl through. The fragments of wood around the edges are black and charred. There's definitely been a fire, but maybe the water butts prevented it from catching. And then it hits me. I must be responsible for all this. And if I did this, what else have I done? I check under my nails again and recoil in disgust when I still find traces of skin and dried blood.

I pull myself upright and tread cautiously, with shuffling side-steps, towards the front door of the cabin. I stop for a moment to take it all in, then push it open and step inside.

As my eyes adjust to the gloom, I scan the kitchen and sitting area and see the orange gas canister lying on its side. I barely have time to digest this when the door unexpectedly bangs shut. It's the wind, I tell myself. My breath quickens as I walk towards it. Fear is a state of mind. I think it was Joe who had a theory that you could control fear by thinking about all the people who love you or could love you. *Mum, Dad, Joe, Maudie, Mo.* I say their names, over and over again, like a mantra, as I lift the latch and slowly open the front door.

On the ground a small wooden doll stares up at me. Its arms are made of bones and the skull of a *Pica pica* magpie sits on its head. It's completely creepy. Hands trembling, I pick it up to take a closer look. It has hair, like my hair. Eyes, my colour. It's wearing a denim dress that looks familiar. I lift the skirt and see a blood-stained hole below the belly button. Shit-scared, I drop the doll onto the floor. I feel like I've seen something like this before, but I can't remember where or when. I'm just turning this over when it hits me that this doll wasn't on the ground when I came in. There's a piercing scream that sends the birds screeching into the sky. I hardly recognize the sound of my own voice.

6

Then

According to Dad's schedule, we were meant to get up at sunrise on the day we left to prepare our body clocks for the rhythms of the timetable at the eco-retreat. In the run-up to our trip he'd spent a lot of time learning new skills, including a method of telling the time by measuring the height of the sun in the sky, which Mum joked would fry his retinas. By this stage, Dad was so adamant he'd trained his body to wake up on its own that he didn't bother to set the alarm clock for four forty-nine and we ended up over-sleeping. So, it's fair to say the day got off to a bad start.

When Mum flurried into my bedroom to wake me up, we were already hours behind schedule and there was a parking ticket on the van Dad had unexpectedly bought in exchange for our old car a few weeks earlier. 'Aha! A subliminal message,' Dad exclaimed, as he tore it up and threw the pieces into the air. The fine seemed simultaneously to infuriate and gratify him because it confirmed all his opinions about the futility of modern life and why we needed to embrace a purer existence in the natural world.

Such was my excitement about seeing Mo again that I was already dressed under my duvet, with my bags lined up at the end of the bed. Mum and Dad twittered about my maturity and thoughtfulness, but it was one of those clumsy lumps of parental praise that was really about the failings of another family member – in this case Joe – who not only wasn't ready but was also still in bed with a girl who wasn't Eadie or Dana.

I knew this even before I heard Dad yell and the girl scuttle downstairs because Joe had caught me test-driving outfits in the bathroom mirror when he arrived home at two in the morning. Having no faith in my own opinion, and confident Joe was so off his face he wouldn't exploit my self-doubt, I'd forced him and the girl to help me choose between a pair of boyfriend jeans and white vest top or a button-down denim mini dress.

As I closed my door wearing the denim dress, I felt nothing. I didn't mind packing up my room or that some-one else would be sleeping in my bed for the next two months. I didn't mind missing the first two weeks of term. I didn't mind having said goodbye to my friends. 'Not caring is a superpower,' Joe used to say, when I questioned his lightness of being. Finally, I understood what he meant.

Cara held open the back door of the van as I tried to force my bags into the available space. Dad reminded her that she needed to be out of the house by midday. 'No worries,' Cara said, in a deflated tone. I hugged her, which made the denim dress ride up my thighs and caterpillar uncomfortably around my stomach.

'Don't worry, it's all going to be fine,' she said, putting her arm around my shoulders. 'Time will fly.' I felt bad for Cara because the words of comfort she offered me were really meant for her.

Dad twitched around making the final adjustments to his rucksack. Touchingly he'd unearthed the same rucksacks he and Mum had used during their South American travels. Although it was really hot, he was wearing embarrassingly new Haglöfs hiking boots, khaki shorts, and a matching shirt with long sleeves pulled down to his wrists. The only time Cara smiled was when she saw him.

'He looks like the bastard child of Ray Mears,' she whispered to Joe. I felt sorry for Dad because I recognized hope in an outfit and, if anything, his was begging for approval even more than mine. If it hadn't been for the wet patches under his armpits, I'd have given him a hug. He'd worked so hard to get everything ready and already his plans were unravelling.

In spite of Dad's carefully drawn-up packing plan it was impossible to fit all our stuff into the van. Several of the things he'd listed under Large Essential Items, including an orange propane gas canister and his Reliance Rhino five-gallon water container, were still lined up on the pavement.

In the end we had to unpack everything and start from scratch. During this process Dad discovered that Maudie had secretly packed three extra bags for herself. One held all the dressing-up clothes that Mum had expressly told her not to take, including a flamenco dress and our grandmother's wedding dress. The other two contained her entire collection of stuffed toys. Maudie put on the flamenco dress, climbed into her seat and refused to take it off. There was a standoff, during which Dad pleaded with her to leave the stuffed toys behind. We all knew it was futile. He always gave in. So in the end – as usual – it was me who was called upon to make the biggest sacrifice. The orange gas canister was heaved into the well of my seat and Maudie's bags took its place in the back. I spent the entire journey straddling the gas canister with my fat sweaty thighs. It banged against my legs and pinched my skin every time Dad turned a corner, and although in time

I grew to see it as an ally, during that journey I hated it with more passion than I thought was possible.

If I'd known how long it would be until I saw my aunt again, I would have hugged Cara a little longer and thought more carefully about my final words to her as we settled into our designated seats in the van.

'Call me. Whenever, especially if –' Cara was still speaking when Dad slammed the door. I think right to the end she was holding out hope that Mum and Dad might invite her along for the ride. But I could see it could be good for my parents to have a break from her. Cara was the cause of virtually every argument they had.

'Thanks for everything,' I heard Mum whisper to her, as they hugged each other goodbye.

'I'm always there if you need me,' said Cara, her voice taut with emotion. 'Always.'

I didn't get why Mum was thanking Cara when it should have been the other way round. Mum climbed upfront with Dad.

'You'll be back before you know it,' Cara shouted, with false cheer, over the noise of the engine. Joe and I sat beside each other in the back seat opposite Maudie. Her rabbit cage took up the space between us, and the only part of Joe that was visible was his curly black hair. Even he seemed excited about our first road trip in the van. He'd given it a name – Rory. Eadie and Dana were already ancient history and before we'd reached the outskirts of the city, he was making bad jokes about hippies and free love and wondering if there would be any girls his age at the Haven. I messaged Mo. It took me an hour to settle on the final wording. I was torn between whether to say *See u tonight* or

Be with u tonight. I stuck with the first option and then felt deflated when he wrote back, *Can't wait to see you all.*

The argument later that day started over something insignificant. It kicked off at the service station when we finally stopped for lunch at half past three. Stressed that we were four hours behind schedule and still only halfway through the journey, Dad reversed too quickly into a parking space, mounted the kerb and ripped off Rory's bumper.

The impact sent Juniper and Jason scurrying round their cage in panic and the jam-jar lids that Maudie was using as bowls for her plastic dogs were flung into the front of the van, tipping water over Mum and Dad. Dad got out, collected the bumper and wordlessly placed it over Joe's lap as if it was his fault.

Joe, who'd been asleep for most of the journey, finally stirred and unfurled. 'Chill out.' His face looked weirdly misshapen, in part because the wire pattern of the rabbit cage was indented on his cheek, but mostly because it was doughy with hangover. 'Is this our last meal in civilization?' he rasped, half opening one eye. 'In which case can I have anything and chips?'

'How about chips and chips?' suggested Maudie, excitedly. She did her saucer-eyed thing and pleaded with Mum and Dad to grant her one last strawberry milkshake. Mum reluctantly conceded that McDonald's might prove the quickest option. To our total astonishment Dad agreed.

'I told the folks at the eco-retreat we'd be there by six,' he said, peeling a twenty-pound note from a wad of cash in his pocket. I braced myself for the inevitable explosion about capitalist banks screwing over their customers, but it never came.

'What time does Reception close?' asked Mum.

'Not sure,' said Dad. 'Probably before sundown. I think they're early-to-bed-early-to-rise kind of people.'

I couldn't ever remember eating in a fast-food restaurant with my parents. I wolfed an extra-large portion of chips and ordered another without a single eyebrow being raised. Joe polished off a double burger without Dad mentioning how much soya a cow had to consume in its lifetime to produce just thirty burgers. Even Mum devoured a Big Mac.

Dad didn't eat anything. But it wasn't for ideological reasons. It was because he was filled with restless energy. He sat beside me poring over the map and directions that Mo had sent him in the post. *The Haven,* it said at the top, in his strangely neat, sloping script.

The map was hand-drawn with trees and hedges shaded in with different colours and tiny buildings outlined in black ink. *Mo's tree-house,* it said, beneath a house on stilts. There were round timber-framed cabins with grass roofs, chimney pots with smoke billowing out and intricately drawn goats, cows and chickens. It was beautiful. Above one of the smaller houses he'd written Drift Ridge Cabin with our names beneath. I traced its outline, remembering the way his finger had run along my hand at Maudie's party. Mum asked to take a closer look. 'Wow! That's quite something. Do you think he does this for all the guests?' she asked.

I shook my head. 'Definitely not.'

'Why us, then?' asked Mum, doing that thing where she raised one eyebrow.

'Because we're special,' said Dad and I, simultaneously. It was rare that we hit the same beat at the same time and we laughed.

'I doubt many of the other guests knew him as well as we did before they arrived,' said Dad, proudly.

Mum shot him a lingering look over her sunglasses. 'We've met him once. For six hours in total. I'm not sure you can tell anything about anyone in such a short space of time.'

'It's not the quantity of communication, it's the quality of the connection,' I said, parroting one of Cara's favourite observations. 'You got with Dad the same day you met him, didn't you?'

'Who told you that?' asked Mum.

'Cara,' I said.

'Bloody typical,' muttered Dad. He pored over the map again and calculated that it could be another five hours before we arrived, which meant we would almost certainly be too late for dinner. 'Come on, folks! Let's get this show on the road!'

'Otherwise we'll arrive in the dark.' I shared his impatience. I was desperate to see Mo again.

We'd all finished eating, apart from Maudie, who was trying to make her strawberry milkshake last as long as possible. After the earlier spillage, Mum and Dad had ruled that no one should eat or drink anything in the van.

'Please let me drink it during the journey. Please! I'll keep the lid on,' she begged, between birdlike sips through the straw. 'What's the point of a table if we never get to use it?'

'Come on, Maudie,' Dad protested, but she sensed the defeat in his tone.

Mum attempted to placate her by introducing a compromise. 'Why don't you put your milkshake in the cool box and drink it once you get there?' she proposed. Truly

Mum was a born diplomat. Maudie refused and kept up her campaign of tiny sips.

'That drink is two hundred millilitres, and you're drinking around one millilitre every two seconds, which means at the same rate you'll take an hour and a half to finish,' said Joe. 'Stop being a dick.'

He reached across Mum to seize the milkshake but missed his target and instead tipped it onto Mo's directions and Maudie's flamenco dress. I grabbed the soggy map while everyone else leapt away from the table to avoid the pink froth dripping over the edges. Maudie stood rigid, nostrils flaring. Her face went pale, then slowly turned redder and redder until eventually her skin was the colour of her hair. She clenched her fists.

'Incoming,' Joe warned.

'Shut it, Joe,' snapped Dad.

'Count to twenty, Maudie,' said Mum. 'One. Deep breath in. Two. Deep breath out . . . Come on, you can do it.'

But she couldn't. Or wouldn't. It was difficult to tell with Maudie. Her eyes glazed, her breathing became faster, then she burst into tears, threw herself onto the floor and beat her fists on the picture of Ronald McDonald.

'You'll pay for this, Joe. You'll pay for this,' she screamed. She howled with rage. A couple of boys on the neighbouring table started sniggering and pointing. Everyone in the restaurant was now staring at her. This was Maudie's superpower. Making sure she was the centre of attention at all times. I saw Dad march towards my brother and grip his upper arm, just inside the sleeve of Joe's T-shirt, out of Mum's sightline. My stomach turned over with anxiety.

'Stop causing trouble,' said Dad, tightening his grip

around Joe's arm, his fingers pinching the skin so tightly that his knuckles turned white.

'All anger is entitlement,' said Joe, pressing his lips together. He squared up to Dad. If Dad was hurting his arm, he wasn't going to show it. Neither of them backed down. I noticed for the first time that Joe was taller than Dad. I looked round to see if anyone was watching this sideshow, but everyone's eyes were on Maudie, who was still hammering the floor with her fists. I made a beeline towards Dad.

'It's Maudie's fault, not Joe's,' I pleaded with him.

He ignored me. Once again, I was invisible, which should be a superpower but isn't. I looked at Mum to intervene, but she was frantically dabbing at the map with the edge of her T-shirt, like a picture restorer trying to save a masterpiece from a flood.

'You can break my arm and I won't get angry,' said Joe, through clenched teeth. 'I won't ever be like you.' Dad finally let go.

'Come on, Maudie! I'll get you another milkshake!' Mum tried and failed to persuade Maudie off the floor.

I picked up the map from the table. The green trees and hedges had turned pink, and the inky outlines of the houses and animals had run into each other to create an impressionistic murky mess. The instructions at the bottom were still legible but there were gaps at key points in the middle. At the top, the letters had been rubbed out, and where it had said THE HAVEN, it looked as if it said HEAVEN.

'Hope it's not a subliminal message that we're all going to die there,' said Joe.

'If we can't work out how to get there, I'll kill her,' I said ferociously.

While Mum and Dad were distracted, I went into the service station and bought as many packets of Maoams as I could with the twenty-five pounds Cara had given me for emergencies. On the way back to the van, I tore open five sweets, crammed them into my mouth and chewed until the sugary sweetness turned sickly and I felt normal again. The rest I hid at the bottom of my backpack. I didn't want anyone to know about them, mostly so I wouldn't have to share them, but also because I couldn't face the way Dad's gaze would drift from the sweets to my stomach. I pulled down the front of my denim dress where it had hiked up again and tightened the belt to remind me to breathe in.

Joe noticed the extra bulge in my backpack as soon as I sat down in the back of the van. He squeezed the bottom corner so that the packets of sweets crunched between his fingers. 'I think Cass has news to share with the group,' he said triumphantly. Everyone turned towards him and then me.

Something made Joe stop in his tracks. I liked to think it was compassion but more likely it was a sense that he might need an ally over the next two months. 'She's found a USB port,' he announced, flipping open a hidden compartment beneath the table. Dad had made a big thing about how we wouldn't be able to charge our phones at the Haven.

'It'll only work if the engine's running and I'm keeping hold of the key,' said Dad.

I could tell by the way his jaw had set that he was irritated. Since Maudie's party I'd noticed he'd become somehow simultaneously thinner- and thicker-skinned.

By way of apology for his meltdown at the restaurant Dad tried to press the directions into Joe's hands and asked him to sit up front to help navigate the final leg of the journey. In the past this kind of peace-offering might have won over my older brother. Of all of us he had the easiest temperament. 'Slow to rage and quick to forgive,' Mum always said. Like her, although she never said that. Maudie was more Dad than Dad. Quick to rage and slow to forgive. I wasn't sure what I was. I was unformed or maybe slow to form. But, as it turned out, this was my superpower.

'No, thanks,' said Joe, in an even tone. 'I prefer the back.'

'How about you, Cass? Will you help your old man?' Dad asked.

'Sure,' I said, gratified by my sudden promotion in the family hierarchy. Joe smirked. No one who'd known me for more than five minutes would trust me to navigate. I literally had no sense of direction.

'It's going to be difficult to piece together the section that drowned in the tsunami,' Dad cautioned, as I got into the van beside him. I turned the map in my hands. Even if the words hadn't bled into each other and the carefully painted landmarks blurred into different shades of strawberry milkshake, I still wouldn't have been able to fathom it out.

'I'll do my best,' I promised.

Initially I didn't need the directions because the route was obvious. Busy dual carriageways gave way to quieter roads framed with unruly green hedges until eventually we found ourselves on a remote country lane where there was so little traffic that a strip of dry grass tickled Rory's underbelly. Outside the air got cooler as we snaked higher and higher into the hills. The drop outside my window became more and more vertiginous until the angle of the corners was so sharp that Dad had to execute terrifying three-point turns to make it round the switchbacks. Maudie covered her head with the skirt of her soggy flamenco dress and kept worrying what would happen if we met a car coming the other way. But apart from us, the only signs of life were sheep scattered over the bald hills. Eventually even the screen of the satnav turned green.

'We're officially off grid,' announced Dad. 'I am reborn.' He was choked up. Mum and Maudie cheered from the back of the van. I buried my excitement in case Joe saw it as betrayal.

'It's like the trees and grass have swallowed the road,' said Maudie, peeking out to show her two favourite dogs the view.

'The air is purer already,' said Mum, closing her eyes and leaning her head against the window so her face was bathed in sunshine. She looked so peaceful and beautiful. Mum was such an easy-going person. Her cup was always half full. She sang when she cooked and believed that things always had a way of sorting themselves out.

I started to measure the hours in playlists. Joe's was called Get Me Out of Here and started with 'Home' by the Foo Fighters and ended with 'Home Sweet Home' by Mötley Crüe. He nudged my shoulder to make sure I appreciated this act of subliminal rebellion. Dad remained oblivious. He chose Queen's *Greatest Hits* and we all sang 'Bohemian Rhapsody' from beginning to end with the windows wound down. '"He's got a moose, got a moose, can you do the banned tango,"' sang Dad at the top of his voice.

Many playlists later we found ourselves in a lush green valley nestled between two enormous hills. The route followed the curves of a river that wound through a tiny village where half a dozen dilapidated stone houses straddled either side of the road. We pulled over to consult Mo's directions. The section we needed to examine was impossible to decipher.

'What now, folks?' asked Mum, cheerfully.

'We've got a fifty-fifty chance of getting it right,' said Joe.

I passed the soggy piece of paper back to Mum. The sun had dropped behind the hills and the light was starting to fade. Sensing looming tension, I turned towards the passenger window and pretended to watch the river, while secretly unwrapping more Maoams. Mum spotted an elderly woman sitting in a rocking chair, smoking a cigarette with her eyes closed, on the pavement outside one of the houses.

'I'll ask her for directions and report back,' Mum offered.

It took a while for Mum to return. 'It's all a bit odd. She has no idea what an eco-retreat is and has never heard of the Haven. She says we're the first people to come through the village for months, apart from a few hippies and some Jehovah's Witnesses.'

'That's weird,' said Dad, pulling an old-fashioned Ordnance Survey map from the glove compartment. 'There's no other way in. Anyone who goes to the Haven has to travel through this village.'

I remembered Mo explaining how it would be impossible for me to visit after the rains started because of flooding and suggested we should probably turn right and follow the river upstream.

'If we reach the tree tunnel, we'll know we've called it right,' I said.

'What's a tree tunnel?' asked Maudie.

'It's where the branches of trees meet overhead to form a natural tunnel,' I explained.

'How do you know all this?' asked Mum.

'It was on Mo's map,' I babbled.

'Then why didn't I notice it?' said Dad, grimacing so hard that his forehead resembled the contours on the map. He turned on the engine and took the first right. I wasn't used to my opinion holding so much sway and it felt good. We continued in exhausted silence. The bare scrub slowly turned into more unruly woodland and forest. By this stage all we wanted was to get there.

We climbed up a meandering road through thick forest. The terrain became rockier and the road got so narrow that the branches of the trees locked together to form a tunnel over our heads.

'Goddamnit, Cass, you were right!' yelled Dad, in excitement.

'Can you see the light at the end of the tunnel, Dad?' joked Joe.

From where I was sitting, I could see Dad's jaw was still set hard. Was it the anxiety of us being late? Or the discovery that his son no longer cleaved to his word? Or was there some latent stress inside him, like the heat at the earth's core, which would always threaten to bubble to the surface and consume us all? I wondered if all dads were like him. The truth was we didn't have many points of reference. There were no other men in our family. He was a late-born only child, whose parents had died years ago.

Mum read out the surviving three lines of instructions at the bottom of the map. *Climb Drift Ridge ¼ mile. Sharp right in gap in hedge between blackthorn and hazel. Continue to the Ends of the Earth.*

We pressed our noses against the window of the van

searching for the mystery opening in the hedge with a renewed sense of purpose. None of us wanted to spend the night in Rory. Not even Dad.

'What about there?' I tentatively suggested, pointing at a gap in the hedgerow, a little wider than Rory. We all got out to have a look.

'Well done, Cass,' said Dad, patting my head. I leant into him.

'If you were a dog, you'd be a Labrador,' said Joe. That hurt, but he'd stepped through the hole in the hedge and was swallowed by the forest before I could retaliate.

'What's it like on the other side, Joe?' Maudie called.

'There's snow everywhere and I think I spotted Mr Tumnus taking a shit in a composting toilet.'

Maudie giggled.

'Maybe it's a test and the guests who are clever enough to find the place are the ones who get to stay,' wondered Dad.

'What's that?' asked Maudie, suddenly. She knelt in front of the hedge, slipped her hand inside and pulled out a small wooden doll with a skull covering its face. It had dark brown hair that appeared real, a headdress of tiny bones made to look like antlers and a white dress embroidered with flowers. Its arms were covered with tiny hieroglyphs, triskelion, conjoined spirals and mandalas that were identical to the tattoos on Mo's arms. Maudie placed the doll in the palm of her hand and held it up for us to inspect.

'That's horrible,' declared Mum.

'Really spooky,' I agreed.

'I kind of like it,' said Maudie. 'Can I keep it?'

'No!' Mum tried to grab the doll from her hand, but Maudie stuffed it deep into the pocket of her flamenco dress. A branch snapped in the woods on the other side of the road. We all jumped and turned, but could see nothing.

'What was that?' asked Mum, nervously.

'Probably an animal warning us to get out of here before nightfall,' said Dad, trying to make light of the spookery.

After that we didn't need much persuading to get back into the van. It took Dad several attempts to persuade Rory through the narrow opening in the hedge and I wasn't even sure when he succeeded whether it was something to celebrate. I think at that point if one of us had suggested we went back to the nearest town everyone except Dad would have agreed.

'There's ruts,' Dad triumphantly declared.

'Ruts. Sweet,' said Joe sarcastically.

As we progressed, the furrows became deeper and craggier. The trees huddled closer and closer together, their branches entwined in ever more complicated embraces until it was so dark that Dad had to turn on the headlights to see the route ahead. There was a new noise, an eerie high-pitched screech that sounded like hundreds of fingernails scraping the side of the van. My heart raced. Dad crunched down the gears until we were making such slow progress that even I could have outrun Rory. But the noise didn't stop, just changed tempo.

'What is that?' I asked nervously. No one replied.

'I feel as if I'm in *Wrong Turn*,' said Joe. He placed the rabbit cage between him and the window, pulled Maudie onto his knee for protection and started to outline the plot of his all-time-favourite horror film. 'It's about six teenagers who get hunted down by inbred cannibals after their car breaks down in a forest.'

'Please stop,' begged Maudie, burying her face in his shoulder.

'You'll be all right, Maudie,' said Joe, 'You're skin and bones. It's Cass they'll go after!'

Instead of being irritated by Joe's put-down, I found its predictability comforting. The van started to list towards my side. The scraping noise got louder. Dad pressed down the accelerator, but we continued at the same speed, as if something was holding us back.

'We're going to roll! We're going to roll!' shrieked Maudie, who'd been thrown against me and was sandwiched on the other side by her rabbit cage. 'Please stop, Dad! I'm begging you!'

'This can't be right, Rick,' yelled Mum, bumping her head on the windscreen as she tried to peer out.

'We have to keep going.' Dad was clinging to the steering wheel to stop himself sliding towards Mum. 'Maybe this is a private road that leads to Mo's house and everyone else goes in the main entrance.'

'Maybe we should check out what lies ahead before we go any further and get stuck,' said Joe. 'In case maybe we can't turn around and end up spending the rest of our lives here. Just saying.'

'Maybe we should walk the rest of the way,' suggested Mum.

Hoping to impress Dad with my superior courage but also resolve the mystery so I would get to see Mo that night, I decided to take action. I slid open my door and leant out to check out what was making the noise. Thorns like scalpels ripped open the flesh on my right arm and thousands of tiny black insects flew into the van, covering my face and hair.

'Brambles,' I confirmed to Dad. My eyes filled with tears of pain.

'Well done, Cass,' he said gruffly. 'Well done.' But still he didn't slow down.

Instead he accelerated and tried to pick up speed. Rory roared in protest. Mum shrieked at Dad to stop. The noise got louder. This time it came from underneath the van. My head thumped against the window and the gas canister pinned my right leg against the sliding door. Maudie sobbed in my ear. Then suddenly the van was on its side and Joe, Maudie and the rabbit cage were all on top of me. I looked up and remembered dreamily thinking how strange it was that the van now had a sunroof.

'Fucking fuckers!' Maudie shrieked in my ear. 'We've capsized!'

My face hurt like hell where the rabbit cage had hit it and my leg was going numb beneath the gas canister. But all I could focus on was how it was looking less and less likely that I'd get to see Mo that night.

7

Now

It's not whether you get knocked down, Cassia. It's whether you get up. I hear Mo's voice and spin round the kitchen, hoping he's come to help me. But the voice isn't real. It's in my head. Something rustles and I jump again. The poster on the wall is flapping in the breeze. *The Rules of Threes* it reads across the top. Then underneath: *You can survive 3 minutes without air; 3 hours without shelter in a harsh environment; 3 days without water; and 3 weeks without food.*

Three minutes without air. I feel the sensation of hands gripping my neck, squeezing hard until my vision narrows and I have a head full of stars. This time grainy details flash before me: a gold ring on one of the fingers; the smell of incense; a blurry disc of light that fades the deeper I sink into the black vortex. I'm suffocating! *Breathe, Cass, breathe.* I come up for air and find myself panting like a dog on the kitchen floor, all sweat and wheeze. I'm completely alone. Mo isn't here. I'm crushed by the weight of my disappointment.

I warily look round our cabin. That policewoman wasn't exaggerating. It's a total shithole. Broken furniture, unwashed dishes, and the remnants of a fire on the floor beside the hole where the wall used to be. Fuck knows how I'm going to find the first-aid kit in this mess. I pick up an upturned stool, sit at the table and thirstily gulp down the dregs of a glass of water. My attention turns to four plates of leftover pasta encased in a dried red sauce. I'm starving. I grab a fork that still has cylinders of pasta stuck on its prongs from the nearest plate and swallow so fast that I imagine the *penne* queuing to get down into my stomach. The pasta is stale, and the tomato sauce tastes rough, but I don't care as long as my stomach's full. I can tell from the way my ribs stick out that I've been hungry for a while.

Then it hits me. It's all wrong. I'm in Dad's seat but there's no place laid for him . . . Bloody bandages litter the floor . . . There are piles of filthy clothes. Thoughts gallop across my consciousness but I can't connect them to anything specific. It's like my memories are shapes, not events. I find one of Mum's hair toggles with a knot of her hair knitted into the elastic and put it on my wrist like a bracelet. My body aches with the missing of her.

I get up too quickly, overturning the stool, and head towards a row of nails on the wall by the bedroom door. There are a couple of jackets and a grimy old backpack with a Danish flag on the front but no first-aid kit. I rifle through pockets, like a thief, stuffing loose coins, used tissues, matches, a pen and bits of paper into the backpack. I check in the store cupboard but it's empty, apart from a half-finished packet of soya beans and three cans of chopped tomatoes that I pack into my bag.

I catch sight of a wooden crate under the sink and crawl over, slating myself for prioritizing food when the light is fading fast, and I don't have a torch. The police have taken everything out of the Ziploc bags and tossed it onto the floor. I stuff an unused blister pack of water-purifying tablets into my pocket. My luck improves: two plastic bags.

Plastic bags are like gold in these parts. They have multifarious uses. Water storage. Boot liners. Leak pluggers. I carefully fold them, corner to corner, making them as small as possible and tuck them in the inside pocket of my jacket.

Then the main prize. A head torch. JS, it says on the elastic in big black letters. I can't allow myself to wonder why only Joe's head torch has been left behind. I flick it on, cup my hand around the bulb and point it towards the floor so that its underwhelming beam won't be visible to anyone watching the cabin. The batteries are on their last legs.

The first-aid kit must be in Mum and Dad's bedroom. Spooked by what I might find, I lift the latch and shove open the door so that if anyone's hiding they'll be more surprised than me. But apart from the mattress on the floor and a broken table lying on its side, it's empty. It's really dark, and I realize it's because the windows are boarded up from the outside.

I peel back the grubby layer of blankets on the mattress. The sheet beneath is filthy. There are different-coloured stains that merge into each other. I sink onto the mattress on my knees. Memories collide in painful fragments. A withered hand. Burnt flesh. Maudie screaming. I sniff the blankets and they smell like family. I'm suddenly exhausted and want nothing more than to lie down and sleep.

My head throbs with a thumping beat, and when I touch the top of the hood it's damp again with fresh blood. I flail around and find the small red first-aid kit hidden behind the broken table. But someone has got here before me because it's empty, apart from Mum's sewing pouch. I force myself upright and stumble back into the kitchen.

The mirror to the left of the sink is dark and sticky with smoke and cooking oil. I wipe it with the glove in small circles and slowly my face reassembles. My skin is pale yellow, as if it hasn't seen daylight in a while. My left cheek is covered with dried blood. My lower lip is swollen so that I have an overbite like a pug. And there are bruises on my neck. I'm unrecognizable even to myself.

I cry out when I pull down the hood because the fabric has stuck to the wound. It's the first time I've seen my injury and I'm shocked at the way the cut gapes open like a broken zip. Needs cleaning. I look down and see a saucepan of water sitting in the sink that looks reasonably clean and a dry dishcloth that doesn't. I dip the grubby cloth in the water and start to rub my face in small circles. The dried scabs of blood above my lip and in the channels beside my nose peel away relatively easily. When I reach the hairline, it becomes trickier. A good chunk of my hair is purple and stiff with dried blood.

I pour water and salt into a plastic bag, make a tiny hole in the corner, and hold it above my head to flush the wound with saline. Leaning over the sink, I let the water flow through until the red dribble fades to pink.

Teeth grinding with pain, I keep rinsing the wound until the throbbing in my brain becomes unbearable. When I look into the mirror again, I'm panicked by the depth of the ragged gash that starts just above my hairline and continues as far as my left temple.

I line up the needle, black thread and matches on the kitchen table and rest the mirror against the backpack, with the torch on top so it points at my head. I struggle to thread the needle because of my mangled finger. It doesn't hurt, but I have no feeling in it. Eventually I manage to tie a big black knot at one end. I strike a match and hold the flame against the needle until my fingers burn. It's as sterile as it will ever be.

Using my left hand, I pinch together the two flaps of skin as best I can and brace myself before sticking the needle through the flesh, around half a centimetre from the edge of the cut, through the upper layer of the skin. I cry out. It's a strangled sound that comes from deep inside, the kind of noise an animal makes when a hunter fails to get a clean kill. I count to ten, pull the thread tight and somehow manage to stick the needle into the flesh on the opposite side of the cut. I tighten it as much as I can to bring the two pieces of skin close together so it's secure enough to seal the wound but not to kill the tissue. I repeat this process four more times until it's as if all I've ever known is this pain.

My head is bleeding again but this time it's from the puncture wounds of the needle. I turn off the torch and sit until I can stand without feeling faint. I, Cassia Sawyer, am stronger than I could ever have imagined. When I pull myself up my eye is drawn to a hunting knife hanging on the wall. I take it down, run my finger along the blade and shove it into my backpack. I catch a glimpse of myself in the mirror. My vision blurs. *Am I the hunted? Or the hunter?*

8

Then

For a moment there was beautiful silence. I looked up through the window of the van and saw the same branches that had viciously savaged my skin minutes earlier now swaying gently in the breeze against the red and orange sunset and wondered if we'd all died and gone to Heaven. But it had been a cartoonish accident in slow motion and, other than a few scratches and Dad's bruised ego, we didn't have a lot to show for all the drama.

It took me a moment to get my bearings and understand that my door was now the floor of the van and the window facing the sky was in fact the passenger window. My spine pressed uncomfortably against the gas canister. I couldn't move because Joe was wedged in beside me.

'Are you all okay?' Mum cried, from the front.

'Yeah,' groaned Joe, as he struggled to pull himself upright.

'I didn't spill my drink,' stammered Maudie, who was sprawled across us both, milkshake in one hand, the handle of her rabbit cage in the other. The rabbits stared at us, wiggling their noses in quiet disapproval. It unnerved me that Juniper and Jason never showed their feelings. According to Maudie, they only made a noise when they were shit-scared.

'This is a disaster,' muttered Mum.

'Life's greatest lessons are learnt from the worst mistakes,' proclaimed Dad.

'What if you die making the mistake?' panted Maudie, as she struggled to manoeuvre herself towards the door of the van.

'Look, I'm really sorry,' said Dad.

'It was an accident, Rick,' said Mum. 'Could have happened to any of us.'

Not true. Not true. It occurred to me, in the adrenaline-fuelled clarity that often follows a shock, that the strategy Mum used to soothe Dad was the same approach she adopted with Maudie. I wondered if Mo required similar management. Did all men? It was a horrific thought.

'God, this is so embarrassing,' I sighed. 'What are the eco-retreat people going to think?' I was really worrying about what Mo would think of my useless family.

'Hopefully, we'll never know because they'll never find us,' muttered Joe.

'What happens if we're lost here for ever?' panicked Maudie. 'How will we feed Jason and Juniper?'

'We'll eat them before they get hungry,' said Joe, smacking his lips.

'If you touch my rabbits, I'll kill you!' she threatened.

'Don't worry, Maudie. When we don't turn up, they'll send out a search party,' said Mum, leaning over to stroke her hair.

'Mo won't abandon us,' I said resolutely, my faith absolute. 'He could find us anywhere. He can track the same animal for days.'

'And let's look on the bright side! At least none of us is hurt,' said Dad, from the front of the van. He'd already let himself off the hook.

'Rory might not agree,' said Joe.

This was true. Our poor van lay compliantly on its side, wheezing its final breaths. I couldn't understand why Dad was so relaxed about trashing Rory and felt suddenly tearful. Our van might have refused to bow to Dad's will, but it had perished in the process. I felt there was a lesson in this for all of us but there was no time to think anything through.

'We need to get out of here right now,' declared Dad, as he hid the key of the van behind his sun vizor. 'Two bags each. No arguments.' There was never going to be any resistance to his plan. It was obvious we couldn't spend the night in Rory and there was no way we could take all of our luggage with us.

Joe manoeuvred the rabbit cage until he could stand on it and stretched up to the sliding door to ease it open. The cool evening breeze fanned my face and soothed the bleeding cuts on my arms. I closed my eyes for a moment. So much had already happened that I felt as if I'd been away for months. It was curiously liberating to know that the past could be obliterated so easily. My heart soared at the thought that I was finally close to Mo.

'Great job, Joe,' said Dad. He jumped down to the ground and urged us to throw our luggage to him. My dress had lost several of the buttons at the bottom, so it now gaped open as high as my knickers, highlighting my non-existent thigh gap. I grabbed my backpack with the Maoams.

One by one, we hauled ourselves up towards the door, climbed out and jumped to the ground. Dad stood below us, arms wide open, ready to catch our bags, as if he was the hero of a disaster movie. Maudie insisted her rabbits

73

didn't count as a bag, draped their cage in the wedding dress and persuaded Joe to carry it, which meant she got to bring everything apart from her plastic bags of stuffed animals. Maudie, it struck me, was the most adaptable of us all.

I turned around, trying to work out the route back to the road, but everywhere looked the same. The trees and bushes that the van had forced apart were once again locked together in their companionable embrace. It was as if the forest had closed ranks around us.

Gripping Maudie's hand, Dad advanced with a sideways shuffle along the shallower of the two ruts to protect Maudie's crazy dress from being torn apart by the brambles. I cursed my choice of shoes as I tried to stick close to Dad and Maudie. The wedge heels sank into the soft ground, throwing me off balance, and the bare flesh around my toes and ankles was soon peppered with nettle stings and insect bites. Occasionally Joe nudged me forwards. He and Mum were so close behind I could feel their breath on my neck.

'What's that?' asked Joe, after we'd been walking for about half an hour. He squeezed my shoulder and pointed into the forest. I squinted at the shape-shifting trees. He turned my head towards a tree with a trunk so wide that even if we all held hands around it, they wouldn't meet. 'Can't you see?'

'Stop it, Joe,' I said angrily, assuming he was winding me up with one of his horror-film moments. But as he held my head in place, I saw three willowy girls slowly step out just a few metres away and stand stock-still in a line staring at us. They had similar flat faces and long tangled dark hair with badly cut fringes and were wearing variations of the

74

same voluminous long-sleeved shift dress in a grubby brown shade, which had probably once been white, over trousers with flowers painted on them and leather boots. They all had the same tattoo of a triple spiral on their arm, although the tallest girl had several others, including a cross inside a circle surrounded by black dots. They looked improbably cool in a grungy sort of way. Even without the lookalike outfits it was obvious they were sisters.

The youngest one picked up her headdress and jammed it back on. She was wearing a necklace made of animal teeth and three blue feathers. I saw them eyeing my cuts, the torn denim dress, the shoes, and felt the hot burn of their pity.

'Are those angels?' asked Maudie, untangling herself from Dad and stepping towards the girls. She wasn't even scared.

'Welcome to Heaven,' said the eldest girl, who I guessed was more or less the same age as me. She slowly lifted the floaty shift dress above her head and flapped the corners, seemingly unaware or not caring that we could see her bare chest.

'Look at my wings!' She laughed. She turned around and showed off her double-jointed shoulder blades, then pirouetted back to face us again.

Dad turned around so he didn't have to look, and I loved him for that. Joe, on the other hand, was transfixed by the girl. He didn't even stop gawping at her when I nudged him in the calf. I could hardly blame him because she was staring straight back at him. In the end Mum stepped forward and walked towards her, wordlessly took the corners of the dress from the girl's hands and covered her again, without embarrassment, in the same efficient way she might tuck a sheet into a bed. The youngest sister giggled.

'Shut up, Skylar,' warned the girl in the middle, slapping her hand over her sister's mouth to smother her laughter.

'Who are you?' asked Maudie.

'We're the Vivian sisters,' said the one in the middle. I frowned. Mo hadn't mentioned anything about these girls in any of the hundreds of messages we'd exchanged since Maudie's party.

'We're very pleased to meet you,' Dad replied awkwardly.

'We're looking for the Haven,' said Mum, politely, as if nothing had happened. 'Perhaps you could guide us to Reception?'

'Reception?' repeated the oldest girl.

'So they can direct us to our eco-cabin,' explained Mum.

'Eco-cabin?'

I wondered if she was taking the piss, but she just looked confused.

'Maybe we should take them to the Spirit House, River?' asked the middle sister.

'No, Lila. I'm not doing that,' said River, firmly.

'As you like.' Lila shrugged as if we'd failed some test and were no longer interesting. Her billowy top slipped down revealing a shoulder that was as shiny and hard as a marble.

'What else can we do?' asked Skylar. 'We can't just leave them here. The growers might find them.'

'If we take them with us, we'll get into trouble,' warned River. 'You know the rules about outsiders. It would be a transgression.'

It was weird the way they spoke about us as if we weren't present. At the time I thought they were being rude. Later

I realized it was because they'd been cut off from the out-side world for so long that they were only tuned in to each other.

'Piper!' called Skylar, hugging a man who'd emerged from the trees. Dad stepped forward to introduce us, but Piper wasn't interested.

'What is your purpose?' he interrupted. His question could have sounded aggressive or challenging but his tone was peculiarly formal.

'Our purpose is to get out of here as fast as fucking possible,' growled Joe, from behind me.

'We're booked in to stay at the Haven,' said Mum, trying to pull the situation back to centre. 'And I would really appreciate it, Piper, if you could direct us to the people who run the eco-retreat because, frankly, it's been a really long day, our van has broken down and we all need to get a good night's sleep if we're going to be on form for tomorrow's activities.'

He shot her a quizzical look. I took advantage of the lull in conversation to check him out. He was wearing a long jacket with colourful tassels that hung from the collar and sleeves. It was decorated with bells, strips of leather and feathers. His hair was in dreadlocks tied at the back with red wool and he had a thick beard. He had a kind, ruddy, weather-beaten face and when he smiled his wrinkles smiled with him.

'I'm sorry but I don't quite understand.' Piper paused again. 'How did you know about us?' He sounded almost fearful.

'Mo invited us to spend the summer with you,' Dad explained. I was suddenly aware that none of us knew his surname.

'Hmm,' said Piper, noncommittally.

'He told us about the retreats you run to allow people to experience life in an environmental community. We're very eager to get started. Aren't we?' Dad turned to us for back-up.

'Can't wait.' I nodded enthusiastically.

'I mean, it's not exactly what I was anticipating but now we've made it here, I'm very curious to learn more,' said Mum. She gave my hand a quick squeeze. Piper didn't reply. I could tell he was one of the few people who were immune to her balm for the soul.

'Did Mo tell you how to get here?' Piper asked.

'Yes, yes, exactly,' said Dad, beaming broadly, as if now we all understood each other, and everything was going to be fine. 'He sent us a map with directions, although I have to say we weren't sure we were going to make it because my son spilt milkshake all over it!' Dad gave a forced laugh, and Piper reciprocated with a quick smile that didn't quite connect with his eyes.

'Maybe you could take us to Mo so he can explain,' proposed Mum.

Piper frowned deeply. Dad started talking again and Piper put up his hand to tell him to stop. Amazingly, Dad fell silent.

'Mo isn't with us at the moment,' said Piper. 'And he didn't mention anything about you coming before he left.'

'Where is he, then?' I cried, unable to disguise my disappointment. It hadn't occurred to me that he might not be here. None of his messages had suggested this. Just yesterday he'd said he'd see me in a few days and described all the things we'd do together when I arrived, like showing me his tree-house and taking me to the lake to swim.

'Why would Mo leave when he knew we were arriving today?' asked Maudie.

'He always has a lot of stuff to do,' said River, vaguely.

'What kind of stuff?' asked Joe. I didn't think he was particularly interested in the answer to his question. He just wanted River's attention. She opened her mouth to reply but Piper shook his head and she fell silent. He plucked leaves from a bush beside him, rubbed them vigorously between his hands until they disintegrated, and threw the pieces over our heads, then closed his eyes. The smell was intoxicating.

'Here's what we're going to do,' he said finally.

He explained he would take us to Mo's old cabin for the night. There would be food in the store cupboard, and we could refill our water bottles from the river. He would communicate our presence to the other members of the Haven. I waited for Dad's response. To either disagree with Piper's plan or suggest some amendments. But instead his eyes went watery. 'So be it,' he said calmly. 'Thank you, Piper.'

For me, the let-down of Mo's no-show was slightly softened by the prospect of staying in his old cabin. Joe was less enthusiastic, especially when Piper told River and her sisters to go home. He took Mum aside and tried to convince her that we should take our chances and find our way back to the road. 'There's something weird about this place,' he whispered to her.

'It's just one night, Joe. Then we can take a rain check.' Mum was neither agreeing with him nor disagreeing with Dad. 'It's not what we signed up for but we don't have much choice right now.'

We followed Piper deeper into the forest. It was getting

dark, and with only the torch on our phones to light the way, our progress was painfully slow. Maudie's flamenco dress kept catching on the undergrowth and Piper ended up giving her a piggyback. At some point, she fell asleep, her cheek nestling in his dreadlocks. Eventually we came to a cluster of buildings in the centre of the community and walked past a group of seven or eight people playing Johnny Cash round a fire. A couple lying in a hammock sat up and stared at us as we passed, but not in an unfriendly way.

'At least it's not "Kumbaya".' I nudged Joe.

We then trudged uphill for another half an hour or so until we reached an enormous oak tree that Piper said was called Old Big Belly. He turned right, and twenty minutes later, at the bottom of the valley, we arrived at Mo's cabin. By this stage, we were all exhausted. We dumped our luggage inside the door and huddled together while Piper carried Maudie into a small bedroom and laid her on a grubby mattress on the dirt floor. He pulled out some musty-smelling blankets from a cupboard, tenderly covered her up until only her frizzy red hair was visible, then came back into the kitchen.

'Welcome to Drift Ridge Cabin,' said Piper.

Drift Ridge Cabin. In spite of the calamitous day, I felt a shiver of excitement. Finally, I was here.

While Piper tried and failed to get the solar-powered electricity to work, Dad used his phone to illuminate the tiny room. Shadows danced across the wall, but I could make out a wooden table with five stools made from tree stumps on one side, and on the other, a countertop with a hob, a sink with a tap attached to a hosepipe and a shelf with saucepans, pottery plates and mugs, all neatly lined up. There was a mezzanine with a makeshift sofa built out of pallets with room for one person. It was small but perfectly proportioned.

'I'll share the bed with Maudie,' I offered quickly, because there was no way I was going to sleep on the mezzanine alone.

'Bravo,' said Dad.

Joe headed towards a cupboard in the corner. Inside were jars of honey, pickles, dried beans and kimchi.

'Interesting minibar,' said Mum, under her breath.

'Welcome to the luxury eco-pod,' declared Joe.

'It has a certain rustic charm, doesn't it?' Dad said hopefully to Mum.

'Ten out of ten for authenticity, but I think we should ask for an upgrade tomorrow,' she whispered back.

The cabin smelt of so many things: dust, damp, pine and sweat. But it was Mo's scent, a heady blend of smoke, patchouli and coffee, that lingered in the air. I recognized it right away and breathed in with my eyes closed, grateful for the way it instantly brought me close to him. He must have been there recently, which surely meant he'd be back soon. I looked for other signs of him around the kitchen and saw the knife he'd brought to Maudie's party hanging on the wall.

'He comes here to dress his kill,' said Piper, watching my face. He missed nothing. 'It's too difficult to carry the carcasses up the steps of his tree-house.'

'Where's the bathroom?' asked Mum.

Piper pointed outside into the forest. 'Composting toilet. Ten metres to the left. There are two buckets. Piss in the right and shit in the left. Cover your shit with sawdust to help it decompose. There's a bucket shower in the outhouse.' He shone his torch outside and we could just about see the outline of a small shed-like structure. 'Do you have any other questions?'

'Might it be possible to move closer to the centre of the community tomorrow?' Mum asked hopefully. 'Or do you have a family glamping field? I feel this cabin is a little isolated. And unloved.'

Piper looked at her blankly.

'Where do the other guests stay?' she persevered.

'Outsiders don't usually come here.' Piper spoke slowly and deliberately. 'Mo should have consulted us before inviting you. All decisions at the Haven are reached by consensus. Everyone who has come of age has to agree. I'll call a processing session to discuss and let you know what we decide as soon as we can.'

'What's a processing session?' asked Joe.

'It's how we resolve problems between us,' he answered vaguely. Piper was halfway out of the door when he turned around.

'Apologies. I almost forgot,' he said in a kindly tone. 'Do you mind giving me your phones, please? It's one of our rules. To prevent outsiders tracking us. And they don't work here anyway. There's no coverage.' He gave a broad smile.

'I'd like to keep mine to take photos,' said Joe.

'Taking photos is a transgression,' said Piper. Joe looked puzzled. 'It's against the rules of our community.'

Dad immediately gave him Maudie's pink brick phone, which made it difficult for the rest of us to put up a fight. One by one we reluctantly handed them over. Only Mum said anything; 'Will they be kept in a locker?' Piper nodded and gave one of his enigmatic smiles before closing the door behind him.

'We've just handed over thousands of pounds worth of iPhones to a complete randomer,' said Joe, clearly wondering if we'd become victims of a sophisticated scam. Dad warned him about cynicism being the ninth deadly sin.

I couldn't be bothered with another argument and climbed fully clothed into bed with Maudie. Even though I was dog-tired, I couldn't sleep. I couldn't believe that I'd finally made it to the Haven. And I was confident that as soon as Mo heard I was here he would come and find me. By tomorrow everything would fall into place. For so long I'd felt like Maudie's spilt milkshake, leaching in and out of other people's lives, but now, finally, I was someone of consequence.

9

Now

I wake with a jolt and my body snaps into action. I hear rain manically tap-dancing on a roof above me and the howl of the wind outside. The entire room seems to be swaying but somehow I manage to crawl to a broken window. The wind roars so hard in my face that it sucks the air from my lungs. The creaks and groans of this room aren't familiar, and cloud shrouds the almost-moon. When I turn on my head torch to look outside, I'm astonished to find myself high in the tree canopy buckling and bending alongside the kings and queens of the forest. And then it comes back. I'm in Mo's tree-house . . . I came here to look for him . . . to ask for his help . . . Mo always knows what to do . . . He always protects us. If anyone can find out what's happened to my family, it will be him.

I pull myself upright. The tree-house lists from side to side. I stumble slowly around the tiny space longing to find Mo grinning back at me. But the hatch is bolted and the rope ladder lies in a tangle on the floor beside me. I'm all alone. I feel the tears coming and this time there's nothing I can do to stop them. The beam from my torch spotlights the kitchen area with its small Primus stove, a couple of saucepans and a shelf of food. There's a jerry-can of water and a pile of plastic boxes, each one carefully labelled. Clothes. Tools. Batteries. Crockery. Sleeping-bag. The police haven't been here. But judging from my lonely footprints in the dust, neither has Mo.

The sight of his green backpack in the corner of the room puts me on edge. No one from the Haven ever goes into the forest without their pack, which means he left in a hurry too. I hold his bag tight to my chest, smell it and close my eyes, willing myself to pinpoint the last time I saw him. I remember us dancing round a fire . . . hurtling down a mountain track in his truck . . . running through the forest. But the edges of these memories are blurry and float away, like clouds, before I can make sense of them.

I touch my uncooperative head. The injury burns red hot and the throbbing seems higher-pitched, maybe because the stitches are too tight or because I didn't clean it properly and it's getting infected. I kneel on the grubby mattress to catch my breath and spot a large red-brown stain on the floor. I touch it. It's damp, and when I lick my finger I know that it's fresh blood.

My throat constricts and my breath thins, like I'm in the dead zone at the top of a mountain. Something bad has happened to Mo. There can be no other conclusion. And in the gap where memories should be I start to wonder what role I played in all this. I'm wild with fear.

My eye is drawn to a makeshift bookshelf constructed from crates the other side of the mattress. I crawl over and frantically start pulling out books and magazines. *The Complete Guide to Medicinal Plants.* Carlos Castaneda, *The Teachings of Don Juan. Understanding the Radical Environmental Movement. Poisonous Plants.* A faded Spanish magazine falls out of one of the books. The pages in the middle have been carelessly ripped out. I barely have time to consider why

Mo would have this when I come across his beaten-up notebook with the brown leather cover.

My hands shake as I turn the first page. There are dates handwritten in Mo's tiny, sloped writing and a few sentences beneath, like a diary. I read slowly. I don't know if it's concussion but my brain is fried and I have to put my finger under each word to keep my place. The first entry is 27 September 2017. *Arrive the Haven.* The next 4 October 2017. *Processing.* Sometimes instead of writing there's a drawing. An entire page is dedicated to a description and diagram of a complicated drip-line irrigation system for watering crops. Environmental catastrophes are noted: *9 February, plague of locusts Kenya. January 2020, 18 million hectares burn Australia, bushfire. Floods Pakistan.* There are shopping lists with ticks and crosses beside weirdly unrelated items. *Netting 10; Stakes 200; 25 pairs latex gloves; 10 shears; twist ties; phosphate.* I'm totally thrown by this. Isn't going to the shops against the rules? And I don't recall ever seeing any of this in the community, let alone in these quantities.

I search to find an entry for the date we arrived. Nothing. It's difficult not to feel insulted. But I find the date of Maudie's birthday party. Our names are written in tiny handwriting but only mine is circled. I flick through to the end of the notebook.

> *I was a drop-out*
> *I've been an addict*
> *I've been in prison*
> *I've had problems with alcohol*
> *I have taken life to give life*
> *Now, I'm a spiritual warrior.*

This completely throws me. Especially the mention of prison. I've learnt more about Mo in the last five minutes than I have in all the time I knew him. Filled with apprehension, I turn to the final page.

There is no place to hide. Wherever you are I will find you. And when I find you, Cassia, I will kill you. My mouth goes dry. I try to swallow but I can't. I keep reading. *I will remove the heart of stone from your flesh and give you a heart of flesh. You will pay for what you've done.*

My entire body quivers as if I've touched a live cable. It's like every worst fear rolled into one. It's not just that Mo wants to kill me and I have no idea why. It's that I got him so wrong.

10

Then

Ironically Dad was the first to break the rules at the Haven. Fuelled by paranoia that we might disgrace ourselves by sleeping in, he'd compromised his radical self-reliance by hiding his phone to use as an alarm clock. But, as it turned out, he was caught off guard anyway because on our second morning, well before his alarm went off, there was a muffled knocking at the door.

'What's that?' asked Maudie, gripping my upper arm. We'd spent the past couple of nights clinging on to each other in jittery fear at the barks and screams that came from the woods outside our cabin and the sudden skirmishes on the roof. Too scared to leave the bedroom, let alone the cabin, we resorted to peeing in a plastic container that we emptied out of the window in the morning. I could never have imagined it would be comforting to share a double bed with Maudie, but I couldn't have got through that first forty-eight hours without her.

'Don't worry,' I whispered, peeling her fingers from my arm as the knocking got more insistent. 'It'll be Mo. He's come for me.'

'For you?' Maudie looked puzzled.

'For us, I mean.'

I jumped out of bed, pulled on my jeans and white vest top and forced myself to walk slowly towards the front door. But instead of Mo, the youngest of the three sisters stood there, dressed in the same grubby smock, trousers and boots that she'd been wearing that first evening.

'Oh.' I tried not to sound disappointed.

'They've sent me to show you the way to the Spirit House for the processing meeting,' explained Skylar, winding her hair around her finger as she stood in the doorway. 'The community has made its decision and we weren't sure you'd remember the way because you walked here in the dark.'

Maudie came out of the bedroom smiling broadly and clutching her favourite toy from Dog Show, the pink plastic spaniel with the plaited blue tail.

'Meet Hilda,' she said, holding out the dog's paw for Skylar to shake.

'We don't play with plastic toys,' replied Skylar.

'Why?'

'They're bad for the environment. And for our imagination.'

Maudie gave her a long, hard stare. I waited for her to kick off. Instead, she pressed Hilda into Skylar's stomach. 'Keep her. I won't say anything.'

Skylar checked over her shoulder, grabbed the plastic dog and stuffed it into the top of her two-sizes-too-big left boot.

'Good sharing, Maudie,' said Mum, who'd emerged from the bedroom holding hands with Dad, like a honeymooning couple. God, they were so embarrassing. 'It's good of you to come and get us.'

'I didn't want to come. My parents told me to fetch you,' said Skylar. 'We're a bit more open to outsiders than some of the others.'

At the time, apart from being struck by Skylar's unflinching honesty, I didn't take much notice of her comment because I was doing my usual anxious review of what my parents were wearing. Mum was an almost acceptable seven out of ten in her patchwork denim skirt and halterneck top, managing to be both hippie and elegant, although the skirt was a little try-hard. Dad, however, was dressed in his new trousers and shirt, looking like Indiana Jones, but not in a good way.

'Oh, my God! What's with all the pockets?' I whispered to Joe, who'd emerged in yesterday's clothes. Everything about my brother looked crumpled, even the bridge of his nose.

'In a previous life he was an advent calendar,' he replied. Fuelled by a combination of exhaustion and stress, I started giggling uncontrollably.

Fortunately, Dad had woken up in one of his superlative moods and roared with laughter too. Everything was the most, the greatest, the best. So, he treated Joe's quip as 'the best joke ever' and kept excitedly saying, 'Center Parcs this ain't,' without noticing the slightly wistful look in Mum's eyes every time he mentioned Center Parcs.

'What's Center. Parcs?' asked Skylar. She said it slowly, with a full stop between Center and Parcs.

'That's the best question I've ever heard!' Dad exclaimed. 'Totally reinforces why I wanted to come here. This is going to be the most original holiday we've ever taken. The best ever! Shall we get going, folks?'

We all trailed obediently behind Skylar back into the forest. It felt a little weird putting our trust in this small girl especially because it seemed she was taking some utterly random route up the steep hill. But as we progressed, I could see she was following a rough path that meandered around trees and rocks where the bracken had been flattened, and across makeshift bridges constructed from planks that had been strategically placed over the widest streams. It occurred to me that Mo must have made this same journey every day. He'd probably built the bridges.

'How do you know the way?' called Maudie.

Skylar picked up a handful of leaves. 'If the leaves have been disturbed the trail is darker.'

'How does that work?' asked Joe.

'When you tread on the leaves that face the ground they absorb more moisture, which makes them turn browner.'

'That's astonishing,' said Dad, as we bent to examine them.

Fuelled by the hope that Mo might be waiting for me at the Spirit House, I tried to match her pace. But even in her chunky boots, Skylar had an economy of movement that made it impossible for any of us to keep up with her. Her feet barely seemed to touch the ground. She raced between trees and over streams like a goat, whereas we had to use the bracken to pull us uphill as it got steeper. Every ten minutes or so she stopped to allow us to catch up, but no sooner had we reached her than she set off again and it wasn't long before I was a sweaty, breathless mess. Even worse, an itchy heat rash was creeping up my torso. I cursed my white vest top. Its paleness highlighted the red blotches on my arms, and I was a walking target for insects and brambles.

Maudie was the only one who came close to keeping up with her. The early-morning sun shot spears of light through the thick canopy of leaves creating natural spotlights and she leapt from one to another, pretending she was on stage, and reciting lines from her last school play, which happened to have been *Alice in Wonderland*. Skylar shot her a quizzical glance. '"Curiouser and curiouser,"' she said.

'You know it too!' Maudie exclaimed excitedly. 'Did you read *Alice* at school?'

'Not school-school,' said Skylar, cautiously.

'Where then?' asked Maudie.

'At home-school with my mum.'

'I would love not to have to go to school and have Mum as my teacher,' said Maudie, sorrowfully. She hugged Mum, who looked appalled at the idea.

'I know. I'm really lucky,' said Skylar.

'You see!' said Dad to Mum, as if he'd just won an argument. 'You see!'

When we reached the top of the hill, I was relieved to hear Dad begging for a water break. We slumped to the ground and looked across to the other side of the valley. The vegetation endlessly repeated itself in different shades of green down to an enormous lake, whose surface glistened in the sunshine. On the other side the same green tapestry of hills and mountains continued as far as the eye could see. The only sign that anyone lived there were the plumes of smoke that rose from the basin of the valley, the occasional crow of a cockerel or a dog barking.

'Do you ever go across the lake?' asked Mum.

'No. It's against our rules. It's too dangerous. Bad people live in the forest on the other side.'

'The view is amazing,' I said, taken aback by the way I felt it physically inside me. 'The most incredible I've ever seen.'

Joe kicked my ankle. 'Stop being a bum-licker,' he panted.

He fired questions at Skylar as a delaying tactic. 'How long have you lived here?'

93

'Since for ever.'

'Have you ever been to a city?'

'Never. But in my dreams many times.'

I thought the way she talked in riddles was to make her seem more mysterious and wondered if it was a trait I should copy as part of my de-Labradorization process. As the small line on her forehead deepened, I realized these questions stressed her out because she couldn't answer them. Mum sensed this too.

'The noises we hear in the night . . . what are they?' asked Joe, desperately trying to win a few more minutes of reprieve. He was almost as unfit as me, not because he was overweight but because of the oil slick that coated his lungs from the vaping.

'Which ones?'

Maudie did a poor imitation of the screeching noise we'd heard. Skylar cupped her hands together and made a sound so similar that I could feel the same fear creep up my body again.

'That's crazily realistic,' said Joe, admiringly.

'That noise is a muntjac,' declared Skylar.

'What's that?' asked Mum.

'It's a type of small deer that originally came from China. They escaped from a park years ago and started breeding in the wild. They're what you call an invasive species.'

'What's an invasive species?' Maudie asked.

'Something that doesn't belong here.' She paused and looked up at us. 'An Outsider. Like you.'

I saw Mum trying to catch Dad's eye, but he rigorously ignored her.

'Was it being attacked?' asked Maudie.

Skylar snorted with laughter. 'No! They do that to let

their family know where they are or as a warning signal that something has come into their territory that shouldn't.'

There wasn't much time to process any of this because Skylar was on the move again, and although the walk down the other side of the hill should have been easier, the faster pace meant the brambles and tree roots were like tripwires. All of us fell at least twice. Occasionally Skylar stopped to point out something that might interest us, an elderberry bush laden with purple berries that could be turned into juice, or an irrigation channel made out of a hollowed tree trunk to divert water to the settlement area.

'It's so impressive the way you work with the landscape rather than against it,' said Mum, in her teacher voice, as she examined one of the handcrafted irrigation channels. 'I can't believe you managed to carry these huge tree trunks up here.'

'A community is greater than the sum of its parts,' responded Skylar. She said it unthinkingly, like the responses during a church service, and fell silent again.

Shortly after this we arrived at a clearing. A man lifted his hand and waved at her.

'*Hola, Skylar! Cómo vas?*'

'*Muy bien, Juan!*'

'Why's he dressed up as an astronaut?' whispered Maudie.

'He's a beekeeper.' Skylar gestured towards half a dozen hives sitting in a neat row at the back of the clearing. 'Juan knows everything there is to know about bees. He even has a family of European black bees.' We looked at her blankly. 'They're endangered. Practically extinct. He keeps them apart from the others in a secret place where they can't catch the diseases transmitted by the hybrids, like varroa mites . . .'

'*Cuidado con . . .*'

We couldn't hear the rest of what Juan said because a dog had appeared and started a noisy but half-hearted round of barking that sent the bees frantic.

I moved close to Dad to protect him from them.

'Quiet, Chester,' Skylar ordered. The dog gave her an embarrassed look and slunk towards a cabin I hadn't even noticed, set back about ten metres from the clearing. It was camouflaged with mosses and vines, and its roof was covered with long green grass, so it seemed to emerge from the hillside itself. Smoke poured out of a tiny chimney pot. Joe nudged me and pointed at the window. I saw a figure staring at us on the left of a dirty glass frame.

'That house looks as if it's alive,' said Maudie. 'Like it might chase us down the hill.'

'You say the strangest things.' Skylar giggled. 'It's where Aida lives in her shipping container.'

'Who is Aida?' I asked. Mo hadn't mentioned her either.

'One of our elders,' said Skylar.

'It's amazing how well disguised it is,' said Mum, admiringly. I was baffled that she was still so upbeat when this was clearly not the experience she'd been expecting. It dawned on me that she was happy because Dad was happy, which should have been romantic, but instead filled me with a dizzy unease. Mum's happiness shouldn't depend on Dad's mood. Hadn't Cara said exactly that during one of her many rows with Mum about coming here?

Skylar's pace slowed as the track widened into a more obvious path that curved down the hillside into an orchard. The stitch in my side finally eased.

'Apples, pears, plums, gooseberries,' said Skylar, pointing at different trees and bushes like a tour guide. Their

96

branches were so heavy with fruit that they almost touched the ground.

'It's an ancient orchard,' said Skylar. 'Piper thinks it was probably planted by Aida's family hundreds of years ago.'

'I can't believe people have lived in this forest for so long,' observed Mum.

'We are its gatekeepers,' said Skylar.

She stopped and stood on tiptoe to pick five pears off a tree. They were bigger and plumper than any pear I'd ever seen. I bit into the flesh and the juice dribbled down my chin.

'We grow all our own fruit and vegetables here,' said Skylar. 'We have goats and cows for milk and cheese, chickens for eggs, and catch fish from the rivers and lake. The meat eaters rear pigs and hunt wild animals, like deer and wild boar. If we don't produce our own food, we don't eat.'

'You mean you never go shopping?' asked Joe.

'I think someone went once,' she replied vaguely.

'Nectar of the gods,' proclaimed Mum, as she bit into her pear. Skylar smiled. I could tell she was comfortable with Mum. People generally were. I wondered how it felt to be someone who never had to make any effort to be liked. As we descended into the valley below the orchard, the stream widened into a large pool. Skylar stopped and we watched exotic insects with fluorescent wings expertly skim the surface of the water.

'Sometimes we swim here,' said Skylar. 'We dive from that rock.' She pointed towards a narrow ledge halfway up the steep rock face. 'But you have to be careful. Kaia's son Jorn broke his leg.'

'How did you get him to hospital?' asked Mum.

'We didn't,' said Skylar. 'The healing is in the forest.'

Mum looked doubtful and Dad muttered something about the ninth deadly sin.

'Will you look at that dragonfly!' he said, pointing out an elegant insect with a bright metallic green body and blue eyes. 'That's the most beautiful creature I've ever seen.'

I looked at him and saw that his eyes had that misty quality again. Perhaps Mum was right. The Haven was exactly what he needed. I suddenly felt proud that we were here because of me.

'Actually, it's a damselfly,' said Skylar, almost apologetically. 'It's an easy mistake to make.'

'It's still the most beautiful creature I've ever seen,' said Dad, crouching to get closer. 'Apart from Mum, of course.' He gave her a lingering kiss on the lips.

'Sorry.' I apologized for Mum and Dad.

'It's understandable. All mammals have sexual needs,' said Skylar, in a matter-of-fact tone. 'It's part of nature.'

'How can you tell it's a damselfly?' Dad asked.

'They rest with their wings closed and they have much longer, thinner bodies. This is an emerald damselfly, and the blue eyes mean it's a male. They're endangered. You're really lucky to see it.' She took out a notebook from her bag to record the sighting. Her enthusiasm for the little damselfly was infectious.

'It's like being with David Attenborough,' observed Joe. He pulled off his hoodie, knotted it round his waist and puffed on his vape.

'Why do they risk flying so close to the surface?' asked Mum.

'Because they're laying eggs in the water,' explained Skylar.

'Gross,' said Maudie.

'Actually, damselflies and dragonflies show us the water is clean. They don't lay eggs in dirty water,' explained Skylar.

'Do they sting?' asked Maudie. 'My dad got stung by a bee and almost died. At my birthday party.' She started to tell Skylar about the shelter she'd built with her friends and the pink Barbie cake.

'I know all about it,' said Skylar, a little too quickly.

'You do?' said Maudie, deflated by this failed attempt to divert attention back to her.

'How?' asked Mum.

'My sister River told me.'

'How did she know?' asked Joe.

'Mudder told her.'

'Who on earth is Mudder?' Dad asked.

'The man who lives up in the trees. Some people call him Badger or Motley Joe,' said Skylar. 'Some call him Mo.'

I felt myself flush. Luckily, I was already bright red with heat rash, so no one noticed.

'Why does Mo have so many names?' asked Joe.

'Sometimes people who don't want to be found have lots of names,' said Skylar. 'To throw outsiders off the scent.'

'Why would he not want to be found?' asked Mum.

'We are not what happened to us. We are what we choose to become,' said Skylar, pressing her hands together as if she was praying.

'What do you mean?' I asked.

'You should accept people for what they are now, not define them by their past,' replied Skylar, slightly robotically.

'The child is a genius!' proclaimed Dad.

'It's a nice idea in theory,' observed Mum, 'although perhaps not always sensible in practice. If someone has a history of violence, for example.'

'Where exactly does Mo live now?' I was relieved Maudie had asked this question so that I didn't have to.

'In a tree-house up on Blood Mountain. Around a half-hour walk from you. One Way Will helped build it.'

Maudie interrupted again: 'One Way Will? Why do you call him that?'

'Because he went on a trip and never came back,' said Skylar.

'What kind of trip?' asked Mum in confusion.

'Hallucinogens,' said Skylar. 'We don't approve of taking drugs, but we have compassion for those who try to stop. One Way Will used to work with the growers. We took him in.'

'Who are the growers?' Mum pressed her.

'Outsiders who farm marijuana on the other side of the lake. But they're a long way away from here so we don't have to worry about them.'

The forest gave way to a track that took us past a small round dome cabin made from bent wooden poles.

'Is that a turf roof?' Dad asked excitedly. 'And cob-wood walls?'

Skylar nodded. 'Juan built it himself.'

'Wow,' said Dad. 'It's like episode seven of *Off the Grid* when they construct the bender in the woods.'

The track curved to the right and we came across a cluster of cabins, almost identical to ours, except they were hooked up to solar panels and a wind turbine, which Skylar explained meant they had electricity and hot water most days. She explained that, apart from Mo and Aida, everyone else lived around this settlement area. 'Do you want to see inside my home?' she asked.

'That would be great,' said Mum.

We followed her into the largest cabin. There was an expansive kitchen and sitting area with a comfortable-looking long wooden sofa covered with throws and sheepskins, and a wood-burning stove. There were masks and woven wall hangings, wind chimes and dream catchers. Hippie shit, as Dad would say. At the back a beautiful terrace was shaded with sweet-smelling climbing flowers and vines.

'It's wonderful,' said Mum. 'So peaceful.'

'We do home-school on the terrace. The Danes live next door and One Way Will on the other side.'

We went back out. I heard voices in the distance and saw we'd arrived in the same dusty clearing surrounded by trees where we'd briefly stopped on the way to our cabin that first night. At the centre was the large semi-circular construction, only now I could see that it was in fact three distinct buildings. On the left side was a large, perfectly round dwelling, with a neat thatched roof so it looked like a small house wearing a floppy hat. 'Spirit House' read the lopsided hand-carved wooden sign over the door. To its right was a covered outdoor dining area with a long thin table. I stopped counting the spaces on benches and chairs when I reached thirty. And beside this there was a long, thin rectangular building with a corrugated-iron roof. Judging from the number of huge saucepans hanging from hooks on the ceiling I guessed it was the community kitchen. I glanced inside and saw neat rows of kitchen utensils, crockery and cutlery. A poster stuck on the wall said, *A place for everything and everything in its place*. It was impressively clean and tidy.

'This is the most beautiful building I've ever seen,' said Dad, as he squinted up at the roof of the Spirit House in the early-morning sunshine.

'Mudder helped to design it,' said Skylar, as we stood in an arc outside. I felt a surge of pride that Mo was responsible, and growing excitement that he might be waiting for me inside.

'It's a cross between a Celtic and a Native American round house,' boomed a voice behind us. We all turned at the same time.

'Hello,' said Mum, politely.

'Greetings,' said Piper, pressing his hands together in the same way Skylar had done.

'Greetings,' said Dad, giving an awkward half-clap.

'Are you all well rested?' Piper beamed and I noticed his teeth were brown, like the water we fetched from the river. 'Did you sleep well?'

'Yes,' we all lied, apart from Maudie.

'It was the worst night of my life,' she declared. 'Apart from the one before that.' Piper roared with laughter and rocked backwards and forwards on his sturdy, muscular legs. I examined his flip-flopped feet and found myself mesmerized by his toes. The flesh was stained black and full of crevices and the long nails were thick and yellow, like a separate eco-system from the rest of his body. I took in the necklace with a large bronze pendant that hung around his neck, like a medal, and saw it was carved with hieroglyphs and inlaid with red stone. I noticed he had a tattoo with the same markings as his daughters on the top of his shoulder. *Definitely different*, as Dad would say, usually when he disapproved of someone.

'We're very grateful to you for sending Skylar to help us get our bearings. I'm not sure we'd have made it on our own.' Dad laughed nervously. I'd never seen him so eager to please. It was like he was turning into me. For the second time in three days, I felt sorry for him.

'Come,' Piper said, gesturing towards the Spirit House with a broad smile. 'Our community has reached consensus. You are welcome to join our processing session.'

Piper strolled towards the Spirit House, while the rest of us lagged behind with Skylar. A huge piebald carthorse lumbered towards us.

'This is Gaia,' explained Skylar, encouraging Maudie to stroke her nose and neck. 'I'll teach you how to ride her if you like.'

'That would be amazing!' Maudie brimmed with excitement.

We passed an outhouse where four people were scrubbing and rinsing clothes in old-fashioned steel tubs.

Mum gave a whistle of approval. 'That's quite a system you've got there.'

'Laundry is a community activity,' explained Skylar. 'We all take turns.' A tall man with long, wavy blond hair wheeled a barrow piled with damp laundry towards a woman waiting beside the longest washing line I'd ever seen. A boy with a bad limp trailed behind them holding a bunch of dead fish knotted together with string while a smaller girl, who I guessed was his sister, carried a fishing rod twice her size.

'Magnus, Kaia, Jorn and Lucia,' said Skylar. 'They're Danish.' They waved at us.

'Their children are so sweet,' I said.

'They're not their children,' said Skylar. I was puzzled. They were exact replicas of their willowy blond parents. 'Children don't belong to parents at the Haven. We belong to each other.'

We passed a pile of suitcases, plastic boxes and canvas bags to the right of the dining area. I nudged Joe in the ribs. 'Told you. We're not the only people staying here!'

'It's our luggage, you fool,' said Joe.

'Gaia carried everything from your vehicle,' explained Skylar.

'Why's the zip on my bag open?' I heard Joe ask. He knelt down beside his black backpack and manically checked inside for his vape refills, stuffing any spares into his pockets.

'You've never knowingly zipped up a bag in your life,' teased Mum.

I watched the way she wrung her hands and realized that she did this when she was doing balm for the soul. I wished I hadn't noticed because it made me aware that Mum's effort to make everything feel better for everyone was fuelled by the same anxiety that made me eat whole packets of Maoams in the middle of the night.

'It's very kind of you to have brought our luggage,' Mum called to Piper, but he was already inside the porch of the Spirit House. We followed him.

'This is where we hold all our community get-togethers,' Piper explained, as he kicked off his flip-flops. 'Musical evenings, parties, processing sessions . . .'

Skylar crouched down to remove her boots and hid Hilda deep in the toe. Dad instructed us to do the same even though we'd already started to pull off our trainers.

'It's always important to show respect for other people's customs,' he whispered.

'Stop behaving as if we're meeting some undiscovered tribe in the Amazon,' muttered Joe.

Dad didn't reply. Instead he pointed to a sign just inside the door and then back at Joe: *A cynic is someone who, when they smell flowers, looks around for a coffin.*

'You need to go into this with an open heart, Joe,' warned Dad. 'Like Cass.'

I didn't want to enjoy his praise, but I couldn't help it. Truth be told, I was relishing my new status as favourite child too much.

Inside the Spirit House it was gloomy, which was a relief because it dampened the glare of my heat rash. I was always happiest skulking in the shadows. I stuck close to Piper as he led us through a crowd of adults and children, perhaps two dozen in total. I scoured the room for Mo but couldn't see him. Piper directed Mum and Dad to a threadbare sofa beside an open fireplace while we settled on the floor at their feet. Mum and Dad sat down and smiled so hard that the muscles in their cheeks twitched with the effort. My face burnt red. It was worse than school assemblies because, instead of rows, we were in a circle, which meant I was visible from all angles. The Vivian sisters sat opposite and I saw the glint in Joe's eyes when River grinned at him.

There was stuff everywhere. Enormous baskets hung from ceiling hooks. A guitar painted in psychedelic colours sat in an armchair as if it was the rightful owner. The shelf that ran the entire circumference of the circular room was overflowing with books. *The Bean Cookbook, Bushcraft for Beginners, Poisonous British Plants,* On the wall a poster in large multicoloured capital letters said: *PRIORITIES 1. Earth care 2. Cooperation. 3. Friendship.* Except, judging by all the crossed-out numbers and arrows, there was some disagreement over what the priorities should be.

A tall woman came over and introduced herself to us as Piper's partner, Sylvie. She had the same dark hair and brown skin as her children. Her shoulders were broad, and her arms and legs had a solid quality, like a piece of old furniture. 'Welcome to our community,' she said, in a deep, rich voice.

I nudged Joe to get him to look at a blackboard propped up behind a plastic barrel with 'Rainwater' written on the side. *What's Happening?* it said at the top, in bright orange chalk. *Non-aggressive communication workshop. Gong bath. Spinning. Fermenting for beginners.*

Joe groaned. 'What's happening is I'm getting the fuck out of here and going back home as soon as I can,' he whispered.

'You can't. The house is rented out for the next two months.'

'Cara said I could move in with her.'

'She doesn't have anywhere to live either.'

'Other people offered.'

This took me by surprise. 'Like who?'

'Marco's parents. Dana's. People who know what's been going on with Dad.'

'What do you mean?' I asked in confusion. 'What's going on with Dad?'

'Come on, Cass, get your head out of the sand,' hissed Joe. 'He's having the mother of all mid-life crises.'

Piper stood up and explained that we should all join hands and sit in silence for a moment to direct positive energy to the processing session. I put out my hand and Joe pinched the tip of my finger. My stomach rumbled with hunger.

I followed Piper's instructions to close my eyes and take

deep breaths. A gentle breeze floated across my face and I half opened my right eye. Piper was waving a charm made of short twigs tied in the middle with the same red thread knotted through the hole in the doll that Maudie had found in the hedge. He started chanting. I glanced over my shoulder at Dad and saw him staring at Piper in a state of dazed wonder. Even Joe sat in open-mouthed silence.

> *'I place the Rowan and the thread before you,*
> *A charm between this house and harm,*
> *Against storm,*
> *Against flood,*
> *Against disease.*
> *Then into the forest I go . . .'*

'. . . to lose my mind and find my soul,' responded a woman on the opposite side of the circle. She stood up. A ray of sun shot through the window infusing her with early-morning light. Everyone turned towards her. She put up her hand, palm facing towards us, closed her dark eyes and bowed her head slightly. The room fell silent. Even the small children were still. It wasn't an aggressive or attention-seeking gesture. It almost felt private, as if we shouldn't be watching. Except it was difficult to take your eyes off her. Everything about the woman was uncompromising, from the silver streak in her long black hair to the severe middle parting that divided it into two long curtains that reached her bum. She was wearing a tight vest top, skinny black jeans and scuffed leather boots, yet the gold chain around her neck was elegant and delicate. When she bent down to put her hand on Piper's shoulder, I could see the sinews in her muscly tattooed arms. Her bony shoulder blades were like wings. If she was a bird, she would have been a raven.

'I am Aida,' she introduced herself to us and smiled, so all the angles of her face were momentarily softened. 'Your arrival has come as a surprise but, nevertheless, we welcome you to the Haven with open hearts.' She spoke in a slow, gravelly voice.

'That's very kind of you,' said Dad, bubbling over with enthusiasm. 'It's a magical place.'

'We're very grateful,' Mum chipped in.

'It's many years since outsiders last came here, so please forgive us if we appear unfriendly,' she continued. 'The forest depends on us for protection, and we are wary of those who mean it harm.'

She informed us that, after a day of processing, consensus had been reached and everyone had agreed we should be allowed to stay for two months. In return for food and lodgings we'd be expected to donate thirty-five hours a week of our time to community projects. She pointed to another list on the wall: gardening, cooking, farming, chopping wood, home-school, childcare, laundry and security. There were names beside each job, including ours. Dad was put in charge of the vegetable field behind our cabin that Mo usually looked after; Mum was to be part of Juan's beekeeping team; Joe was with the fertilizer unit; and I was placed in the kitchen with River. Maudie would attend home-school with Skylar.

'Any questions?'

'What is this place?' asked Joe. 'What are you into? Are you survivalists? Off-gridders? Preppers? Eco-warriors?' There was an uncomfortable silence. 'Basic hippies?'

'We produce our own food. We create our own heat and light from solar panels, wood and a water wheel. We make and repair our own clothes. We tread lightly upon this earth,' explained Juan, in his thick Spanish accent. Now he was out of his protective gear I could see he was short and stocky with the same solid build that everyone at the Haven seemed to share. He pulled his thick dark hair back into a ponytail as he spoke. '*Cuidamos a la madre tierra.* We look after Mother Earth.'

'Most problems on our planet come from thinking we are superior to the natural world. Epidemics, climate change, intensive farming. These are the dangers of a life divorced from nature,' added Aida.

'And why do you need security?' asked Joe, pointing at Mo's name beneath security.

Dad shot Joe an irritated look.

'The forest is a sacred space,' said Juan. 'And we are its gatekeepers. Our purpose in life is to protect it.' He had that rare quality of being gentle and calm without being a pushover. Even Joe melted when he spoke.

'This is all wonderful,' gushed Dad. 'We're very grateful to you for giving us this opportunity. Honestly. We'll do our best to make sure you have no regrets. Apologies for my son's nosiness.'

'Please don't worry. We encourage a full expression of viewpoints at the Haven,' said Aida. She paused. 'One last thing. There are no secrets here.' Her eyes bored into me and I felt she could tell I was thinking about Mo. 'Our sense of security comes from our relationships. We would ask you to respect that spirit of openness and share any shadow-side issues in our processing sessions.'

'How does that work?' asked Joe.

'It's a simple community meeting, like this, where we share our problems and ideas about anything that has resonance in the life of the Haven. For example, if you have interpersonal problems with a partner or anyone else in the community, this is the forum to resolve them. If you've committed a transgression, it gets discussed here.'

She gestured towards another poster on the wall. Transgressions: Taking drugs. Mobile phones. Stealing food. Crossing the lake. 'Or if you wish to embark on a new sexual relationship with someone or have a child, everyone has to agree first.'

I saw Mum catch Joe's eye and wink.

'Of course.' Dad nodded feverishly.

'This lifestyle is not for everyone. The Haven is either your greatest dream or your biggest nightmare. It's down to you. It's whatever you want it to be.' Aida walked towards us and crouched in front of my parents, smiling serenely. Her movements were liquid.

'Do you have the map that Mudder sent you?' she asked Dad. I could tell from the way she said Mo's name, as if she was sucking on a lemon, that she didn't like him. Dad pulled the directions out of his pocket and she took them. I willed Dad to ask her where Mo was, but he was too focused on smoothing out the map.

'Did you make a copy?'

'No,' said Dad.

'Or show it to anyone else?'

'Absolutely not.'

She lit a corner of the map with a match and held it in her hand until it had almost completely burnt before throwing it into the fireplace.

I I

Now

Mo's threat has shot a painful blade of terror straight through me. I need to get away from his cabin as quickly as possible. As soon as the storm blows itself out, I unbolt the hatch, feed the rope ladder through the opening, and step out onto the top rung. My bag weighs heavy with new kit: sleeping-bag, camping stove, flint and steel for making fire, binoculars, tarp. Plus three Ready to Eat Meals. One each for Mum, Joe and Maudie. For when I find them.

Outside it's cold as hell. The flimsy ladder twists and lurches in the breeze. I stare down at the forest kaleidoscoping below and calculate it's around forty vertigo-inducing feet to the ground. But the terror of Mo's threat neutralizes all other fears. I climb down, my throbbing head boiling over with wild theories about what I could have done to make him hate me so much, until it feels as if it's going to explode. The only real explanation can be that I put his beloved community at risk. I force myself to remember all I know to be right and true about Mo. He brought us to the Haven to show us a new way of life. He protected us all from the growers, from outsiders, from ourselves.

When I finally hit solid ground, I hide the ladder where I found it, in the branches of a blue fir, and crouch down to do the checks. It's good terrain. The soil is springy with pine needles and leaves, which makes it easy for me to leave no trace. There are no broken twigs or snapped branches on trees, no leaves that have been turned over, damp side up, no damaged cobwebs. Once I'm convinced no one has been here I set off back down the mountain towards the settlement area. My plan is to leave Mo's notebook somewhere obvious for the police to find, so they see his threat against me and focus all their efforts on finding him rather than me. The sense that I've done something bad eats at my soul again. I can't give up until I know what it is. I stop just once. To pick oyster mushrooms from the trunk of a fallen beech. My stomach rumbles. I bite into one but it's too metallic to eat raw. *Stop thinking about food. Need makes you weak.* I guess I've learnt that one the hard way.

As I get closer to the centre of the community, the ground becomes more waterlogged, and my pace drops to a slow trudge. I line my boots with the plastic bags and visualize my family waiting for me in the Spirit House. I say their names out loud, willing them into existence. 'Mum. Joe. Maudie. Mum. Joe. Maudie.' Not Dad. Never Dad. A cartoonish image of Dad's face, cold and hard as a glacier, flashes across my mind and fades.

The settlement area is gloomily silent in the early-morning fog. It's immediately obvious everyone has abandoned the community. There are no barking dogs. The cowshed is empty. The goats have disappeared. Only the white hen is left in the chicken hutch, sitting on a pile of eggs. Seven in total. That's one egg a day, which means it must be at least a week since anyone was last here. She lets me lift her to take my share and when I stroke her feathers she clucks with pleasure. She's weak and hungry like me. I feed her corn and she gratefully pecks it from my hand.

I pass the cabin where River lives with her parents and sisters. The front door is half open. I glance inside. Everything that can easily be taken has gone. There are owl pellets on the floor and a family of woodlice has made itself at home under the sink. The musty smell of neglect fills my nostrils.

I think of River and remember the way she threw her head back when she laughed, how she smelt of lavender and roses and could float like a cork in any water. It's the first time I've really considered her, which is weird, because I think she was my best friend. Until she wasn't. I frown. *We fell out!* This memory pierces my consciousness, sharp and painful like a shard of glass. Did I do something bad to her too? Does she hate me, like Mo? I feel sick with guilt. The fear spills over again, drowning all the details.

I creep back outside and edge through the narrow gully between the chicken run and the cow shed towards the Spirit House. The carved door is closed. The frame at the bottom has been gnawed by either rats or squirrels. I carefully ease it open, slip inside and turn on my head torch. On the table seeds lie scattered beside neatly labelled envelopes. Beans. Tomatoes. Beetroot. A list of winter chores hangs on the wall, but only three have been crossed out. *Move solar panels for winter sun; clean wood-burner; chop wood.* In the fireplace half-burnt logs lie in a pool of water.

Mo's threadbare armchair sits in the middle of the circle. A faded blue hoodie is draped over the arm. I recognize it immediately. It belongs to Joe. He wore it all the time. Every worst fear floods my brain. My scalp tingles and the sensation spreads over my entire body. I start to tremble. I press the hoodie against my nose and mouth, inhaling Joe's scent until I feel almost lightheaded and the panic subsides. I put on the hoodie under my jacket and glance at the blackboard where the Haven rules are written. TRANSGRESSIONS, it reads across the top in angry capital letters. Underneath everything has been rubbed out, apart from one sentence. TRUST NO ONE, it says, in Joe's messy handwriting. A beam of sunlight shoots through the window. It's getting light outside. I need to go.

I pull out Mo's notebook from my backpack and scan the room. The police mustn't realize someone has put it here since their first search. Impulsively, I tuck it into the back of the old armchair, hoping they'll assume they missed it the last time they checked the Spirit House.

When I go outside again everywhere is blanketed in mist. Apart from the demented scream of a muntjac it's unearthly quiet. I take a different route back up Blood Mountain, trying to calm myself by breathing in the pure scent of the early-morning air. The river makes a garbled noise and I guess it partly iced over during the night. I cut left and head for the densest part of the forest where the evergreens will give me cover. I touch them as I pass. Holly. Pine. Yew. Juniper.

Ahead of me a twig snaps. I drop down behind a bush and pull the knife from my bag, hoping it's a boar. They're crazily short-sighted and I'm downwind. But as I peer through the fog, I see a shadowy figure running straight at me through the mist. I freeze for the time it takes them to clock me and for a split second we stare each other out from a distance. Our faces are mostly covered to protect us from the cold so all I can see is a pair of eyes. I cut right and break into a run. Behind me I hear the light crunch of boots chasing after me. I sprint as fast as I can, making lightning-fast switchbacks, like a hare.

'Hey!' It's a woman's voice. I didn't expect that. I'm way ahead of her now. 'Wait,' she cries out again.

'Shut the fuck up,' I mutter to myself, as a pheasant torpedoes out of the bracken on maximum alert to the left of me. I might have outrun her, but she seems immune to the fact that her ruckus is likely putting us both in danger. Swearing under my breath, I turn and half jog back down the hill towards her, pressing my hand to my throbbing head. As I get closer, I see she's wearing a grubby jacket with a broken zip and a long hippie skirt, with a frayed fringe caked in mud. She's no more than a girl like me! Her spindly legs are bare and covered with scratches above the rim of a cheap pair of rubber boots. The boots are a giveaway. She's likely one of those hippie chicks who work as trimmers for the growers on the other side of the lake. Bad people. I slap my hand over her mouth and push her to the ground.

'Promise you'll be quiet,' I hiss at her. She nods feverishly. I take my hand away.

'Are you from the Haven?' she asks. My turn to nod. She clumsily pulls herself up and places a protective hand over her stomach. I'm shocked to see she's pregnant.

'What happened to your head? And what are those marks on your neck?' she asks. Her gaze darts nervously around. I touch my neck, but I don't know what she's talking about. 'Who did this to you?'

'My turn to ask questions,' I interrupt. She's put me on the back foot. 'Did you escape from the growers?' I try to avoid staring at her stomach.

'Yes,' she whispers. 'They're after me because I overheard them talking about how someone got killed.' She's breathing so shallowly she's almost hyperventilating. I show her how to calm her breath.

'Who got killed?' My mind goes straight to the darkest places.

'A man. That's all I know.' She sobs. 'Can you take me to the road? Because if they find me they'll kill me too.' She tugs desperately at my coat sleeve.

'How old was the man?' I press her for more details.

'I didn't see him. I just heard them talk about it.'

I explain that my family is missing and I'm searching for them in the forest. I describe them to her.

'I haven't seen them. There was a bad storm about a month ago. The people from the Haven left for higher ground. Maybe your family went with them.' I want more but she's too scared to focus on anything apart from her own shit.

'Take me to the road,' she pleads. I put my hands on her shoulders. 'Please. Take me to the road.'

'Listen.' I point up at the North Star and explain how she can use it to navigate west. I give her a can of tomatoes and one of the ready meals. 'Go back down the hill to the settlement area, cross behind the kitchen. Keep straight until you hit the stream and follow its course to the road. It's around a two-hour walk.'

'Thanks,' she says, her eyes filling with tears again. She gives me a quick hug.

'Have you come across anyone else?' I ask her.

Her voice lowers to a barely audible whisper. 'The man with a tattoo on his hand crossed the lake yesterday.'

'What did the tattoo look like?'

'Three triangles.'

It's Mo.

12

Then

What was most surprising about that first week at the Haven wasn't how strange everything felt, but how quickly nothing felt strange. Within days, a routine of sorts had taken root. We woke at sunrise, when the robin started tapping on our window, and rushed to be first in the queue for the composting toilet. 'Shit and chip! Shit and chip!' Joe shouted outside. On the way back I would collect an icy pail of water from the stream, rig it up in the outhouse and shiver under the bucket shower for exactly four minutes. After that we'd walk through the forest to the settlement area for breakfast. The route soon became second nature and within days I could do it on my own in half the time it had taken that first day with Skylar.

Every morning I set off in hope that Mo would be waiting for me at the Spirit House and every evening I returned to our cabin disappointed. When Piper got us to join hands in a circle to thank Mother Earth for her bounty before we sat down for breakfast, I would manifest to see Mo instead.

No one from the community mentioned his absence. When I plucked up the courage to question River, she told me that just because you couldn't see someone didn't mean they weren't there. 'Mo is everyone and no one, everywhere and nowhere.' She laughed. Which made just about as much sense as him not showing up.

Luckily, there were plenty of distractions. The settlement area was always buzzing with people, who were for the most part friendly. Animals roamed freely. Not just the three dogs – Chester, Micky and Snack – who stuck close to the food action, but also the enormous carthorse, Gaia, and George, a sweet little runt from a new litter of pigs, who needed bottle-feeding three times a day. Maudie was over the moon when she was put in charge of the chickens, and Joe helped River milk the cows and goats. He was shameless when it came to making a good impression on girls.

Skylar hadn't been exaggerating. The community was almost entirely self-sufficient. If there was something you needed there was someone who could sort it. New jumper? Go and see Kaia, who spun wool from the fleece of the small flock of sheep on an old-fashioned loom. A fruit bowl? Try One Way Will, who could carve anything in wood. When I got period pains, Aida soothed them with a tincture made of valerian, motherwort and rose. Anything broken was recycled or mended. Absolutely nothing was wasted. Leftover fruit and vegetables from the polytunnels behind the Spirit House, and the field where Dad worked, were fermented and pickled and stored in an underground root cellar. Fish was smoked in a home-made smoker that Piper had built. Milk was turned into cheese, yogurt and butter.

There were two main meals a day, one in the morning and one in the evening, served in the community kitchen. Kaia ran the cooking team with ruthless efficiency. Endless lists of supplies and meal plans hung on the wall. Most were a variation on the same ingredients. So, breakfast was eggs, beans and bread, and dinner was curry and bakes. We were blown away by their work ethic and commitment.

By the end of the first week, even my own family seemed to have forgotten about Mo. To be fair, we were pretty much occupied from dawn till dusk. There was always more to do than time to do it, and I guessed the people who'd been most uptight about us staying were finally persuaded because all of us, apart from Maudie, pulled solid eight-hour days, six days a week. No one slacked.

As soon as breakfast was over, everyone got down to work. Dad headed back to Drift Ridge Cabin where he spent every daylight hour digging, hoeing, weeding and irrigating Mo's vegetable field until his hands were cut and scarred, his fingers and nails stained black. Mum spent the day with Juan, looking after the different beehives scattered through the forest, and came home talking about royal jelly, drones and brood rooms, as if she was learning some new mysterious language. Maudie studied poisonous plants at home-school on Sylvie's terrace with Skylar, Jorn and Lucia.

I was put on kitchen duty with River under Kaia's watchful eye. Our job involved picking, peeling, chopping and fermenting hundreds of newly harvested onions. My eyes watered constantly, and even after swimming in the river, I couldn't get rid of their cloying stink. It was hot, hard work, but as Joe pointed out when we arrived back at our cabin in a state of exhaustion every evening, it beat shovelling shit. It turned out there was nothing scientific about being a member of the community fertilizer unit: Joe's job consisted of either carrying buckets of shit from the toilets to the barrel composter or spreading shit in the orchard. 'Everyone here talks shit,' Joe deadpanned, at the end of each day.

'Juan says you're a hard worker,' said Mum, giving him a

hug. That was the highest compliment at the Haven. Dad tried to convince him that turning human waste into something valuable was a miracle resembling alchemy but that didn't land. Things seemed better between Joe and Dad, in part because they were too tired to fight, but mostly because Dad was still in a state of ultra-positivity. Even Mum, who monitored his moods like the weather, thought that coming to the Haven might have shifted the dial for him. We were all, in our different ways, happy.

The upside of onion duty was that I got to hang out with River most of the day. She was the friendliest of the Vivian sisters. Skylar was only interested in Maudie, and Lila was haughtily indifferent to us all. But River took it upon herself to be my guide to the forest. She explained how to spot the hidden vines that lay coiled under the soil, the giant hogweed, with sap that caused skin lesions, and the poisonous hemlock that disguised itself as wild carrot. She taught me the difference between the sweetly frantic trill of the robins, the exuberant song-thrushes and the melancholic quickfire of the blackbirds. She showed me how to distinguish deer tracks from badger trails and recognize the heart-shaped hoofprint of the roe deer and the clumsy big-toed track of the muntjac. She talked all the time as she did this. 'The further apart the prints, the greater the speed . . . Running prints are always deeper than walking prints . . .' Eventually she showed me how I could recognize which humans had been in the forest by the tread of their boot. When she told me I was a quick learner I blushed with pleasure. 'Always take a second look at everything you see, Cass. Nothing is as it seems.'

River was a strange mix of characteristics. On the one

hand she was the first truly free spirit I'd ever met, and I envied her lightness of being. For a Labrador like me, she was a good person to hang out with because she didn't overthink. She was funny without meaning to be and clever without making me feel stupid. 'Do you know your onions, Cass?' she joked every morning. 'Fact: the ancient Egyptians used to worship onions.' 'Fact: they buried the pharaoh with onions in his eye sockets.' 'Fact: the more the onion makes you cry, the healthier the crop.' Somehow, she made peeling onions feel like the best job in the world. Yet at the same time I always felt she was holding something back. It was like her lightness disguised a darkness.

River was the only person who questioned me about life as an outsider. I gave over-elaborate descriptions about anything from TikTok to Alexa so she would have to give equal detail when answering my questions about Mo. The way he'd persuaded me to come here then failed to turn up was as hurtful as it was incomprehensible. But after a week of drilling down, all I'd learnt was that Mo had arrived at the Haven 'four winters ago', and that River thought Piper might have come across him at a gathering of the Rainbow people in Romania before she was born, or maybe Juan had met him in Spain. Or perhaps Denmark. Because, according to One Way Will, Mo was at least half Danish. A typical conversation went something like this.

'Why did Mo come here, River?'

'Because the winds of change were upon us.'

'What does that mean?'

'It means we'd lost our way and needed guidance to get back onto the right path.'

Then she would do something crazy, like shove onions in the old bra I'd given her as a present, call Joe over to take them out and fall around laughing when he blushed and looked away. I could tell she didn't want to talk about Mo. 'When someone isn't here, it's better to think they don't exist,' she said.

'Why?' I persisted.

'So you live in the present and not the past.'

They were circular conversations that got me nowhere.

Otherwise River was much more open about life at the Haven than anyone else. I learnt that, before Sylvie, Piper had been in a relationship with Aida for eight years. When I mentioned it must be difficult for Sylvie and Aida to live so closely alongside each other, River had looked astonished. 'We don't own each other. Why would people stay together if they're not happy?'

She told me Sylvie had also been in a sexual relationship with another woman at the same time as she was with Piper. 'They were really happy until they weren't.'

'And what did they do then?' I asked.

'There was a processing session and everyone agreed they should end the relationship.'

'Sounds complicated,' I commented.

'Nothing's more complicated than unhappiness.'

'What do you mean?'

'Do you think your dad makes your mum happy?'

'Of course,' I said a little abruptly.

'Well, I'm not so sure.'

'What do you mean?'

'I see your mum spending too much of her energy keeping your dad happy instead of keeping herself happy. She should bring it up during processing.' I couldn't help feeling annoyed, not because of the implied criticism of my parents but because I'd never worked this out for myself.

When we sat down for breakfast at the end of that first week, River let slip that Mo had been gone for two full moons, which meant that for most of the time he'd been messaging to say he couldn't wait to see me, he wasn't even at the Haven. My fork dropped from my hand and hit the table. It made no sense.

'He comes and goes all the time,' she quickly added. 'He'll definitely be back by the end of October.'

'Why October?' I blurted out, failing to hide my despair.

'Because that's when we celebrate Samhain.' I stared at her blankly. 'It's a festival to mark when we move from the lightness of summer into the darkness of winter.'

'But we'll have left by then!'

'Well, stay longer,' she replied.

'How can you be sure he'll come back?'

'Mo will never leave us. He protects us all.'

I couldn't ask any more questions because other people, including Mum, had sat down to eat with us. Kaia was next to me. She spoke to us in English and to Jorn and Lucia in Danish.

'Do you and Magnus speak in Danish with Mo?' I found myself asking. If River couldn't be more expansive about Mo, then I would outmanoeuvre her.

'Nope. Or rather *nej.*' Kaia smiled. 'Why would we do that?'

'Because he's Danish, isn't he?'

'Only in his dreams.'

Annoyingly Mum changed the subject by telling them she'd had a dream about her espresso machine magically appearing in the cabin. The story fell flat when no one understood what an espresso machine was.

The conversation turned to how long they'd all been living in the community. Aida's family had settled in the forest generations ago. Piper and Sylvie had come here as children after their parents met Aida's at Firefly, a hippie gathering in the Pyrenees. River, Lila and Skylar had all been born at the Haven. A fourth child, a boy, had died during childbirth. Juan was sent from Cazalla, an international community in Spain, to pass on his knowledge about permaculture. He'd met Kaia and Magnus at a gathering of the Rainbow people in France during his journey north.

'And I never went home.' He beamed.

I was about to ask about Mo again, but Lila had left the table and was squinting up at the brilliant blue sky. She called Aida over.

'What's wrong?' I nudged River. She didn't reply.

'Quiet,' ordered Aida. She cupped her ear with a hand. I couldn't see or hear anything.

'The noise is coming from over there.' She pointed in the direction of the lake. In the distance a small black speck appeared at the crest of the mountain on the other side of the water. 'Outsiders!'

Everyone got up from the table and started rushing around in a state of focused hyperactivity.

'Quick, Cass.' River tugged at my arm. 'We need to make sure they can't see us from the sky.'

We dragged the kitchen table under the trees. Aida covered the solar panels with branches, Juan and Sylvie pulled a green tarp over the roof of the outdoor dining area, Lila herded the chickens into their pen, while One Way Will coaxed the goats and cows into their shed. It was obviously a well-rehearsed routine.

'Get inside the Spirit House, everyone!' ordered Aida. She was the only one who spoke, and even in our short time in the community, I knew that where Aida led, the rest followed. We crowded into the Spirit House in complete silence and stood by the windows craning our necks towards the sky as the black speck got larger. By this time the gentle vibration of an engine was clearly audible. The fear and tension were almost palpable.

'It's the metal bird again,' whispered Skylar, clinging to my arm. I'd never seen her scared before. I looked up and, to my astonishment, saw a microlight flying towards us.

'Don't worry,' I reassured her. 'It's not dangerous. It's like a bicycle with an engine and wings.' It occurred to me, looking at Skylar's vacant expression, that she'd likely never seen a bicycle.

'It can't hurt you,' said Maudie, giving her a hug.

'What does it want with us?' asked Skylar. 'Why does it keep coming back?'

It seemed insane that everyone was so scared of a microlight, but when it started to fly back and forth over the settlement area, I got worried too. What was it doing? At one point it hovered so close to the trees that the branches shimmied in its drag. There was one person on board. Judging from his bulk, I assumed it was a man, although it was difficult to tell because his face was hidden by a helmet. He held the control bar in one hand and a camera in the other and was clearly filming the ground below.

'What do you think?' Piper asked Aida. They both stared skywards.

'Best-case scenario, the authorities have had a tip-off about the growers,' she replied, in her calm, even voice.

'Worst-case scenario?' Piper responded.

'They've had a tip-off about us,' said Aida.

'Do you think someone followed Rick and Eve to the Haven?' Piper eventually asked. My back stiffened. They obviously didn't realize I was standing right behind them. 'Or that they told someone else how to get here? Maybe they were lying and gave a copy of the map to someone.'

'Mo should never have brought that family here,' said Aida, ferociously. 'It's a transgression. They're the kind of people who sow bad weeds in good soil. The father is as easily provoked as an Africanized bee!'

'Mo said he needs someone like Rick on board to help him deal with outsiders,' countered Piper.

'Haven't you noticed how Mo is the biggest rule-maker, but he's also the biggest rule-breaker?' Aida hit back. 'You have too much faith in his opinions and ideas.'

'And you don't have enough,' Piper said firmly. 'We have to take into account everything he's done for us.'

'At what cost? We were a harmonious community. Now there are arguments all the time.'

'We're not meant to have this kind of discussion outside processing,' warned Piper.

'We used to communicate just fine without those sessions,' Aida replied.

They fell silent as the microlight buzzed over the Spirit House and swooped back up the hill. As it veered left to climb, it made a wheezing sound, like it was having an asthma attack, before finally sinking below the treeline and disappearing. There was a collective sigh of relief.

When River and I went back outside the only sound was

the chorus of birdsong. 'Warblers . . . skylarks . . . field-fares . . .' she said. 'Telling us everything is fine.'

I wiped my forehead. It was already blisteringly hot.

'Let's go for a swim,' suggested River, linking her arm through mine. 'No one's going to get any work done now.' The man in the microlight was already ancient history.

Twenty minutes later we were halfway to the lake. The first part of the hike was familiar because it was the same route we took back to our cabin. But instead of tacking right by Old Big Belly, we continued up Blood Mountain. Skylar led the way, carrying Maudie's backpack filled with the plastic figures from Dog Show, while Maudie tucked in as close as she could behind her, carrying nothing. Irritatingly, at the last minute, Joe had decided to tag along and had managed to insert himself between River and me.

The air seemed cooler, as if we'd entered a separate microclimate and the earthy mint smell of the pine forest became headier. A sound like hundreds of people whispering filtered through the trees. Skylar stopped for a moment and looked up at the wide-skirted fir trees hula-hula dancing in the breeze.

'What is that noise?' asked Joe, nervously. I was beginning to notice that he was more scared of the forest than I was.

'It's the pine trees gossiping,' said Skylar, putting her fingers in her ears. 'They're such attention-seekers.'

'That's fucking freaky,' said Joe.

'Are you frightened of trees?' teased River.

'I'm getting Evil Dead vibes,' Joe gabbled. 'Do you remember that scene where the tree rapes the woman, Cass?'

'What's he talking about?' Skylar asked her sister.

'No clue,' said River, giving a lazy shrug.

'Horror films,' explained Maudie. 'Joe is obsessed with them.'

The frown line between their brows and the quizzical way the Vivian sisters cocked their heads to the right was now familiar to me. I understood it wasn't disapproval, but an expression they adopted when we started talking about something they'd never heard about. Like sexting. Or Netflix. Or Donald Trump. I liked interpreting our world for them and began explaining about horror films before realizing that neither of them understood what rape meant either.

'Rape is a sexual act inflicted on someone without their consent,' I explained, hoping they wouldn't ask me any more questions in case I said something that revealed my lack of first-hand knowledge about sex.

'So, in Joe's film a woman is . . . violated sexually by a tree?' asked River, hesitantly. I nodded.

'It's not real,' said Joe, sensing the conversation slipping away from him.

'Human beings rape the natural world,' said River, fiercely. 'Not the other way round. They're the most destructive species on the planet. They burn down rainforests, poison the sea and lakes, farm and kill animals without compassion . . . Why don't you portray human beings raping nature in one of your horror films?'

'It's not real, it's just stupid make-believe,' said Joe, nervously. 'And it's not my film.'

I almost felt sorry for Joe because it was impossible to imagine that something so apparently trivial would have provoked such a strong reaction.

'I get you have a close relationship with the natural world,' said Joe, frantically trying to claw back. 'It's really . . . cool . . . and I'd like to know more about it. Become a pine whisperer myself . . .'

God, he was so obvious it was embarrassing. Even Maudie gave an eye-roll. The pines were now whispering louder than ever.

'But every tree has its own voice,' said River, in a more forgiving tone. 'You just have to learn to listen.'

Joe laughed, unsure if she was still angry or teasing him again. 'What do you mean?'

'Birch trees whistle, pines whisper . . . If their leaves are dry, they sound more sorrowful,' she explained. 'Do you know you can actually hear a tree dying?' She stopped to press her ear to the trunk of one of the pine trees. 'Listen, can you hear how it makes a popping sound? It's telling us it's thirsty.'

'You're shitting me,' said Joe, pressing his cheek against the tree, his face so close to River's that their lips were almost touching. When he pulled away his cheek was mottled brown and yellow from the bark. River rubbed it off with her hand.

'It's to do with the xylem,' she explained. 'They're like arteries. If they have to work too hard to get water from the soil, the sides collapse and tiny air bubbles get in. The popping noise is the sound of the air bubbles bursting.'

'Even when a tree dies it lives on,' said Skylar. 'Piper told me that in the outside world you get rid of the dead trees. But you also flush away your shit with drinking water so maybe it's not that surprising.'

She swerved sharp left and disappeared from view between two huge boulders that acted as bookends to a scree path that led down to the lake below. We followed close behind.

'Don't look down,' warned River, pointing at the dizzyingly steep drop to the right. 'It'll tempt you in.'

We copied the way they turned their backs to the gully and carefully side-stepped down the slippery scree. Occasionally fragments of stone came loose and clattered towards the lake. From a distance the water was inky black, but as we got closer, it became a shimmering constellation of dark greens, blues and even reds. 'It's so beautiful.' It wasn't simply the colours of the lake that made the words catch in my throat. It was the scale of the endless collage of trees, bushes and vines that covered the mountains the other side.

'Why is the lake so many colours?' I asked, when we reached the shore and they kaleidoscoped once again. We took off our boots and trainers and stripped down to our underwear to bask in the sunshine. I slumped down on a patch of mud that had been baked dry by the heat and thirstily gulped down water from my bottle.

'It's the iron and manganese from the limestone,' explained River, as she lay down beside me.

'Have you ever swum across to the other side?' I asked. It didn't look far. Twenty minutes' front crawl. Max.

'Too dangerous,' she said. 'There are invisible currents and whirlpools that drag you under.'

'Has anyone from the Haven gone across?' asked Joe.

'Dad went there once. He says there are old mineshafts everywhere, like hungry mouths, ready to swallow you up,' said River.

'You could fall in and never be seen again,' added Skylar, dramatically. 'There are bad people too ... outsiders ... growers –'

'But we don't talk about them,' interrupted River.

Skylar tugged at Maudie's arm. 'Come on. Let's build mud kennels for the dogs.' They headed towards the shore. I loved the way Skylar pivoted from adult to child with such ease.

'What's the best thing about living here?' Joe asked River.

'You're never lonely,' she replied.

'And the worst?'

'You're never alone.'

'Do you ever think about what you've lost?' Joe asked, turning onto his side to face her.

'No. I think about what I've gained,' she said.

I lay on my back, enjoying the way the hot dry mud soothed my aching muscles. My body started to relax, and my mind felt deliciously clear and free from worry. 'It smells so good,' I sighed.

'It's the pine resin,' said Skylar. 'It's released from the cones, the needles, the branches. It reduces stress. Helps people to heal.'

'You know so much,' said Joe.

'Aida taught me. Aida knows everything. She's learnt about science from books,' said River.

I closed my eyes and imagined myself as a confusion of cells and wondered how long it would take for my body to decompose and become part of the earth beneath. I focused on licking each single bead of sweat from my upper lip and noticed that even my sweat tasted of onion. I wanted to ask River if she tasted of onions too. Her arm rested gently against my shoulder. I imagined leaning over and licking the skin on the inside of her wrist. Somehow I knew she wouldn't find it weird. She had an intriguingly impersonal relationship with her body. There was no vanity, no shame, no self-consciousness, just an appreciation of its mechanics and functionality. Earlier in the week I'd made the mistake of mentioning that her eyes were a beautiful hazel colour. 'So what?' she'd responded almost aggressively. 'How does that help my life? Eyes are for seeing, not for being seen.'

I must have fallen asleep for a while. When I woke up, I saw that Joe and River were swimming in the lake in their underwear, floating on their backs like starfish. Joe's body was ridiculously white against River's tan. I stood up to wave at them and noticed that the tips of their fingers were intertwined. *Jerk.* I couldn't help feeling angry with Joe. He knew I found it difficult to make friends and I didn't want River to start spending the little spare time we had with him.

Maudie and Skylar lay on their tummies at the edge of the water. They'd constructed a complicated network of mud kennels for the dogs and were taking each one of them out to swim. I thought Maudie was staring at me, but her gaze rested on the undergrowth behind me. I turned round. The leaves rustled and Lila emerged to stare unblinkingly at us.

'You shouldn't have brought them here,' she said disapprovingly. As usual she only spoke to her sisters.

'They wanted to swim in the lake,' shouted River.

'They don't know what they're getting themselves into,' she warned.

'Why do you hate us so much, Lila?' Joe teased, as he came out of the water and shook himself over Maudie and Skylar, like an old dog. They laughed and threw mud at him.

'Did you at least do the checks?' asked Lila, as she scrambled down the bank towards us.

'What are the checks?' Joe asked her.

'For protection,' muttered Skylar.

She removed Hilda from the mud kennel and took her to the edge of the lake to wash the dog's mud-caked fur. Something caught her attention, and she dropped the plastic dog head first on the ground and zigzagged along the shoreline.

'Come, Lila!' she called.

We all trailed over and Skylar pointed at footprints in the mud.

'Must have been us,' said Joe, dismissively. River, Lila and Skylar crouched on the ground.

'Nope.' River shook her head. 'We've been walking around barefoot. This tread is from a boot or trainer. What do you think, Lila?' She examined the ground.

'They're fresh tracks,' she eventually replied. 'Long, deep footprints. Widely spaced. See how the left foot is deeper than the right? Judging from the size, they belong to a man who was running, who either has a right-sided injury or is carrying a heavy load.'

'Could it be someone from the community?' asked Maudie, nervously.

'They're wearing trainers,' said River. 'No one wears trainers here, apart from you guys, which means it's an outsider.'

'How can you tell?' asked Joe.

'Mo taught us how to recognize the different treads,' said River.

'He told us that on the outside there's a machine with every shoe print known to mankind inside it,' explained Skylar.

'How would he know that?' Joe asked.

'Probably because he used to be in the army.' They all stared at me.

'Who told you that?' questioned Lila suspiciously.

I started to backtrack. 'Mo mentioned something about it when he was at Maudie's party . . .'

'Oh, yeah, I remember now.' *Thank you, Joe, thank you.*

We trailed after Skylar as she traced the footsteps along the muddy bank of the lake for a couple of hundred metres to the point where the pine trees abutted the water. Then the tracks abruptly changed direction.

'Look,' said Maudie, pointing downstream. A cream sweatshirt floated on the surface. Skylar pulled it out and held it up. 'Make Every Day Earth Day,' it read on the front. On the arm was a Sierra Club logo. Joe wrung it out and put it in his backpack.

'What do you think?' Lila asked.

'I think the person was being chased and dropped the sweatshirt. Which means someone else was here too,' said River. 'But that person has covered their tracks.' She stood up and shielded her eyes from the sun as she scanned the shoreline on the far side of the lake.

'Do you think he got away?' I asked. We followed the tracks into the water until they disappeared beneath its murky surface.

13

Now

The red kite is all of a flap, which can only mean one thing. I've got company. Shaking with cold and fear, I drag myself out of Mo's sleeping-bag and pull on my boots. I'm deep inside Old Big Belly, the ancient oak, whose heartwood has rotted to create a natural hollowed-out room in the trunk. I pull myself up inside the tree, using the rot holes in the sapwood as foot and handholds until I reach a natural lookout point roughly four metres from the ground. The effort makes my head throb, and when I touch the wound a tiny worm of blood oozes out. I scan the forest and see the police truck from the other day, snaking its way through the undergrowth towards our cabin.

Four people climb out. Three are in uniform. The fourth is my aunt. A swell of emotion surges through my chest as Cara reels around, struggling to absorb the epic scale of the forest. I can't believe she's here, so far from her comfort zone, dressed in her glamorous fake-fur coat and purple lea-ther ankle boots, clutching a framed photograph of us to her chest. I stuff my gloved hand into my mouth to stop myself crying out.

Cara stands apart from the others while they banter together, as if she knows she's not from their tribe. They're about a hundred metres away but I hear everything.

'It's like looking for a bloody needle in a haystack except you've got to find the haystack first . . .'

'The search area is infinite . . .'

'Another inch of rain and we won't make it through that river again . . .'

They stamp their feet and clap their hands to keep warm. The cold is getting to them and there's already a note of defeat in their tone, as if they've given up before they've even started. Cara's determination to find us moves me utterly. It's a measure of her love. But even as I long to go to her, I know I won't. If the police aren't prepared to do what it takes to work out what's happened to my family, it's down to me. It's not that I don't trust them. I don't trust anyone.

'Don't you feel as if you're being watched all the time?' asks Kovac, the policeman with the hipster beard. He looks round nervously, his anxious gaze settling right where I'm perched. 'It's like the crazies who live here knew we were coming before we did. I bloody hate forests.' I feel sorry for him because I once felt the same terror.

'That kind of fear comes from the primitive part of the human brain, Kovac,' says Wass. 'It's your inner caveman grinding into gear.'

She calls them to attention, outlining the plan for the rest of the day, directing them to widen their search to other dwellings. 'Log everything, even if it seems trivial.'

She asks O'Hara if she's had any luck putting together a list of people who've been living at the Haven.

'So far, we've only identified a thirty-two-year-old male, who goes by the name of One Way Will. We found him by the road. He says he doesn't know his real name or how long he's been living here or where everyone has gone. He mentioned a flood. Named a few people.' She glances down at her notes, 'Piper, Motley Joe, Sylvie, Juan and three girls, all minors, called River, Lila and Skylar. No surnames. No addresses. No phone numbers. I'll cross-reference what we've got with the public records office when I get back to the station. But my bet is we'll find nothing on them in the system.'

'No mention of the missing family?'

'He says he knows nothing about them,' O'Hara confirms. Like we never existed either. 'But he also asked me if I spoke to the little people, so he's not reliable.'

'Any luck with the people in the village at the bottom of the valley?' Wass turns to Kovac.

'An elderly lady confirmed a family matching this description passed through a few months ago. They were lost. A woman stopped to ask for directions. She says they never came down.'

'Something bad has happened!' Cara cries out. It's the first time she's spoken. 'That whole eco-retreat thing wasn't right from the start. The guy who persuaded them to come here was a total fraud. I should never have let them go!'

'Unfortunately, feelings aren't facts.' Wass is doing her best to be kind but she's in more of a hurry today. 'A bit of background, people.' She pulls out a file from one of the folders she's holding under her arm and starts flicking through a slim report. 'There was a missing-person investigation a year ago, north of the lake. Before my time. A young woman disappeared. We launched an operation to crack down on guerrilla growers and one of the suspects we picked up mentioned forest people who'd been living here clandestinely for years. There was an aerial police search, but nothing came of it. No trace of the woman or the forest people was ever found. Case closed. We need to re-interview the suspect. See if he recognizes any of these names.'

'Guerrilla growers?' questions Cara. 'Who are they?'

Bad people. Outsiders. Dangerous folks with guns. I wonder if the girl made it out of the forest and why the police didn't find her on the road. My foot slips.

'Drug-traffickers who farm marijuana illegally in the north-west area of the forest,' she explains.

'People who spend their life on the outlaw side of the coin,' says Kovac, pedalling hard to win back Wass's approval. 'The soil here is ideal for the green gold.'

'Are you thinking these growers might be involved in the disappearance of my family?' asks Cara, anxiously.

'At the moment there's no concrete evidence that any crime has been committed,' explains Wass, cautiously. 'Your family could be lost in the forest. Or they might have decided to move to higher ground after the flood.'

'What hope is there of finding them over such a huge distance?' Cara gesticulates wildly. 'They could be anywhere. Maudie's only eight. She won't stand a chance out here in this cold!'

I have no idea where Maudie is. Or who she's with. But if I had to place bets on which member of our family could survive on their wits in the wild, it would be Mauds. She's like a cockroach.

'We'll do everything we can to find them. But if they don't want to be found, it's more difficult,' says Wass, choosing her words carefully.

'What do you mean?' asks Cara.

'Some people want to vanish,' explains Wass.

'I don't understand.' Cara sounds bewildered.

'Disappearing off-grid has its upside. You get rid of the mortgage, become self-sufficient, spend more time together as a family. Life becomes simpler, perhaps even happier. The truth is the mainstream doesn't work for everyone. Among the many possibilities, we have to consider that your sister and brother-in-law may not have wanted to go home.'

'My nephew Joe definitely didn't want to stay,' Cara says emphatically.

'You mentioned you were worried about some phone messages your nephew sent,' says Wass. 'Can you please run through the ones that gave you most cause for concern?'

'Of course,' says Cara, rummaging in her coat pocket for her iPhone.

Wass explains to Kovac and O'Hara that Cara had given her nephew a spare mobile phone for emergencies. I'm in total shock. I had no idea. Phones are a transgression. Plus there's no signal at the Haven. It hurts like hell that not even my own brother trusted me. I pinch my arm to force myself to re-focus as Wass runs through the details with her team. *Pay as you go. Nokia brick phone. Sim serial number.*

'At the beginning Joe didn't message a lot. It wasn't until late August that things got strange.' Cara starts reading. Her voice is shaky. 'On the twenty-sixth he wrote, *Hey C. Weird shit hapning. Just to let u know.*' She looks up. 'I didn't see the message until the following morning.' She holds up her phone so the police can grab a screenshot before continuing. 'I write back *What way weird? U all ok??* I didn't hear anything again for another couple of weeks. I tried calling but it went to voicemail.'

139

'Why did you give the phone to Joe and not your niece Cass?' asks O'Hara.

'I'm closest to Joe. And he's the smartest. If there was a problem, he'd know what to do. Cass is different. She finds life more difficult, and she's more easily manipulated. She's fragile.'

It's painful to hear this. I didn't realize other people could see my insecurities as vividly as I lived them. I swiftly push away the thought because, of course, I'm no longer that person. I'm no longer the weak one.

Cara continues. 'In early October, Joe messaged again. He was worried his dad didn't want to leave the community. So I got in touch with their school to double-check if they'd had confirmation from Rick and Eve that the children would be starting back. The school told me Rick had emailed to confirm they'd be home at the beginning of November. So, at that stage I guess I was more reassured than worried because they'd been in contact with the school.'

How would Dad have sent an email when there's no signal on this side of the lake? And didn't someone take his phone? Nothing makes any sense. My head pounds painfully.

'It wasn't until later that month that I got properly concerned. There were several short messages that worried me. Then on the twenty-second of October at two seven a.m. Joe wrote, *Need ur help.*'

This was a week before we were meant to go home.

Cara continues: 'I messaged every day that week. Joe didn't get back in touch. I knew he had to go miles to get a signal. Then at the end of October there were two more messages sent the same night, the first at six minutes past three said, *Call police*, and the next at four thirty-six said,

Spill it. I don't know what that means. It's obviously a typo. I called the police right away. I was told there wasn't enough information to launch an investigation, and then last week on the fifth of November I got a message saying, *C missing*. That's when I got in touch with you again. And you finally reacted.'

C missing. The news makes me feel almost dizzy. Joe must have meant me. I am missing. Cara points at my face in the photo and they crowd around to stare at me. I feel as though I exist in some liminal space where the only reality I inhabit is my own.

A crackle of voices filters through Wass's walkie-talkie and I realize another team is reporting to her from a different part of the forest. I can tell from the way her body tenses that she's had news.

'They've found some passports,' Wass explains to Cara. 'Does the name Mo mean anything to you?'

'Yes,' says Cara, emphatically, 'that's the guy I mentioned who came to my niece's birthday party. Rick was obsessed with him. He was the one who lured them here.'

'How about the names Moses Bentley, Mauricio Castellar, Morits Jensen or Morden Spilid? We think he uses those names too.'

Cara shakes her head.

Wass shows her a photo on her phone. 'Is this him?'

'Yes.' Cara nods vigorously.

It makes me super-anxious that the more I learn about Mo the less I know. I try to convince myself that it's better to know a little about someone and be scared, than know nothing and be naïve. Like I used to be.

'Why do you think he wanted your family to come here?' asks Wass.

'He chose them. That's what Rick said. I thought it was peculiar even then.'

Wass's radio beeps again. She puts it to her ear to listen and swears under her breath.

'Photograph every page and seal it up,' Wass orders the person at the other end of the radio. 'And run a background check on him.' She turns to the others. 'A diary belonging to this man with clear and specific threats against Cassia Sawyer has been found in one of the buildings. It's a shame you missed this the first day.'

'Where was it?' asks O'Hara.

'On the table just inside the door of the meeting house.'

I frown. That's very much not where I left it yesterday.

'I'm sure we looked there, ma'am,' counters Kovac. Wass ignores him and turns to Cara. *Sorry, Kovac.* I almost feel bad for him.

'I'm upgrading this search to a high-risk missing-persons inquiry with immediate effect.' She barks orders into the walkie-talkie. I smile with relief. Finding Mo has become their priority too, and I'm going to do everything in my power to deliver him.

14

Then

We were told we could talk about anything during processing, then nothing was ever said about anything that mattered. At our first session a couple of days after the outsider flew over in the microlight, I was on the edge of my seat waiting for the community to discuss what had happened. Instead all the chat was about how to stop wild boars crashing the pig pen at night. When River picked up the talking stick, I felt sure she would at least mention the footsteps and sweatshirt we'd discovered by the lake, but instead she made a big deal about how many jars of fermented onions we'd stored in the root cellar. Even worse, Mo's name didn't come up once. And he was meant to be in charge of security. It was all really weird.

During feedback, there was a lot of praise for the hard work Dad had put into the vegetable field by our cabin. 'We commend you for your efforts, Rick,' said Aida. She'd braided black and white magpie feathers into her hair and looked more birdlike than ever.

'You've already more than justified your presence here,' added Piper. It was true. Dad spent every daylight hour digging, hoeing, weeding and irrigating that bloody field, starting earlier and finishing later each day. If the criteria for living with the community was how hard someone worked, then he deserved to stay for a lifetime. He'd even taken to working in the dark, using his head torch to illuminate the vegetables. He was worried because they didn't appear healthy. Their growth was stunted and they had warty deformities. Although none of us said anything in case words made it real, there was growing anxiety that the shifting sands of his mood were changing yet again. Even an amateur psychologist could see Dad's emotional state was connected to the success or failure of the field.

'Thank you,' said Dad, his voice catching. He went all misty-eyed and I knew we were right about his frame of mind. 'I'm grateful to you for entrusting me with such an important task.'

Mum nudged him. On the way to the Spirit House, I'd overheard her urging Dad to warn the community about the mutant vegetables. Dad shook his head.

'We are of the firm belief that many hands make light work,' continued Aida. She paused and observed him with her inky black eyes. Dad didn't respond. He saw it as weakness to admit to any problems. There was an embarrassed silence.

'We were wondering if you could do with an extra pair of hands, *compadre*?' Juan finally intervened. He was still dressed in his white beekeeping suit, although the front zip was half undone, and a distracting froth of chest hair poked out of the gap. 'Eve mentioned you're putting in a lot of extra hours and I'd be really happy to pitch in.' He smiled and everyone smiled with him, except Dad.

I tensed, knowing it would be bad for us all if Dad's mood darkened, but especially for Mum, who would have to try to coax him out of it. 'Thank you, Juan. But that won't be necessary,' he said, in a tight, clipped tone.

Juan ran one hand through his thick woolly hair and

allowed Chester to lick the other. I felt bad for Juan. Of everyone we'd met at the Haven, he most closely resembled people from our old life. Probably because he'd once been an outsider too. We even joked about setting him up with Cara. He wore jeans with frayed hems and played Nick Cave on his guitar. He knew everything there was to know about bees and kept us all entertained by telling terrifying stories about deadly genetically modified Africanized bees. He understood how living in close proximity to your family didn't necessarily bring you closer; that relying on candles and oil lamps for light in the evening quickly became a pain in the arse; that the novelty of hauling water from the river to wash and drink, and collecting firewood so you could cook on the outdoor stove wore off after a couple of days. But he also revealed to us the beauty of a clear night sky by teaching us about the constellations, showed us how to use the North Star to navigate and, best of all, sent Mum home almost every day with treats like home-made hazelnut butter, or bread he'd baked in his outdoor oven. But none of this moved Dad, who seemed to have irrationally taken against Juan.

'We're in for a fun evening,' whispered Joe, shooting a sideways glance at Dad. I saw how Dad's jaw had set hard and his leg was jiggling. By the time we got back to our cabin his mood had curdled. But thankfully he went straight back into his field, so the storm didn't break until the next morning.

'Wake up! Get out of bed!' A torch blazed in my face.

I used one hand to shield my eyes from the glare and the other to scour my madly itchy calf, which was lumpy with fresh bites. Maudie clung to me. I shook her off, annoyed that she must have opened the window during the night and let in all the insects.

'What's up, Dad?' It was so dark inside the cabin that it was impossible to guess the time. His face hovered over me, glowing with sweat. The mercury thermometer in the cabin regularly nudged over a hundred degrees and even at night the heat was suffocating.

'Have the outsiders come back?' Maudie's voice was shrill with fear.

'My field is under attack! I need you all right now! Look lively!' yelled Dad. The beam from his torch strobed dizzily around the room. 'Head torch. Matches. Water-bottle.' He threw each one at me. The head torch painfully clipped my shoulder bone.

'Stop!' ordered Mum. I hadn't even heard her come into the room. 'You need to get a grip!' she blazed. 'We all need sleep, especially you.' But Dad had the wild-eyed look that rendered him immune to any form of reason. He'd gone beyond the point of no return already, and not even Mum could do anything with him when he was trapped in that kind of darkness. It was always fight with Dad. Never flight. I waited for Maudie to throw her own tantrum. That was what usually happened at this point. Instead, she rubbed the sleep from her eyes, scrambled out of bed and pulled on yesterday's clothes. We followed Dad into the kitchen. He shot up the ladder to the mezzanine to wake Joe.

'Get out into that field, now!' he shouted.

'Jesus fucking Christ!' Joe sleepily protested. Dad shook his shoulder.

'What is wrong with you, Rick?' Mum screamed at him. 'You're acting like a complete nutter.'

'That's because he is a complete nutter,' yelled Joe, but he didn't dare disobey Dad. He climbed down the ladder deliberately slowly while Dad paced up and down the tiny kitchen, getting himself even more fired up. Why did Joe fan the flames of his moods? It was an insane tactic.

Dad steamed outside and we all trailed after him towards the goddamn vegetable field. The sun was just rising and I guessed it was about five in the morning. The air was still and humid. Nothing moved. Even the burp of our flip-flopped feet was stifled by the heat.

'Can you please explain what we're all doing here?' demanded Mum. It was good to be out of the cabin. I felt protected by the trees and the birds, who'd temporarily suspended their dawn chorus to watch our pitiful display of family dysfunction. Dad fell onto his knees between two rows of feeble-looking cauliflowers.

'What exactly are you looking for?' asked Maudie, impatiently. Dad stood up. A plump hairy black and yellow caterpillar squirmed between his thumb and index finger. We all recoiled.

'I've found the culprit,' he announced triumphantly, as it struggled to escape. 'Cabbage white caterpillars!'

'Well done,' I exclaimed, assuming the crisis had peaked, and we could now go back to bed. Every hour of sleep counted at the Haven. Dad didn't react. Instead he started furiously crawling up and down the furrows between the vegetables, picking off caterpillars and throwing them into a plastic plant pot.

'Can we go back inside?' I asked. 'Please, Dad.' It was Sunday, our only day off work, and I could see my lie-in slipping between my fingers.

'No time like the present,' declared Dad, beckoning us

over. He showed us the seething mass of caterpillars spilling over the side of the plant pot and shook it in a recriminatory way that sent them delirious with fear. I knew exactly how they felt.

'Gross,' said Maudie, jumping back as one landed on her foot.

'I think you should take up Juan's offer of help. This is too much work for one person,' said Mum, tautly.

'Can you stop talking about bloody Juan for one minute? I've had enough of you badmouthing me to him,' Dad pushed the pot towards Mum and somewhere in the space between his anger and her nervousness it dropped to the ground and the caterpillars fell out, wriggling and squirming in a frothy heap on the dusty soil.

'All you do is watch me work, Eve!' yelled Dad, turning his back on Mum and stomping further into the field. 'You bloody well pick them up. It's about time you started pulling your weight around here.'

Mum looked shocked. I'd never heard him get angry like that with her before.

'Hey,' said Joe, who'd caught up with Dad and was tugging at the back of his T-shirt. 'Hey, you can't speak to Mum like that!'

'Leave him, Joe. He needs to cool down.' Mum tried to intervene.

'Please don't,' I pleaded with my brother. 'Please. Not now.'

'He's bang out of order, Cass,' said Joe. I knew he was right but the gnawing sensation in my stomach was making me feel sick and all I wanted was for it to stop. So, I got down onto my hands and knees and braced myself to scoop up handfuls of the disgusting caterpillars. It was worth it to prevent another row. But as I was about to pick up the first one, Dad's booted foot landed on top of them and he furiously started to stamp on them all, accidentally crushing my finger in the process.

'Fuck!' I cried out, but he was too focused on his caterpillars to notice what he'd done to me. My finger throbbed with pain.

'Stop it, Rick!' Mum screamed at Dad. 'Stop it!' But he wouldn't. Or couldn't. The red mist had descended.

Joe lowered his left shoulder, dropped his head and barrelled into Dad as hard as he could. There was a crack, like a stick breaking. Dad cried out in pain as blood started to dribble out of his nose. Mum tried to drag Joe off him. 'Stop it!' she screamed, so loudly that they must have heard her during morning meditation all the way over at the Spirit House.

I didn't mean to leave without telling anyone. In fact, I was almost hoping someone would call to ask me where I was going. But no one noticed apart from the robin eyeing me from the blackcurrant bush. I wondered if families like mine existed in the animal world and decided that if they did they would probably be killed by predators. Divided we fall and all that.

I puffed my way up the hill, looking back just once to see Dad sitting on the bench outside the cabin, head tilted back, while Mum tried to plug his nosebleed. Fuelled by a potent combination of anxiety and anger, I made quick progress. The anxiety was familiar, but the rage was something new and made me uncharacteristically decisive. A plan crystallized in my head: I would walk to River's house and convince her to go to the lake to swim again. Under the surface of the water all would be cool silence and the turbulence in my head would be stilled.

I no longer worried what River might think of my pale pink body with its rolls of flesh cutting into the elastic waist of my knickers. There was no judgement about personal appearance at the Haven, just curiosity about some of my clothes. *Why would you buy jeans that already have holes in the knees? What is the purpose of shoes that don't protect your feet?* I hadn't seen a single mirror since I arrived.

I'd tried to explain selfies to River during one of our onion-chopping marathons. It was impossible for her to get her head round a world where happiness was measured in likes and an entire day could be ruined by a careless Snapchat. 'I've never seen a mobile phone,' she confessed.

When I crested the hill, I scanned the valley below and decided to take the shortest route rather than the more meandering path we usually followed. As soon as I started walking down the other side of the hill into the wood, however, I was no longer above the tree canopy and almost immediately lost my bearings. I decided that as long as I kept going downhill, I would eventually reach the settlement area and find my way to River's house. After half an hour I realized I was properly lost. I couldn't work out where I'd gone wrong or how to retrace my steps. *Stupid, stupid, stupid,* I told myself.

Occasionally I paused to touch a tree trunk, trying to read the wrinkles on the bark, like a blind person reading braille. I listened to the sound of the leaves. I could tell the difference between the whisper of a pine and the watery lisp of an aspen. *The world does not need words when every tree has its song.* I heard River's voice in my head and understood the truth she spoke.

I'd reached the most ancient part of the forest. It was exactly as River had described to me. Everything was oversized, from the towering trees with their gnarly fat trunks and arthritic branches to the huge boulders decorated with intricate bright yellow and green veils of lichen.

I took a break on one of the boulders to unwrap five of my Maoams and crammed them into my mouth until it was so full that I could only breathe through my nose. I closed my eyes to focus on the way my jaw ached with the chewing and the roof of my mouth burnt with the sugary sweetness. I hated myself afterwards. But just as the heat was preferable to the insects, the self-loathing was better than the anxiety.

Sometime during my second round of self-abuse with Maoams I noticed a clearing in the distance. It was perfectly round and illuminated with a beam of sunlight that highlighted a single tree at the centre. I kept walking towards the light, but it was like a mirage: every time I thought I was close it seemed to be further away. I pushed myself on. Already I felt more light-footed than I had when I arrived. My movements were more instinctive, my body more receptive, as if it was working with me rather than against me. I no longer needed to stop every few minutes to catch my breath. It was as if the forest breathed energy into my very being.

I heard it before I saw them. The sound of chanting followed by a woman singing pierced the air. Her voice was so pure and ethereal that, for an instant, I felt as if I was connected to everyone I'd ever known, to the future and the past, the living and the dead, and everything in the forest.

When she sang, the leaves above me seemed to quiver in response and the fronds of the bracken arch towards the sound. I let her voice guide me towards the glade. As I edged ever closer, I saw a large group of adults and children standing in a circle around the biggest tree I'd ever seen. They were bathed in an orange glow, as if they were aflame. The tree was too tall for me to see its crown, and its branches hung low so that even the smallest children were shrouded by its leaves.

The woman singing stood slightly apart with her back to me, arms lifted towards the sky, encircled in a perfectly cylindrical sunbeam, lost in her song. She was wearing a long white dress embroidered with flowers, and a mask made of a deer's skull and antlers similar to the one that had toppled from Skylar's head that first day, except the antlers emerged from a huge garland of feathers and wildflowers, so she looked like a mystical creature. I hid among the bracken. I knew instinctively that I wasn't meant to be there, and my presence wouldn't be welcome. I tried to listen to the words but could only make out snatched phrases. 'I thank you, Mother Earth, for the bounty you give us ... Bless the land of many trees ... Protect me with your primal love ...'

The voice fell silent for a few seconds and a new sound filled the air as hundreds of birds started their own song. When they stopped the woman began again, and when she fell silent, the birds responded. Sometimes other people standing in the circle joined in. This beautiful exchange seemed to go on for ages. I didn't understand what was happening, but I knew without a doubt that I had never in my life wanted so much to be part of something.

When the singing finally quietened, I tentatively parted

the bracken to peer out of my hiding place. The singer
lowered her arms and the long sleeves of her dress slipped
down to cover her hands. I scanned the crowd dancing
around her to see if I could recognize anyone. Most were
wearing masks or had painted their faces. I spotted Lila
right away. She walked towards the tree, hiding something
in her cupped hands, and knelt to press the object into a
hole at the base of the trunk. 'Have no mercy for those
who think they are superior to the natural world.' Just
behind her, I thought I saw Juan's long wild black hair
spilling out from beneath a crown woven from ears of
corn, and recognized Piper's filthy feet. Skylar was instantly
identifiable because she was wearing Maudie's flamenco
dress. The lace frill at the bottom was hanging off and the
dress was covered with mud. I didn't want to be around
when Maudie saw that.

Four small fires had been lit around the tree and a delicious smell wafted through the air towards me. I breathed
it deep into my lungs and my body responded with a contented sigh. Every now and then someone stepped forward
away from the group of dancers, head bowed, to touch the
tree with the palm of their right hand and hide something
in the trunk until eventually the entire group was shrouded
beneath its branches. An enormous gust of wind surged
through the forest. Branches cracked, leaves shimmered,
and a mighty chorus of animals and birds started up.
Everyone waved their arms in the air, faces tilted towards
the sky, smiling and laughing.

A man stepped forward and took Skylar's hands. She
grinned broadly at him and they spun in a circle until her
feet left the ground and she was spinning through the air.
The man laughed loudly and threw his head back. I knew

it was Mo even before his wooden mask fell to the ground. There was something about the graceful, liquid way he moved as he threw Skylar around. I heard myself gasp. Had he just arrived at the Haven?

A weird confusion of feelings flooded through me: elation that Mo was back and anxiety that he hadn't come straight to his old cabin to find me first. I remembered the words of his last message: *need to see u.* For once, elation trumped anxiety. I stood up ready to join him, convinced it was our destiny to meet here like this and that everyone would understand we belonged together. He was my twin flame. I would join the Haven and become part of a single organism working for the common good, like the bees in Mum's hives.

Just at that moment the girl who'd been singing turned towards me. Our eyes met. River's transformation was extraordinary. I froze in awe. I'd never seen her dressed in anything apart from her worn trousers and grubby shift top. Now she looked as if she was about to get married. She shook her head as vigorously as she could with the weight of her headdress and waved me away with her arm. There was no mistaking the expression on her face. She looked terrified. 'Go,' she mouthed. 'Go.'

I dropped down again. A twig cracked underfoot.

'Did you hear that?' Lila cried. I froze.

'I saw something move over there,' said River, pointing in the opposite direction from where I was hiding.

'Don't worry,' said Juan. 'It's probably a muntjac or a badger. You know how noisy they can be.'

'Did you do all the checks?' Mo asked tersely.

'Of course,' said Piper, smoothly. 'We followed a deer

track, so we didn't leave footprints and avoided going close to any water.'

'How do we know the outsiders didn't follow us?' asked Lila. It took a moment for me to realize she was talking about my family, and that in the eyes of the community we were no different from the man in the microlight.

'They would never find their way here,' said Aida, scornfully. 'They aren't of the forest.'

'Plus they'd never keep up,' declared Magnus.

'Why have they even come here?' asked Lila, gruffly.

'They're searching for the answer to something without knowing what the question is,' Aida replied. 'They're lost. Like all outsiders.' She gave an ambivalent shrug. Her opinion didn't hurt as much as it should have because on some level I knew she was right.

'There's something desperate about them,' said Lila.

'What do you mean?' asked Juan. I wished someone valued my opinion, like Juan valued Lila's.

'They have a bottomless well of need,' agreed Aida. That stung more because I recognized myself in the description.

'Why did you bring them here, Mo?' Piper asked.

'Because that bottomless well of need makes them useful to us.'

I felt his words physically. Like a punch in the stomach. I hadn't expected Mo to speak so dismissively about my family. Especially me. But perhaps he had no choice. He couldn't reveal the truth – that we were here because of our relationship – if it hadn't been approved by the community during processing.

'I heard something again,' said Skylar, cocking her head.

'Quiet,' Mo ordered.

Everyone instantly fell silent. I made myself as small as I could. *Please, God, don't let them find me! Please, God, don't let them find me!* I could hear my heart thumping in my chest and worried that the Maoam wrappers would rustle in my pocket and give me away. But even as my shoulders ached from the awkwardness of prostrating myself on the cold ground, and pins and needles numbed my legs, I knew I was less afraid of being caught spying by the community than of Dad's anger that I'd done something that might threaten our stay here.

Suddenly pandemonium broke out.

'Over there,' shouted Lila.

'Behind the oak,' said River.

I closed my eyes, like I used to when I was little, and waited for them to find me. But no one appeared, and when I looked up, they were heading away from where I was hiding. It was close to miraculous. I'd never considered myself a lucky person, but this seemed to indicate that a change in my fortunes was possible.

Mo was at the front. I was vaguely aware of One Way Will and Lila tucked in close behind. But I couldn't take my eyes off him. He set off at a steady jog. I watched his chest rise up and down and the muscles in his arms contract from the weight of his backpack. He stopped for a moment and stared at River, who was pointing towards a dense area of woodland. I didn't feel sorry for the person who'd saved me. Just relieved I hadn't been found.

I don't know how long I waited in my hiding place. I only climbed out when I was certain I was alone. Coming here suddenly seemed utterly reckless. Yet in spite of what Mo had said about us, I felt curiously elated. It wasn't simply that Mo was back. It was the sense that I'd discovered something on my own that had shifted my perception of the world and somehow changed the very essence of me. I remembered Aida's words. *Into the forest I go to lose my mind and find my soul.* I wasn't really sure what I'd witnessed but I felt changed on some fundamental level.

I walked towards the tree and ducked my head so that I could stand beneath its branches. It was eerily quiet. Even the birds had fallen silent. On the ground I saw what looked like ash spread in a perfect circle around a metre away from the trunk. As I got closer, I could see that small strips of material were tied to its branches and different objects stuffed into every nook and cranny. There were multicoloured stones, feathers, small bundles of what looked like human hair, tied with the same red thread that was woven into Piper's hair. I even found one of Maudie's plastic dogs wedged in an opening close to the bottom of the trunk. I stood where Lila had been standing and nervously put my hand into a narrow gap where two vines of ivy converged in a hairy mass and pulled out a small doll, like the one we'd found in the hedge the day we arrived, except this one was wearing a denim dress and had lighter hair. When I lifted its skirt, I noticed a small hole above its legs, like a vagina, with a whispy red thread knotted through it. I stuffed it back into the tree, feeling a strange blend of shame and disgust, as if somehow my sexual longing was visible to everyone.

15

Now

Leaving Mo's notebook for the police to find has turned out to be a dud strategy. It's focused practically all their attention on me because, apparently, I'm now officially a 'minor at risk of serious harm'. Plus, plus – and I probably should have said this first, except my head is in chaos mode – although the photo in the stash of passports found by Wass's team was always the same, the nationality, date of birth and name were different each time. I can't believe I didn't find these passports myself, and if I missed them, what else might I have missed? *Sharpen up, Cass.* I'm not thinking straight. And I'm burning up, which likely means the wound on my head is infected. Not good, not good.

I'm outside the old shipping container where Aida lives. Every part of its surface drips with mosses, fungi and lichens. When I try to shove open the door a confetti of dead leaves and live woodlice fall around my head. I knock gently and give it a push. To my surprise, it's firmly bolted from the inside. There's no response. I spot a tiny up-cycled window cut into the wall to the right of the door and stand on tiptoe to rub the cobwebs and vines from its surface.

'What do you want with me, Cass?' Aida's sandpapery voice is a muffled whisper but even so I almost jump out of my skin.

'Please, Aida,' I beg. 'Please, can I come in? I need your help . . . I'm hurt. Badly.'

Nothing. For a moment I wonder if the fever has made me delirious and I've imagined her. A memory comes back . . . of Maudie towards the end . . . when she started talking gibberish . . . . . . before they took her away . . . after Joe disappeared. There's a narrative of sorts emerging, which should make me feel good, but if Aida doesn't let me in, it won't matter. Even if I manage to shake off the police, I won't make it through another night in the wild. I thump the door again and scream like Maudie in full throttle. Birds explode from nearby trees. Anyone could hear me. The police. Cara. Mo. But I'm all out of options. I press my hot forehead against the cool steel of the door in exhaustion.

'Please,' I sob. 'Mum told me to come to you if I ever had any problems.'

There's another long silence.

'Are you alone?' Her voice is so close. She must be just the other side of the metal door.

'I've never been more alone.'

'Did you do the checks?'

'Yes.' It's a half-truth. My backpack wasn't zipped properly and I think something has fallen out. But I have an excuse because my brain is on fire.

The bolt grinds open. Aida holds the door just wide enough for me to slink in sideways, scans the forest to make sure I've been true to my word and quickly bolts it again at the top and bottom.

'Thanks,' I say, through chattering teeth. Because now I've properly got the shivers.

'Sit.' She directs me to a low bed in the corner of the

kitchen and points at a crochet blanket. I wrap it round me, close my eyes and imagine the warmth comes from Mum hugging me.

Aida touches my forehead with her hand and frowns. 'You're running a fever.'

I jump. I'd almost forgotten she was here. She reaches up for a small tin on the shelf above and takes out what looks like a strip of bark.

'Chew it. It'll help lower your temperature.'

'What is it?' I ask.

'Black willow bark. Nature's aspirin.'

'How do I know you're not trying to poison me?'

'You don't.' She gives a quick grin. 'That's what happens if you hang out with someone like Mudder too much. You end up thinking his shadow-side thoughts.'

I try to act normal by looking round her container. I've only ever seen it from the outside. Inside it's even darker and tinier than our cabin. There's room for a small square table with two chairs, and a narrow counter with a stove and a sink. At the end an even smaller room is separated from the main living space by a macramé curtain. Three long shelves stretch across the back wall. One has supplies of food. Another crockery, including a couple of surprisingly delicate china plates and teacups. The top shelf has a series of tins. *Tools. Seeds. Pens. Medicine.* Each one is labelled. It reminds me of a doll's house.

'It's eight foot six tall,' she says. 'Standard shipping size.'

I spot a home-made 2016 calendar hanging on the wall. Only two dates are marked.

'What happened on the fourth and thirty-first of July?' I ask.

'It was the first time outsiders brought their ways of

destruction to us. We lost some old friends that day. Trees my family had known for generations. All burnt down by the growers so they could plant their filthy crop.'

'And on the thirty-first?'

'Mudder arrived.' Her eyes narrow and she stares at me as if she's drilling into my very soul. 'Or Mo. As you prefer to call him.'

The mention of Mo makes me feel queasy with anxiety. I fall silent and look down. My gaze lands on a pot of moisturizer and a silver necklace sitting on a table made from a tree stump. I recognize the necklace immediately. It was a present from Dad to Mum. Her initials are engraved on the pendant.

'Mum's been here, hasn't she?'

I pick up the moisturizer and open the lid to breathe in the scent of her.

'She used to visit. Occasionally.'

Aida is being evasive. It's painful that Mum kept this from me. Aren't mothers and daughters meant to have this unshakeable bond? I swallow my tears. She didn't trust me either. 'Why did she come here?'

Aida shrugs and turns away.

'Let me take a look at that.' The dried blood on the hood of my jacket has caught her eye. She tenderly pulls it down. Her nose wrinkles. I know the wound smells bad. To her credit she doesn't flinch. 'You stitch this yourself?'

I nod.

'Good work,' she congratulates me. I can't help feeling pleased. 'Why don't you explain what happened while I get this cleaned out?'

'I was hoping you might be able to tell me. The final days are a bit of a blur.'

She puts her hands on my shoulders and stares uncompromisingly into my eyes.

'I left the Haven weeks ago. When everyone stopped listening to me.' Her look suggests I was one of those people. 'Took refuge in the northern part of the forest. We've found sanctuary there before. When I came back a few days ago, everyone had disappeared.'

'Have you seen any of my family?' I ask, clutching her forearm.

'Joe came by a few days ago.'

I choke up. She pulls away.

'How was he? Was he okay?'

'He stayed for just a few minutes. He looked very thin. He wanted to know if I'd seen you or River.'

'What about Maudie? Did he say anything about her?'

'Nothing. Try not to worry about Maudie.' She fixes me with her dark eyes. 'She's a survivor.'

'Do you know where Joe has gone?'

'I don't. He didn't say. It's better that way.' She pauses. 'Cass, why don't you tell me what you can remember?'

'I think I was attacked or involved in some sort of fight. I woke up in the forest with this injury on my head and everyone gone. There was a fire in our cabin. I don't think it was an accident.'

'Why would anyone want to hurt you?' she asks.

I tell her about the threat to me in Mo's notebook and the red stain on the floor in his tree-house.

'Are you trying to tell me Mo attacked you? Why on earth would he do that? His job was to protect us.' She snorts dismissively. 'Maybe you upset other people.'

'I'm worried I might have done something really bad,' I blurt out. 'I found skin and blood under my nails. Will you let me hide out here so the police don't find me, Aida? Please? I need time to find out what's happened.'

'If the authorities discover you here with me, it puts me centre stage and I don't want that kind of scrutiny. They'll come back and take me away for questioning. They could force me to leave the Haven. As far as they're concerned, this is an illegal settlement. I'm a gatekeeper of this forest, just as my family were before me. It's my sacred duty to take care of it. Nothing else matters.'

'They'll never find your container. It's too well hidden.'

She turns her back on me and lights the rocket stove to melt pine resin for the wound on my head. 'This is how the Egyptians treated infections,' she explains, as she stirs the mixture. 'The resin comes from a Norway spruce . . . It has more terpenes than a Scots pine.' The scent of pine fills the container. I close my eyes, breathe it in and feel my body properly relax. 'Once it's boiled, we need to strain it, add the beeswax and let it cool. It's going to take a while. Is that okay?' I feel her hand on my shoulder.

'More than okay.' My voice quivers. I wasn't expecting such tenderness from Aida.

'One night,' she says eventually. 'I'll give you one night. In honour of your mum. And then you have to go.'

'Thank you,' I whisper.

'There's something I need to show you,' she says. I follow her into the bedroom. It's a tiny space, no wider than the foam mattress that takes up most of the floor. Every square centimetre is accounted for and it's ruthlessly tidy. Her clothes hang from a pulley system attached to the ceiling: three pairs of black jeans, four green T-shirts, five pairs of socks, and four hand-knitted jumpers. A heap of carefully folded blankets lies at the end of the bed. A shelf runs along the width of the mattress. There are three wooden boxes that I guess she made; one contains hair toggles, another a brush and comb. I'm taken aback to see a moon cup because I can't imagine Aida going through an off-grid period. She's too ethereal for the mess and grub of bodily fluids. She stands on the mattress and stretches up to the bracket that holds the pulley system in place to pull down a small parcel taped to the ceiling.

'Joe left this for you.'

I take the parcel from her hand. It's taped up at the ends like a badly wrapped present. 'How did he know I'd come here?'

'Everyone comes here in the end,' she says.

'Do you know where he's hiding?'

She stares at me long and hard. Her upper lip twitches slightly.

'I really need to find him, Aida. Please.'

'He doesn't want to see you at the moment, Cass.'

What have I done that my own brother doesn't want to see me? Why does no one trust me? I blink back tears and open the parcel. I'm hoping there might be a note from Joe inside, explaining everything. It's wrapped in several layers of pages torn from a magazine. I take out my knife, slice it open and an old-style brick phone, partially covered in masking tape, slides out.

16

Then

So much for my big disappearing act. When I finally made it back to our cabin after the ceremony in the forest, no one seemed to have even noticed I'd been missing most of the day. Mum, Dad and Maudie were still in the same field where I'd left them. Dad was telling his favourite joke. 'How do you eat an elephant?' His bruised, swollen nose gave his words a honking nasal undertone and they hung embarrassingly long in the heavy evening air. 'One bite at a time,' Maudie chipped in. Dad was always disarmingly good-humoured and emollient after one of his meltdowns, like he'd lanced a boil. He even acted hurt if anyone mentioned his behaviour, as if he was the victim. It was always someone else's fault. Usually Joe's.

I felt sorry for Mum, constantly having to navigate the highs and lows of Dad's mood swings. Living on top of each other had made me appreciate what hard work he could be. I wandered past the front of the cabin amazed at how quickly we'd come to resemble one of those off-grid families from the TV shows we'd watched before we came. A solitary saucepan of water bubbled away on the wood fire of the outdoor cooker. Damp clothes that never seemed to dry hung on the line. We all smelt of eau de Haven, a musty marinade we never managed to shake off. Jason and Juniper were in their run, basking in the late-evening sun. Gaia was tied up in the shade, swishing her tail to get rid of the flies. She was the closest thing to Uber at the Haven and I guessed that someone from the community was visiting Mum and Dad.

I felt alive in a way I'd never felt before without being certain exactly how the tectonic plates had shifted inside me. I'd witnessed something magical, and it had infused my soul. That was the only way I could explain it. I cut down the side of the cabin, past my bedroom window, enjoying the sensual way the cow parsley licked my thighs. For the first time I felt perfectly at home in the forest. It was a weirdly unexpected sensation.

I focused on the night chorus of birds warning it was time to return to the safety of their nests before it got dark. The mewing of the little owls who lived in the tree outside our bedroom, followed by the squeaking lisp of their recently fledged babies, who'd been banished to a neighbouring tree last week and were begging their parents to bring them food. The night shift had started.

'Let Maudie make the tea,' I heard Dad honk, as I turned the corner and headed towards the vegetable field.

'It's fine. I'd like to stretch my legs,' Mum replied evenly.

'It's Maudie's fire. She collected the wood, she helped build it and she lit it on her own with a flint and steel. She'll be fine.' Dad's voice brimmed over with pride. 'Maudie learns faster than the rest of us put together.' I couldn't help feeling insulted, but I could tell this had nothing to do with how he felt about Maudie or me: it was about how it made Dad feel better about himself. Classic head-fuckery.

'Please, Mum, please,' Maudie pleaded. 'I'll be really careful.'

'Okay,' Mum reluctantly agreed. In any case Maudie had already disappeared.

As soon as I went into the field, I saw that the visitor sitting cross-legged on the ground opposite Dad was Mo. Even though I'd seen him at the ceremony, I wasn't expecting him to come for me so soon. But I buried this thought alongside the anxiety and paranoia caused by his recent no-show: all that mattered was that he was right here right now. Feeling almost lightheaded, I continued into the field and spotted Mum and Dad sitting on a fallen branch by the hedge. Dad's upper lip was swollen into a trout pout and his nose had a large purple-grey bruise from the fight with Joe.

Mo didn't see me at first, which gave me time to relish the way his T-shirt had slipped off his shoulder, showcasing the hard line of his clavicle with the soft shadow of muscle in his arms to most excellent effect. His dark curly hair had grown and framed his face beautifully. He was hot. He made me hot. I wanted him. I was paranoid that the surprise of seeing me might mean he'd betray his feelings in front of Mum and Dad, but he looked up and shot me a slow, languid smile.

'Hey, Cassia,' he said. 'Long time no see.'

Fortunately, Mum used the distraction of my arrival as an excuse to check on Maudie. Joe had done his usual disappearing act. Which left Dad to contend with, but he was too consumed by his deformed carrots to grasp what was unfolding right under his nose.

I felt Mo's eyes consume me. Even in the heat of his gaze, I didn't look away. We walked towards one another, half laughing. I sucked in my stomach and was pleased there was no longer so much to suck in. The walking and physical labour had shrunk and hardened my body already.

'Why are there ants *and* aphids?' Dad asked Mo. 'What have I done to deserve that?'

'Ants feed on the honeydew that the aphids produce so you'll need to get rid of both,' advised Mo, without taking his eyes off me. 'Try to encourage natural predators. Like ladybirds.'

'Is there anything this man doesn't know, Cass?' said Dad. 'They don't teach you this stuff at school, do they?'

'He's the best.' I grinned at Mo. Dad wasn't concerned with my opinion. He was trying to make sure I was good with him after what had happened earlier that morning. That was how he made us complicit in his shitty behaviour. While Dad searched in vain for ladybirds, Mo stepped forward and wrapped his arms around me.

'Why did you take so long?' I immediately regretted the question because it made me sound so needy. *Bad Labrador.*

'Time doesn't exist for those who are meant to be together,' said Mo. A tiny part of me imagined Joe's bullshit detector ringing off the scale but I wanted to believe more than I wanted to be right. I looked up at him and decided that if he tried to kiss me I wouldn't care if Dad saw or what he thought. In fact, I wanted everyone to know about us.

'Where were you?' I whispered. *Bad, bad Labrador.*

'We had some problems with growers in the northern area of the forest on the other side of the lake.'

It was then I spotted the rifle lying on the ground beside him.

'Why do you have that?' I asked nervously. I'd never seen a real gun before.

'It's my Remington 700. Your dad wants to learn to

shoot with it in case his vegetables are being eaten by rabbits.' My heart sank.

'That's not a good idea,' I blurted out. Of the many things I didn't understand, it was obvious to me that one of life's great certainties was that someone who couldn't reverse a van into a parking space should emphatically not be in possession of a gun.

'If you like, I can teach you too,' he offered. He picked up the gun and casually slung it across his shoulder.

'Right now?' I hesitated.

He pointed towards the woodland that marked the boundary between the field and the dense forest beyond. I got it. He was trying to find a way for us to be alone. We traipsed across the withered vegetables, kicking up a cloud of dust. Dad gradually faded from view. Mo steadied my nerves with his constant chat.

'When you're hunting deer, always stay downwind. Their vision isn't up to much but upwind they can smell you a mile away . . . If you keep the wind in your face, you'll always be the hunter. Never the hunted. Got that, Cassia?'

I nodded a little too eagerly and he grinned at me. 'I'm so glad you're here,' he said.

My stomach somersaulted. I couldn't stop smiling. When we reached the trees, he paused and handed me the gun. It felt awkward and heavy in my arms. 'How do I even hold it?'

'Like this.' He stood behind me and pressed himself against me, lifted the stock into my right shoulder and demonstrated exactly how to balance the barrel between my left thumb and swollen index finger. Then he raised the gun to my right eye and put his finger on top of mine on the trigger. The air around us became thick and syrupy with desire. Every tiny movement of his body triggered a disproportionate reaction in mine. His breath on my neck sent shivers down my shoulder, between my breasts, down my stomach and straight between my legs. I remembered a line from a poem we'd learnt at school and understood it for the first time. *I love thee to the depth and breadth and height my soul can reach.*

He pulled the trigger. Click! It was a tiny noise, but it was so unexpected that I reeled right back into him. He caught the gun and roared with laughter. I turned to face him.

'Don't look at me. Look into me,' he said. He took my hand and pressed it against his chest so I could feel his heartbeat. We must have stood like that for almost a minute. His green eyes burnt into me. I felt as if he'd turned me inside out so that every nerve was exposed and every dark secret I'd ever hidden inside me was visible to him. For the first time in my life, I'd met someone who totally accepted me.

'So, where have you been all day?' he asked casually. 'I've been waiting here for ages.'

Remembering the terrified look on River's face at the ceremony I held back for a second. And then I weighed up the importance of honesty in relationships at the Haven.

'I went into the forest . . .'

The rest of my words were drowned out by the terrible sound of Maudie screaming. It was a harrowing noise that pierced the still night air. I understood right away that she wasn't having a tantrum. It was the sound of someone in terrible pain. Mo untangled himself from me, Dad stopped massacring aphids and we all sprinted to the front of the cabin. I'm ashamed to say that I couldn't help feeling irritated that yet again Maudie had managed to divert everyone's attention back to her. If ever there was a moment that was meant to be mine, then surely this was it.

As soon as I turned the corner I saw Maudie kneeling on the ground, writhing in agony, cradling her left arm. The saucepan, which had contained boiling water, lay empty beside her. The fire was still burning and a couple of logs smouldered on the ground. Maudie's head was tilted skywards, and her eyes were wide open as she wailed like a banshee. Every so often she gulped for breath and made horrible gurgling noises that were even more unbearable because she sounded as if she was choking. Mum was crouched beside her, gripping Maudie's good arm to still her. But Maudie screamed even louder.

'Oh, my God, oh, my God, oh, my God,' Mum cried over and over again. I'd never seen her at such a loss. She generally had a solution to every problem.

'What should I do, Mum?' I shrieked.

'Cold running water! We need cold running water!' Mo yelled, over Maudie's screams.

There was running water in the cabin that came out cold, but only in a trickle, because the water pressure was so low, or there was lukewarm rainwater in the big orange winter storage butts that sat in the porch. I dithered pathetically, unable to decide if I should hook up the hose to the tap in the cabin or run to the river at the bottom of the vegetable field to collect a big bucket full of ice-cold water.

'Attach the hose, Rick,' Mum bellowed, 'and, Cass, fetch Aida. Tell her it's urgent.'

'Why do you need Aida when you've got me?' questioned Mo.

'Because Aida always knows what to do,' roared Mum.

I glanced from Mum to Mo, conflicted about who I should listen to as Dad frantically fed the hosepipe through the window of the cabin.

'Look at me, Maudie!' Mum tried to tilt Maudie's face towards her, but she kept howling at the sky. She didn't blink once.

'Mauds, I need to cut the sleeve off your dress!' Maudie was in too much pain to take in what Mum was saying. Still dithering about whether to fetch Aida, I stepped forward and bent down to try to get through to her. I almost gagged at the smell of burnt flesh and realized that, as well as tipping the saucepan of boiling water over herself, she'd burnt her arm on the open fire. Her hand was a horrible shiny purple colour.

'Please let us help you.' I couldn't bear to see Maudie in such a state. She was the bravest of us all. I stretched out my arm towards her good hand. 'Give the pain to me, Mauds,' I pleaded, remembering how Mum and Dad used to do this when we were little. 'Squeeze my hand.' But she didn't look at me or anyone else. She was trapped in her own private hell of shock and pain.

'Shall I get the scissors, Mum?' She gave me a quick nod. Dad ran over with the hose and started spraying it over Maudie's arm. She desperately tried to turn away from him.

'*Stoooop!*' she cried, in a single long moan. '*Stoooop!*'

'I'm so sorry, Maudie, but we have to,' said Dad.

'It will stop the burn getting worse and make it feel cool!' Mum put her arms around Maudie's waist to hold her in place. 'I'm so sorry.' Mum's voice was almost a whisper.

174

I headed into the cabin and closed the door behind me to muffle the sound of Maudie's screams, feeling guilty that it was such a relief to have time out from the crisis. I suddenly remembered how Dad had hidden his mobile phone from Piper the day we arrived. I lurched into my parents' bedroom, threw myself onto the dirt floor and used one hand to lift the mattress, the other to search for the phone. The floor was a graveyard of dead insects, mouse shit, dustballs and feathers, but the phone was there. I pulled it out and miraculously turned it on. *Emergency calls only*. I touched the screen. Nothing. My heart sank.

'What are you doing?' Mo was in the room with me.

'Trying to dial nine-nine-nine!'

'There's no signal, Cassia.' God, I loved the way he said my name. 'You look beautiful when you're scared.'

He put his arms around me, leant towards me and kissed me hard on the lips, his tongue pressing my mouth open. His lips were soft and he tasted exotic. Smoke, coffee and a hint of patchouli. I'd kissed boys before but there had been something more mechanical about their tongues inexpertly sweeping back and forth across my gums, like windscreen wipers. This was different. He ground against me and grabbed my T-shirt, twisting it in his hand until he could reach my breast. There was a hungry impatience to his approach that made me falter, and a kind of disinterest in my reaction. I froze in confusion. This wasn't what I'd imagined.

'We need to help Maudie,' I floundered. But when he pulled away, I felt almost bereft.

'Don't worry, Cassia, the community will deal with Maudie's injury. We always do.' He gave me a reassuring hug. 'Your dad shouldn't have kept his phone. It's a transgression.' He held out his hand. I'd like to say I thought for a moment before handing it over. But I didn't. I gave it to Mo unquestioningly and he slipped it into his pocket.

I found Mum's scissors in the first-aid kit beside the bed. Mo grabbed a container of cooking oil from the shelf in the kitchen and we rushed back outside. Maudie was still kneeling on the ground crying, but her voice was quieter and throatier. She looked paler too, and even though it was so humid that I was covered in layers of sweat, I noticed she was shivering.

'She's in shock,' wailed Dad, who now looked really shaken.

'Hold her still, Cass, and I'll try to cut off the sleeve,' Mum instructed.

Mo stepped towards us, undid the lid of the cooking oil, and tilted it towards Maudie's arm.

'What are you doing?' Mum yelled at him. It dawned on me that no one really knew what they were doing. We were all flailing around.

'It'll help ease off the sleeve,' he barked.

'Stop!' a voice ordered. I couldn't see where it came from. Mo squinted towards the composting toilet as Aida emerged from the bushes and headed towards Maudie. 'If you put oil on a burn, it retains the heat and makes it worse,' she yelled. 'Keep the hose on it, Rick. Cass, give me the scissors.'

I glanced at Mo and saw a shadow pass over his face. Aida calmly bent down beside Maudie, put her hands on either side of her shoulders and tilted my little sister's chin towards her. She was half sobbing, half groaning and trying to say something indecipherable. I could see the terror in her eyes.

'Do you trust me, girl?' Aida asked. Maudie bobbed her head. 'Here's what we're going to do. We need to get this sleeve off or it'll stick to the burn and cause an infection. You need to count to twenty in your head and keep as still as you can while I cut. Can you manage that?'

To my astonishment Maudie nodded again. I noticed that the hand that emerged from the sleeve had turned into a bubble wrap of blisters.

'You help her count, Cass,' said Aida. We all knelt in a semi-circle around Maudie, as if we were worshipping a living god, and began counting together. Only Mo didn't join in.

'One – two – three . . .' cried Maudie. Every number was an anguished scream.

'You're doing great, Maudie,' said Mum.

'My brave girl, my brave girl,' said Dad, on repeat. He looked awful, ashen, even beneath his deep tan. Aida made slow progress with the scissors up the sleeve of the dress. As the material parted, the true extent of the injury was revealed. The burn started on the inside of Maudie's arm, just below the elbow, coursed all the way down her forearm as far as her knuckles and edged into her thumb and index finger.

When Aida had reached the shoulder of the dress, she efficiently cut off the sleeve and threw it onto the ground. Dad put the hose back on the burn and Maudie started screaming again but, compared to the horrible gurgling a few minutes earlier, her high-pitched shriek was almost a relief.

'Keep going with the hose for at least half an hour and then we'll seal her arm in a plastic bag to stop it getting infected,' said Aida.

Maudie's screams turned to tears of pain. She sobbed and sobbed, and when I touched my own face it was damp with tears. I couldn't bear to see my brave little sister suffer so much.

'We need to call an ambulance,' Mum babbled.

'How? There's no Wi-Fi or phone signal,' I pointed out.

'Then we need to get her to a hospital,' said Mum, frantically.

'How are we going to do that?' panicked Dad.

For the first time since we arrived it occurred to me how vulnerable we were. With Rory dead in a ditch, the only way to get medical help would be to cart Maudie through the forest to the road and pray that a passing truck might pick us up. I remembered how we hadn't passed a single vehicle on our way here. Besides, it was beginning to get dark and there was only a feeble crescent moon to light our path.

'We need to carry her to the road,' insisted Mum.

'It's a two-hour walk and that's in daylight,' said Dad.

'Could she ride on Gaia?' I suggested.

'*Noooo*,' wailed Maudie. 'Too sore. Too sore.'

I was encouraged that she was responding to what everyone was saying.

'She's not going to hospital,' said Mo, firmly.

'What do you mean?' shrieked Mum.

'We can look after her here,' said Aida. 'We have our own medicine.'

'Don't be ridiculous!' shouted Mum.

'She's young. She'll heal.' Mo took my hand and gave it a reassuring squeeze.

'This is crazy!' cried Mum, looking at Dad to back her up.

I didn't know what to think or who to believe or what to do.

'Why don't we see how she gets on tonight and if she's not any better we can take her at first light?' suggested Dad.

'We can't afford to wait,' yelled Mum.

'She can't go to hospital,' repeated Mo, more firmly. 'They'll ask too many questions, Eve.'

'What do you mean?' asked Mum.

'They'll get social services involved. They always do if a child has an accident at home. They'll want to know how she hurt herself, where it happened, who she was with. They'll send people to look for us,' he explained.

'It could put the Haven at risk, Eve,' said Aida. 'No one must know we're here.'

'Especially when we've had so much trouble with outsiders recently,' added Mo. 'That guy in the microlight has filmed us before.'

'A decision of this magnitude would have to be discussed in processing and the community won't agree to you taking her,' said Aida, a little more gently. 'There's too much at stake.'

'It's Maudie's life at stake!' shrieked Mum. 'There's no time for discussion.'

'We're like the bees, Eve. We have to focus on the collective good, not individual need,' said Mo. 'Juan must have told you this.'

'Couldn't we go to the hospital tomorrow morning and pretend it happened somewhere else?' Dad pressed them. He was trying to find a middle road.

'We could say we did it on a camping holiday, somewhere closer to town?' Mum quickly interjected.

'Great idea,' I said. I couldn't help thinking how Mum and Dad's absence would make it easier for me to hang out with Mo. Then Aida threw a curve ball.

'If you leave you can't come back. And if one of you goes, you all have to go. Every time someone arrives or leaves the Haven we attract unwanted attention and increase the risk of being discovered.'

God, she was annoying.

'That's fine.' Mum shrugged. 'We'll all leave now.' I couldn't believe this was happening. There was no way I was going to bail just when Mo had finally returned, and I could tell Dad felt the same. And Joe wasn't even here.

'Don't want to,' burbled Maudie.

'I think Maudie would prefer to be treated in the community,' Mo observed.

'She's eight years old! She doesn't know what she's talking about!' snapped Mum.

'Why don't we give it a couple of hours and see what happens?' suggested Dad, putting his arm around Mum in an attempt to soothe her.

Mum was having none of it. She stepped away from Dad and shot him a look of pure hatred.

I hesitated for a couple of seconds, then said, 'That sounds like a good plan, doesn't it, Mum?' If it felt like betrayal, that was because it was. Mum looked at me in total shock as it dawned on her that no one was going to help take Maudie to hospital and that she couldn't even rely on me to back her up.

'Where's Joe?' Mum kept asking. She knew Joe would side with her.

'Gone walkabout,' I said.

'As usual,' Dad chipped in.

'Being self-sufficient means dealing with the good and the bad on your own. You can't just run for help the first time something goes wrong,' said Mo, smoothly. He pulled a blister pack of pills out of his backpack. 'These will help with the pain.'

It took me ages to get to sleep that night. Every time I breathed in the muggy night air the smell of burnt flesh filled my nostrils. Maudie was in Mum and Dad's room, doped up to her eyeballs on the painkillers Mo had given us. My thoughts churned into a thick soup of worries about Maudie's burnt hand, the way Mo hadn't made a plan to see me again and the fear on River's face when she saw me at the ceremony, until they congealed into a single fat-berg of heavy immovable worry.

Daydream drifted into a vivid nightmare about River. Wherever I turned, her face stared back at me. I saw myself tugging the sleeve of her white dress, begging her to answer my questions. *Who is Mo? Does he love me or hate me?* She said nothing and kept beaming at me with her strange enigmatic half-smile. She allowed me to brush her hair and I discovered that the antlers weren't part of a headdress but were growing out of her skull. *What are you?* I screamed at her. *Tell me what you are!* She said nothing and instead took my hand and pressed my fingers to my temples: I could feel hard bumps beneath the skin where my own antlers were growing. *We are as one*, she said. As she opened her mouth, a swarm of bees flew out. I screamed but there was no sound. I couldn't breathe. Someone's hand was covering my mouth.

'Cass!' Joe's voice whispered urgently in my ear. 'Cass, wake up! I need to talk to you. Do you promise to stay quiet?' I nodded.

'What the fuck, Joe?' I said breathlessly, as soon as he took away his hand. I was angry with him, not just for scaring me shitless, but for interrupting my dream about River at the very point where it seemed some vital truth was about to be revealed. Joe sat on the edge of my mattress, head bowed, as if he was praying. His clothes were soaking wet, and he was shaking.

'Where have you been?' I asked, suddenly incensed at the way he always managed to disappear when the shit hit the fan. 'Maudie nearly died!'

'What do you mean, she nearly died?' His voice quivered.

When I turned on my head torch and shone the beam at Joe's face I saw he was crying. I'd never seen my brother in such a state before. I got out of bed and sat on the edge of the mattress with my arm around him. He rested his head on my shoulder. I could feel the damp of his tears through my T-shirt. I'm not proud to admit that although the better part of me was alarmed the worst part couldn't help feeling pleased: I'd always wanted Joe to need me, like I needed him.

'What's wrong with Maudie? Is she missing? Have they taken her?' He sounded petrified. I described the accident and how no one apart from Mum wanted to take her to hospital, and Joe instantly blamed Dad. It infuriated me that his first reaction was to blame rather than worry about Maudie, especially when he'd managed to avoid the whole trauma. I tried to remove my arm because it was beginning to cramp, but he clung to me.

'He's going to get us all killed,' he said.

'Maybe you'll kill him first,' I whispered, trying to make light of their fight earlier in the day. 'His nose is badly messed up.'

'There's something I need to tell you, Cass!'

'Let's go outside,' I suggested, thinking of the flimsy plywood walls. 'We mustn't wake Maudie.'

'No!' He got up and closed the shutters. 'The fields have eyes, and the forest has ears.' I assumed he was taking the piss.

'Is that a line from a film?'

'It's what River says.'

'It's meant to be comforting, not threatening,' I said, irritated at the way Joe talked about River so intimately. He picked up a rug and draped it over our heads until we were cocooned in a hot, airless, makeshift tent at the end of the bed.

'Someone tried to kill me.'

He put his hand over his mouth as if just saying it meant something bad would happen. I could tell his fear was genuine but at the same time it seemed absurd. I gave a jittery laugh.

'I'm not joking, Cass.'

'We're in an eco-community, not a war zone.' An image of River's terrified expression passed like a shadow across my consciousness and faded.

'You have to believe me.' His teeth were chattering.

'Tell me what happened,' I urged. I shone the torch in his face and noticed how wild-eyed he was. 'Are you bunning?' I asked, suspicious that he'd been smoking the last of his stash of weed.

'No!' His gaze darted about so that the whites of his eyes flashed with fear, like in those awful online videos of animals being forced into slaughterhouses.

'Stop it, Joe, you're freaking me out!'

'This is a bad place, Cass. We need to leave!' He put his hand over his mouth again.

I pulled it away and pushed his hands onto the mattress in an effort to ground him. 'You haven't given it a chance.

Mo came back today. Everything will get better now he's here. He was asking about you. He taught me how to track deer. And use a gun.'

I tried and failed to hide my excitement.

'Has Mudder got to you too, Cass?' hissed Joe. I was annoyed he was using the name River used for Mo. It sounded disrespectful. 'Don't you get that he manipulated Dad into coming here? He wants something from him. Or from one of us.'

I wanted to explain that coming to the Haven had nothing to do with Dad and everything to do with my relationship with Mo. But something made me hold back. I was afraid my brother would laugh at me for thinking someone as attractive as Mo would be interested in me, or that he might disapprove of the fourteen-year age gap. I tried a different tack.

'Maybe you need to open your heart to new experiences, Joe. If you'd witnessed what I saw today, you'd understand. There was a ceremony in the forest. River was there, all dressed up. She sang with the birds. It was the most beautiful thing I've ever seen or heard in my entire life.'

'I did. I was there too.'

'Bullshit,' I said incredulously.

'I came to look for you because I was worried you might have got lost.'

That pissed me off. My useless sense of direction was part of family folklore. Mo had explained to me during one of our messaging sessions that you can only grow as a human being away from your family. I now understood exactly what he meant. I wanted to change and evolve, and my family were holding me back. They were the impediment to my happiness.

'You weren't there! You're winding me up,' I snapped, as I pulled away.

He grabbed my arm. 'I saw her in that crazy outfit, Cass. I heard her sing. I watched all the woo-woo stuff just like you did. I saw the bits of material tied to the trees. You saw me, Cass. You know you did.' I looked at his jacket and remembered the flash of blue streaking through the undergrowth. He gripped my arm. 'I tried to distract them after they heard you. I was terrified what they might do if they found you.'

I finally realized he was telling the truth. 'Where did you go?'

'I headed back into the forest. They tried to follow me, but I was too far ahead for them to catch up. But when I got to the river, someone else was waiting for me. I ran along the bank and another person appeared. It was impossible to shake them both off. So when I got to the river I jumped in and held onto a branch by the bank. I was almost completely under water. I could hear them looking for me the whole time. Whenever they got too close, I had to go under and hold my breath. It was fucking freezing.'

His breath quickened and he started speaking faster, the words tumbling over each other like the water in the river.

'I stayed there until I thought my bollocks were going to drop off. When I was sure they'd gone I tried to swim back across, but the current was really strong and carried me downstream. I thought if I kept floating, I might reach the village where we saw that woman in the rocking chair and then I could escape, get help for you all. But it was too cold. It was just too fucking cold.'

His eyes glazed, and he stared straight through me as if he was in a trance.

'Go on,' I urged.

'I swam back to the place where I'd been hiding. It was really difficult to get out of the water because my clothes were so heavy. When I stood up one of them was waiting for me. It was like they knew where I was going to be even before I'd made the decision myself. I started running again but I kept tripping on the vines.'

'Could you see who was chasing you?'

'It must have been Mo and One Way Will. But their faces were covered.'

'Did you recognize their voices?'

'They didn't speak. They communicated with hand signals.'

He began sobbing again. I hugged him and stroked his hair and he calmed down a little.

'It's all right, Joe. You're not there any more. You're with me in my room and everything is fine.'

'I'm injured, Cass. Not badly. But it hurts like fuck. They could have killed me.'

He lifted his T-shirt. There was a deep gash across the top of his arm, just below the shoulder. It was a clean cut and perfectly straight.

He rummaged in the back pocket of his jeans and put something into the palm of my hand. I examined it with my torch. It looked like an arrowhead. Its steel edges were so razor sharp that when I turned it in my hand it sliced through the skin on my fingers.

'If I hadn't swerved to the right, it would have gone straight into my spine.' He started to tremble again.

'What is this?' I'd never seen anything like it.

'It's a crossbow bolt. Hunters use them to kill wild animals.'

Joe's distress was next level. I knew that what he described was real, but I couldn't believe that anyone from the Haven would have tried to hurt him on purpose.

'Maybe the person with the crossbow thought you were a deer.' It seemed an obvious possibility.

'Do I look like Bambi?' Joe tried to laugh. 'There's no way they thought I was an animal. You've got to believe me, Cass. You've got to persuade Mum and Dad to leave before something even worse happens to one of us. Dad won't listen to me.'

'Maybe you should mention it to Mo or bring it up during processing,' I suggested.

'Not a word to anyone,' he said emphatically. 'You promised. I don't trust anyone here.'

'But there might be a logical explanation.'

'What logical explanation could there be for firing a crossbow at someone?'

His exasperation cheered me up. It had unnerved me to see him so scared.

'Maybe they thought you were one of the bad people. Or maybe it was one of the bad people shooting at you and not someone from the Haven at all. It could have been one of the growers. Or an outsider.'

'You can't just go around killing people. If you think that then you're as crazy as they are.'

My head swirled.

'Has it occurred to you, Cass, that maybe they are the bad people and you're beginning to sound like one of them?'

His criticism stung. I removed the blanket from our heads. 'You can't ask me for help and then get angry when I don't say what you want to hear,' I said sulkily. 'You're beginning to remind me of Dad.'

'How many more weeks have I got to put up with this shit?' Joe lay down on the mattress beside me and closed his eyes. 'I'm not sure I can handle it any more.' He started listing all the things that reminded him of home, and this seemed to soothe him. 'Man City. Music. Fifa. Snapchat. Eadie and Dana. Nandos. Five aside.' He wanted me to add to the list, but I couldn't think of anything. 'Maoams?' he prompted.

'Definitely Maoams.'

It wasn't the first time in my life that I'd noticed how someone else's experience of the same event could be so entirely different from my own. But it was probably the first time that I was the one who'd had the better time. I lay down beside Joe and felt something spiky on my pillow. When I picked it up I saw it was a dead bee.

17

Now

'Do you think Joe will come back?' I do my best to sound casual, waiting until Aida's back is turned before asking so she can't see the desperation on my face. I nervously scratch the last remnants of masking tape from Joe's phone with my nail as I wait for her to answer. I'm surprised by the effort he's put into wrapping it properly. That kind of attention to detail isn't something I'd associate with my careless brother.

Aida hums as she stirs the melted pine resin in the saucepan. She definitely knows more than she's letting on. I try not to take it personally. By the time things turned dark at the Haven, it was wise not to trust anyone.

'Won't Joe want to check on you?' I blurt out. She keeps humming. I turn the phone in my hands, trying to work out why my brother would want me to have it instead of keeping it for himself.

'You really think I need anyone to look after me, Cass?'

Her words are coated in sarcasm. It's okay. I deserve it. Everyone knows Aida is a survivor. That's the biggest compliment you can pay anyone at the Haven. She's got through more winters than any other member of the community. She knows everything there is to know about plants and trees. She's a brilliant tracker.

Someone once told me the best way to determine

someone's weakness is to identify their worst fear and Aida's greatest fear is being forced to leave her beloved forest. Which is precisely why she'll want me gone from her container as soon as possible.

'Joe knows better than to visit me when the forest is crawling with police,' she says, throwing shade on me. She brings the bowl of resin over to the table and lays out a pair of nail scissors, lint and salt water. 'Sit.'

I know what's coming and she gets I can't handle it.

'Those stitches have to come out, Cass. The wound has swollen around them, and the longer you wait, the more infected it'll get.'

She scrapes my hair back from my face, cuts through the first two stitches and pulls the thread through the tiny eye holes in my skin. I cry out and then retch but nothing comes up because it's so long since I last ate.

'Put yourself outside the pain, Cass. Hold it in your hand, pretend it belongs to someone else and blow it away.'

I follow her instructions. She removes two more stitches. I imagine myself lying in Old Big Belly listening to the whisper of leaves and the chatter of warblers. I try to speak but no sound comes out. Aida gives me another piece of willow bark to chew, then takes out the last two stitches so fast that it's a single high-pitched note of agony. It's over. She gently flushes out the wound, fills it with the warm pine resin and puts a dressing on top.

'Leave it in place for three days.'

We sit in silence. It feels comfortable to be with her and say nothing. Her fingers touch the side of my neck. I jump and she frowns.

'Those marks. What are they?' she asks.

'Bruises from when I was attacked, I guess.'

She gently covers each mark with a fingertip, like she's measuring. 'Big hands. Those marks are older than the head injury.'

Something else catches her eye. She gets up and walks over to the barometer hanging on the wall, taps it with her knuckle and knits her brows as if she doesn't quite believe what it's telling her. 'If this is right, there'll be a foot of snow by morning. What are you going to do then, Cass?'

'Cold environments carry fewer scents than warm ones. It'll make life more difficult for the police dogs.' I'm trying to impress her even though the truth is I don't rate my chances in the snow. 'I'll shake them off and head to the other side of the lake.'

'The cold holds the scent for longer and makes the environment more sterile,' she counters.

'But the snow will cover any new tracks,' I argue back.

She pauses. 'Why don't you just give yourself up to the police?'

'I'm too scared about what I might have done.' It's that simple. 'And I don't trust them to find out what's happened to my family. The only way I'm going to untangle it all is to find Mo.' I choose my words carefully. 'If the police pick me up, they'll take me away and I'll spend the rest of my life trying to fill in the gaps.'

'You could be back in your cosy set-up in the uncivilized world in a couple of days.' It makes me smile that Aida's concept of an uncivilized world is one where people live a life divorced from nature.

'I don't want to leave. I want to stay here. The world outside has no meaning for me. The forest is my home.'

She fixes me with her piercing dark eyes, trying to gauge

my sincerity. 'If you want to stay, you'll need to find Him before He finds you.'

I nod in agreement, noting there's no offer of help.

'So, are you going to look at that device?' She points at Joe's phone.

I turn on the phone, half expecting it not to work. The screen lights up and my stomach flutters. The battery shows four per cent. God, Joe, you could at least have made sure it was charged! My fingers fumble over the keypad. It's a long time since I used a phone, let alone a brick with its tiny keys. And my bent finger won't co-operate. Then it comes back. Dad stamped on my hand! *I'm sorry, Cass. It was a mistake.* He was always sorry. It was always a mistake.

Inbox. Forty-seven messages. Sent, twenty-seven. I need to make wise choices about where to focus my attention. I go to the inbox. There are literally dozens of messages, almost all from Cara. I flick back to the beginning. It's pre-dictable stuff. *How's it going? Did the badger turn out to be a weasel?* She never liked Mo. *Mum ok? Dad calmed down? Maudie?? Cass??* I can tell from different variations of these messages over the next couple of weeks that Joe didn't respond right away. That makes sense. There was no signal on our side of the lake.

I'd forgotten how brick phones keep sent and received messages separately, and waste time cross-referencing Joe's responses. *Fine. Good. Fine. Dad about to blow. Maudie = natural-born survivor.* There's a break in communication for a couple of weeks. Then Joe writes back: *Weird shit. Will explain.* Except he doesn't.

Towards the end of August there's a flurry of messages. He tells Cara about Maudie's injury. Cara sends medical advice from Alessia about how to treat burns. This means Joe must have been crossing the lake almost every other day to get a signal. I glance at the battery. Three per cent.

It's five days before Joe is back in touch. *Can't wait to get home.* Cara asks, *When u coming?* Joe replies, *Dad wants to delay. Maybe 3 weeks??* Cara writes back, *You'll have enough good stories for a lifetime!!* She's trying to keep his spirits up. *Am bringing a girl with me.* He must mean River. I don't recall River ever mentioning this to me. And I was meant to be her best friend. Why wouldn't she tell me? It's like no one trusts me. I start to feel panicky. My breath gets shallow. Then everything goes black. I feel the sensation of the hands around my neck, of not being able to get any air into my lungs, of drowning. It's the same memory from before.

'Breathe, Cass, breathe!' Someone violently shakes my shoulders, and when I open my eyes again Aida is staring at me.

'Where did you go?'

I shake my head to force myself back to the present and Joe's phone. I notice how the tone in Cara's messages gets more frantic. *For sale sign gone up outside house!!!!! What's going on??? Does Mum know? When u leaving???* Joe gets back to her a week later. *WTF? Mum knows nothing. 4 days. All packed* (^-^). I think he's trying to do a smiley emoji. *Dad resistant. Mo controlling him.* I check the battery. Two per cent. *Can you describe how to get there? EXACT ROUTE?* A few days later Joe gives a pretty good description of what he remembers of our journey to the Haven. Then another bombshell. *Sold sticker on house!!!!* In some recess of my mind, I had half imagined Mum, Joe and Maudie lined up outside our old home to give me a hero's welcome when all this is over. I try to process what I've just read. Our house no longer belongs to us. We have no home.

'You okay?' Aida asks.

'Dad sold our home without telling Mum. Or us.'

'That would be worth a lot of money, right?'

I nod. I note this down, but I can't take it in. It's like Dad knew we were never going home.

'What do you think he did with it?'

'I don't know. He closed his bank accounts. There was a big row.'

'There were lots of big rows,' says Aida. 'Noise travels in the forest. There are no secrets here.'

'Why didn't Joe tell me any of this?'

'Either he wanted to protect you. Or he didn't trust you. Take your pick.' I glance down at the phone. One per cent. There's another message from Joe to Cara: *Need help. Call police.*

Hold out. Getting help, Cara writes back. Then *U look so thin!!! Am worried!!!* It hadn't crossed my mind there would be any photos. I make a snap decision to abandon the messages and press the camera icon. There are only two pictures in the file. The first is of Joe standing on one of the rocks in the lake. Judging by his contented half-smile, I guess River took it. Cara is right. He looks really thin. How did I not notice? I click on the next photo. This hasn't been sent to anyone. The screen is tiny and the photo slightly blurry. I know instinctively that this is what Joe wants me to find. I check the date and calculate it was taken six days ago.

At first, I think it's someone lying on their side asleep under a tree. The person's head is tucked towards their chest, their knees are bent, and their hands are furled into fists. Apart from an average-looking chin, no feature of their face is visible. The way the light throws late-afternoon shadows makes it difficult to work out where their body ends and the forest floor starts. I can't even tell if it's a woman or a man, although I'm certain it's not a child.

I squint at the picture. There's something off about the shadow of the figure lying on the ground. It doesn't match the outline of their body. I show Aida.

'That's because it's not a shadow, Cass. It's blood.'

18

Then

The following week Joe and I crossed to the other side of the lake with the Vivian sisters for the first time. Everyone else was so focused on Maudie's injury that no one seemed to notice what we were up to and we went to the lake to swim every afternoon. None of us needed much persuasion. I was off my tits bored with fermenting fruit and vegetables for winter supplies I'd never eat, and Joe had stirred enough hot shit to last a lifetime. Even the law-abiding Lila left work early. In any case, by midday it was too hot to do anything except be in the water.

So, when Joe pointed out that the water level was now so low we could probably wade most of the way across, there was little solid opposition to his plan. I was glad to have something to occupy me. Mo had been on another trip to investigate reports of outsiders on the outer reaches of the forest, and Joe and I tried to avoid spending too much time at home: Maudie's dressing needed changing three times a day and her screams during this process were unbearable. At least at night the painkillers kicked in. Although as soon as Maudie was quiet, we could hear Mum and Dad arguing about whether the burn was healing and whether she should go to hospital. They only stopped when Dad got up to patrol the field.

'We need to play Worst Death Ever before we swim. It's

our ritual,' Skylar anxiously reminded us. She'd invented the game after the accident. All of us were freaked out by what had happened to Maudie, and Skylar was obsessed that if we didn't play, it would bring bad karma. We each had to come up with the most horrific and gruesome way we could die and then vote on a winner.

I think it was our way of making Maudie's injury less frightening to us. That Friday my Worst Death Ever was being eaten alive by wild boars. Skylar's worst scenarios always involved outsiders. She came up with a tragic tale of an outsider poisoning Old Big Belly by hammering copper nails around their trunk. Joe tried to argue this didn't count because it didn't involve her dying, but Skylar insisted that if her favourite tree died she would too. Lila's scenarios almost all involved terrible accidents: she mistook a deadly webcap for a wood blewit and died of kidney failure. River said that was impossible because Lila knew everything there was to know about mushrooms and would never make such an amateur error.

Joe usually won, mostly because he'd watched so many horror films that it was easy for him to come up with sick ideas that were inconceivable to the rest of us. He described freezing to death in the river after being hunted down by a madman wearing a mask and armed with a crossbow. He paused to stare at the sisters, but if they knew anything, they gave nothing away, even when he pulled up his T-shirt and showed them the scar on his shoulder. 'That's horrible,' gasped River, running the tip of her finger along the perfectly straight line.

But that day victory belonged to River. Her Worst Death Ever involved giving birth in the forest and the baby getting stuck in her pelvis. You could tell right away this was going to be a good one. 'So, my Worst Death Ever would be discovering I'm pregnant with the Devil's baby.' I guessed Joe had helped her because it was a classic horror theme. 'I'm in labour for days and days, screaming in agony until the animals and birds disappear, the sky turns black, and the rains come so I can't leave. Aida wants to cut me open with a kitchen knife to get the baby out, so I have to hide in the forest on my own. I push so hard to give birth that my internal organs turn inside out so when I put my hand between my legs, I feel my intestines as well as the baby's head. They get infected. I die. And the baby dies too.' We looked at her in awe.

'Fuck.' Joe grimaced. 'That's so bad.'

'You win,' said Lila.

'Hands down,' said Skylar.

'What happened to the father?' I asked.

'I killed him already,' said River. She gave a little shrug and stood up.

I got up too. I was relieved it had taken so little time to choose a winner because some days we wasted hours wrangling. I wanted to get back to the Haven as quickly as possible because after breakfast when I bumped into Mo, as I was hauling jars of onions down into the root cellar, he'd casually asked if I might like to hang out at his tree-house that night. I'd been longing for him to suggest this since the day he returned. Although we'd seen each other every day, and he sat next to me at most mealtimes, we still hadn't carved out nearly enough alone time. There were always too many people nosing around. But now that he'd posed the question, instead of euphoria I felt slightly sick.

'Do I sense from your hesitation that you're not comfortable with that idea?' Mo had asked, as he followed me down into the root cellar.

'No! Of course not. I absolutely want to come. One hundred per cent.'

I knew why I'd hesitated: I'd never had sex with anyone.

It was dark and musty in the cellar, and I couldn't see clearly. Mo took the jars of onions from my arms and pulled me to him. I felt his mouth kiss my neck over and over again and my body shivered with pleasure. 'This is what it can be like,' he whispered. He suddenly took my hand and pushed it against his groin. His breath went heavy. His cock was hard. I was half into it. And the half that wasn't made me feel I was hurtling too fast down the scree towards the lake.

'Cass,' River called down into the cellar. 'Where are you? We're all waiting.'

'Just coming.'

'Let's go,' I said briskly to the others. We all got up and stood in an arc, shielding our eyes from the fierce midday sun, trying to plot the best route across the lake. I copied Skylar and tied my boots around my neck, then stepped into the water. I felt the silt at the bottom squelch between my toes and tried not to think about the leeches and snails that lived in the muddy sediment beneath.

'It's not as cold as last time,' I said.

'The temperature goes up every year,' said Lila. 'Aida keeps a record. That's why we get the green algae. The fish that like the cold die and we're left with the carp, who like the warm and eat all the zooplankton, which control the algal blooms.'

'Sometimes I think the best thing for the world would be if human beings became extinct,' said Skylar, mournfully.

We waded deeper, skirting the right-hand side of the lake towards the pod of rocks. Skylar forged ahead until the water lapped at her thighs. River and I hung back.

'It's great that Mo's here again all the time, isn't it?' I asked.

'Yeah,' she said noncommittally.

I felt his reappearance gave me a reasonable excuse to talk about him. 'Did he come back because he wanted to see you sing at the ceremony in the forest?' I asked.

She didn't reply. It wasn't the first time I'd tried to talk to her about that. Each time she went quiet and looked so uncomfortable that it felt almost cruel to keep asking. Even when I said something complimentary – like telling her that her voice was so good she could put out a song on Spotify, or that she looked like a goddess in her white dress – she didn't react.

'You shouldn't have been there,' she said fiercely. 'The ceremony is just something we do. It's private.'

'Did Mo come back that same day?'

'You don't get it, do you?' she now asked, flicking water at me with her hand.

'Don't get what?'

'I . . . don't . . . want . . . to . . . talk . . . about . . . Mudder.' She swiped her hand across the surface of the water and splashed me in the face each time she said a word. It seemed aggressive, but she didn't stop giggling.

'You don't understand,' I said, wiping my eyes. This seemed like the right moment to tell her everything. 'He's my . . . I mean . . . We're together . . . That's the whole reason my family came here. Except none of them know. So don't say anything. Especially not to Joe.'

She froze on the rock in front of me, then turned round. Her expression was difficult to read. It seemed to combine anger and fear and something more indefinable, which could have been pity.

'You don't know what you're getting into.'

She dived into the water. I thought I'd gone too far. I always found it difficult to read how much I was meant to reveal to friends. Too little and they thought I was boring. Too much and I risked being unfiltered. Both accusations had been thrown at me in the past.

'Maybe you should talk to Joe. I'm not in a position to give advice,' said River, when she broke to the surface, hair all slicked back, like an otter.

The conversation was over. I'd expected River might feel happy for me or even happy for herself, because my relationship with Mo meant that I might come back during school holidays or even stay at the Haven when the rest of my family went home. Instead, it was like I'd pushed her too far. My attempt at intimacy had created more distance.

I couldn't believe how easy it was to get to the other side of the lake, which made it even more puzzling that no one had crossed before. There were none of the dangers Mo had warned us about. No razor-sharp rocks hidden under the surface. No currents. No algae. Our biggest problem was the sun reflecting heat onto the water during the half-hour it took to cross. Once we reached the narrow strip of beach on the other side, we slumped in a hot mess under a tree and downed half our water supply. My arms were already bright red. Skylar offered to paint our faces with mud to protect against sunburn. She drew three lines across our foreheads, a line under our eyes and then a circular hieroglyph that matched the tattoo on their arms. We looked so cool, like a beautiful tribe.

As she painted my face, I stared across the water at the Haven. From a distance I could see how the outer boundary of the community nuzzled the most sheltered corner of the lake. The trees merged into a single solid green mass, so it looked tiny and strangely uniform. 'Like Planet Earth from the Moon,' observed Lila. The epic scale of the rest of the forest was more apparent from this side. I could see how the lake covered a vast area to the west before eventually tapering into a wide river that presumably flowed down into the village where we'd seen the woman in the rocking chair.

'If you want to escape in a hurry, you could float downstream from here,' said Joe. 'It's much less rocky than the river at the Haven.'

'You know this is a transgression,' Skylar pointed out. 'We'll have to bring it up during processing.'

'If it's a transgression why are some people allowed to come over here and not others?' asked Lila. 'And why do some people get away without reporting this during processing?'

'What do you mean?' asked Skylar.

'Mudder crosses the lake all the time, so why shouldn't we?' asked Lila. 'And he's obviously lied about how dangerous it is.'

It pissed me off that Lila was always so negative about Mo, but especially when she was right.

'Mudder gets to cross because he's looking after us. He keeps the bad people away. Protects us from outsiders,' Skylar intervened. 'He saved us.'

'What exactly has he saved you from?' asked Joe. None

of them responded. They were doing that thing where Joe and I ceased to exist, and they only heard each other.

We'd been so focused on making it across that we hadn't planned what we were going to do when we got to the other side. I think at that moment if someone had suggested we should turn back no one, apart from Skylar, would have kicked up much of a fuss. But she was already gazing longingly up the steep hillside in front of us. She was literally the most hyperactive person I'd ever met.

'What's that?' she asked, pointing heavenwards. We craned our necks and saw black smoke billowing from the middle of the forest.

'It's either a wildfire or maybe they're clearing more land. We should let Mudder know,' said River. Her attitude to Mo always confused me. On the one hand she seemed to dislike him but on the other she always deferred to him.

'We can't wait for Mudder to get here. It'll be completely out of control by then,' said Skylar, disappearing into the undergrowth before the rest of us had a chance to give an opinion. We all followed her. As my eyes adjusted to the dappled light, I spotted a smooth dirt track around forty centimetres wide that snaked up the hillside through the dense undergrowth.

'What if we come across the people who made this track?' I asked nervously.

'We won't! It's a badger run, stupid,' teased Skylar. 'Come on, we'll get to the fire quicker if we use it because the badgers have cleared the undergrowth for us.'

She scrambled up. The smell of smoke got stronger the higher we climbed. After half an hour or so we came into a clearing where rods of sun beamed down onto a pockmarked landscape of holes and hummocks that resembled a First World War battlefield.

'I've never seen such an enormous badger sett!' exclaimed Skylar. Her excitement made me realize how subdued she'd been since Maudie's accident. 'There could be four or five clans living here alongside each other. If Maudie gets better, I'll bring her here.'

'When she gets better,' I firmly corrected her.

'Hey!' Lila shouted. I looked around but couldn't see her. 'Come over here!'

We all assumed she'd found the fire and ran towards the sound of her voice, heading into the dense woodland on the west side of the sett. There was a definite trail through the undergrowth, but it didn't have the smooth, polished quality of the badgers' run. The stems of the bracken and nettles had been more carelessly trampled.

'Wild boar?' suggested River.

'No sign of rooting,' said Lila, 'no scat, no wallows or rubs. More likely humans.'

A heady odour filled the air, like warm hay with notes of something more earthy and sweet. It became stronger the closer we got. I saw Lila standing in the middle of rows and rows of identical bushy plants with spiky leaves and powdery flower heads. The smell was intoxicating. Some were bigger than Joe, which meant they were more than six feet tall. Every couple of rows there was a shallow trench lined with plastic drainpipe that carried water from higher up the hill to a series of smaller trenches so that every plant had its own water supply. The ground was littered with empty fertilizer bags. Joe picked a few flowers from the top and sniffed them.

'Marijuana,' he said appreciatively. He picked more and zipped his haul into the side pocket of the backpack.

'Don't, Joe,' warned Lila. 'They'll know the grow has been disturbed. These are shadow-side people. You need to be careful.'

We hurried across the hill, through the field of marijuana until the glade became forest again. Wafts of smoke occasionally drifted through the air. We were getting closer to the fire. Now that it was a reality, I knew with absolute certainty I didn't want to find it. It hadn't rained in months, and the trees and vegetation were tinder dry. It was ridiculous to think we'd be able to put it out. Plus seeing Maudie in such agony had made me terrified of getting burnt.

Then we came across unmistakable signs of human activity. Skylar noticed a couple of cigarette butts and a plastic water-bottle. I found an old rusting saucepan. The undergrowth started to thin out and, in the distance, a cockerel crowed. I thought I heard a baby cry.

'We need to get out of here right now,' hissed River.

'Why don't we cut back down the hill? Eventually we'll hit the lake.' I was beginning to feel scared and wanted to go back to get ready for Mo. It was dawning on me that tonight could be the most significant moment of my life so far. There were so many things to sort out: should I search Joe's bags for condoms, or would Mo have his own supply? The Haven definitely wasn't self-sufficient in condoms. Could I tell Mo I'd never had sex or might that put him off? Would he want me to spend the whole night with him? Or would I have to walk home through the forest in the dark?

There was more litter. Tin foil; beer cans; crisp packets; a worn-out trainer; and a chair leg. It was the kind of rubbish

I hadn't seen since I'd left the city, and the sisters had never come across half of the products that littered the ground.

'What's this?' asked Lila, picking up an empty Red Bull can.

'You're so pure,' said Joe, as he explained the concept of energy drinks to her.

Skylar found a bicycle chain and draped it round her, like a necklace.

'You look like a rapper,' I teased her.

'What's a rapper?' she asked. Joe ruffled her hair affectionately, but Skylar froze in her tracks.

We were at the back of a caravan. I followed her gaze. A blond-haired boy with bright red chubby cheeks was watching us. His face was pressed against the glass so that his nostrils were monstrously flared, and every time he breathed out, the window fogged. His face was expressionless. Then suddenly all hell broke loose. A dog on a chain lunged at us snarling and barking and, seconds later, someone grabbed Joe around the neck.

'What the fuck are you doing here?' We saw the gun on the man's shoulder. 'Come with me. No dicking around.'

Skylar held my hand tightly and we followed the man as he shoved Joe round the side of the caravan. His brown hair was tied in a limp ponytail that bounced angrily from side to side. Terrifying scenarios played out in my head. He would shoot us dead. Keep us prisoner. Enslave us. Sell us to sex traffickers. I saw the fear in Lila's eye and felt even more scared because I'd never seen her afraid of anything.

There were four or five more scruffy dwellings close to the trailer and a barn that was bolted and padlocked. There was so much stuff everywhere that it was difficult to know where to look – piles of tyres, empty oil cans, a broken lawnmower and rusting tools. Some kids were pretending to drive a broken-down car. One of them, who couldn't have been more than about ten years old, was smoking a rollie.

'What is this place?' Skylar whispered. 'I don't like it.' She looked terrified.

'A growers' settlement,' River whispered back.

'Where have you come from?' asked the man. 'Do not bullshit me.' His tone was marginally less aggressive. He was skinny but strong-looking and had improbably luscious long black eyelashes. A woman headed towards us from the other side of the settlement and eyed us up and down. She was wearing a grubby orange mini dress and heavy boots and had the same stress lines on her forehead as Mum.

'Who've we got here, JJ?' she asked. 'You Mo's people?'

'You know Mo?' Skylar asked in astonishment. On the one hand Mo had legendary status so it wasn't surprising that everyone knew him. On the other, he'd never told anyone at the Haven that he'd met the growers.

'Everyone here knows Mo. He's the main man. Are you one of his girls?' asked JJ. He stared at me and gave a hollow laugh. I looked at him in queasy confusion. *I'm his only girl,* I wanted to say. But I stayed quiet. I guess I was too afraid of what his response might reveal.

The older sister of the boy we'd seen at the window came to the trailer door. I peered past her into the kitchen area. The shelf above the cooker was filled with prescription drugs. Above the table a crossbow hung on a hook. I nudged Joe. 'Take a look at that,' I whispered, then wished I hadn't when I saw Joe's terrified expression.

The girl eyed us suspiciously. She was wearing tracksuit

bottoms that used to be pink but were now covered with stains and layers of dust and grime.

'So, what brings you here?' asked the woman, who introduced herself as Em.

'We saw the fire,' said Skylar, pointing in the direction of the smoke. 'We wanted to help put it out.'

'That fire is at least five miles west of here.' JJ snorted with laughter, as he put down his rifle inside the door of the trailer. 'There's nothing you can do about it. It'll either be growers looking for new land or wildfire because of the drought. It's the burning season.'

'Are you the Bad People?' interrupted Skylar. River shot her a furious look.

'What kind of question is that?' asked the man. His tone was amused rather than angry.

'If trying to survive makes us bad people then we are the bad people,' Em cut in. She looked much younger than JJ. 'We came to the forest to work as trimmers after we got into debt and lost our home. We've been here five years now. Ryan was born in this trailer.' She was much less hostile and I could sense she was eager for chat.

'Shut it, Em!' muttered JJ.

'That must have been terrifying,' said River.

'When I saw those two blue lines on the pregnancy test, I cried my eyes out,' said Em.

'What's a pregnancy test?' asked River.

'Are you for real?' exclaimed Em. When she realized River wasn't taking the piss, she explained the mechanics.

'Where we come from, everyone has to agree before someone gets pregnant,' said River. 'The forest is no place to have a baby.'

'Fucking weirdoes,' muttered JJ.

'Rosealea came out like a dream,' said Em. 'Ryan, on the other hand, was an awkward bugger, just like he is now.' The blond boy in the caravan flipped the bird at her. 'I lost a baby in between these two.' Her eyes glistened. 'The cord got stuck round her neck. I didn't make it to hospital.'

'Because you couldn't get a phone signal to call for help?' I asked, thinking of Maudie.

'You can get a signal on the escarpment over there.' Em pointed to a tall rockface in the distance. 'I didn't go to hospital because these bastards wouldn't let me.'

Another man appeared from the trailer opposite and hurtled towards us, arms pumping like pistons. He wore no clothes apart from a filthy pair of denim shorts and leather boots. From a distance it looked as if he was wearing a necklace but when he got closer, I saw it was a tattoo of a dotted line that said, 'CUT HERE'. He came to an abrupt halt in front of us and started running his hand obsessively through his long, limp hair.

'This guy is loony tunes,' Joe whispered in my ear.

A hard wedge of anxiety settled in my stomach as the man's gaze flitted from me to River and back again. We huddled together and Skylar shrank into my side.

'Under whose authority have you come here?' he yelled. It was an oddly complicated question that none of us were sure how to answer.

'These are forest people, Kyle, from that weirdo hippie community the other side of the lake,' explained Em, calmly. 'They're just kids. They're not here to steal the grow.'

'Did the authorities send you?'

'We have no contact with anyone outside our community,' said River, nervously.

'Then why are you here?'

'They know Mo,' said Em.

Kyle's focus flipped to Joe's backpack. 'Give that to me!'

Joe held out for a few feeble seconds before handing it over. Kyle unzipped the top pocket and immediately found the grass that Joe had picked. He waved it triumphantly at Em and JJ and stuffed it in his pocket.

'They know where the grow is. They'll have to stay until after harvest.' His voice had pivoted from angry to excessively calm. Both were equally threatening. My intestines convulsed. I needed the toilet.

'We can't keep them here, Kyle. We don't have enough food for ourselves, let alone five extra kids,' said JJ.

'We won't tell anyone about the grow,' panicked Joe. This was the wrong thing to say because it drew attention to the fact that we knew where the crop was located.

All riled up again, Kyle squared up to him. 'They can eat each other.' He cackled hysterically.

He was off his head. Loco. And you can't reason with someone who is crazy. I could tell we were all thinking the same thing. I saw River desperately looking around, trying to work out how we were going to get out of this.

'Calm yourself, Kyle,' said Em. She was like Mum, doing balm for the soul.

'Okay. Then one of them has to stay to guarantee the rest won't squeal.' He stared unblinkingly at Skylar. 'I'll keep that one.'

'She's a child. Her parents will worry and send people to look for her,' said Em, smoothly. 'They might contact the police.'

'Let me stay instead. I can help with the harvest,' offered Joe.

'I want *her* to stay,' said Kyle, in a way that suggested he usually got his own way.

I felt a wave of relief that he hadn't selected me, then guilty at my total cowardice. 'She can cook and clean for me and share my trailer. If the others say anything she'll get hurt.' I felt sick with fear, but Skylar didn't flinch.

'Off with his head!' she said pointing at the tattoo round his neck.

'What do you mean?' Kyle clearly wasn't familiar with *Alice in Wonderland.*

'It takes all the running you can do to keep in the same place. If you want to get somewhere else, you must run twice as fast as that,' said Skylar. She kicked him hard in the shins, spun round and sprinted downhill away from the settlement with the rest of us following. We ran clean through the first patch of nettles and brambles. I didn't even feel them. I glanced back and saw Kyle and JJ chasing us. But JJ was overweight, and Kyle was wearing shorts, so his legs got shredded, which gave us the advantage. *Know your enemy*. That's what Mo said. And Skylar did.

We chased down the hill after Skylar, weaving in and out of the taller brambles and nettles. When eventually we reached the lake Joe threw himself on the ground and lay there panting.

'I can't go on.'

'Come on, Joe,' pleaded River. She reached for his hand and pulled him up.

'What's wrong with him?' asked Lila, impatiently.

'He vapes too much,' I explained. Lila pressed her finger to her lips. We instantly fell silent. She used her fingers and thumb to indicate she'd detected voices. I listened hard. It was such a still day that even the trees had stopped whispering. But I couldn't hear a thing.

'They'll be here soon,' whispered Lila. 'We need to cross the lake right now.'

It was a scramble to get back to the other side. We had to keep stopping to help Joe, and in our exhausted, filthy, sunburnt state, all of us, except Skylar, either fell in the water or stumbled on the hard rocks.

By the time we got home it was almost dark. I gently pushed open the door of our cabin and was taken aback to find Magnus, Kaia, Piper and Sylvie sitting round our kitchen table with Mum and Dad. I scanned the room for Mo and felt the cold sting of his absence. Either he'd given up on me hours ago or he was still looking for outsiders.

They turned towards us. Even in the flickering candlelight I could see Mum's face looked strained. Piper managed a quick smile but not long enough for it to reach his eyes. Sylvie nervously twisted one of her plaits around her fingers.

We waited for them to reproach us for our irresponsibility, to demand to know where we'd been, and why we were so late, but they said nothing.

'Is Maudie okay?' I blurted out, suddenly spooked that something awful had happened to her while we were away and none of them wanted to be the one to tell us.

'She's asleep,' explained Sylvie, gesticulating towards Mum and Dad's bedroom.

'There's been an incident,' said Piper. 'We held an emergency processing session this afternoon. It's all sorted.'

I glanced from Mum to Dad but neither of them would look me in the eye.

'What kind of incident?' asked Joe.

'Mum has let us down,' said Dad, tightly. 'Again.' The vein in his head was throbbing but I couldn't tell if this was because he'd already detonated or was about to.

'What happened?' I asked. I tried to catch Piper's eye, but he avoided my gaze.

'You explain, Eve,' urged Dad. Mum turned to us. She looked dreadful. Her eyes were bloodshot and there were dark bags underneath them.

'I tried to leave,' said Mum. 'With Maudie.'

'Can you believe it!' Dad exploded. 'She put Maudie on Gaia! They almost reached the road. Luckily Mo found them.'

'Maudie needs to go to hospital,' said Mum, emphatically.

'You've committed a transgression,' Dad hissed at her. 'It reflects badly on us all.'

'Why is it a transgression to want to get help for Maudie?' asked Joe, angrily.

'She didn't ask the community for permission,' explained Sylvie. 'It has to be agreed during processing. Eve understands this now.'

'I didn't realize we needed permission to leave the Haven as well as to come here,' observed Joe, sarcastically.

'There's no way she could have got Maudie up on that horse on her own. But she won't tell us who helped. We've been sitting here for three hours trying to get it out of her.' Dad stared long and hard at Joe. But I knew it wasn't Joe because he'd been with me all day.

19

Now

'Police! Open up!' My heart beats in time to the pounding on the door. Joe's phone is still in my hand and I'm staring at a photo of a dead body. It's like holding a hand grenade with the pin removed. I can't believe they've found Aida's container so easily. Either they tracked the mobile signal, or I slipped up with the checks. I turn off the phone, wrap it back in the paper and stuff it in my backpack.

'Come on! We know you're in there! It's locked from the inside!' Kovac's adrenalized voice is instantly recognizable. My mouth goes dry, and my spine turns to liquid ice. I glance at Aida. Her face is still but her eyes dart nervously around the room.

I open my mouth to tell Aida I'm going to hand myself in. That I don't want to create any more trouble for her. That my family has been a curse on the Haven. She quickly presses her fingers to her lips and shakes her head. 'No,' she mouths. Instead, she kicks my muddy boots under the kitchen counter and gestures towards her bedroom.

'We've got a few questions for you, Aida!' Kovac shouts through the window. I catch her eye. *Sorry,* I mouth and put my hand across my heart. I crawl across the floor towards her bedroom with my backpack on my shoulder.

Once I'm there, she pulls the curtain across, carries a stool to the corner of the room, and stands on it to unpin a corner of an Indian throw that covers the entire ceiling to reveal a small hatch. She pushes it open.

Thud, thud, thud!

'We need to talk to you, Aida! We need your help!' This time Wass speaks. Her tone is more measured and less hectoring.

I climb onto the stool, push my backpack through the hole and pull myself up through the tiny opening to find myself on top of a flimsy false ceiling made of plywood that sits about two feet clear of the metal roof of the shipping container. Aida closes the hatch and I flip onto my back and lie as flat as I can, spreading my weight to prevent the ply from sagging.

As my eyes adjust to the darkness, I spot a small circle of light on the far edge of the false ceiling where the ply has expanded and contracted and cautiously slide towards it. The further I move away from the hatch, the more claustrophobic it gets, but once I've managed to drag myself across, I discover there's a natural peephole in the wood to the kitchen below. Desperate for fresh air, I press my lips to the hole, then watch as Aida unbolts the door.

'Aida?' asks Wass. She nods. 'Do you mind if we come in for a moment?' She's already got one foot through the door. 'We're following some leads in a missing-persons inquiry. Five members of the same family. Mother, father and three children.' She's inside the container before Aida has a chance to respond.

'I'm not sure how much I'll be able to help . . . I haven't been here in a while,' says Aida.

'When you say you've been away, can we assume it wasn't a package holiday to Tenerife?' Kovac says sarcastically, as he gets out his notebook and pen. Aida looks confused. My sympathy for her is equal to my irritation with Kovac. His pen doesn't work, which puts him on the back foot. He shakes it, sucks at the nib, and suddenly he's wearing blue lipstick. Aida offers him her pencil.

'How long were you away?' asks Wass.

'More than a month,' replies Aida, without missing a beat. 'Since the last full moon.' Wass looks at the chronology of the case in her notebook. 'Which means you left before the family were meant to go home?' She's trying to gauge how much Aida knows.

'If you say so,' says Aida.

'Why did you leave?' asks Wass.

'To spend time alone in the forest. I do the same every year. But this time when I came back everyone else had disappeared.'

'Why do you think that is?'

'People here tend to go to ground when trouble comes their way.'

Wass looks around the shipping container, but it's a respectful kind of curiosity. There's no judgement. The dainty teacup drying by the sink catches her eye. Her radio crackles and beeps. She's directly below me, so close I can see her highlights need redoing.

'Perhaps they got lost hiking on the windward side of the northern pass,' suggests Aida. Wass holds her gaze and places an empty tomato can and my sock on the table in front of her. 'We found these less than fifty metres from here.' I remember the open zip on my backpack and inwardly swear at myself for my carelessness. 'And we picked up a signal earlier today from the father's mobile, just north of the lake, less than a mile away,' she adds almost casually. 'There's a search team in the area already.'

My heart starts pumping again. And then it comes back. I gave Dad's phone to Mo. It's not Dad who's in the area. It's Mo.

'I don't need to tell you the mercury's dropping,' says Wass, tapping the barometer. 'The little girl, Maud, is only eight years old. She won't make it outside in this cold . . .'

She's trying to draw in Aida by appealing to some higher maternal instinct that she doesn't possess. Aida steps towards the window and stares skywards, brow furrowed. 'You've got about twenty-four hours before the wind changes direction.'

Wass is losing patience. 'Not to put too fine a point on it, but in the eyes of the law this is an illegal settlement,' she snaps. 'I could get an eviction order sent over by the end of the day and put a stop to anyone ever living here again. But if you cooperate with us, I'll ask the authorities to look at your situation more favourably. I respect what you're trying to do to protect the forest even if I can't condone it.'

'You can't evict people who don't officially exist.' Aida remains expressionless.

'Did you spend much time with Eve Sawyer?' Wass asks.

'Not really,' says Aida.

'Then why are so many of her belongings here?' Wass dangles the necklace in front of Kovac so he can see Mum's initials engraved on the silver heart. 'Why would she leave something so personal?'

She doesn't miss a thing and I respect that. So does Aida. She pauses as if weighing up two heavy alternatives. 'Eve sometimes came by when there was trouble at home,' she says eventually.

'What kind of trouble?'

'Her husband had bad mood swings. Got angry a lot.'

'And violent?'

'Sometimes.'

I knew this already, but somehow it's more shocking when someone outside the family articulates it.

'We had a report this morning that Eve was sighted in the village down the valley two or three days ago.' Wass abruptly turns to face Aida again. I wasn't expecting this and, judging by her surprised expression, neither was Aida. The tears pour down my cheeks. To know Mum was alive so recently is overwhelming and makes me realize how much I thought the opposite might be true. I've been trying to put my family to the back of my mind, but now my stomach aches with missing her.

'Well, that's great news,' says Aida, in a neutral tone.

Wass flicks back through her notebook. 'She was dishevelled but mentally alert . . . had notable swollen red bumps on her arms . . . mentioned her youngest child was sick and her older daughter had gone missing more than a week ago. She asked everyone about Cassia.'

I've been missing for at least nine days. If I subtract the four days I've spent hiding in the forest, then that's five days I can't account for. I think of the clothes I'm wearing that don't belong to me, the gunk under my fingernails, and feel sick all over again.

'What happened to Eve after that?' asks Aida.

'She disappeared back into the forest,' says Wass.

'The people in the village thought she was just another of the weirdos hiding out from the authorities in the woods,' says Kovac.

'There've been no sightings of the children or the father. Have you seen anything that makes you think they might be in the area?' Wass presses her.

'Nothing.'

'We know the family was lured here by a man called Morden Spilid,' says Wass. 'What do you know about him?'

'Never heard of him,' says Aida.

'You might know him as Mauricio Castellar,' says Kovac. 'Or Mo.'

'Ah, Mudder,' says Aida, as the penny drops. 'He's a member of our community. He rolled into the Haven four winters ago.'

Wass turns to Kovac. 'Any news on when Spilid first came into the country?'

Kovac shakes his head. 'We're still waiting to hear from Interpol. We can't access the SIS II database any more. We've asked them to look at the Passenger Name Record data instead. It takes a lot longer.'

'I want to be straight with you, Aida.' Wass tries a different tack, trying to make Aida feel she's sharing a confidence with her. 'The dogs have picked up the scent of human remains. This could turn into a murder investigation and then the forest will be crawling with police.'

'I'd be very surprised if the dogs didn't pick up the scent of human remains,' says Aida, calmly. 'We've buried our dead in this forest for hundreds of years.'

'Fresh blood was found in Morden Spilid's cabin. Can you explain this?'

'Mo is a hunter,' says Aida. 'Perhaps he dressed his kill at home.'

'How would you carry a dead deer up a rope ladder?' says Kovac.

'What kind of person is Spilid?' I notice how Wass asks more open-ended questions and how effectively Aida neutralizes this strategy.

'Do you like him?'

'He's a member of our community. We have to get along.'

'When did you last see him?'

'The day I left.'

Wass is distracted. She's fixated on a dusty area under the bed in the corner of the kitchen. I watch as she bends down awkwardly on one knee and pokes her head under. 'Gloves,' she orders Kovac. 'And an evidence bag. With a label.' She's spotted something. I press my eye to the hole. Kovac pulls a box of turquoise latex gloves from his bag. Now on all fours, Wass reaches under the bed and pulls out something and drops it into the evidence bag. It's the *Pica pica* doll that looks like me. It must have slipped out of my pocket when I was crawling across the floor. My stomach somersaults.

'Can you explain why this is under your bed?' Wass turns to Aida, who looks equally rattled by the discovery.

'I don't know. Maybe one of the kids from the community left it behind. Some of them come here for my classes on medicinal herbs.'

'That's some weird witchy black-magic shit,' mutters Kovac, who is now completely on edge.

Wass turns the bag in her hands, scrutinizing every detail of the doll.

'Looks like real hair,' says Kovac.

'What bird do the feathers come from?' Wass asks Aida.

'Magpie,' she confirms. 'The black on the tip and the white on the tail is a dead giveaway. The skull in front of the doll's face is magpie too.'

'What might that mean?' Wass asks.

'Some people think magpies have protective qualities,'

explains Aida. 'The white on the feather could symbolize purity, and the black protection from evil spirits. I'd say the doll was made to protect rather than threaten.'

Wass tips the bag upside down and the doll's denim dress flies up to reveal the small hole with the red stain.

'Get this swabbed for DNA,' Wass orders.

'What are you thinking?' asks Kovac.

'I think the hole has some kind of sexual significance,' says Wass. She pauses for a moment. 'Give me the photo of the family.'

Kovac pulls it out of his file. Wass scrutinizes it. 'Look,' she says, tapping my face with the tip of her index finger.

'What do you see, Kovac?'

'I see that Cassia has the same colour hair, that she's in a denim dress identical to the one the doll is wearing, and they both have the same necklace.'

'Whoever made this was trying to protect Cassia,' says Wass.

20

Then

A couple of days after our trip across the lake, I was woken at first light by an ear-splitting crack outside the bedroom window, like a firework or a car backfiring. I heard Maudie whimper on the other side of the plywood wall and Mum trying to comfort her.

'What the fuck was that?' hissed Joe, who'd fallen asleep on the mattress beside me in the middle of another late-night discussion about Maudie. Crack! The same noise blasted through the still night air and then again. Crack! We flipped onto our fronts and lay as still as we could.

'I think it's someone shooting,' I whispered.

'No shit, Sherlock!'

'Do you think JJ and Kyle have discovered where we live?'

He gave my hand a reassuring squeeze. The gunfire stopped and the usual early-morning crew filled the vacuum as if nothing had happened. A fox barked, our robin trilled, and a pheasant squalled through the undergrowth. I rolled onto my side and knocked gently on the wall to let Mum know we were okay. She knocked back and Joe and I edged nervously towards the bedroom window and peered out. Through the mist, we saw a bare-chested figure we immediately recognized as Dad running around the field holding the Remington tight against him. We watched in spellbound horror as he darted up and down furrows, occasionally stopping to examine something in the soil. Eventually he came to a halt in front of a row of potatoes, clicked off the safety, pointed the barrel towards the ground and this time fired at almost point-blank range.

'Oh, my God!' I cried out. Dad's head turned towards our window.

'He's lost the plot,' said Joe.

Since Mum's failed attempt to leave with Maudie, he'd been way more volatile again.

'Stop!' I yelled through the open window.

Another voice had joined in my cries and before I knew it Mum was racing barefoot into the field. Dad's attention flitted to her. For a split second I was terrified he might think she was the predator and shoot her.

'I saw something eating the potatoes, Eve. Its head came up from the soil.' Dad stabbed his finger at a wilted potato plant. 'Fucking fuckers!'

'Only Dad could get angry at a potato,' said Joe. We laughed until there were tears in our eyes, and then we hugged each other and cried a bit. Fear does that to you sometimes.

'What do you think is wrong with him?' I asked Joe.

Incredible as it sounds, we'd never properly considered this before. His temper had always been terrifying, but Mum had somehow managed to protect us from its excesses by smothering it and absorbing its heat. But coming to the Haven had somehow distilled him into a concentrated version of himself that exposed a darkness in his soul that we hadn't fully noticed before.

'Do you think he'd ever hurt us?' I asked, forgetting that Joe had been at the wrong end of Dad's temper more times than I could remember.

'I won't let him,' said Joe.

'Come back inside, Rick. You need to sleep!' Mum yelled at Dad. When he didn't react she put her hand on his shoulder. Dad stopped digging and seemed to melt into her. It was like witnessing a miracle. The sense of magic was heightened by the way Mum was now so willowy that she seemed to sway in the breeze.

'You've been out here all night. Come and get some rest!' Mum urged. 'You're scaring Maudie.'

'I don't need sleep like normal people, Eve.'

Dad trailed back to the cabin after her, and I headed to the outdoor washroom, peeled off my clothes and stepped naked into the open-air bucket shower, laughing at myself for the way I used to keep my underwear on in case someone saw me. I released the valve. The icy water gave me brain freeze and made my nipples ache. But it did the trick. For a few minutes I forgot everything apart from the delicious sensation of cold numbing my body. I noticed how the soft creases in my stomach and thighs had disappeared and that although my legs and arms were scarred and scabby with cuts and bites, they'd become strong and muscular.

The only towel smelt too disgusting to use so while I drip-dried, I searched the dirty clothes pile for my denim mini dress. I hadn't worn it since the day we arrived, which made it the cleanest item of clothing in my possession by some margin, and I wanted to smell good when I saw Mo again. Since I'd failed to turn up to meet him two days ago, he'd completely blanked me. I did up the buttons from the top down, leaving the first couple open so he'd catch a glimpse of the curve of my breast. When I caught sight of the broken buttons above my knees, I noticed a small rectangle of fabric had been cut out of the hem. Someone had mutilated my favourite dress.

I went back into the cabin and found Maudie sitting upright on the makeshift sofa in the kitchen, bookended by two large cushions, her toothpick legs dangling over the edge. I was relieved to see Mum had already changed the dressing. Careful not to touch her arm, I gave Maudie a half-body hug, and was cocooned in a heady cloud of anti-septic, infected skin, damp clothes and the musky smell of the long-term unwashed.

'How are you feeling, Mauds?' I asked, stroking her hair.

'It doesn't hurt as much,' she whispered. Her cheeks were rosier than I'd seen in a while, and she was brushing one of her plastic dogs. I unwrapped a couple of my sweets and she opened her mouth like a little bird to allow me to pop them in.

'Heaven,' she tweeted, closing her eyes in pleasure as she chewed.

I hugged her again until she pleaded to be released.

'Can you give me a hand, please, Cass?' Mum called, from just outside the front door where she was hanging clean bandages on the washing line. She glanced over and gave us a quick smile. I was shocked at how frail she looked. Her patchwork skirt hung around her hips, her fingers were raw from washing dressings, and her eyes were sunken. I went to help loop the bandages around the wash-ing line and persuaded her to sit down for a minute on the bench. She leant back against the cabin wall and allowed herself to bask in the sun.

'Are you okay, Mum?'

'Cara was right. Coming here was a terrible mistake.'

Her gaze flitted around as if she was scared someone might be listening. 'Dad's getting worse, not better.'

'We'll be home in less than four weeks,' I tried to reassure her.

'We're not spending another month here!' I was taken aback at her vehemence. Mum was usually so go-with-the-flow. 'I'd leave with Maudie today if I could. But they won't let me. They watch what I'm doing all the time.'

'Maudie seems a bit better.'

'That's because she's taking so many painkillers.'

'Don't you want to stay for Samhain? Mo says it's amazing. Everyone dresses up to frighten away the evil spirits. He says the veil between present and future is so thin that night that some people have second sight. Maudie will love it.'

This triggered another wave of worry. 'That man has made everything worse . . . I thought he might help Dad but it's like Dad's in thrall to him . . . He won't even do what's best for Maudie any more. Mudder is eating his soul.'

'Actually, Mo is a pretty interesting person,' I said.

Mum must have heard the hint of defensiveness in my tone because she looked horrified. She put her hands on my shoulders and shook me. 'Has he got to you too, Cass?' she demanded. 'Tell me, has he got inside your head?'

Thankfully Maudie started coughing, which made her retch, so Mum hurried back inside as the deep rhythmic boom of the Nordic gong began reverberating through the forest, calling us to an early-morning processing session. Dad rushed into the kitchen.

'We mustn't be late!' he panicked. Not being on time had always triggered him. But his desperation to impress people at the Haven had made being late more dangerous than it used to be.

'You know what,' said Mum, quickly, 'I think I'll stay here with Maudie.' The gong continued to echo through the forest.

'If Maudie doesn't go to processing, everyone will assume she's still really ill,' replied Dad.

'She is really ill,' snapped Mum.

'Actually, I'm feeling a bit better,' Maudie whispered. Mum kissed the top of her head.

'You can pass that on to them, Rick,' said Mum.

'They need to see her with their own eyes,' insisted Dad.

'Why would we risk Maudie's health to take her to some stupid meeting about issues that don't affect us, with people we'll never see again because we're leaving in a month?' Dad shot Mum a furious look.

'People are in a heightened state of paranoia because of the security situation. They don't want anyone leaving the forest until things have calmed down, especially with a sick child. It would attract all the wrong attention,' countered Dad. 'Let's give her a couple of painkillers. If people see she's well enough to come to processing, they'll stop worrying that you'll try to do another runner. I'll bring her back as soon as it's over, Eve. You know I love Maudie more than life itself.' His voice quivered.

'It's a strange kind of love when you won't let your own daughter see a doctor,' retorted Mum. She was pulling away from him and he couldn't see it. There was a whinnying sound outside. Gaia had mysteriously appeared and stood patiently under a tree, flicking away flies with her tail.

'Did someone order an Uber?' Joe riffed.

'I did,' said Dad proudly. 'I asked Mo to bring her.'

Maudie squealed with excitement as she saw the horse. 'Please let me go! Please let me go!' She started to curl her fists. 'I want to ride on Gaia.' A tantrum was brewing. All of us apart from Mum agreed this was a positive sign.

'We can bring Maudie back if she feels ill,' I suggested.

'Please, Mum,' she begged.

'Okay,' Mum finally relented.

The walk to the Spirit House was uneventful compared to everything else that had happened earlier that morning. Having got his own way, Dad had returned to centre, and we were all relieved to see Maudie leave the cabin for the first time in weeks. She sat on Gaia's wide back, cradled from behind by Mum, and the rhythmic shire-horse plod rocked her into a deep sleep.

We were the last to arrive. When Dad carried Maudie across the Spirit House and placed her in the string swing seat by the fireplace, a ripple ran through the circle of people sitting cross-legged on the floor. She sat unnaturally straight-backed looking tragic, her injured arm draped across her lap.

My heart soared as I spotted Mo through the crowd on the opposite side of the room, sitting in the beaten-up armchair, one leg casually draped over the arm, whittling a piece of wood with his pocketknife. I forced a casual wolf lope towards him.

'Hey! I'm sorry I was too late to see you the other evening.'

'Late for what, Cassia?' he asked, in a bored tone, without looking up. I stared at him in confusion. I couldn't work out if he'd really forgotten about our date or if he was messing with my head because he was annoyed with me for not turning up. He continued whittling.

'I thought we had a plan,' I said, awkwardly shifting from one foot to the other in my nervousness.

'What kind of plan?' asked Mo. He finally peered up and narrowed his eyes. 'You took so long I've forgotten the details.'

How was it possible to swing from euphoria to despair so quickly? I didn't know how to respond. Fortunately, just at that point, the sun rose above the trees on the east side of the Spirit House and beams of light radiated through the multicoloured glass window onto the wall above the fireplace. It was the signal for processing to begin. Everyone fell silent. We stood in a circle, holding hands, Joe on one side of me and Lila on the other. Mo sat opposite between One Way Will and River. The weirdest thing about this part of processing was that it no longer felt weird.

It was Aida's turn to guide the session. She placed the talking stick in the middle of the circle, picked up a small clay bowl and lit a sage smudge stick. 'Let us begin,' she rasped. She closed her eyes and wafted smoke over her face with the palms of her hands until the smell infused every corner of the Spirit House.

'I thank Mother Earth for providing us with the necessities for life, the plants, the birds, the fish and the animals,' she said. 'Show us the way of life we need to follow to provide a future for our young people. Teach people that the healing is in the forest. Teach those who consider themselves superior to the natural world the wisdom to understand the folly of their beliefs. Let us send those who would destroy nature towards the light.'

She bowed her head. All of us repeated what she'd said apart from Mo, who altered the words of the final sentence. 'Let us destroy those who would destroy nature!' He said the same phrase several times over. Other people joined in, including Dad. Hoping for Mo's approval, I did the same.

'We choose the path of righteousness,' Aida countered. 'We reject violence.' Mo talked over her again. An undercurrent of conflict crackled between them.

'Stop!' Juan angrily ordered Mo. 'This isn't the way we do things here. We work together.'

Aida slowly walked around the circle to bathe our faces with sage. I hadn't seen her in a while, and I couldn't help staring as she stood in front of me holding the bowl. She had a silver lip cuff on her lower lip, long earrings made from animal bones, and feathers woven in her long dark hair. Her whole vibe was a challenge, as if she defied anyone to find her attractive. She might have been trying to look like a scruffy old crow. But she radiated strength and beauty.

'Purify your soul from negative thoughts, Cass,' she said, as she wafted the smoke over my face. I looked into her dark eyes and tried, but all I could think about was Mo's coldness towards me. Once the room was infused with sage, Aida instructed us to walk anticlockwise in a circle twelve times in silence.

'Let us still our unruly thoughts so we can work in the dynamic moment,' she said. Only Joe broke the rule of silence. 'She's triggering my guru radar,' he whispered in my ear. We sat down and One Way Will picked up the talking stick. I knew from previous sessions that whoever held this stick had the right to speak without interruption.

'I want to give thanks to Mo for protecting our community from incursions by outsiders,' he said. Will's allegiance was clear. 'His sacrifice allows us to live a life of peace and harmony and all of us, from the mightiest oaks to the weakest saplings, owe him a debt of gratitude.'

'We give thanks.' There was a loud chorus of applause and murmured appreciation from around three-quarters of those sitting in the circle. Mo basked in the heat of their approval. He smiled warmly at everyone but when he caught my eye his gaze iced over so that even in the sweaty atmosphere of the Spirit House I shivered. I'd entirely blown it with him by not turning up. I felt sick inside.

Magnus had picked up the talking stick, so everyone's attention turned to him. 'I want to give thanks to Juan and Eve for all the work they've put into the hives over the summer. It looks like we're in for a bumper crop of honey.'

I glanced at Dad, expecting him to be pleased that Mum had restored family dignity, but instead he looked as if he was chewing a bitter blackthorn berry. Magnus handed the stick to Sylvie.

'I want to give thanks that Maudie has recovered and is well enough to come to processing,' said Sylvie, smiling broadly at her. 'And thank her for the wonderful poster she started the last time she came to home-school. We hope you come back very soon, Maudie. It's good to see you're on the mend.' She held it up for us all to see. 'WILD PLANT RUSSIAN ROULETTE', it read, in big letters across the top of the page.

'Are you well enough to explain it?' asked Sylvie.

Maudie nodded. 'I drew the poisonous plants in one column and the edible ones they imitate in the other,' she said softly. Everyone leant forward to hear her properly. 'Deadly plants are very clever. Hemlock disguises itself as wild carrot. Death cap mushrooms look just like ink caps. It's a matter of life and death if you get it wrong.'

'What lesson did you learn from doing this?' asked Aida.

'I learnt that plants are no different from human beings,' said Maudie. 'Bad people disguise themselves as good people and you have to learn to look long and hard to be able to tell the difference.'

There was more applause. It went on until almost everyone in the room had been thanked for something, no matter how trivial.

Kaia picked up the stick. 'Winter food supplies, folks,' she announced. 'I've done a comparison with our position at the same time last year and, apart from dry cured pork, smoked trout, apples, pears and honey, we're not hitting any of our targets. It's the worst situation in the twenty years I've been living at the Haven. I don't need to tell you what this means with winter round the corner.' A worried murmur of overlapping voices threaded its way round the room. No one picked up the stick.

Piper put up his hand. 'What are the implications in terms of winter supplies?'

'If the figures are correct, it means skipping one meal a day for at least four months,' said Kaia, consulting her notebook. 'We'll have to rely on hunting deer and wild boar, and smoke fish twenty-four/seven until the weather turns. We'll have our usual supply of eggs and milk, but we won't be able to eat vegetables every day and there might not be enough wheat to bake bread more than once or twice a week.'

'I don't understand how this can happen when all we do is work,' complained Magnus.

'The field up at Drift Ridge Cabin isn't producing the kind of yields that it did last year,' explained Kaia. This was the field that Dad was looking after. I glanced over my shoulder and saw his jaw tighten. My body tensed. It was incredible how such a tiny gesture could have such a big impact on my mood.

'Perhaps Rick can update us on what's going on with that field,' suggested Sylvie. 'Is harvest late? Are you still having problems with caterpillars?'

She handed Dad the talking stick and everyone turned to him. He cleared his throat. 'Er, it seems to me that something else might be affecting the vegetables. The cauliflowers, cabbage and broccoli aren't growing properly. The radishes and beetroot have been gnawed. There are a few bare patches. I'm out every night keeping watch but every morning I find partially eaten vegetables on the ground.'

'What about the potatoes?' asked Skylar. I could hear the desperation in her voice. Potatoes were the mainstay of almost every meal.

'The earlies failed completely,' said Dad. 'I'm working on saving the maincrop, but something is eating them from beneath the surface of the soil.' He pulled out a couple of potatoes and carrots from his bag and handed them round the group.

'This is an easy one,' said Juan, in his sing-song voice, as he held up a sick-looking carrot. 'That's vole damage. They tunnel underground and nibble the vegetables from below. If you don't deal with them early in the growing season, they're impossible to get rid of because they breed five times between spring and autumn. So, there are likely hundreds, if not thousands living under the soil in that field.'

I couldn't believe that Juan had come up with an explanation so easily. It all made perfect sense.

'I think perhaps what you're trying to highlight, Rick, is that we need to prepare for crop failure across the board in that field,' said Juan. His tone was kindly. But for someone so quick to point out the failings of other people, Dad was exquisitely over-sensitive when it came to anyone questioning his own. He jiggled his foot and turned the talking stick round and round in his fist. The tension was almost palpable.

'Why didn't you call a processing session to discuss these problems?' Aida asked gently.

'I guess I thought I could turn it around,' said Dad. 'I've been shooting the rabbits and rats and picking off the caterpillars. Perhaps that will improve the situation.' He sounded so hopeful that it hurt my heart.

'Didn't Juan offer to help you weeks ago?' Kaia suddenly asked him.

'Why didn't you accept his offer?' Piper pressured him. Dad remained silent.

'It's the nature of processing that we have to help each other learn from our mistakes, Rick,' said Aida, eventually. 'That's how we grow as individuals within our community. Questioning our own motivations and decision-making is a crucial part of processing.'

This was the first time I'd heard anyone, apart from Mum and Joe, really call Dad to account. I caught a glimpse of his jaw again and understood there would be a price to pay later.

'I was confident in my strategy,' Dad persisted.

'You haven't lived here long enough to think collectively but we can't help noticing that you use the pronoun "I" a lot when you speak,' said Sylvie.

'The most difficult aspect of community living is putting aside ego,' said Kaia, in a kindly tone that would grind Dad's gears. 'Altruism doesn't come easy to human beings.'

'We have to learn from the bees,' suggested Juan. 'Their survival and stability depend on their ability to listen, collaborate and focus on the common good. They share information freely with each other and make decisions by majority.' Everyone stared expectantly at Dad. I could tell he wasn't going to concede anything. He slammed his fist on the arm of the wooden chair. Everyone jumped.

'Do you have problems with controlling your emotions, Rick?' asked Aida. Her tone was curious, rather than confrontational. But I knew Dad wouldn't see it that way. His fist furled and unfurled. 'We can help you with this. It's not fair on your family. Especially Joe.' This was cataclysmic. It hadn't occurred to me that anyone outside our family was aware of Dad's aggression towards Joe and no one, not even Cara, had ever dared be so direct with him.

'I don't need your help. Thank you,' said Dad. His face was so rigid that his lips barely moved when he spoke.

'We need to be clear that Rick inherited a lot of problems with this field. He didn't create them,' warned Piper. 'His mistake was not keeping us informed.'

'Mo should never have handed over such a big responsibility to someone with so little experience,' Sylvie agreed.

'I did my best,' said Dad, his head bowed in defeat. No one could argue with that. No one could have worked as hard as Dad. His efforts had been superhuman.

'The truth is Mudder didn't put in enough work at the beginning,' said Juan. 'He didn't fertilize the soil before planting, he didn't water consistently during the spring drought and, most importantly, he did nothing to enclose the field with wire to protect it from voles in the first place.'

Juan was trying to make Dad feel better. But I knew Dad wouldn't see it like that. I understood enough about human relationships to sense that Dad felt inadequate beside Juan and was involved in some ridiculous power struggle that he could never win because Juan was too cool for mind games. The foot-tapping became more frenzied. For a few awkward minutes the talking stick sat in the middle of the circle. I looked at Mo and was surprised to see he was smiling.

'I think everyone needs to get some perspective,' he said languidly. 'What's more important? Protecting the Haven from outsiders, or weeding a field of vegetables? Not that I'm belittling the weeders of this world. At the beginning of the year, we agreed my priority should be the security of our community.'

There was silence as this contribution was digested.

'Maybe he's right,' said Skylar, eventually. 'I'd sooner starve than let the outsiders get a foothold in our forest.'

'Think of all the issues we were dealing with back in March,' said Mo. 'The felling and burning of the copse of ancient oaks by the growers . . . the man in the micro-light flying over . . . trimmers camping in the pine forest . . .'

There was a lot of nodding and murmured agreement. 'We've had double the number of incursions this year compared to last, and more wildfires, because of the drought, and floods, because of the heavy rain.' He pulled out a notebook from his pocket and began reading out a list of specific dates when trees were felled, bits of wood-land burnt down, and when the microlight flew over. It was relentless. He cleared his throat. 'I've even had a report that, for the first time, a group of people crossed to our side of the lake a couple of days ago.' He caught my eye and I flushed. He knew what we'd done.

'This is terrible news,' cried Piper.

'How can you be so sure?' asked Joe.

Honestly, why couldn't he ever keep his mouth shut?

'The fields have eyes, and the forest has ears,' Mo told him with a half-smile. 'I found five sets of tracks down by the lake. And this.' He pulled out a bag of weed.

I nudged Joe.

'I didn't leave that,' he whispered. 'They took it from me.'

'It must be the growers!' said Sylvie, in horror.

I glanced at the Vivian sisters to see if any of them was going to admit that it was us. But they stared resolutely ahead, their strange expressionless faces revealing nothing.

'This changes everything,' declared Kaia. 'Mo is right. Our focus has to be on protecting the forest.'

'I can't keep on top of this on my own any more,' said Mo. 'It's pointless for Rick to work in the vegetable field. It's a lost cause. I want to ask permission for him to join me.'

'We're leaving soon,' interrupted Mum.

'Maybe you should extend your stay, Rick?' suggested Mo. 'Help me out until things are more under control.'

'Sure,' said Dad. Mum shot him a belligerent look.

Aida lit more sage to give the community silent time to reflect on the situation. A few minutes later everyone voted unanimously in favour of Dad helping Mo with security. Mo then requested the talking stick.

'Of course, there's a very simple solution to the problem of food shortages,' he said breezily. I was in total awe of the way he hadn't let the negativity bring him down.

'But it requires people to be less rigid in their thinking.' He waited until he had everyone's full attention. 'Why don't we take a trip to the supermarket in town and stock up on supplies to make up for the shortfall? Simple.'

There was a shocked silence.

'That's against all of our rules,' spluttered Sylvie. 'We've always been completely self-sufficient. Dependent on ourselves rather than other people.'

'And when we've had crop failures in the past we've done without. It was tough but we got through.' Kaia backed her up.

'What's the point in suffering for the sake of it?' Mo argued. 'Some people might call that masochism.' Someone on the opposite side of the room laughed.

'What's the point in principles if they're abandoned the first time we bump up against a problem?' countered Aida. 'Some people might call that hypocrisy.'

'This is an emergency that threatens the very existence of our community,' insisted Mo.

'How could we even afford to buy food from a supermarket?' asked Magnus.

'I've got money from selling our produce at the festival where I met Rick,' said Mo.

'Talking hypothetically, how would you even get to a supermarket, let alone bring back the amount of food we'd need to buy to make up for the shortfall?' asked Piper. As soon as he posed these questions, I understood Mo had won the argument.

'I've got a friend with a truck,' said Mo. 'I borrowed it for the trip in March.' He had a solution to every problem.

'This is a transgression on two counts. One, we never buy food. Two, we never use fossil fuels,' said Lila, firmly.

'We can go to a chemist and get silver sulfadiazine to heal Maudie's burn,' said Mo. I glanced at Dad and saw he was nodding vigorously in agreement.

'That would be really helpful,' murmured Mum. She avoided catching Aida's eye.

'Say your piece, Aida,' said Mo.

Her eyes were dark as ink. 'This isn't about whether we shop in a supermarket. It's about who we are. Our community lives by simple rules according to our respectful relationship with Mother Nature. The forest provides our basic needs: we build shelter from its wood, drink water from its streams and grow food in its soil. We create energy from the sun and wind. We rely on no one apart from ourselves. This is what makes us free. Buying food in a supermarket won't simplify our life. It will cause more complications.'

'I'm with Aida,' said Lila.

'I think we're ready to vote,' said Piper. 'All those in favour of restocking supplies from a supermarket, raise your hand.' Everyone put their hand in the air, apart from Aida and Lila. Aida's arms hung stiffly by her sides. Lila indicated that she hadn't decided either way.

'Who would you take with you?' Piper asked. 'Most of us attract the wrong kind of attention. None of us have papers.'

'Cassia and River,' said Mo, without missing a beat.

I flushed red but this time it was with relief and joy that not only had Mo seemed to have forgiven me but he was also trying to find a way for us to be together for an entire day, using River as cover. Awesome.

'Why Cass?' River blurted out. 'Joe would be more useful for carrying the heavy stuff.' I seethed at her treachery.

'Cassia knows how to find her way round a supermarket and she's good at blending in,' countered Mo.

'Joe knows his way round a supermarket too,' said Mum. I couldn't believe how they were trying to sabotage this chance for us to be alone and half wondered if Mum suspected something about Mo and me.

'Cassia does what she's told,' countered Mo.

Aida stood up. 'In five years' time, when fuel crises have become routine, when food runs short every winter, when people are experiencing unsurvivable heatwaves and flooding, what will you be wishing you had done now? If we don't make these sacrifices and find our own solutions to problems, then no one will, and the forest will be lost.' She scanned the room. Everyone studiously avoided her gaze.

'If you all refuse to go, this won't happen.' Aida's eyes bored into me.

'I want to go.' I gave an apologetic shrug. Mo grinned at me.

'Be careful, Cass,' warned Aida. 'He comes from the shadow side.'

Mo roared with laughter and other people joined in.

Aida's face twisted with quiet fury. 'My family have lived in this forest for generations. We have never relied on food from the outside for our survival. It goes against all our most fundamental beliefs. There's no way I can agree to this plan.' She spoke loudly and steadily over the noise. Then she slowly stood up, stared us all down and pushed through the circle of people sitting on the floor. There was a moment of stunned silence as the community absorbed what was happening. Then everyone started talking at once.

'If we don't buy food, we'll starve . . .'

'If we don't stick to our principles, the Haven could collapse . . .'

'If Aida leaves, we will lose our way . . .'

'Aida is leaving because we have lost our way . . .'

Sylvie rushed after her. 'Aida, don't do this!' she pleaded, tugging at her arm. This was the closest thing to a crisis that I'd seen since we'd arrived.

'Please don't go,' begged Piper. 'Let's keep talking until we find consensus.'

'I will never agree to betray the most basic principles of our community,' declared Aida. She walked out of the Spirit House in dignified silence, head held high, and didn't look back.

'The time for talking is over. It's time for action,' said Mo.

Soon after this Mum and Maudie left on Gaia. Dad's mood had flipped again. Not only had bringing Maudie to processing proved to be the right decision, because the community would now stop worrying about her, but he no longer had to stress about the failed field of vegetables. Better still he could spend his days helping Mo with his security patrols on the other side of the lake.

Aida didn't come back for the rest of that day, and when Juan went to her container to look for her later that night, it was padlocked from the outside.

We stayed at the Spirit House late into the evening. No one mentioned Aida again. It was as if as soon as she left the Haven she ceased to exist. When I quizzed River, she explained that now consensus had been reached, the subject was closed. There was a strange energy in the air that I hadn't felt before, a kind of reckless euphoria.

'It's because it's the last full moon before Samhain,'

explained River, matter-of-factly. 'It creates a strange other-worldly energy.'

We helped cook dinner together in the kitchen as we always did but for once no one noted down what ingredients we'd used in the inventory, or bothered to ration the quinoa and rice, which were already in short supply. Aida's absence left the community unmoored. Only Lila protested. 'Why are you using up the vegetables that we're running out of?'

No one responded apart from Mo. 'Why so serious, Lila? We can replace anything you like when we go to the supermarket, sweetheart. You name it and we'll get it for you.' He looked at me and grinned.

At dusk, One Way Will fetched the home-made mead from the root cellar that was meant for Samhain and poured generous tumblers for everyone, including Skylar. No one questioned him, and the fermented honey made the mead so sweet that we all drank too much too fast.

As it got darker, Magnus suggested we build a fire. Everyone formed a line to pass dry logs from the winter store to an enormous pyre that eventually stood higher than us. Mo sparked a flame with his flint and steel and the tinder-dry logs at the base quickly started burning.

Kaia climbed onto a tree stump and everyone fell quiet as she recited a poem. The trees swayed, the red kite mewed, and for once Joe said nothing. By the time she had finished, the flames licked so high above us that we were all bathed in a warm orange glow. Sylvie went into the Spirit House in search of an old CD player that I hadn't seen before and hooked it up to the solar-powered battery. The sound of Woody Guthrie singing 'This Land Is Your Land' drifted through the night air. Everyone moved in time to the music. Several couples danced together. Sylvie and Piper embraced and danced so slowly they barely moved, their cheeks pressed together.

Mo asked me to dance and somehow I didn't feel self-conscious as we twirled and spun around the fire. At one point I felt his lips brush mine. He whispered in my ear about our connection and how I was his twin flame.

'You need to learn to breathe the air of inner freedom, Cassia,' he told me.

I searched for River and saw her dancing alone, eyes closed and arms swaying in the air as the flames cast wild shadows across her body. She was wearing her headdress of antlers, one of my T-shirts, and a long skirt that skimmed her ankles. The way she moved was hypnotic and I couldn't stop watching. Neither could Joe. I caught his eye and he quickly looked away.

As the moon waned, the crowd thinned and the vibe mellowed. Some people fell asleep around the fire. Joe and River were curled up under a rug. Dad, in contrast, was still wired. I kept waiting for Mo to take me back to his tree-house, but Dad wouldn't stop talking and kept wanting to discuss plans for catching the people who'd crossed the lake. In the end, I sat down beside them and watched as Mo packed what looked like recently mown grass into a curvy glass pipe with a long thin stem and a wide round chamber. 'Light it, inhale as deep as you can and hold for twenty seconds.' He winked at Dad. 'Take three big hits.'

'What are you doing?' I asked Dad.

'It's something to help him relax. You need to chill out, don't you, Rick?'

I couldn't argue with that. Dad was fully focused on lighting the pipe. I guessed Mo had loaded it with weed, which was confusing because, according to the list of transgressions on the wall of the Spirit House, taking drugs was against the rules. Dad sucked hard on the pipe and held his breath while Mo counted to twenty, and then breathed out, coughing gently. He repeated this process a couple more times and started singing. 'Sweet dreams are made of cheese ...' I groaned with embarrassment. 'Maybe you should slow it down, Dad?'

'I don't feel a thing!'

'What's in the pipe?' I asked Mo, trying to sound cooler than I felt.

'*Salvia divinorum.* The plant that saves. Used by Mazatec shamans to create a visionary sense of consciousness ...'

'You mean sage?' I was confused. We cooked with sage in the community kitchen almost every day.

'It's a special kind of sage, like weed. Except better.'

'Isn't taking drugs a transgression?' I was now getting properly worried about what was going on.

'*Salvia* is entirely natural,' smiled Mo, as if that meant it wasn't against the rules.

I was confused. Swimming in the lake was natural but was against the rules. Having a phone was unnatural and a transgression but didn't Mo have Dad's phone? And he hadn't shared his relationship with the growers during processing, which was also surely a transgression. The contradictions sent my head spinning. I remembered what Skylar had said about Mo having the right to bend the rules because he was the one who protected us.

I couldn't follow this thought to its logical end because Dad was trying to speak. He opened his mouth to form words, but his lips moved in slow motion and no sound came out. Then slowly, like melting cheese, he slumped over onto the ground and lay on his side facing me without blinking. I tried to pull him upright. It was hopeless. All his strength had gone. No sooner had I lifted him into a sitting position than he toppled the other way.

'Dad, are you okay?' He didn't respond.

'Don't worry, Cassia,' said Mo. 'He's on the journey of a lifetime.'

Dad muttered something that sounded like 'swish'. I glanced down at him and he lifted his right arm towards me. His gaze was fixed on his fingertips, but it was as if the rest of his body was rooted to the ground. I tried to hold his hand. His fingers were frozen in a rigid claw.

'Dad, Dad, can you hear me?' He didn't react. I lifted his T-shirt. His heart was beating so fast that I could see it pumping in his chest. I shouted again and he didn't respond. A small dribble of spit leached out of the side of his mouth, like sap from a tree.

'Is he meant to be like this?' I was trying to keep a lid on my panic because I didn't want to risk pissing off Mo again.

'Relax, Cassia, you'll freak him out,' said Mo. 'He's sliding into a state of divine inebriation.'

Then to my relief Joe was beside me. He looked round and got it straight away. He clicked his fingers in front of Dad's face. Nothing.

'What's in here?' Joe picked up the smouldering pipe and gave it a sniff.

'*Salvia divinorum*,' said Mo, squeezing my hand. 'Diviner's sage.'

'You're fucking kidding! That's a really powerful hallucinogen.' Joe was completely strung out. He tried and failed to rouse Dad again. 'It's like extra-dimensional torture. No one who has tried it once ever wants to take it again. This is the last thing he needs.'

'*Tranquilo*, kids, I'm an experienced sitter,' said Mo.

'What's a sitter?' I asked in confusion. Everything was getting out of control so quickly.

'A spirit guide who sees someone through an experience with hallucinogenic drugs,' said Mo.

'I'm sinking! I'm sinking!' Dad cried, even though he was as still as a statue. It was the first time he'd spoken. He opened his eyes and looked straight through me. He sounded completely terrified. 'It's so dark . . . I can't feel anything . . . I can't see anything . . .'

'You're not alone, Dad!' I said.

'It's all right! We're with you,' said Joe, trying to rest Dad's head on his lap. His tenderness towards him scared me even more.

'Will he ever come back to us?' I sat on the ground beside Dad.

'Don't worry, Cassia. The divine insights last about twenty minutes,' said Mo, draping his arm around me. 'Unless you're One Way Will. In which case you never come back because you were never really there.' He roared with laughter.

'You're so full of shit,' said Joe, angrily.

'He's reaching a state of universal consciousness,' said Mo, calmly. He addressed Dad. 'You're in a safe place to face your fears, Rick. Tell me what you see, and I'll write it down.' Mo took his notebook out of his pocket.

'I no longer exist!' Dad squirmed on his back, like an upturned woodlouse. Joe tried to restrain him, but Dad violently shook him off. It was as if he possessed superhuman strength. 'I'm sinking into the forest floor. The colours are too bright. I'm unravelling. I'm no longer whole!' He held his head in his hands.

'What can you see?' asked Mo.

'Bees! Bees!' cried Dad. 'Everywhere bees!' He writhed around on the ground, arms flailing so violently that all we could do was watch from a distance. He hit himself in the face over and over again, until his nose bled and the scab on his lip opened up. I started crying and saw Joe was crying too and remembered what he'd said about none of us making it home from the Haven and wondered if he was right.

Then suddenly it was over. Dad still looked anguished, but at least he could speak again. 'I thought I'd be trapped there for ever,' he sobbed. 'It was like a fragment of Hell...'

I gave him a hug. 'You're back with us now, Dad.'

'I left my body and thought I was never going to get back,' he whispered. The whole experience had lasted less than twenty minutes, but it took a good couple of hours for him to sound remotely normal again.

'Thank fuck Mum's not here,' muttered Joe.

Mo was right. Over the next few days, something shifted in Dad, but not necessarily in a good way. His emotions were still close to the surface but instead of anger he seemed more vulnerable. When something moved him – the delicate trill of the wood warbler or Maudie's bravery – tears would pour down his cheeks. But with Mum he became clingier and more jealous of Juan. He wanted to know where she was all the time. She could no longer soothe him when he became agitated. He started accusing her of stealing his energy. When she tried to persuade him to go to sleep in their bed, he said she was trying to imprison him. During the day, when he wasn't with Mo, he spent hours boiling the heads of the animals he'd killed and hanging their skulls across the windows of our cabin, like bunting.

'Why bother when we're going home in a couple of weeks?' Joe asked him.

'Maybe we won't go.' Dad laughed.

We never told Mum what had happened. We pretended Dad had cut and scratched himself falling from a tree. We didn't want to add to her worries, and I knew that if she found out what Mo had done, she would have brought it up in processing and banned me from having any more contact with him. And she would have been right to do that. After what he did to Dad, I should have stayed away from him. But I couldn't. No one had ever made me feel so seen before.

21

Now

Wass and Kovac are impatient to get back to the police station to get the *Pica pica* doll swabbed. As soon as they leave Aida's container, I know it's time for me to go too. I'd give anything to stay in her cosy, warm home for the night, but I've caused enough problems for her already. She doesn't try to change my mind when I explain that I'm going to cross the lake because that's where the police picked up the signal from Dad's phone, which means Mo is surely in that area.

'I've got to find him before he finds me,' I explain. 'Only Mo has the answers to all the questions.' She gets it.

'Careful he isn't fucking with your head,' she warns. 'Psychological warfare is his speciality.'

I glance out of the small window. The sun tells me it's about two in the afternoon, which gives me a couple more hours of daylight. It's not that I mind walking in the dark. I know how to see without being seen. It's more that, with the temperature already hovering just above freezing, I'll need to build a shelter before nightfall.

'Remember, dry fluffy snow . . .'

'. . . is a good insulator.' I finish the sentence for her and we laugh.

I pack up my stuff as quickly as possible. Aida forages through her belongings. She gives me a box of matches, a tarpaulin, and her own two-litre cow-hide waterskin.

'I can't take all this,' I protest. 'It's too much.'

She doesn't reply and instead adds a pair of socks and an extra jumper to the haul. She insists I choose any food I want from her supplies. I pick out bread, home-made goat's cheese, smoked fish and apples. Finally, she hands over what look like two comedy furry slippers made of carpet.

'What are these?' I ask in bewilderment.

'You put them over your boots to mask your prints. The growers get the trimmers to wear them when they carry the grow out of the forest. So they leave no trace.'

'Where did you get them?'

'They were a present.'

'Who from?'

'I helped a girl escape. She gave them to me to say thank you.'

'Are you sure you won't need them?' I ask, as she helps with my backpack. Her kindness makes me feel fragile.

She reaches up for one of her hag stones and ties it on a thread around my neck for protection. 'This is to remind you never to give your power away to anyone again. You have courage, Cass.'

I try to say thank you, but the words get mangled in my throat. Emotion at this point feels like indulgence. I turn on Joe's phone to look at the photo again in case I missed anything the first time. But the screen flashes blue and the battery dies on me before I've reached the picture of the dead body.

'How did Joe get round that?' Aida asks.

Of course. It makes complete sense that Joe must have found a way of charging the phone to be able to send all those messages to Cara over such a long period of time. *Think, Cass, think!* My mind races. Then it comes to me.

'The van.' There was a USB port in the arm rest of our van. 'I think Dad hid the key behind the sun visor. If I can get the engine to turn over, maybe I'll be able to charge the phone and cross the lake at first light tomorrow morning.'

Aida cautions me to walk along the lakeshore, sticking close to the edge of the forest, until I reach the Teg, a huge granite rock that sits at its widest point.

'The terrain is easier. From the Teg you head directly north for about twenty-five minutes. The van is in a ditch close to that point. We covered it with pine branches.'

I glance out of the window and see the first flakes of snow falling.

'Thanks for everything,' I tell her. 'You saved me.' It's true. My fever is dropping, and although my head still aches, it's more like background noise. And I'm remembering more. I hug Aida. This time she doesn't pull away.

'You've saved yourself, Cass,' she says, as she unbolts the door. I head outside and pull a scarf across my face to protect it from the bitter wind that whips my cheeks and hike up the hood of my jacket. I clutch Aida's arm.

'Why does no one trust me?'

'Because of your closeness to Mo. People are scared of him. He's very manipulative.'

For the first couple of hours I'm completely alone. Even the buzzards and red kites are quiet. I hope the swallows managed to leave on their journey south because the north wind is a bitter and treacherous enemy. The only parts of my body exposed to the elements are my eyes, and they soon water and ache from the cold, especially when the sun drops below the trees. There are a couple more snow flurries, but they're half-hearted and visibility is generally good. After a while, I start to sweat. I don't think it's the fever coming back, more that I'm moving at a half-jog. I stop to remove a layer. Sweat is a fickle friend because it heats you up, then gives you the chills when you cool again.

When I reach the lake, the wind hardens across the vast expanse of water. But Aida is right: the lake helps me keep my bearings and it's easier underfoot. The snow is coming thicker and I put on the overshoes she gave me so I don't leave footprints.

I haven't been walking along the shore for long when a line of people emerges from the forest on the opposite side of the lake. I immediately crouch down behind a boulder and take out Mo's binoculars to get a closer look. Thirteen people in total, all walking in the same westerly direction that I'm headed, hunched over, not just because of the wind blowing off the lake but because of the heavy loads on their backs. I guess they're trimmers carrying sacks of marijuana towards a boat I spot waiting further downriver. The bad weather must have delayed the process of getting the grow out of the forest.

A few minutes later a quad bike appears from the undergrowth and bounces past them, stirring up a fine powder of snow. I adjust the binoculars and recognize the long-haired man carrying a rifle across his back: it's Kyle. I duck down, heart pumping.

I lose valuable daylight waiting for Kyle and the trimmers to get ahead of me. I stamp around and clap my gloved hands to get the circulation flowing again. The light is fading as I make my way along the shore, and by the time I reach the Teg, it's almost dark and I've no choice but to turn on the head torch to navigate my way back up the hillside through the forest. As the temperature drops, the snow falls thicker and starts to settle. I don't fancy my chances outside tonight, even with a tarp for shelter. I check the compass to make sure I'm heading in a straight line and pick my way uphill through the undergrowth. After about half an hour I find a small snow-covered mound with pine branches crisscrossed beneath, just as Aida described.

I pull off the branches. Underneath, our poor van lies on his side in the ditch, held in a straitjacket of snow-coated brambles. His lovely bright red surface has turned green and yellow with lichens, moss and liverworts.

'Sorry, Rory,' I mutter. I bend down and feel my way along the side until I find the handle of the sliding door. I ease it open and crawl inside. By this time, I'm breathing so unevenly from the combination of fear and exertion that the windows are soon fogged up. It's not as warm as I'd hoped but it's dry and clearly a better option than rigging a tarp for the night. The way Rory is tilted on his side is disorienting. I clamber clumsily into the front of the van and pull down the sun visor in front of the driver's seat. There's no key.

I turn on my torch and rummage desperately under the seats, in the glove compartment, the side pockets, inwardly cursing Joe for not hiding it somewhere obvious. The torch spotlights a beautifully woven orb spider's web, a bird's nest lined with mud and cemented with saliva that I guess belongs to a song thrush or blackbird, and tiny pellets of dormice scat. Rory has grown his own eco-system. The beam of the torch settles on the floor behind the front seat. I shine it underneath. No key. Instead, a pile of dolls, like the one I found in my pocket, stare back at me.

They're carefully laid out, face up. Nine in total. All

female. They're really disturbing. I know immediately this has nothing to do with Joe. I force myself to pick up the first doll. She has long dark hair held in place by a pair of perfectly carved miniature antlers and a white dress embroidered with wildflowers. Her stomach is made to look as if she's pregnant. The doll beside her wears an ugly, stiff dress that reaches just below her knees. It has tiny indentations all over it, almost like polka dots, and a piece of red thread knotted through the hole drilled between her legs. Then it hits me. It's been made to look like Lucia, the ten-year-old daughter of the Danish couple. I frantically examine the other dolls. There's one wearing a delicate skirt made of damselfly wings and another with a headdress created from tiny bones. The next has red hair and is wearing an exact miniature copy of the wedding dress Maudie loved so much. It dawns on me with a slow, sickening dread that these are all girls from the community.

22

Then

After the trip to the Spirit House for the processing session, my little sister took to her bed and refused to get up again. Mum was crazy with worry. And because Dad was now out all day patrolling the forest with Mo, she had to stay back at the cabin looking after Maudie. She gave up helping Juan with the bees and missed them like they were old friends. We should have called Dad out for putting it all on Mum, but it was such a relief not to have him around that we let it go.

'Maybe we should talk to Juan.'

'Dad won't listen to Juan. He's jealous of him.'

'True. How about Piper and Sylvie?'

'Like we can trust people here.' Joe snorted sarcastically.

'Why don't we at least discuss it with Mum?' I urged Joe.

'She's got enough worries on her plate,' he said.

'What worries could Mum possibly have?' a voice demanded. My stomach knotted. We hadn't heard Dad come in. He paced up and down the kitchen waiting for our response. The main side-effect of Dad's new sage-induced state of universal consciousness seemed to be a complete inability to be physically or mentally still. It was like he was bubbling over. He spoke quickly and urgently, as if everything was of vital importance, flitting from one subject to the next, so it was impossible to follow the thread of any idea or conversation to its logical end. He hardly seemed to sleep and had become obsessed with digging a well so the cabin would have its own permanent water supply.

'She's worried Maudie's getting weaker,' I said haltingly.

'She's over the worst.' Dad always said the same thing. He pulled out a piece of paper where he'd written our weekly timetable of chores. He was big into rules. There were now so many that even he struggled to remember them all. Get water; lay vole traps; update the food inventory; record everything we eat; note the internal temperature of the cabin; look for signs of outsiders . . .

When I mentioned to Mo that I was worried about Dad's state of mind since he'd smoked the sage, he told me to go easy on him because Dad was on a long journey to find his inner truth and doing incredibly important work for himself and the community. I asked Piper for advice. 'Mudder's helping him figure out his life, so he doesn't have to,' he tried to reassure me.

Mum came into the kitchen clutching a flannel. 'Maudie's losing sensation in her fingers,' she said, without turning to look at Dad.

'She's over the worst!' he said again. He rolled his eyes behind Mum's back and looked at me to back him up. I didn't even blink.

'The wound smells bad,' Mum kept wringing the flannel, long after any drops of water came out.

'You're such a downer, Eve!' Dad erupted. His moods came upon him without any warning. 'You're like a noose around my neck, a forcefield of negativity stealing all the positive kundalini from my body.' He suddenly punched himself hard in the stomach. I jumped and my body went completely rigid. *Here we go*, I thought. *Here we go*. His mood had pivoted again. 'That's what being with you feels like.' Dad punched himself a second time. Even Joe cowered against the wall. I reached out for Mum and put my arm around her. I felt terrified that relationships were like icebergs and that what might be going on beneath the surface between him and Mum could be even scarier than what we witnessed. I promised myself it wouldn't be like that with Mo and me. Although my parents hadn't passed on the template for a happy relationship, we could build our own version from the ground up.

'Get a hold of yourself, Rick,' ordered Mum. She was usually fearless with him but there was a tremor in her voice I hadn't heard before.

'It's impossible to live with someone who spends so much time on the shadow side,' declared Dad. None of us dared point out that he was the cloud who stole the sunshine from our lives. His eyes flitted around the cabin and fixed on a jar of honey on the kitchen table.

'What's that?' he asked menacingly. It was crazy he could see evil intent in a jar of honey.

'Honey,' said Mum, sharply. 'From the black bees. The rarest ones.' It clearly said 'Honey' on the jar, so I knew his question was cover for some other warped strand of paranoia worming into his brain.

'Who gave you this honey, Eve?' Dad persisted. I imagined the dark thoughts burrowing into his grey matter, like the maggots I'd seen eating the flesh on the ram's head that he'd brought home the previous week.

'Someone brought it over to put on Maudie's burn,' said Mum, careful not to mention Juan by name. 'Apparently honey can help skin heal.'

'Has Juan been here again?' growled Dad. 'As soon as I go, he's sniffing around you, like you're a dog on heat. You must be giving off some kind of fuck-me pheromones.' I felt as if all the stiflingly hot summer air had been sucked out of the cabin and my chest was being compressed by a heavy weight. I looked out of the window towards the green of the forest and felt comforted by the gentle rocking of the trees.

'Juan has been bringing us food ever since we got here.' Joe spoke in a low, calm tone. This was too much for Dad. The lines on his forehead concertinaed. 'For us all. Not just Mum,' Joe added quickly. It was too late. I wanted to dive under the kitchen table to brace for the inevitable explosion. Dad didn't disappoint. He grabbed the jar of honey and threw it at Joe, except Joe ducked and it caught Mum on the side of her head before shattering against the wooden partition. The honey dripped down the wall onto the floor. I rushed over and wrapped myself around Mum.

'I hate you!' I screamed. Dad ignored me. Not even my hatred was worthy of his attention. Joe came over with a dingy cloth and wiped a trickle of blood from Mum's face.

'I'm sorry,' Joe whispered. 'I shouldn't have wound him up.'

'I'm fine. Honestly,' said Mum. 'It's just a shame about the honey. It might have helped Maudie.' The sound of Maudie crying came from the bedroom.

'I know how you rush to see him every day!' Dad shouted at Mum. 'I know how you try to get as close to each other as possible while you're looking at the hives.'

'Don't be ridiculous, Rick! We're head to toe in protective clothing.'

Mum stood her ground. Dad turned to me. I made

myself as still as possible by shallow breathing. I didn't even blink. He grabbed my wrist and stared into my face. His eyes flashed black and he was close enough that I could see his pupils were totally dilated. For a split second, I thought he was going to kill me. The most frightened animals always die first. I saw it all the time in the wild.

'Tomorrow is the day,' he pronounced. He'd moved on to something else. Juan and the honey were already ancient history.

'Do you know what I'm talking about, Cass?' I was struck dumb with fear. I managed to shake my head and he flew at me for being slow. He didn't get that it was the anxiety he created that caused my brain freeze. 'Crank that very slow brain of yours into action, Cass.' I waited for his usual flabby-body-flabby-brain comment, but it didn't come. 'Mo asked me to tell you that he's borrowed a truck to go to town early tomorrow morning and he wants you and River to meet him by the road at first light. I'm so proud that he chose you to go with him, Cass.' His eyes were watery with emotion.

'That's great, Dad,' I said nervously. And it was. Not only could I escape Dad's craziness, but I'd finally get to spend a whole day with Mo.

At first light I got up and crept out of the cabin. I was half-way through the vegetable field when I heard Mum's voice. I turned and saw her stumbling towards me with Maudie in her arms. I groaned. Was it too much to ask to have a day off from my family on this day of all days? Maudie was slumped across Mum's chest with her eyes closed, head lolling, her heavily bandaged arm banging into Mum's side like a giant club.

'You've got to persuade Mo to take her with you,' Mum panted, as she got closer. 'She needs to see a doctor. You understand that, don't you, Cass?'

It was true that Maudie had been sleeping a lot more the past week, but we all put this down to exhaustion after the excitement of the processing session.

'She's on the mend, Mum.' I stroked Maudie's sweat-soaked hair. 'She's definitely crying less.'

'Maybe it's because she's getting weaker.'

'Or because she's not in as much pain.' I tried to reassure her.

'You don't get it, Cass,' said Mum, fiercely. 'If someone has a third-degree burn, it can damage the nerve endings, so they don't feel anything. Maudie needs skin grafts. And antibiotics to help fight the infection. Touch her forehead. She's burning up.' I was impressed with her sudden knowledge of burns, but not surprised because Mum was one of those people who quietly knew everything rather than noisily knowing nothing.

I felt so sorry for her and Maudie, but I knew if I gave in to that feeling I would never go. It wasn't her desperation that was so upsetting, although it was awful to see her so worried. It was more her delusion that I could carry Maudie for two hours through the forest to meet Mo, persuade him to take her to hospital, no questions asked, when none of this had been approved by either him or the rest of the community. I glanced eastwards and saw the sun rise through the trees. 'Mum, I'm so sorry, there isn't enough time. I can't carry Maudie to the road because she's too heavy, and if I'm late Mo will go without me. The whole community is relying on me to help. I'll talk to Mo about Maudie. See what he can do to help us. How about that?'

'You don't understand!' She gently laid Maudie on the furrow of what might once have been a row of carrots and started to unwrap the bandage. *Dermis. Epidermis. Second degree. Third degree. Skin grafts. Streaks.* The words poured out of her mouth, like she'd become fluent in a new language. As she got closer to the wound, she became more frantic, especially when it became apparent that the bottom layers of the recently changed dressing were already stuck together with pus. She pressed a piece of paper into my hand. 'This is the address of the hospital. Go straight there.'

'How did you find this out?' I looked at the writing and recognized it as Joe's. 'This is crazy, Mum. I'm a minor and Maudie's eight. Even if we made it, which we wouldn't, the hospital would ask a whole lot of questions and get social services involved.'

'Tell the doctors I'll be there by the end of today.'

'How will you do that?' I pressed her.

'Joe will help. He understands.'

The implication was that I didn't. I tried not to let it bother me. Mum and Joe were tight before we came to the Haven. Now that Dad was losing the plot they were practically telepathic. But Mum had let slip that she viewed my judgement as more questionable. She saw me as one of those trees whose roots hadn't established properly, so they swayed wherever the breeze took them.

'Mum, I've got to go,' I pleaded.

She gently pulled off the final strip of Maudie's bandage.

'Look, Cass!'

To placate her, I bent down to examine the burn. I regretted it right away. Maudie's wrist was soaked with wet

263

pus and the wound glistened and gleamed as if it was alive. There was a horrible white, waxy area by her thumb, and a dark brown patch that turned purple as it crept up her wrist with a brown crust, like grilled cheese. And then there was the awful smell. It stank of rancid meat. I looked away and slapped my hand over my mouth to stop myself retching.

'Oh, my God, Maudie!' I cried.

'You see. It's badly infected. She needs antibiotics,' said Mum, firmly, as if my reaction proved her right and I would fall into line.

'Today is all about buying food supplies,' I panicked. 'It's what everyone agreed during processing. The most I can do is use my time with Mo to persuade him to take her another day. Maybe even tomorrow.'

'Another day might be too late . . .' Her voice trailed off in exhaustion.

For a split second I almost caved in. Mum was right about Maudie needing help. But her plan was flawed because if I didn't turn up Mo would simply leave without me.

'I'm sorry, Mum, there's nothing I can do right now. But I promise I'll speak to him.'

I'm ashamed to say that at this point I ran into the forest to meet River. It was only later it occurred to me that Maudie hadn't stirred once during this entire exchange.

Mo had instructed us to wait for him on the side of the road by the opening in the hedge. *Between hawthorn and hazel.* His directions were etched on my memory. But at this time of year, with the nettles at their most vigorous and the bracken and brambles having reached their late-summer peak, I would never have found my way from Old Big Belly to the road without River. They were almost as tall as us and covered any previous tracks. We picked our way through the undergrowth, elegantly lifting our legs like storks, edging forwards by degrees. After the stress of the previous evening, I felt as if I could finally breathe again.

When River found the opening in the hedge, I saw it was completely overgrown. 'Cover your face and go through backwards,' she instructed. We barrelled our way to the other side and found ourselves standing on a grass verge beside a tarmac road, staring at a signpost warning drivers that the speed limit was 30 m.p.h. It was the first time in more than two months that I'd left the forest and I stood in silence taking it all in. The road looked even rougher than when we'd first driven along it. There were deep potholes and a long strip of tall weeds running down the middle. We sat on the verge to catch our breath and wait for Mo, but after half an hour he still hadn't turned up.

'Maybe the truck has broken down. Or his friend refused to lend it to him.'

'Don't worry. He'll find a way. Mo won't let me down,' I said confidently. I smiled at River expectantly, waiting for her to grip my arm and beg for details, like I'd seen the girls at school do. Instead she got up and started picking blackberries.

'Make the most of them. They'll be gone in a month.'

'So will we,' I said mournfully.

'That's not what your dad's told us,' she replied.

I wanted to ask her more but Mo had pulled up beside us. I put my fingers in my ears to muffle the noise of the truck. My hearing was definitely more sensitive. I wasn't like the Vivian sisters, who could detect a baby little owl from a hundred metres, but I could make out sounds that Joe and Maudie couldn't hear, and the truck was an assault on my senses.

'I said you were one of us the day I met you,' Mo grinned, as he screeched to a halt and wound down the passenger window. He pointed to the seat in the middle and I scrambled in beside him. River slid in the other side. She stared in wonder at the dashboard and asked Mo to explain all the dials.

'I can't remember the last time I went in a ve-hi-cle.' She said 'vehicle' as if it was three different words, which made me laugh. Looking to impress River, I turned on the radio and tuned in to Radio 1. I couldn't think of a single situation over the past two months where my knowledge had exceeded hers and it felt good to be the one in control for a change. One of my favourite Tame Impala tracks was playing. I sang along. It was as if everything was conspiring to make the day perfect. My anxiety over Maudie diminished in direct proportion to the growing euphoria I felt to be hanging out with Mo and River. I began to wish that the rest of my life could be this journey and that the three of us could live like this for ever, away from all the stress of my family. I imagined us heading to France, Spain, catching the ferry to Morocco, and driving through Africa, further and further away from Dad.

'I'm going to miss you guys so much when we leave,' I said wistfully.

'Well, don't go,' said River.

'We need to get back to school,' I said.

'Why?' asked Mo. 'What could you possibly learn at school that's more useful than what you learn here?'

'The answer to everything you need to know is in the forest,' said River. 'Everything you need is here.'

Mo drove recklessly fast along the narrow mountain road, rollercoasting us from side to side as he navigated the vertiginous bends. I found it exhilarating but River got car sick and had to hang her head out of the passenger window, like a dog. This worked out fine for me because my legs were pushed right up against the gear stick and she was so busy focusing on not throwing up that she couldn't see how Mo's hand lingered between my thighs whenever he crunched up and down the gears. He was into me again. Nothing else mattered. As we started to go down into the village at the bottom of the valley, I noticed how the river level had dropped since our journey here and the fields and hedgerows had turned from yellow to brown.

'Drought,' observed Mo. 'Every year it's worse.'

Closer to town, the effects of the heat became more dramatic. The road straightened and as we got lower the terrain became flatter and there were fewer trees. We passed a smouldering field that had burnt in a wildfire and hedges with sun-scorched brown leaves.

'Makes your dad's field look almost healthy,' observed Mo.

'It's a shame no one knew about the voles,' I said. I didn't like the way people had only started referring to it as Dad's field after everything had gone wrong. There were more voles than ever in the field. They were quite sweet with their tiny round faces and little ears. But the rotting vegetables attracted less appealing scavengers, like the rats and mice that had started to find their way into our cabin. Last night a rat had even jumped out of the composting toilet.

'They first appeared back in March,' said Mo. 'It's amazing the way they breed.'

'You knew about the voles back then?' I asked in confusion. I worked out this must have been around the time he'd come to Maudie's party.

'Yeah,' said Mo, noncommittally.

'Then why didn't you warn Dad?'

He glanced at River to make sure she was asleep. 'Because then we wouldn't be going on this trip to town together, sweetheart, and Aida would still be in charge!' He laughed and planted a quick kiss on my bare shoulder. 'It's like the badgers. You have to get rid of the old boar to become head of the clan for the sake of the youngest.' I couldn't relish his kiss because I was trying to process what he'd just said. He'd used Dad to get rid of Aida. I shivered even as the temperature gauge hit thirty. I thought of Dad's angst over the field and all the fights caused by his stress. I knew in my head it wasn't right, but I didn't want to argue with him in case he went cold on me again.

River lifted her head from the edge of the passenger window and declared she no longer felt sick. Outside it got hotter as the hills turned into plains. I tried to turn on the aircon but it didn't work: 34 degrees, read the temperature on the dashboard.

'How does the car know that?' asked River. I laughed.

'What else does it know?'

'It knows that you are the hottest thing to have graced the passenger seat,' teased Mo. River glared at him, and I glared at her, consumed with an unexpected violent jealousy. My emotions were off the scale.

'Play nice,' Mo teased.

He turned off the main road and we soon found

ourselves negotiating a roundabout on the outskirts of a small town.

'You don't drive like someone who's spent most of their life in a forest,' I said.

'That's because I haven't spent most of my life in a forest.'

'Where were you before you came here?' I asked.

'Travelling.'

'In Colombia?' I said, remembering the conversation he'd had with Dad at Maudie's party.

'God, no! Asia mainly. I've never been to Latin America.'

We passed a police station and then the hospital. I felt a pang of guilt that I still hadn't raised the issue of Maudie with Mo. The high street that cut the town in half was the usual mix of boarded-up windows, betting outlets, pound shops and piri piri chicken joints. The only real action took place on a large industrial estate on the other side of town where we found the huge supermarket, a DIY store and a chemist. The more urban the landscape became, the more River shrank into her seat.

'Will you show me how to buy things, Cass?' she asked timidly.

'Buying something is easy, River. Planting and growing it yourself is way more difficult and much more impressive. Don't get seduced by stuff.' I put my arm around her shoulders. 'The way you live is so cool.'

Mo pulled up in the supermarket car park and reversed into a space. As we climbed out of the truck, I saw people nudge each other and quickly look away. I tried to see us as they saw us. The fact that all our clothes were washed together in the copper rich water from the river meant that they'd all turned the same sludgy beige. Our hair was wild.

Mo's was in dreadlocks and River's tangled black mane hung down as far as her buttocks. Mine was kind of greasy, even though I'd washed it that morning, because I'd finally run out of shampoo and was trying out River's raw honey and rosemary concoction. Then there were the tattoos that ran up and down River and Mo's upper arms. We didn't look strange to each other, but we stood out against the bland sameness of the other shoppers.

I found a trolley and pushed it towards the door of the supermarket. River was glued to my side. She was utterly out of her comfort zone and twitchy about everything from the squeaky wheels of the shopping trolleys to the automatic doors that slid open to let us in. Even I felt overwhelmed. There was too much noise, too much dust, too much concrete, too little nature, and way too many gaudy colours. It was at this point that Mo announced he was leaving us to it and would pick us up in a couple of hours.

'What do you mean?' I asked, taken aback. I'd imagined us walking round the supermarket hand in hand, choosing food like a regular couple. 'Where are you going?'

'We have multifarious tasks,' he said, with a wink.

'You can't abandon us here!'

'You look just like your dad when you're angry,' he teased. 'Stick to the lists and make sure you don't miss anything.' He pulled a scrappy pile of shopping lists from his pocket and a wad of twenty-pound notes tied with an elastic band, pressing them into my hand.

'Did you make all that money at the festival?' I gasped.

'Let's just say someone owed me.' Then he walked back to the truck, jangling the keys in his hand.

River and I had no choice but to go ahead on our own.

I ground to a halt just inside the door, momentarily dazzled by the combination of very bright lights and the endless rows of products. River did a slow pirouette, struggling to take it all in.

'What do you think?' I asked.

'It's a vision of Hell,' she said.

Mo had given me about twenty lists. Everyone was allowed to request ten items. The only people who hadn't got involved were Aida, Joe and Mum, although on the same piece of paper with the address of the hospital Mum had written 'GET SULFADIAZINE.' Flicking through the lists, I saw there were at least four or five products that everyone wanted – toothpaste, condoms, tinned tomatoes, matches and rice – and that my time in the truck would have been better spent compiling one long list. The novelty of discovering that One Way Will wanted nail varnish and remover, alongside his ten kilos of rice, and that Piper had requested a pink tangle-tease hairbrush like Mum's wore off pretty quickly. Mo's list was all the things I guessed the community needed for Samhain, like rum, candles and paraffin. I felt reassured that he was always thinking of ways to make things better for other people.

The layout of the supermarket was unfamiliar, so it took a long time to locate anything. Plus River was no help whatsoever. If I asked her to find cooking oil, she just stared at the shelves in confused silence, overwhelmed by the choice. Olive, sunflower, coconut or rapeseed? One, two or five litres? Spanish, Italian or Greek? She carefully read every label from beginning to end. I could see people staring at her, but she was oblivious.

'What happens to all the plastic?' she asked fearfully. 'Don't they realize?'

271

'They realize but they don't care. They're only really interested in making money.'

'Aida is right. We're selling our souls by shopping here.' River sounded despondent.

She asked endless questions. Does everyone have to walk round in the same direction? Is there a limit to what you can buy? Why does the fruit look so perfect? What is a sell-by date? When I explained that any damaged or out-of-date fruit and vegetables were thrown away, she fell into another slump. 'Truly we are a species in decline,' she said. She stared at the onions and found it upsetting that it didn't say how long it took each one to grow. An hour later, we were still only a quarter of the way around the shop, and I hadn't completed anyone's list.

Just when I thought it couldn't get worse, we turned our trolleys into the meat aisle.

'This is a place of death!' she cried in horror. Several people, including a couple of shop assistants, shot us disapproving stares. River walked slowly taking in the different sections and subsections, touching packets of chicken drumsticks, flaccid sausages, worms of mincemeat and bloody steaks. The whole aisle must have been about thirty metres long. For a while we walked in silence. Then I heard her start to mutter.

'Why does the meat have a different name from the animal apart from chickens?'

'So people don't think about what they're eating. People think chickens are stupid so they're less bothered about them.'

'How can they think that?' she asked.

'Because they've never hung out with chickens.'

My entire view on chickens had changed since I'd lived

at the Haven. They all had their own personality. Some were chatty. Some let you pick them up. Some were nervous. I loved the way they created dust baths in the soil to suffocate mites and fleas in their feathers, and their raw crow of pride whenever they laid an egg.

'Where do all these dead chickens come from?' asked River.

'Thousands and thousands of them have lived in sheds where they never saw the light of day. Most of them only live for thirty days. They're bred to grow quicker, and by the end of their life they're so heavy they can't move so they sit in their own shit and get sores on their legs. The egg-laying hens have it worse because they live longer. Their beaks are clipped because they get so stressed they turn on each other.'

A woman beside us picked up a packet of chicken thighs.

'Why do you not raise and kill your own animals?' River asked her politely. She quickly wheeled away. We continued down the aisle, past endless packets of bacon and pork chops.

'Who kills these animals?' asked River.

'They take them to places called abattoirs. The sheep, calves and pigs get funnelled into cages where they're either electrocuted or stunned with a gun, although sometimes it doesn't work. Some religions don't believe in stunning them, so they slit their throats and bleed them while they're conscious.'

River looked as if she was about to cry. 'It's so cruel and wasteful.'

'Better to be a dead animal than a live one.' I started to tell her how the soya to feed them was imported from countries that cut down rainforests to satisfy our appetite for chicken, and how some people who worked in slaughterhouses suffered from PTSD, but she looked so depressed that I took pity. Human beings can only cope with so much reality.

It took a good couple of hours to get everything on the lists and we spent ages in the check-out queue. To the amusement of the check-out guy, who was trying to flirt with River, we packed everything into huge hessian sacks that Mo had found in the root cellar, then manoeuvred our ridiculously overladen trolleys into the car park. I glanced around hoping Mo had reappeared but there was no sign of either him or the truck.

Outside it was unbearably hot. I squinted up at the sun shimmering overhead and guessed it was about two in the afternoon. I looked for a tree or a bush to sit under but there was concrete as far as the eye could see. Nothing that would create shade or breeze. So, we decided to take advantage of the aircon inside the chemist. River asked me for money.

'I want to buy something without your help,' she said.

The clinical interior of the chemist with its steel counters, pristine white shelves, and shop assistants dressed in white coats made us stand out even more. The woman behind the counter tracked us with narrowed eyes.

'Oh, wow!' River had spotted the nail-varnish section and seen the rows of false nails painted in different colours. 'Look at that, Cass!'

She touched each colour reverentially with the tip of her index finger as if they were precious stones.

'You can try them out,' I explained, showing her the testers.

'I'm going to use a different one on each nail,' she said, lining up potential colours into neat rows.

I headed to the medicines shelf and packed my basket with any products I thought might help Maudie: antiseptic, sterile wound dressings, bandages, aloe vera and saline. I couldn't find the sulfadiazine Mum had requested although I did come across some vitamin E cream for the scarring on Joe's shoulder. The fact that the day hadn't evolved into a date with Mo in the way I'd imagined meant I still hadn't tackled him about helping Maudie.

At some point I went back to find River, but she'd disappeared. I finally located her at the prescriptions counter, talking earnestly to a female pharmacist. I guessed she was discussing nail varnish.

'How old are you?' the woman asked. Stranger and stranger. Her tone was kind, but River still rocked nervously from one foot to the other.

'Sixteen.'

'You look much younger. Do you want me to give you the number of someone you can speak to in confidence?'

'I just need to know how to use it,' River said impatiently.

'The instructions are inside but basically you pee on the stick.'

I approached the pharmacist with a fixed smile. This is my best friend, I wanted to tell her, and I know she's unworldly but if you mess with her you mess with me.

'Is there some problem?' I asked, in my most confident tone. River turned round. She tried to hide the package, but I could see right away that it was a pregnancy test. My basket clattered to the floor.

'Maybe you could help your friend,' suggested the pharmacist, swiftly directing us towards a toilet. She'd done her bit and was happy for someone else to take over.

'Sure,' I said, trying to disguise my shock.

We headed back outside and wheeled our trolleys to a toilet in the car park. I locked the door behind us and leant against it. River stared into the toilet bowl with her back to me.

'I can't believe how outsiders shit on clean water,' she commented. She was doing that thing where she tried to avoid dealing with something by changing the subject.

'I can't believe my best friend is worried she's pregnant and doesn't tell me!' I shot back, unable to hide the hurt in my tone.

'I'm sorry, Cass. Please. I need your help. I'm not even sure if that's what's wrong with me. I've been feeling really sick. And tired.'

She carefully undid the pregnancy test, pulled down her pants and squatted over the toilet bowl to pee on the dipstick. She was completely unselfconscious about my presence.

'Am I doing it right? Am I doing it right?' she kept asking.

'I don't know. I've never done a pregnancy test,' I replied sulkily. I re-read the instructions and explained that if a blue line appeared she was pregnant, and if the window stayed clear, it was fine.

'If you're pregnant, who is the father?' I had a good idea of the answer to that question, but I wanted to hear her say it.

She wouldn't look me in the eye. 'Joe said I should do the pregnancy test.'

Fucking idiot. I angrily slammed down the toilet seat and sat on it holding the dipstick with River beside me. In the minute it took for the two thin blue lines to appear in the little windows, I thought how, yet again, I'd been overtaken on the life-experience front by a friend. Even River, who'd spent her entire life in a forest, had somehow managed to live more of life than me. It was a fleeting feeling replaced swiftly by relief that I wasn't the one who was pregnant. River glanced at me for confirmation. I nodded and she covered her face in despair.

For a few seconds I had a romantic image of being an aunt, buying cute little clothes, becoming a key influence in the life of the baby. This vision was immediately displaced by the certainty that River was way too young to have a baby, that the forest was no place to give birth, and the concept of Joe becoming a dad was ludicrous. And there had to be consensus before a couple even got together at the Haven, let alone had a baby. I remembered her Worst Death Ever and realized she must have suspected back then.

'Not a word to your brother. I don't want Joe to know,' she said, in a muffled tone.

'I swear not to say anything.'

'I don't want this. What do I do, Cass? What do I do to get rid of it?'

I hugged her. 'You can have an abortion,' I suggested. I tried to do the calculation in my head. 'You can't be more than about eight weeks pregnant. Joe's only been here since July.'

'How do I do that?' She sounded desperate.

I had no idea, but I didn't want to freak her out even more by exposing my ignorance. 'There's a solution to every problem.'

'Thank you, Cass. I don't know what I'd do without you. You're a true friend.' Her voice caught and she gave a sad smile.

'To every problem there's a solution!' I said, not really believing my own propaganda.

'Why don't we get a bus out of here?' she said unexpectedly. 'Go somewhere else.'

'Like where?'

'Your aunt Cara's house? Maybe she could help me. Joe says she's a good person.'

'She is,' I affirmed, my voice stiff with resentment that the texture of River's relationship with Joe was so much richer than mine.

'I can't have a baby in the forest.' She started sobbing. 'I can't. Remember what that grower, Em, told us. They won't let me go to a hospital if something goes wrong. Look how they've dealt with Maudie.' She was inconsolable. And she was right.

We went to the bus stop at the entrance of the car park and waited all of ten minutes before Mo pulled up in the truck. 'I've been looking for you two everywhere,' he said, getting out to open the tailgate. He heaved the hessian sacks from the shopping trolleys into the boot. Back and forth. The bus arrived and the driver opened his doors beside us.

River leant towards me. 'Go, Cass,' she whispered. 'Leave while you can. Before bad things happen.'

'I'm not leaving you,' I whispered back.

'Not a word to anyone. You've got to promise.'

'I promise.'

'If anyone finds out I'm dead.'

The journey home took way longer. The truck struggled with the weight of our supplies. As well as our shopping, Mo had bought bags of phosphate, netting, stakes and shears, four large bottles of propane gas, new spades in different sizes, saws and dozens of boxes of nails and screws. The final hour or so of the journey was almost entirely uphill in the late-afternoon heat, and steam hissed out of the bonnet as the truck overheated. We had to stop several times to refill the radiator with cold water.

I badly wanted to talk more with River but there was no opportunity. She fell asleep with her head on my lap for most of the journey and I slung a protective arm over her. I couldn't help glancing at her stomach and trying to remember the page in my biology textbook that showed a foetus at different stages. I reckoned the baby was probably the size of a pinto bean and wondered how a pinto bean could make you feel so ill. I tried to work out exactly when she and Joe had started having sex, then felt angry with him all over again. Couldn't he have shown some self-control for once, especially since River was two years younger than him? The fact that she didn't even want him to know was a total stain on his character.

I didn't feel old or wise enough to be dealing with a situation like this and was furious with my brother for his careless selfishness. It would have been bad enough if Eadie or Dana had got pregnant but at least on the outside you could get help. Now I was left clearing up his shit. And, although it was ridiculous, I felt left out and a bit stupid. I couldn't believe that neither of them had told me they were involved.

One thing was obvious. The pinto bean had to go. We would have to come back into town as soon as possible so she could get it sorted. While I was flattered that River had confided in me, I felt weighed down with the burden of such a heavy secret. Plus a deadline loomed: as far as I knew, my family was meant to be leaving after Samhain.

'What's up with you, Cass?' asked Mo. 'You look like you've got the weight of the world on your shoulders.'

'I'm tired,' I said quickly.

'I'm sorry we didn't get to spend much time together.'

'That's fine. Really. It was nice being with River. Where did you go?'

'Hardware shop. How about I teach you to change gear?'

'Cool!' Mo was the only person capable of nudging me out of my funk. He put on the music at full volume and got me to place my hand on the gear stick. He covered it with his, and we crunched up and down through the gears until I could find each one with my eyes closed.

'You're good with your hands, Cass,' he said. I blushed and he laughed. His hand tightened over mine on the gear stick. 'Do you want to come back to my cabin tonight? Or are you going to blow me out again?'

'Sure,' I said, trying to curb my inner Labrador. It was that easy.

River didn't wake up until we reached the hole in the hedge. Mo manoeuvred the truck up onto the verge and we ground to a strained halt. She put her hand across her stomach.

'Almost home,' I said.

We left the truck by the side of the road and made our way back through the forest to the Spirit House, where we were given a hero's welcome. River went straight to her cabin to sleep while Piper, Sylvie, One Way Will and the Danes led Gaia back to the road to collect the supplies from the truck. Mum and Dad weren't there, which was a big relief, because it made it all the easier to slip away with Mo for the night.

23

Now

I can't sleep. I'm lying across the passenger seat but because the van is tilted on its side I keep sliding towards the window. Whenever I close my eyes, the noises start up outside. There's a snuffling sound at the rear door; a branch snaps by my window; and at one point I imagine I hear the door handle crank into action. Everything has an edge to it. In the end I take Mo's knife out of my backpack and hold it against my stomach. I'll search for the key again when it's light and I can see properly.

When eventually it falls quiet, I ease open the door and see footprints in the snow leading away from the van. Totally wired, I slam it shut and lock it again. I keep the torch on a low beam for comfort and it spotlights the dolls that lie scattered around me. I pick up the one that looks like Maudie, examine its hair and realize that not only is it the same auburn colour but it also looks like real human hair.

The attention to detail, the specks of brown freckles across the doll's nose and cheeks, the perfectly drawn big brown Maudie eyes and the careful stitching on the dress point to someone who knows her well. The doll looks so like my little sister that I find myself pathetically hugging it to me.

I lift the skirt of the dress. It feels peculiarly intimate doing this, like I'm violating her privacy. A red thread is knotted multiple times through the hole. I compare it with the doll that looks like River. There's no red thread. I examine all the other dolls lined up on the table. Five have a red thread looped through the hole. Four have a hole without thread, but the area around the hole is stained red. It's truly mystifying.

I decide there's nothing to be gained by waiting until first light to look for the key so I can charge the phone. I put myself in Joe's head and search around the van, trying to work out where he might have hidden it. I recall the chaos of his old bedroom and how no part of the floor had been visible for years. Then I remember with a jolt how Joe's bedroom now belongs to someone else because Dad has sold the house. And then it occurs to me that, maybe right from the start, Dad never intended to go home. Or, rather, maybe Mo never intended Dad to go home.

I rummage through the obvious places: the glove compartment, behind the sun visors, the side pockets of the doors. I find spiders, woodlice, earwigs, but no key. I clamber back into the middle of the van and sprawl on the floor in the footwell to sweep under the seat with my arm. It's filthy and the dust makes me cough. There are some useful finds: a pen, a notebook and a damp but clean pair of socks. There's also a small cloth bag sewn from the same hand-spun wool used by people at the Haven to make clothes. Inside are small scraps of material, including a remnant from my denim dress, different-coloured cotton reels, and a ball of red wool.

I climb into the rear of the van and find a couple of bags containing Maudie's stuffed animals. I prod and poke them in case Joe has hidden the key inside one. In the gully by the rear doors, I come across five distracting prickly balls of hedgehog. The smallest is curled up inside one of Joe's old trainers. I touch the hoglet and its spines ripple in response. I lift it out onto the palm of my hand. Its eyes are tight shut, and its face is scrunched up like an old man's. 'Hey, little fella,' I whisper. When I tip it back into its winter quarters, I tilt the trainer and the key to the van falls out, alongside an adapter for the USB port and the charging cable. *Great work, Cass!* Trainers were always Joe's favoured hiding place for storing weed. He might be a slob but at least he's a predictable slob. And then, hot on the heels of this discovery, another triumph. When I climb back into the front of the van and turn the key in the ignition, the faithful Rory coughs and splutters into life without any argument. I pop in the adapter and wait for the phone to charge.

I distractedly smooth out the paper that Joe had used to wrap the phone, and suddenly notice the text is all in Spanish. I remember the Spanish magazine in Mo's tree-house with the pages torn out from the middle and realize it's no accident that Joe used this paper to wrap the phone: he wants me to read it.

The text and colours have faded along the folds. At the top the date says 11 de julio 2014. I read the words aloud, hoping that by hearing them I might understand. I've learnt some Spanish at school and picked up a little from Juan but not enough to help me fully decipher the content of this article. One word pops up repeatedly during my skim-read. *Cazalla. Cazalla. Cazalla.* The name sounds familiar. It takes me a few moments to remember where I've heard it before. And then it comes to me: it's the name of a commune in Spain that someone once mentioned.

There are several colour photos, mostly with captions I can't translate. One shows the interior of a small cabin.

Another, members of the community swimming naked in a lake. The biggest photo is of a group of men, women and children smiling at the camera as they lean in to each other. *La comunidad de Cazalla*. Everyone is baked brown by the sun. Some are holding tools like hoes and spades. A woman has her arm around a sturdy cow who gazes moonily at the camera. There's a list of names underneath. I skim-read across and one leaps out at me right away: Morden Spilid. I hold the piece of paper close to my face almost fearfully, fully expecting to see a younger version of Mo smiling back at me because, according to my calculations, he should have been around twenty-three in 2014. But while the man in the picture fits the correct age profile, there's nothing about him that resembles Mo. He's tall, with blond hair, round glasses and a soft-featured face. He has a shitload of tattoos across his shoulder and down his left arm.

I iron out the next page and see a photo that is instantly recognizable. I grab Joe's phone to double-check. It's identical, except it's much clearer than the photo on the phone, so the pool of blood is obvious, as is the fact that the poor guy's stomach had been slit from one end to the other. *La Policía Busca al Asesino de Morden Spilid, de nacionalidad Danes*. I don't need fluent Spanish to understand this. The person in the photo is Morden Spilid, a Danish man, and the Spanish police are looking for his killer. Beside this is a photo of his parents, entwined in grief like the conjoined tree outside Aida's container. There's a small picture of a knife. *Posible arma homicida* reads the caption. Possible murder weapon. It's a hunting knife or, rather, a specialized knife for gralloching deer and it looks exactly like the one on the seat beside me.

A queasy feeling starts in my throat, travels down into my stomach and I throw up.

24

Then

Mo's tree-house stood so high that it was invisible from the ground. The only giveaway was the rope ladder he unclipped from the trunk of one of the firs and shimmied up to disappear into the evergreen canopy above.

'Come on!' he called down. 'It's Heaven on earth up here!' I hesitated for a split second, thinking that this moment embodied everything I'd hoped for since we'd first met at Maudie's party, yet still put me totally on edge. Attempting to herd my feelings into something consistent, I nudged slowly upwards, almost hoping that someone nosy, like Sylvie, would stroll past and ask what on earth I was doing. Except we were in the most remote part of the forest halfway up Blood Mountain. Sensing my hesitation, Mo waited for me on the platform he'd built at head height under the main cabin. At one end there were six plastic containers, neatly stacked on top of each other, all labelled in Mo's sloping handwriting. *Tins. Vegetables. Medicine. Tools.* At the other, there was a row of five-litre containers of water. An empty bucket sat on top of one.

'For the ladies. In case you don't want to pee over the edge.' Mo grinned when he saw me staring at it.

He pointed at a wooden ladder that led up to the little cabin and offered to steady it while I went ahead. He radiated confidence, and his certainty gave me certainty. This was meant to be. But I was making the same mistake I always made with boys, looking to them to reflect back to me how I should feel, rather than knowing how I felt. Bad Labrador! I pushed away the thought by shoving open the hatch, and when I poked my head through and breathed in Mo's undiluted musty animal scent, I felt as if I was entering his world. It was a cosy, beautiful space, built entirely of wood, with windows that looked out over the forest, so it was light and airy rather than dank and dark like our cabin.

Mo gave me a jokey micro tour: cooking zone on the right, sleeping area on the left, shelving in between. Everything had been meticulously designed in miniature to fit the tiny space, from the small kitchen table to the wooden stools at each end. It was impeccably tidy. I studiously avoided looking at the mattress on the floor.

He brewed us tea and carefully put away the supplies he'd bought in town. I chirped nervously like the robin outside our bedroom window. I told him how Dad was jealous of Juan and waited for him to laugh but he didn't. As I talked, he removed his clothes, carefully folding each item, until he was naked apart from his underpants. I tried to remember what pants I was wearing, praying they weren't a pair of Mum's that I'd filched from the underwear pile or, even worse, my brother's. He ambled languidly over to the mattress, which consisted of layers of striped blankets on top of a couple of pallets and lay on his back with his hands behind his head, watching me.

I stood completely still, staring at him, reminding myself to relish each moment. I gazed at his body, taking in its raw muscularity and sinewy detailing. I couldn't take my eyes off his broad shoulders and the way his entire body was tanned the same deep colour, like he'd been dip-dyed in treacle, so the tattoos that covered his left arm and shoulders were faded like ancient hieroglyphs. There was a distracting narrow trail of hair that led from his belly button inside his underpants.

'So here we are, Cassia.'

'So here we are, Mo.'

He patted the space beside him on the bed. 'Are you nervous?'

I nodded, feeling grateful that I was with someone who could read my mood and accept me in my entirety.

'Embrace that feeling of fear,' he said, stretching his arm towards me. I took his hand, noticing a thin fuzz of hair across his knuckles for the first time, and lay down beside him. I stared at the ceiling, hyper-aware of my shallow breaths, the rise and fall of my ribcage, the weight of my eyelids each time I blinked. I wondered if this was sexual tension. Except I didn't feel sexual. Just tense. *Don't act weird*, I kept telling myself. *Be normal.* I felt the laser glare of his gaze as he shifted towards me and to relax myself counted the tines on an enormous set of deer antlers that hung on the wall opposite me. Eleven in all.

'Tell me what you're thinking,' Mo breathed heavily in my ear.

'Did you learn to use a gun when you were in the army?' I asked.

'What kind of army would let me into its ranks?' Mo laughed. 'Can you imagine me taking orders from anyone?'

I frowned. This wasn't what he'd told me at Maudie's party.

'Is Dad a better tracker than me?' This was a good diversion. Tracking was Mo's specialist subject.

'Nope.' He laughed again. 'Do you remember? I said

you were one of us, Cassia. That first time I set eyes on you I could tell.'

'How?' I asked, flattered that he remembered so much of our first encounter.

'Your energy and strength set you apart from the rest.' He was a good liar. I'll give him that.

'Look at me, Cassia,' he urged, touching my painfully sore sunburnt shoulder. I tried not to wince in case I sent out the wrong message and rolled onto my side to face him. We lay there contemplating each other without touching. It was a charged moment.

'Do you know what we're doing here, Cassia?' Mo stared at me intently with his luminous green eyes. When I couldn't give a coherent response, he answered his question for me.

'We're creating the future.' I thought of the pinto bean growing in River's stomach. 'Making the dreams of tomorrow.' Everything he said sounded incredibly meaningful. He got up and closed the window. Outside the light was fading. I imagined Mum's worry when I didn't come home before dark but there was no time for guilt because Mo pressed himself against me and began stroking my face and neck. I could feel his dick twitching against my thighs and his breath hot against my shoulder. I waited hopefully for some physical explosion that would neutralize all the thoughts jostling for supremacy inside my head, but all I could think about was what would happen next.

His hand hovered close to my right breast and started playing with my nipple. I hoped his passion might be infectious but instead my entire body went rigid as if I was at the dentist. I'd done some stuff before with boys but nothing with this kind of ambition.

I wanted to appear as if I knew what was going on but how could I when I had so little experience with boys my own age, let alone someone fourteen years older than me? The gap between us felt as wide and unknowable as the lake on the misty mornings when you couldn't see to the other side. My head fizzed as it dawned on me that I was out of my depth. I felt simultaneously too young and too old, too pretty and too ugly, too happy and too unhappy. This confusion sowed further head-fuckery. There was the confusion of wanting to believe but not believing, of wanting to enjoy, but not enjoying. Outside the birds struck up the call to head home for the night. I wondered if I could tell Mo that this was enough for the moment. That I wanted to break the sexual act down into its component parts and stage two was something that really needed to be scheduled for a later date.

'Don't we need to call a processing meeting to tell people we want to start a relationship?' I asked.

'No, because it started outside the Haven,' he said tersely.

'But isn't it part of our commitment to open-hearted communication in the community?'

'What do you want?' Mo couldn't hide his impatience. It was a good question. *I just want someone who sees me*, I didn't tell him. My need was pathetically simple. Simply pathetic.

'How old are you, Cassia?' he asked, tilting my chin towards him.

'Sixteen,' I said.

He smiled. 'You're going to enjoy this.' I hoped he was right.

He leant over and kissed me. I closed my eyes and tried to abandon myself to the moment. I wanted to be turned to liquid. But I had this hyper-awareness of where the hand that wasn't pressing into my back was roaming. His tongue stopped probing my mouth and he disentangled himself. A wave of relief swept over me as space opened up between us again. Except he was only leaning back to pull down his underpants. I gasped in shock. I'd never seen a real-life fully erect penis. He looked at me with lustful intent and urged my hand towards the one-eyed snake. I tried to unfurl my hand from his, but he wouldn't let go.

'I think it's time for me to get home,' I stammered.

'I don't think that's what you want at all,' he said throatily.

He kissed me more roughly, his tongue probing my mouth. His hand returned to my nipple, which he twisted as if he was trying to get the lid off a stubborn bottle. When he pulled away again, he put his hand at the back of my head, slowly increasing the pressure until it was clear to me that he was pushing my head towards his groin. There was a sort of stand-off. If it was a battle of wills I would have won, but it was an unfair fight based on who was physically stronger. I began to get properly scared. No means no.

'I'm not into this,' I said. His breath quickened and I realized my resistance turned him on even more. No one had mentioned that possibility in the consent lessons in PSHE. I tried to yell but the words got tangled in my throat. It was pointless. No one would hear. And if by some miracle anyone came to my rescue, they'd blame me for getting into this situation in the first place. They might not say it, but they'd think it. And, strange as it might sound, I felt some sense of obligation too, as if I was failing to keep my side of the bargain. 'I'm sorry,' I heard myself say. 'I've made a mistake.' I sounded so terrified and helpless that I hardly recognized my own voice. Mo ignored me, grabbed my hair and twisted it round his fist tighter and tighter until my scalp burnt. All the time he was doing this, he stared at me with a strange half-smile. Then he pushed my head towards his groin.

He forced his dick so deep into my mouth that I choked. I even gagged a couple of times. But not even the threat of me throwing up over him was enough to make him stop. My mouth felt as if it was being ripped open at the sides as he pushed deeper. There was a lot of use of imperatives. Suck. Lick. Swallow. But really it was just about him manipulating my body for his pleasure, until I no longer felt human. I focused on breathing through my nose to prevent myself from suffocating. That was the first moment where I thought I might die.

And then I felt his hands tightening around my neck. He started to squeeze. The breathing through my nostrils slowed and my thoughts drifted away. At one point it seemed I'd left my body and was observing myself from above. Everything went red and I remembered thinking that I never thought death would be red. And then the red turned to black until the sour taste of his sperm filled my mouth. Suddenly it was over. He flipped onto his back as if he didn't realize or care that I felt I'd been through a near-death experience. It was a few minutes before I could move.

'We're going to make a whole new tribe out here,' said Mo. He offered me water. I couldn't understand why I was shivering when it was so hot. I swirled the water round my gums like mouthwash and spat it onto the floor to get rid of the taste of him. My mouth was bleeding. I tried to get up from the bed but each time I collapsed back onto the mattress. All I wanted was to get out of that place, but my body wouldn't cooperate. He'd pulled up the rope ladder and locked the trapdoor. He lay down beside me, smoked a joint, and quickly fell asleep. I had no choice but to stay until first light. I didn't cry that night. I was too overwhelmed by my own sense of powerlessness and too afraid that if I made any noise he would wake up and make me do the same thing again, and that this time I might not make it through.

The night I spent at Mo's tree-house marked the beginning and the end of something. When I came round the next morning, I touched my neck. It felt bruised and sore. I sat up, pulled my knees to my chest, and looked out of the window, feeling sadder than I could ever remember. There was no romance. There was no relationship. I bit my lip to stop myself crying.

The red kite, whose photo Mo had shared all those months ago, was eyeing me from her nest, so close I could almost put my hand out and touch her. How could I have got it so wrong? Why didn't I listen to the inner voice that told me not to go up to his tree-house last night? She tucked her head under her wing, and I wished I could do the same, but Mo had woken up and was grinning at me as if nothing bad had happened. I understood three things simultaneously: he would want me to do the same thing all over again; I didn't want to; and he wouldn't care.

'Come here, gorgeous creature.' He pulled me towards him.

'Sorry. I'm not really into this.' I felt furious with myself for apologizing. His face tightened. He put the palm of his hand over my right cheek, just the wrong side of gentle.

'Play nice, Cassia,' he said tautly. It was the same phrase he'd used in the truck.

'I don't think this is how it's meant to be,' I said, trying to sound braver than I felt.

'You know you want it,' he said, increasing the pressure on the side of my face in an attempt to direct me towards his groin.

'I really don't,' I said more fiercely, struggling to escape his grip. His hands moved to the front of my neck and squeezed my windpipe. He increased the pressure. I started choking.

'Come on, Cassia, don't be such a tease.' Then suddenly he was on top of me, pinning me down on the mattress. 'You want this as much as me.'

'There's something you need to know!' I yelled. It was a split-second decision. Not thought through at all.

'Tell me later,' he said breathlessly.

'It's really important!'

'Don't mess with me, Cassia.' I felt him slightly release his grip, enough that my arms were free. I held out for a few seconds, to win time.

'You mustn't tell anyone.' I didn't expect him to keep my secret. I just knew instinctively that this would give it more currency. 'Even during processing.'

'Go on.'

'It's about River.'

'What about her?'

'She's in big trouble.'

'What kind of trouble?'

I paused. 'She's pregnant.'

He finally rolled off me. I quickly stood up and caught sight of myself in a small mirror hanging on a nail. My face was flushed. There were angry red fingerprints either side of my neck and a small purple bruise on the right above my lips. I pulled my hair around me like curtains to hide the marks.

His face betrayed nothing. I kept talking, fleshing out the details to win me time. I explained about buying the pregnancy test in the chemist, going to the toilet together and how River didn't want the baby and Joe had advised her to go to my aunt's house.

He sat up and leant against the wall. I took my time to embellish the details, knowing that every second the focus swung away from me and onto River, my situation became a little less dangerous.

'We need you to drive her back to town. For an abortion. Or somewhere where she can get to my aunt. Will you help?'

Something shifted.

'Sure,' he said, getting up to head towards the stove to boil water for tea. 'We'll work it out. Don't worry.'

The guilt of revealing River's secret was eased by the fact that as well as saving myself I'd also come up with a potential solution to her problem. She couldn't be too angry with me if I'd sorted her a lift back to town.

'Do you know who the father is?' Mo asked almost casually.

I couldn't see his expression because his back was turned to me. 'My brother. They've been having a thing since we arrived.' The words tumbled out.

'Well, isn't he the man,' he growled.

Mo's repressed anger was somehow even scarier than Dad's volcanic eruptions because it was more difficult to read. He began to get dressed. Waves of relief washed over me. The moment of immediate danger had passed. I pulled on my trousers and jacket before he could change his mind, did up my belt on the tightest notch and tugged the zipper right up to my chin, to hide my flesh and make it as difficult as possible for him to reach my body. Mo put on his boots and camouflage jacket. Then he picked up his gun, slung it over his shoulder and knelt to open a wooden box. He took out a head torch, the curved knife with the gut hook that he'd brought to Maudie's party, a longer knife with a straight blade, binoculars, a couple of carabiners, a box of bullets and a hand saw. It was the slasher-movie playbook. I didn't need Joe to tell me how this was going to end.

'What's all that?'

'My gralloching kit for gutting deer.' He carefully put it all into his backpack. 'Let's go,' he said, directing me towards the hatch in the floor.

'Go where?' I asked nervously.

'Hunting. You said you wanted to come.' He seemed freakily unaware or unconcerned about how much he frightened me. It was as if everything from choking me to packing a murder kit was completely normal. There was a moment of blinding clarity. *He's done this before!*

'I think I should get home and check on Maudie.' If he heard the catch in my voice, he didn't show it. All I wanted to do was get into bed with Mum and tell her everything that had happened. I couldn't bear how upset she would be. It would give her no pleasure to know she'd been right about Mo.

'We're going to the other side of the lake,' said Mo. 'Someone informed me they'd seen outsiders there.' His eyes bored into me. 'But you knew that already, didn't you? You seem to know a lot of stuff that you don't tell me.' I felt almost nauseous. Somehow, he seemed to be inside my head.

'I've only crossed once.'

'But your brother has been seen crossing every day this week.'

The journey to the lake was so familiar I could have walked it with my eyes closed, which was just as well because I could hardly see for the tears streaming down my face. Mo moved fast but I was as strong and fit as I'd ever been and had no trouble keeping up with him. I was crying for the loss of something that had never existed as well as the new crisis I'd created by identifying Joe as the father of River's baby.

I might as well have put a target on Joe's back. Even worse, I couldn't tell him what I'd said because it would betray River's confidence, so he would be totally unaware he was in any danger. Telling Mo that River was pregnant had been enough to stop him in his tracks. I hadn't needed to say anything about Joe being the father. That revelation was purely vengeful, the toxic result of my anger with Joe and River for keeping their relationship secret and my jealousy that she was closer to him than I was. If he hurt my brother, it would be totally on me. Shame heaped upon suffocating layer of shame.

I kept fixating on his gun, wondering if being shot was a painless death, and thinking that perhaps it would be best for everyone else if he just did away with me. I noticed he'd mounted a scope on the barrel of the Remington.

'Helps to kill with pinpoint accuracy, Cassia,' he said, when he saw I was looking at it. He took it off his shoulder, pointed it at me and laughed when I recoiled in fear.

In the distance a low growl of thunder echoed through the forest. The sun retreated behind a bank of grey cloud. Mo licked his finger and held it in the air. 'The wind's turning easterly.'

'What does that mean?'

'It means the weather has broken. Autumn is upon us.'

'You know we're leaving next week. After Samhain.' I hoped that reminding him Joe would soon be out of his hair might make him less vengeful.

'The community decides when you leave,' he replied. 'Not you.' He glared at me menacingly and I stared at the ground in fear, hoping not to antagonize him further.

Within a few minutes there was a torrential downpour. It was the first rain since we'd arrived at the Haven and lasted less than half an hour. But in that time the entire landscape was reconfigured. The evergreen firs slumped like depressed teenagers with the weight of the water on their branches, and colours became more muted, as if a veil had been thrown over the forest. Mo instructed me to line my boots with plastic bags to stop my feet getting soaked.

The rain meant it took longer than usual to reach the lake. We emerged from the forest at a point much further west, where it was at its widest, beside a huge granite boulder that Mo said was called the Teg. I'd never been this far before. The hills on the other side were shrouded in mist, but this only amplified the dizzying scale of the landscape that had opened up before me. I stood on the shore in awed silence. Without any trees to provide shelter, I was buffeted by the wind, which whipped across the usually flat surface of the water, creating small, agitated waves that broke by my feet. Mo went into the bushes and dragged out a small wooden canoe and two oars hidden under branches.

'Sit behind me. Copy exactly what I do,' he instructed. 'Don't lean. If we capsize, we're fucked. It's deep in the middle and colder too.'

I'd never been in a canoe before and struggled to paddle in time with Mo, especially because we were heading into the wind. The muscles in my arms soon screamed in protest. The more progress we made the rougher it got. Before long I was throwing up over the side.

'I thought River was the one with morning sickness,' quipped Mo. He was relentless. He breathed in time to the rhythm of the paddles breaking the surface of the water and didn't slow once. I watched the tension in the sinews at the back of his neck and eyed the backpack he guarded between his legs. His obsessive focus filled me with cold terror. When we reached the other side, he hid the canoe and scrambled into the undergrowth. It was a well-oiled routine. I guessed we were due south of the growers. He began to stop at regular intervals, either to examine the ground or check something through his binoculars.

'You need to keep your senses open at all times, Cassia.'

He gave a wild laugh. It was totally intimidating, but understanding how Mo fed off my fear, I attempted to smile back. He walked a little further. Something caught his eye and he indicated I should bend down beside him. At first, I couldn't see a thing. But then he took my middle finger and traced the outline of a track.

'Is it a deer?'

'Adult female, judging by the size. Do you see there are two main toes that come to a point? It's a dead giveaway.

You can tell they're fresh because the outline is crisp, and the track walls haven't crumbled, even after the rain.'

A bellowing roar echoed through the forest. I jumped. It was a primeval sound that seemed to come from the very belly of the earth. There was something soulful in its tone, like a desperate plea for attention after centuries of neglect.

'What's that?' I asked in alarm.

'It's the rutting season. The adult males are searching for hinds to mate with.' Within seconds the same noise reverberated through a different part of the forest.

'Why do they do that?'

'To deter rivals and make themselves attractive to females,' whispered Mo. 'The louder the roar, the bigger the deer. That way, the males can tell if they're in with a chance in a fight. If they don't back down, they battle it out to the end.' He paused to stare at me. 'Pure power, sex and death, Cassia. That's what makes the world go round.'

He instructed me to go ahead and take over tracking. I could feel his eyes burning into the back of my neck. He could bring me to the ground at any moment and no one would ever find me. I focused on the prints, asking him endless questions, hoping flattery and interest would keep him kind. Aida was right. Mo was a shadow-side person. I spotted a pile of small black pellets on the ground close to a print.

'Deer scat?' Mo gave a nod of approval. 'You're a quick learner.' In spite of everything, I still relished his praise and hated myself for it. But when you've invested so much in something over a long time it's difficult to let it go all at once.

As my eyes adjusted to the subtle undulations in the

soil, I spotted smaller tracks close by. Six deer in all. At one point Mo pointed towards a glade and we saw two adult males charging at each other using their huge antlers as weapons, like medieval jousters. Mo looked around like a bird of prey. At times like that, he seemed more animal than human. When he used the binoculars, it was to confirm something he'd already spotted. He pointed at the bushes. All I could see were branches and leaves dripping with rain from the storm. He pressed the binoculars into my hands and directed my face slightly uphill to the right. I saw a huge red furred face staring back at me. Its muzzle was pale, its nose damp and black, like a cow's, its neck thick with fur, but the strangest thing was its head and antlers, which were garlanded in green and brown fronds of bracken, as if it was wearing an elaborate headdress.

'What's it got on its head?' I asked, in astonishment.

'The males try to make themselves look as big as possible to attract the hinds and frighten off the opposition. He's one sexy mother-fucker. And he knows it.'

The stag stared at me, and I stared at him. *Help*, I mouthed.

There was a rustling to our right. Mo pressed his finger to his lips to warn me to stay silent. I glanced over and saw the doe we'd been tracking with five younger hinds skittishly running across the same small glade where I'd just seen the stag. We tracked her in silence.

We kept moving. Sometimes the doe looked back at us, and I was certain she could see me. At one point, I needed to pee. Mo instructed me to dig a ten-by-ten cat hole and cover my piss with earth and leaves. 'That way no one can pick up your scent.'

I was concentrating hard on directing my pee into the

hole when I heard a different sound, like a low whistle. I glanced over. A ghostly figure wearing a long white dress and headdress made of antlers stepped out from behind a tree. I shook myself and pulled up my trousers, floored to see River staring back at me. I turned towards Mo to see if he'd noticed but he was busy tossing fistfuls of grass into the air to check the wind direction. When I looked back, River had disappeared. There was a crack as a twig snapped.

'Quick,' whispered Mo. 'We'll get her soon. She's starting to make mistakes.'

'I don't want to kill her,' I said desperately.

'She's had a good life and she'll have a good death. Better than any animal that ends up on a supermarket shelf. She'll feed us for months.'

We set off and it wasn't long before I spotted River again. This time she was peering out from the side of a beech tree.

'There she is!' said Mo, pointing at the same tree. I overtook him, running as fast as I could. River flew through the dogwood, sidestepping clumsy slabs of fallen rock, and jumping over running streams. This time I didn't lose her. I saw her hide behind another tree but when I slowly circled it expecting to find her, there was nothing on the ground except a black and white magpie feather.

'She's close,' Mo said. He took the gun off his shoulder and loaded bullets into the chamber. *He knows it's her! He wants to kill River!* He overtook me. I stayed close to his shoulder. River reached the depression in the valley and stood with her arms in the air singing. Mo aimed the Remington at her and flicked off the safety.

'No,' I screamed. 'Don't kill her!'

I threw myself at him, but it was too late. He fired. There was a faint cry, like breath leaving someone's body.

'River, River, River,' I heard myself sob, as I rushed towards the spot where she'd fallen. But when I opened my eyes to look at her, it wasn't River: it was the doe we'd been tracking all morning. Blood poured from the wound in her chest. She was still warm, and her fur tickled my face. Her eyes were black and shiny, and so, so sad. It was an illusion. Mo had made me go mad, just like he was making Dad go mad. I hugged her body to mine and cried and cried. I didn't care that there were plenty of deer and she would provide dozens of meals for the community over the winter. She had a beautiful pure soul, while Mo's was warped and dark. Mo wasn't worthy of her. He wasn't worthy of me. I cried for her, for me and for my brother.

'She didn't suffer.' He hauled me off her. I was completely confused by what had happened. It felt as if I was losing my mind. I looked down at my clothes and they were covered with blood.

'Come on, Cassia,' said Mo. 'The work begins now. We need to get her cleaned up to avoid contaminating the meat.'

He got out the saw and cut off her legs at the knee. I put my fingers in my ears to block out the sound of the blade slicing through the bone. Then he attached a rope around her hind legs, tossed the other end over the branch of a nearby tree and hauled it up until the deer was hanging in the air at face height, rocking gently in the breeze. He inspected her mouth, and bent down to look between the cleats on her hoofs, to make sure she was healthy, then pulled out the knife with the long, curved blade from his bag and handed it to me.

'Slit her throat downwards,' he instructed.

'I don't want to.'

He dragged me to my feet and forced the knife into my

hand, keeping his fist tight over mine. He lifted my hand towards her throat and stuck the knife through her skin, into the flesh and sliced downwards. Blood poured out and quickly started to pool on the ground. I touched my face and when I looked at my finger it was red with her blood.

'Now for the gralloch. We need to remove the stomach, intestines, heart and lungs.' He took the knife back and grinned at me.

'I hate you!' I sobbed. 'I hate you!'

'Now you're showing the right kind of instincts.' He chuckled as he cut out the doe's internal organs. It was as if he was controlling my feelings.

Why did he make me do this? I couldn't work out if he was trying to frighten me, to show me what he was capable of, or if he genuinely wanted to teach me how to disembowel a deer. Was it so that I wouldn't focus on what he'd done to me?

He clasped my face between his hands. 'If you say anything, to anyone, about what happened between us, this is what I will do to you.'

I finally understood.

When I got home in the late afternoon, our cabin was eerily quiet. I peeped through Mum and Dad's bedroom window and saw Maudie lying asleep on the mattress, while Lila watched over her. She'd taken to visiting Maudie every afternoon so Mum could sneak off to help Juan get his hives ready for winter. This had to be kept completely secret from Dad, whose jealousy over Juan had spilt over into epic levels of irrationality. Lila had combed Maudie's hair with the brush she used for her plastic dogs so that it fanned out around her head. Maudie's eyes were closed, and both arms, including the bandaged one, rested on her stomach with the palms pressed together as if she was praying. The contrast between her deep auburn hair, pale skin and cotton dress gave her an ethereal look, as if she was between worlds. It choked me up to see her like that.

Lila moved gracefully around her, carefully placing different objects close to Maudie's body without touching her. There were hag stones, a whelk shell, bits of cloth, a sprig of rowan, animal bones, a small bird's skull and Maudie's favourite plastic dog, Hilda. She lit a sage stick and talked under her breath as she wafted it around, calling on the different amulets to help Maudie get better.

'The healing is in the forest, Cass,' Lila said. Her back was turned to me.

'How did you know I was here?' I asked, awed at her hearing.

'I can feel the weight of your sadness.' I scrambled through the window. Lila saw my bloody clothes and didn't ask any questions. Instead, she gave me a hug, helped me pull off my jacket, T-shirt and trousers, swaddled me in a rug and made me lie on the mattress next to Maudie, who didn't stir. She picked up the bird's skull and whispered to it before putting it back down.

'Spirit of the forest protect my sister Maudie.'

'What are you doing?' I asked.

'I'm taking the fire out of her wound.'

Lila brushed my hair and smeared one of her potions on the bruises and fingerprints on my neck and shoulders. She arranged bones and skulls around me and bunches of pennyroyal and teasels. I squeezed my eyes shut but still the tears escaped. My sense of shame over what had happened with Mo felt limitless, as if it could never be contained. I blamed myself. For my poor judgement. For being stupid enough to believe in our relationship. For my gullibility. I felt so raw, like he'd shredded my soul. I would never be the same again.

I breathed in the sweet smell of sage. I think I must have fallen asleep because when I opened my eyes again it was dark outside, Lila had gone, and someone was shaking my shoulder. Wild with fear, in case it was Mo, I lashed out. Maudie stirred beside me.

'What the fuck?' It was Joe. I was safe. He was safe. For the time being.

'What happened to your face?' It took a moment to figure out what he was talking about. 'What are those marks on your neck?'

I opened my mouth. I wanted to tell him. Then I remembered Mo's threat and the words stayed deep inside me, a squalid lump of torment.

'A branch got me.' His eyes narrowed in disbelief. I tried to force a smile but the sides of my mouth hurt too much.

'I need to speak to you, Cass.' Joe's voice sounded weirdly distorted.

I pulled myself upright and followed him into the kitchen. He sat down at the table holding his head in his hands.

'He found out,' said Joe.

'Found out what?'

'Someone told Dad that it was Juan who tried to help Mum and Maudie leave on Gaia. Dad's gone loco.'

'Where's Mum?' I asked.

'I told her to warn Juan.'

'But won't Dad be here soon?' I panicked. Even now, after everything that had happened to me, my primordial fear was of Dad unleashing his temper on Mum.

The door of the cabin slammed open. We flinched as Dad came in and slapped three bloody venison steaks on the kitchen table.

'Congratulations, Cass,' he said, pouring himself a glass of water. 'Mo tells me you learnt to track faster than anyone else he's ever taught. Says you took in everything he said.'

He steamed into the bedroom to check on Maudie. I caught Joe's eye. We tensed, anticipating the inevitable explosion. Within seconds he burst back into the kitchen.

'Where's Mum?' he demanded, his gaze darting from Joe to me.

I fabricated an elaborate story about her going to Sylvie and Piper's house to collect material to make new bandages for Maudie. He wasn't buying it. 'You might be a good tracker, but you're a bad liar. Where is she?'

He came over to me and stood with his face just inches from mine, glaring into my eyes. 'I'm learning to read minds,' he said. 'And I can see that you're thinking Mum is probably with Juan. Is that right?' His voice got louder. His eyes were cold and vacant, as if he'd disappeared. It was like he was possessed.

'Where is that slut?' he yelled, so close to me that I could feel his saliva stick to my cheek.

'Leave her alone.' Joe insinuated himself between us, so Dad's attention pivoted to him. He raised his fist. I thought he was about to hit Joe, so I kicked him as hard as I could in the calf. Dad's knee gave way. This seemed to catch him off guard. He'd never had to contend with both of us at the same time. Instead of hitting Joe, he shoved both of us outside and bolted the door behind us.

'Stay there until you're ready to tell the truth!'

'He's crazy, isn't he?' I asked Joe.

'We've just got to get to Samhain and then we can leave and get help for Maudie. If we're lucky, he won't come with us.' Joe gave a hollow laugh. What about River? I wanted to ask my brother. I couldn't understand how he could so unfeelingly leave her behind. For a while we sat in silence on the bench in the porch.

A short while later, Dad came out. 'I'm going to the well,' he announced. It was as if he couldn't remember what had just happened.

25

Now

I leave the van at first light. My feet seem to know where I'm going better than my head. Just as well, because snow has powdered the landscape, smoothing out its rough edges, blurring the boundary between earth and sky. At least I don't have to worry about leaving tracks. No sooner have I creaked through the snow than my footsteps disappear. I always used to feel invisible. Now finally I am.

It's a bone-chiller of a November morning. Nothing moves, apart from me. There are no birds, no animals scurrying through the undergrowth. Even the leaves are still. As I head downhill towards the lake, I notice its surface is coated with snow. But it's only when I reach the shore and bend down to test the water temperature that I clock it's frozen over. Somewhere towards the middle, I spot a couple of worried-looking tufted ducks slip-sliding around. I'll need an ice breaker, not a canoe, to get to the other side and start the search for Mo.

There's no way I can walk across. I'm at the widest point, and even if I don't fall through the ice, my jacket and blue jeans make me too conspicuous. My mind works fast. It's a simple choice. I'll have to hike further east, where the lake narrows into a series of tributaries. I retreat into the trees to avoid any prying eyes on the other side of the shore and scrutinize the area around the growers' settlement. There's no smoke. No barking dogs. No crying children. The growers always know what's up before the rest of us because they have eyes on the road. Not even a beetle makes it across without them noticing. They'll be raging about the police presence and pissed off with Mo for attracting the attention of the authorities. So, I figure they've gone to ground too.

I set off through the trees trying, as far as possible, to stay parallel to the lake. My body feels liquid and smooth, at one with the natural world. This is my territory now. Occasionally I nudge the branch of a pine tree and a spray of snow slaps my face. As I move, I run through what I've discovered: Morden Spilid is one of the names Mo goes by; Morden Spilid was murdered in Spain. Which means that Mo has stolen the identity of a man who was murdered. And doesn't that likely make Mo his killer? I can't help comparing the neat incision along the man's belly with Mo's forensic approach to gutting deer, and feel the muscle burn of pure fear. If Mo did that to him, what could he do to me or my family? I remember the pool of blood on the floor of Mo's cabin. *Don't jump to conclusions. Keep an open mind. Always.* I pick up my pace, weaving in and out through the trees. I have to get to my family before Mo does.

I've reached the far end of the lake, where I used to cross with Joe and the sisters. I tentatively step onto the ice, using the toe of my boot to sweep aside the snow and crouch to take a closer look. It has a blue tint, which means it's the densest kind. I step onto it and start walking, sliding my feet, rather than lifting them, to keep my weight even, as if I'm gliding. I quickly find my rhythm. I'm aiming for the area where Wass said they'd picked up the signal from Dad's phone because I know Mo was there yesterday.

I'm roughly two-thirds of the way across when I hear the muffled pulse of a helicopter beating its way through the still morning air. I look back over my shoulder. It swoops towards the centre of the Haven, nose tipped forward, skimming the trees to hover above the Spirit House. I freeze. I know it's looking for me and guess Wass has her reasons for escalating the search. The helicopter flies up and down in straight lines, working on a grid system. When it reaches the lake, it'll be game over for me. I'll be seen straight away, and if Cara is with them, she won't let up until they've got me on board.

I try to run but it's an impossible slip-slide. Then another setback as the yelp of excited dogs echoes through the trees. Judging by their hysteria, they've picked up a scent. I change direction and tack eastwards to put as much distance as possible between them and me, even though the ice will be thinner here because it's been warmed by the early-morning sun. There's no time to stick in a knife to test its thickness. There's a creak and a groan. I try to speed up, but the ice reacts faster than I do. Its noisy grumble turns to moans and whines until there's a half-hearted splash and my boots disappear beneath the surface. I find myself standing on the bed of the lake, with icy water lapping my calves. I gasp in shock at the freezing cold and start wading through the broken ice towards the shore. It breaches the top of the plastic bags that line my boots. Each step is colder and heavier than the last and my feet are quickly numb.

When I finally leave the water, I stumble into the undergrowth and collapse onto the snowy ground. I can't feel my feet. It's like they've died. I force myself to stand up and lumber around to restore circulation. When this doesn't work, I frantically pull off my boots and socks. My feet and ankles are white and waxy. I massage them with my hands. Slowly they take on a bluish tinge, which means the blood must be circulating. I pull out the knitted socks Aida gave me, put two on each foot and tie a slightly damp plastic bag on top. My boots are soaked through but at least the plastic bags will keep my feet dry. This whole process seems to take ages.

I feel suddenly thirsty and gulp down water, not caring that if I run out and the temperature stays below freezing I'll have to use the stove to melt snow later. I'm making too many mistakes. I need to recalibrate my priorities. And number one is to put as much distance as possible between me and the dogs. My only coherent thought is that I should stay downwind and climb higher. I set off. The disorienting identical peaks and troughs make it impossible to gauge progress, and because the wind has picked up, it's difficult to work out where I am in relation to the noise of the dogs. Feeling is slowly seeping back into my feet, but the pain is worse than the numbness and every step is agony.

After an hour or so of this grinding struggle I discover I'm almost at exactly the same place where I started. I fall onto my knees in despair. Icy tears pour down my cheeks. The helicopter cruises across the lake towards the growers' settlement, then swoops low over the marijuana fields towards me. It's game over.

A branch snaps close by, a little higher from where I'm standing. I look up. It could be Mo. I unzip my rucksack and pull out his knife. I'm not going down without a fight. There's another crack. I scan the forest for deer and boar. A small branch lands on the ground a few metres away at the foot of a gnarly old oak. I step towards it and see three interlocking spirals drawn in black on the trunk at eye level. The dolls I found in our van had the same markings on their arms, as do the Vivian sisters. I nervously scan the hillside ahead of me and see another tree with the same symbol roughly five metres away. The pattern repeats itself several times. I keep climbing, following the symbols up through the trees until I find myself in the dark shelter of the most ancient part of the forest. Gradually the dogs and the helicopter become an irritating murmur in the far distance. I don't know who's helping me but sometimes there's no choice other than to trust.

I push myself hard, following the trail of triskelions at a half-jog, until I can climb no further because my path is blocked by a large granite boulder. There are natural hand- and footholds in the grooved and fluted rockface and another triskelion. I climb up, and where the rise is steepest there's a sweet V-shaped gap with a flat surface, where a weary soul can rest with a fine view across the entire forest. I spread out the tarp and flop down. The helicopter is a tiny speck in the distance. I examine my feet again, check if my speech is slurred, which might indicate hypothermia, and when it isn't I celebrate by taking out the cheese sandwich Aida made for me and force myself to eat it mindfully, savouring each mouthful. Finally, I pull out Joe's phone and apprehensively turn it on. Battery: 53 per cent.

To my astonishment, I see a flickering bar of 3G. This is where Joe must have come to message Cara. I wonder if the spirals on the rocks were for him? So he could find his way here? I jump as the phone vibrates in the palm of my hand. There are four new messages. The first three are from Cara: GET IN TOUCH!!!! The final one is from Dad's number. Except it's not Dad, it's Mo. *Am watching you, Cassia.* Totally strung out, I frantically look around, almost expecting to find him leering at me with his half-smile. I delete it immediately. Another message pops up straight away.

Then another.

U can run but u can't hide.

26

Then

The sense of something ending hung over us. Summer came to an abrupt close in the wallow of early-autumn rains drumming on the roof of our cabin through the night. The wood warblers and blackcaps retreated from the forest to make their long journey south. Apart from Dad, my family started getting ready to go home. The community had decided to combine the Samhain festival with a farewell party for us in the Spirit House the day before we were due to leave. There was a lot of truth in Joe's bittersweet observation that they were celebrating our departure. I think there was unspoken relief all round that we'd be gone by the weekend and take all our problems with us. 'The Maudie Issue', as Sylvie called my little sister's decline, would only be sorted when she left. And it was becoming apparent in the way people fell silent when Dad appeared and whispered about him during meals that not everyone welcomed his aggressive approach to protecting the forest from outsiders with Mo. Aida's empty seat at the table was a constant reminder of the bitter internal conflict within the Haven.

I was desperate to get away from Mo. Whenever I saw him, at mealtimes or when he fetched Dad in the morning, I felt as if a heavy weight was pressing down on my chest, crushing the air from my lungs. The realization that nothing could trump the strength of a man prepared to use his superior physicality against me left me with a kind of primeval fear I couldn't shake off.

I couldn't believe how Mo acted as if nothing had happened. Even when I didn't see him, the memory of what he'd done agitated constantly inside my head, like a panicked bird that had just discovered it was for ever trapped in a cage. I couldn't stop thinking about it. I woke up at night with the sensation of his hands around my throat. At unexpected moments I found myself inexplicably unable to breathe. The need to get away from him became so overwhelming that it felt as if my life depended on it.

I took to walking through the forest every morning at first light to visit Old Big Belly. I lay on the ground inside the hollow tree trunk with my arms outstretched and my body pressed into the soil and leaves until I felt part of the landscape. The tree's inhabitants got used to my presence. The red squirrels tipped chewed pinecones onto me from their drey high up in the canopy, and their summer-born kits scampered around so close I could feel the draught from their bushy tails. A female woodlouse sat in my hand and when I tipped her over, I saw she kept her eggs in a pouch, like a kangaroo. I spent ages watching a spider pull silk from her fourth leg to spin a gossamer web, and admired her cold-blooded rush to mummify the snoozy wasp that blundered into her sticky lair. *None of my shit matters compared to all this.* The sensation of powerlessness triggered by Mo's attack ebbed a little when I was there. I was part of the natural world, and during those precious moments I could be free again.

The rest of the time I tried to keep busy. To atone for our disastrous family, Dad, Joe and I doubled down on the number of hours we spent helping the community with their winter preparations, even though we wouldn't be there to benefit. Dad hunted and butchered deer with Mo and cured them in salt, spices and herbs to draw out the water. Joe caught and smoked dozens of wild trout. With the Vivian sisters, I loaded up Gaia with logs we chopped from fallen trees until Piper stopped worrying that the community would run out of fuel. He stacked logs outside Aida's cabin in the hope she'd come back. But there was no sign of her. She'd disappeared into thin air.

Mum, who was trapped at home with Maudie, poured all her nervous energy into planning our departure down to the last detail. Rory had a broken axle and not even One Way Will's skills as a mechanic could resurrect him. The community had voted to allow Juan to bring Gaia to our cabin the morning after Samhain to help us get Maudie through the forest to the road. From there he was hopeful we could hitch a lift to town in one of the trucks that would be transporting the grow down the valley.

'And if there's no truck?' whispered Maudie.

'Then we'll walk,' Mum declared resolutely.

'We'll do whatever it takes to get you out of here,' promised Joe, as he stroked Maudie's cheek. 'Hang in there, Mauds.'

Each day the purple stain crept a little further up her arm and the night sweats came back with a vengeance. Mum and Joe had intense conversations about going home. He didn't mention River once and displayed zero guilt about leaving her behind. Instead, he obsessively questioned Mum about our old house. Was she certain we could move back in? Would the tenants really have gone? Was his stuff still there? Yes, yes, yes, Mum snapped at him.

The combined stress of dealing with Dad and Maudie was too much even for someone like Mum. She was at breaking point.

By that stage, Mum's fear and hatred of Mo were equal to my own. After another row about him with Dad, Mum explained to Joe and me that if Dad didn't get away from Mo, he wouldn't recover. This was the first time she'd said she thought he was ill.

I pressed her for details. 'What exactly is wrong with him?'

'I'm not sure, Cass. But whatever it is, this place makes it worse.'

We spoke in whispers in case Dad overheard and went loco. We didn't dare talk about leaving in front of him and he didn't mention it. His attitude was to pretend it wasn't happening.

As the day of our departure loomed, I began to feel more conflicted about giving up on my life at the Haven. When I thought about never seeing the red kites or our robin again or exchanging the soothing green gloom of the forest for the hard grey edges of city life, the drift of flowery scent for the metal smell of pollution, I felt overwhelmed with a kind of cosmic sadness. It wasn't that I didn't want to go back to my old life, it was more that I wasn't ready to walk away from this new one. I didn't want to say goodbye to River and her sisters, and I wanted to hang out more with Kaia and Magnus. I was worried that River wouldn't cope without me and was eaten up with guilt that I'd told Mo about the baby without her knowledge or permission. The need to get away from Mo had become all consuming, but I wasn't ready to abandon my life in the community. And as this realization grew, it stoked my hatred of him. Why should I have to leave because of him?

In the middle of that week, on one of those autumn days when the sun refused to accept it was in retreat, River suggested we go for a final swim in the lake. She claimed she wanted to spend as much time as possible with me before I left the Haven. More likely she was trying to make me feel better that she hadn't told me about her and Joe.

As we strolled down to the lake we didn't chat as much as I'd hoped. Everything about River felt heavy, like she was physically and mentally dragged down. I kept thinking she would rather be spending the day with my brother, even though she kept telling me what a good friend I was, and how much she was going to miss me. If we're such good friends, why didn't you say anything about Joe sooner? I wanted to ask. But didn't I have my own secrets? I'd already decided that I'd never tell anyone what Mo had done to me because to give shape to it with words would give it a life of its own beyond my control. If I pushed it deep enough inside myself, eventually the memory might fade. I told Old Big Belly and that was it. The tree held me in its thousand-year embrace.

Down by the lakeside, the air was cooler. Shivering, we stripped to our underwear ready to swim. I couldn't help noticing the roundness of River's belly. It was sweet and plump, like the chest of a wood pigeon. She caught me staring and tried to hide it with her hand.

'Do you think other people will guess?' she asked apprehensively.

'No,' I lied.

'You haven't told anyone, have you?'

'Not a soul.' The guilt was like sparks exploding in my brain. My face flushed. But what else could I say? I couldn't bring myself to admit I'd told Mo she was pregnant, and that Joe was the father, because then I'd have to explain why. *I landed you in the shit to save myself.* And how could I find the words to describe what Mo had done to me when I couldn't even articulate the experience to myself? I was too terrified how he would hurt me if he thought I'd told River his dirty little secret. The image of the dead-eyed deer with her guts spewed out played on a loop in my head.

'How am I going to get rid of it?' River glared at her stomach. I was relieved at her change of focus.

'Mo told me he's going back into town for more supplies. Maybe you could offer to help him and see a doctor while you're there.' I was trying to give her hope of a way out without revealing I'd told Mo the truth of her situation. But instead of being relieved, she gripped my arm in fear.

'You didn't say anything to Mudder, did you?' When she let go, I saw the imprint of her fingers around my wrist.

'Of course not.' I leant in for a hug so she couldn't see the lie in my eyes. 'It's all cool.'

'If Mudder finds out, it could be really dangerous for us all.'

That was a blow to the solar plexus. I saw the venomous looks Mo gave Joe when he collected Dad in the mornings. But if I told Joe to watch his back I'd be betraying River twice over because she didn't want my brother to know about the baby. By this stage I wanted rid of the pinto bean as much as she did. Then at least I could take off knowing she was safe. A sketchy idea rapidly took shape.

'I've got a plan.' River looked at me watchfully. 'How

about we go to the growers' settlement, find Em and ask her to drive you to town in their truck?' I couldn't believe I hadn't thought of this before.

'Why would she do that for me?' asked River, who was already stuffing our clothes into a plastic bag and eyeing the best route across the water. 'Last time we saw her, her husband and brother-in-law were out to kill us.'

'Because of what happened to her own baby,' I replied.

'You're the best.' River hugged me tightly.

'We'll get through this.' I couldn't fail her. I was her only hope.

The lake was swollen from the rain and crossing was more treacherous than it had been even a week earlier. Some of the boulders had already disappeared beneath the surface and by the time we reached the middle, the water was lapping at our shoulders and we had to hold our bags high above our heads. I could feel the current luring us downstream towards the deeper water.

When we emerged on the shore, we were further west than usual, close to a rough-hewn path that wound up into the forest. I guessed it had been created by the growers. We dried off, threw our clothes back on and set off uphill. The terrain was a little easier now the undergrowth had started its autumn die-back. I listened to the chat of the pines as the wind passed through their long, elegant branches. *We are with you, with you, with you*, they seemed to whisper. My heart lightened a little, and my spirit walked easier.

As we closed in on the growers' settlement, I started to feel on edge again. We were coming at it from a different angle, snaking round the narrow wooden building that had been padlocked the last time we were there. The door was ajar. I glanced inside and saw row upon row of marijuana plants hanging upside down along the walls. River tugged at my arm, but I couldn't tear myself away from the scene inside. A bunch of people sat on stools at either side of a long trestle table loaded with cannabis flowers. Their faces were hidden behind scarves as they snipped and manicured the buds with sharp scissors held in hands protected by latex gloves.

Em looked up and saw us. She barrelled outside and glanced around nervously to check if anyone else had noticed before herding us across the clearing into her trailer.

'What the hell are you doing here?'

'We need your help,' I explained.

'The biggest help I can give you is to tell you to get the fuck out of here before they find you again.' Em slumped onto a wooden chair at the kitchen table. Her bloodshot eyes had big bags underneath. 'A lot of shit has gone down here.'

I efficiently outlined River's problem. 'We need you to drive River into town and help her get rid of it,' I said finally. 'That's the long and the short of it.'

'Who is the father?' she asked. 'Why can't he help?'

'He doesn't know,' said River. That was the only time she spoke.

'I'm driving the grow to town next Tuesday. I'll pick you up on the side of the road at sunrise,' said Em, reluctantly. My plan had worked. It felt so good. But there was no time to celebrate because we could hear raised voices outside the trailer. River and I ducked down, peered through the bottom of the grimy Perspex window and saw Kyle and JJ approaching. My stomach balled. Kyle looked awful. His face was hollow and grey, and he was panting unevenly.

Every so often he stopped and doubled over to grip his stomach. JJ was just behind him, prodding him forward. 'We need to get out of here right now, Fuck-face.' Kyle whimpered, and I admit it gave me pleasure to see him as shit scared as we were.

'How did they find out what we were up to?' he rasped. We watched as he collapsed on the ground just outside the window of the barn where the trimmers were working.

'Because you screwed up,' replied JJ. He glanced over his shoulder at his brother, made a quick calculation and headed into the forest, leaving him behind.

'We can hurt you in many ways.' I recognized Mo's voice right away. *Lick, suck, swallow, bitch.* My chest tightened and my breathing got shallower and shallower until there was nothing left to give. River shot me a sideways glance.

'I'm about to mess up your day!' bellowed a different voice. It was Dad! *What the fuck?*

Kyle crawled towards the trailer. Dad stepped towards him, so close that if the window was open, I could almost have touched him. His eyes were raging. I recognized that look and shrank back. He began kicking and punching Kyle and didn't stop till Kyle fell quiet. I felt completely numb.

'He blazes with madness,' whispered River. 'This is what Mudder does to people. He gives them the *Salvia* and uses it to bend them to his will. He did the same with One Way Will.'

I waited for Em to give us away, to divert Dad and Mo's attention from Kyle to us. But instead she crouched beside us. 'Leave through the window at the back of the trailer.' We went into the bedroom where we'd seen the little boy.

'What's going on?' I whispered, as I shoved open the window and jumped to the ground.

'Mo discovered JJ and Kyle were stealing the grow to make money on the side by selling to another gang. He's threatened to kill them.'

'What's Mo got to do with this?' I asked in bewilderment.

'He runs it all,' said Em. I struggled to take this in. It was like the more I knew about Mo, the less I knew about him. Nothing about him was as it had seemed.

'The other guy is even more nuts than him.'

'That's my dad,' I said mournfully.

'I'm sorry.' She wasn't apologizing for insulting Dad. It was more she felt bad for me having someone like him in my life. That stuck with me. Em felt more sorry for me than she did for herself.

River and I argued about what to do all the way back to the Spirit House. I thought we should call an emergency processing session before Mo and Dad got back.

'He's a total fraud. There aren't any outsiders threatening the Haven. It's all him. He's running the whole show. He is the growers. He probably sent in the microlight to freak out the community into thinking they needed him to save them.' I was incredulous.

'I'm not disagreeing with you. It's just not the right moment,' countered River. 'Let's wait until after Samhain.'

'What's the point in going ahead with a festival to ward off evil spirits when the Devil is already in our midst?' I gave a hollow laugh.

'If we say something now, he might not let you leave. That would be dangerous for Maudie,' said River, 'and it could ruin my plan with Em.'

Mo's hypocrisy and duplicity were like an open sore for me. The gulf between how he talked about women being gatekeepers of the natural world and how he'd treated me was impossible to reconcile. He condemned the growers for destroying the forest when he was masterminding the whole business. I remembered something I'd once read. 'The object of power is power.' It was that simple. Mo wanted power.

'People need to know the truth,' I insisted.

'Once I've sorted the pregnancy, I'll tell them,' said River, firmly.

Back at the Spirit House everyone was preparing for the festival. Sylvie, Piper and Juan were building a huge fire in the centre of the stone circle; Kaia and One Way Will were making fire torches for a procession to the river. Lila and Skylar were putting the final touches to a makeshift altar decorated with skulls, feathers and nuts. I felt suddenly exhausted and wanted to get home to our cabin. I wandered past the fire and saw Piper, Juan and Sylvie huddled together, talking intently. Lila was listening too but from a distance.

'In the fifteen years I've been here, Aida has never missed Samhain,' said Juan. His voice was strained.

'But it was her choice to leave,' observed Sylvie.

'There was no choice,' said Juan. 'They went against her principles. She lost all authority.'

'Mo says he sighted her north of the lake a couple of days ago.' Piper tried to reassure him. 'So we know she's well.'

'And you believe that?' Juan snapped back.

'I have no reason not to,' replied Piper.

'Aida tried to warn us about Mo,' said Juan. 'She saw the darkness in him.'

'Not everyone agreed with Mudder coming to live among us,' Lila pointed out. 'His methods weren't ours. He wanted us to abandon the old ways. Aida was opposed to him right from the start, but she changed her mind after the outsiders destroyed the forest where her ancestors were buried. It was a decision motivated by fear.'

'What did the folks at Cazalla tell you about him?' Piper questioned Juan.

'I left Cazalla a long time before Mo arrived there,' said Juan.

'I'm sure he told us you'd met there,' insisted Piper.

'We both lived there. But not at the same time.'

There was a long pause.

'So how did he find out about the Haven?' asked Lila.

No one had any answers.

By the day of the festival I was totally strung out. I woke with a gut-twisting anxiety at the thought of seeing Mo that even Old Big Belly couldn't soothe. The idea that I could bury what he'd done to me was never going to happen. The caged bird never slept. It flapped and squawked, telling me I was stupid, worthless and didn't deserve to live. I replayed the scene in his tree-house on a loop in my head, and every time I beat myself up for misjudging the risk and failing to put up a better fight. Although there would be plenty of people around, I was terrified he would find a way to be alone with me or hurt me or Joe.

In the days leading to Samhain Dad was eerily calm. He watched us getting Maudie ready for the journey home with detached indifference. I didn't tell Mum what I'd seen him do to Kyle because I didn't want to load her up with even more worries. We were leaving and that was all that counted. Dad was no longer part of our plans. A small part of me felt a kind of pity for him because he was as much a victim of Mo's manipulation as I was. But when I thought about the way he got aggressive with Joe, how we all had to tread on eggshells around his moods, and Mum's full-time job trying to appease him, I realized that Dad wasn't just a danger to himself but also to us. I tried to calm myself with the thought that by first light the following morning we would be gone, and it would all be over.

When Mum announced at the last minute that she and Maudie wouldn't be going to the celebration, Dad was weirdly calm. His obsession that Maudie was fine seemed to have burnt itself out. Maybe it didn't matter any more because we were leaving, or more likely he was happy for Mum to stay at the cabin so she wouldn't see Juan. His hatred of Juan was like a fire he stoked every day. I felt bad for Mum because she wouldn't be able to say goodbye to her friends but there was no way Joe and I were going to kick up a fuss when Dad's mood was so finely pitched.

So, in the early afternoon Dad, Joe and I trudged up the side of the hill and crossed the stream to the Spirit House for the last time. The sun already hung low, and I guessed it was around three in the afternoon. Lila had lent me a dress, but when I'd put it on, it had clung too much to my curves, so I'd opted for a top that belonged to Joe, my baggiest pair of jeans and an old sweatshirt. I wanted to look as shapeless as possible. As we walked past people's cabins, I noticed plates of food and glasses of water left as offerings on doorsteps. 'So far so weird,' muttered Joe, who was desperate to get the ceremony over and done with so we could leave as quickly as possible.

I felt another surge of anxiety when we wandered into

the settlement area. I'd assumed people would be wearing the kind of folksy outfits I'd seen at the celebration in the forest all those months ago. But this was completely different. The whole look was grungier, involving layers of long robes, baggy tunics and oversize masks made of animal skulls, wood and burlap hoods with holes for eyes that made it almost impossible to identify anyone. My lumpy androgynous look fitted in perfectly. Someone touched my shoulder. I jumped and spun round to see two small figures dressed in ponchos made of sheepskins with a hole in the centre on top of shapeless dresses with long caped sleeves. Their faces were covered with deer skulls and long green fringes made of moss and grass.

Lila and Skylar giggled, reminding me of the first time we'd met them in the forest.

'Crazy, huh?' said Lila, in a muffled voice. 'It's to scare away the bad people.'

'Well, you've terrified me,' teased Joe.

'You're not one of the bad people,' said Skylar, linking her arm through his. Her voice caught. 'I wish you weren't going. I don't like all the changes.'

Lila put her arm around her little sister. 'She's upset because Juan isn't coming,' she whispered. 'He's gone to search for Aida again.' She glanced round to check that no one was listening.

'Shall we get something to eat, Skylar?' suggested Joe. 'That will cheer you up.'

We trailed into the covered outdoor eating area. The bulky costumes and heavy masks meant Lila and Skylar moved slowly, heads held high, like royalty. At the centre of the table was more food than I'd ever seen at the Haven, set out in big clay bowls. There were candles everywhere and the table was decorated with pine branches that infused the space with a sweet, calming smell. People milled around chatting and piling food onto plates. There was river trout, potatoes cooked in a spicy tomato sauce, salads, venison stew and in the middle a whole piglet that I queasily recognized as George. We took our plates outside to sit with other people around the stone circle.

One Way Will wandered around with a huge pitcher of mead for anyone who held out a glass to him. There was a sense of exhilarating anticipation in the air. A couple came over to greet us. As they got closer, I recognized Piper's messed-up toes. He was wearing a mask made from moss, ivy and hawthorn and had plaited his beard. Sylvie's face was decorated with three vertical black lines under her eyes. A black and white cloak made of feathers hung around her shoulders.

'Welcome to your first Samhain,' said Sylvie, warmly.

'First and last.' I smiled nervously.

'We're all going to miss you, Cass. Especially River. She's never had anyone close to her own age at the Haven.' For a split second I wondered if I should tell Sylvie about River being pregnant so that someone other than Mo would know. But I'd already broken too many promises to her, so I kept quiet.

'Thank you,' I said, giving Piper a quick hug. 'I'm sorry for all the trouble we've caused . . .'

'You've given more than you've taken.' He smiled warmly. 'We hope you've had a good experience and that you'll pass on what you've learnt about our way of life to outsiders who mean harm to the natural world.'

'I will,' I promised, trying to imagine how I'd persuade friends at school not to shop in Primark and abandon their

Nando's habit. 'I've learnt so much. I don't really want to go.' I was too choked up to say any more. I felt a single tear slide down my cheek. They each put an arm around me.

'What is it, Cass?' asked Sylvie, in concern.

'There's just such a lot to think about.' I wanted to warn them that Mo was working against them. That he would destroy everything they cared about. That everything about him was fake. That he was a curse upon us all. But I'd promised River I wouldn't say anything in case it jeopardized her trip to town with Em to get rid of the pinto bean.

'Like what?' Piper urged me to speak, but I couldn't. Out of the corner of my eye I saw a man in a cloth mask, with two holes for eyes and a hole for the mouth, watching me and knew it was Mo. I was terrified he thought I might be telling Sylvie and Piper about what he'd done to me. He came towards us but at that moment Kaia picked up the huge ram's horn and blew into it to kick off the ceremony. Everyone moved inside the stone circle to watch Jorn light the fire. The flames quickly licked up the side. In the half-light I caught sight of Dad's profile. He stared into the flames, dead-eyed. Sylvie stepped forward to speak. 'May abundance be a constant friend by my heart till winter's end . . .' I couldn't concentrate on what she was saying because I was too worried about where Mo was. It was a *Catch-22* situation. It made me feel sick when I didn't know where he was, and sick when I did. '. . . I thank you, Mother Earth, for the bounty you have given us . . .' After that we lit the fire torches and went to the river to place flowers in the water and watch them float downstream.

River stood inside the stone circle to sing. She was wearing a full-length dress under a long sleeveless robe. Her face was decorated with symmetrical black patterns and her lips were also painted black. She'd never looked more beautiful. She started with a low throaty drone, holding the same note for longer than seemed possible with one breath. When she fell silent, a rhythmic drumming began. Ten people, including Magnus, Kaia and One Way Will, stood in a circle around River, beating deerskin drums while Lila and Skylar banged bones together. This went on until eventually the beat of the drum felt like the beat of my own heart. People danced wildly in time to the rhythm, including Dad.

'Hopefully he'll exhaust himself, forget about digging his well and let us sleep,' Joe whispered in my ear.

River started a song I hadn't heard before, her ethereal voice piercing the night air. I couldn't understand the words. It was like she was speaking an ancient language that could only be felt physically. When she finally finished, she slowly removed her mask, headdress and long sleeveless robe in an almost trancelike state until all she was wearing was a thin white shift dress. In the dappled orange light of the fire, I could see her face glistening with sweat and damp patches under her arms. Her stomach strained against the thin cotton fabric. My pinto-bean calculations had been horribly inaccurate. I looked around in alarm, hoping other people hadn't noticed, but Kaia was already nudging Sylvie and I saw Magnus throw a protective arm around Lucia. Sylvie hurried over to River and pressed a hand on her daughter's stomach. 'Oh, God! Oh, God!' Her expression flitted from horror to fear and back.

'What is this, River?' Piper asked. 'What is this?' He looked hopefully at Sylvie, willing her to provide some alternative explanation for his daughter's round belly, and when she couldn't he put his hands on River's shoulders and tried to speak, but the words got caught in his throat.

'I'm pregnant,' whispered River. 'I'm sorry.'

The news ripped through the community. I watched Joe's face and was relieved when he managed to appear as shocked as everyone else. River glanced fleetingly at me, and I saw the fear in her eyes. *Don't worry,* I wanted to tell her. *I won't say a word about who the father is.* I felt nauseous with anxiety about what might happen next, but at that stage it was more for her than me, because at least her pregnancy was no longer my responsibility. And as this dawned on me, there was a guilt-inducing sense of relief too.

The music and dancing broke off, and everyone fell quiet, until the only noise was the crackle of the fire and the whisper of the wind through the trees. *What now?* Surely Sylvie and Piper would take River home. But the concept of dealing with something in private didn't exist at the Haven and instead Piper called for an immediate processing session. Sylvie attempted to reason with him.

'Aida is right,' he argued. 'Our principles must be immutable.' We all streamed into the Spirit House and sat in a circle. The party vibe had been annihilated and the atmosphere was sombre and tense. I spotted Dad and felt him trying to catch my eye. Lila sat down beside me.

'Did you know, Cassia?' she asked, in a serious tone.

'Absolutely not.' I needed to get my head together because everyone was going to ask me the same question. I waited for her to dig further. When she didn't, I glanced at Lila and saw her eyes were full of tears. I put my arm around her, and she didn't shake me off. In all my time at the Haven, I'd never seen her cry.

'I tried to protect her, but I couldn't.' She sounded petrified and defeated.

'Protect her from what?' I asked.

'From the bad people,' she whispered.

Kaia quickly ran through the usual introduction to processing, although unity, honesty and integrity seemed to have taken a back seat recently, before handing the talking stick to Sylvie.

'Over the years, some of us have given birth in this community. Many of us were born here ourselves. And this has brought us joy and sadness in equal measure. Because being pregnant and delivering babies in the forest can be difficult. And dangerous. And now River is pregnant. She's sixteen years old. Little more than a child herself.' Sylvie's voice drifted away and Kaia gently removed the talking stick from her hand.

'Because of the difficulties of giving birth in the forest, especially during the winter months, and because it's impossible to go to hospital, in case it draws the attention of outsiders to our community, we've always informed each other of our sexual relationships and any desire to have children,' said Kaia. 'River has broken two rules. She failed to inform us that she was involved in a sexual relationship, and she failed to tell us that she fell pregnant. River, what do you have to say?'

River stared at the floor. 'I'm sorry,' she whispered.

'Why didn't you share any of this with us during processing?' Kaia sounded genuinely perplexed.

'A problem shared is a problem halved,' someone called out.

'You were born in this community,' said Magnus. 'Don't you trust us to help you through good times and bad?'

'I was too scared,' said River. 'And now it's too late. I

don't want to have a baby. I don't want to bring a child into this world.' She started rhythmically beating herself in the stomach with her fists. It was too painful to watch.

Sylvie rushed over and wrapped her arms around her. 'Stop, River, stop,' she pleaded. 'We'll work something out.'

I felt Joe shift as if he was about to get up and pressed my hand on top of his to pin him down. But he pulled away and went into the middle of the circle to comfort River. Any hope that he'd stay below the radar evaporated.

'You don't have to have it, River! You don't have to,' he consoled her. 'Leave with us tomorrow and we'll help you. We can take you to the doctor. It's not too late.'

'You know that's impossible, Joe,' said Mo. It was the first time he'd spoken. Mo took the talking stick from Kaia. He was sitting close enough for his patchouli smell to reach my nostrils. I felt the bile rise in my stomach.

'She's too young to have a baby,' Sylvie pleaded with the circle of worried faces. 'It's too dangerous. It's one thing to expect an adult woman to give birth in the forest, but an adolescent girl is different. Look at the size of her hips!'

'The doctors will ask lots of questions because of her age and get the authorities involved,' commented Magnus. There were murmurs of agreement. 'They'll want to know what happened.' They looked to Dad, who always acted as the expert on the ways of the outsiders, for confirmation.

'It's true,' he said.

'I feel bad for River, but we have to think of the common good,' added Mo. 'We'll do everything we can to help her get through this.' His compassionate and reasonable tone was so convincing. For the briefest moment I forgave myself for not seeing through him.

'Who made you pregnant, River?' asked Piper, as he

crunched his knuckle bones with barely repressed fury. I couldn't remember seeing him angry before and was petrified for Joe.

'I can't tell you,' River responded quietly. I felt so terrible for her. It was all so humiliatingly public. I remember Aida explaining how the Haven was a place where joys and sorrows were shared equally, but it hadn't occurred to me that this meant the sorrows would be dissected so publicly.

'You have to tell us so I can kill him,' shouted Piper. He was beside himself.

'Who is the father of the baby?' asked Kaia. Her tone was gentler and kind.

'I don't want to say,' whispered River.

'Why not?' One Way Will pressed her.

'I don't want to create problems for anyone.' She didn't look up. I glanced over at Joe, who looked totally shell-shocked.

'You don't need to shoulder this on your own,' pointed out Magnus.

'Rather than pressuring River to deal with this on her own, why doesn't the father of the baby help her by sharing responsibility and telling us himself?' suggested Kaia. Everyone banged the floor to express approval. This was followed by a hideous vacuum where no one spoke and everyone, apart from me and River, mentally drew up a list of potential culprits. The only man close to River in age was Joe, which must have made for uncomfortable thoughts about the other men in the room. The silence weighed heavier and heavier. Joe sat completely still staring at his toes.

'Truth is courage,' said Sylvie. Still, no one spoke.

Then Mo unexpectedly picked up the talking stick and stood in the centre of the circle.

'He is the father of the baby!' He pointed at Joe. 'It's the outsider.'

My insides turned over.

'What evidence do you have for such an accusation?' asked Piper, shakily.

'I don't like to betray a confidence,' said Mo, 'but in this case collective honesty is more important than protecting an individual.' He paused. 'Cassia told me a couple of weeks ago, the day we went hunting together.'

There was an explosion of outrage as people digested this revelation. The energy in the room took on a menacing edge. That was the moment when I began to feel properly scared for Joe and myself. I would never forget the look on his face when he understood the scale of my betrayal. It was the same stiff, contorted expression he'd worn on the night when he'd been shot at with the crossbow.

'Cass!' River cried out. 'Why did you tell him that?' She snared me in her gaze. Her eyes were filled with tears. A wave of shame washed over me.

'This is bullshit,' shouted Joe. 'Tell them, River! Tell them it's bullshit. It's not me!'

River stared at the floor, her hands covering her face.

'Aida was right. It was a mistake to allow outsiders into our community,' said Mo. He pressed his hands together and bowed his head. 'Heartfelt apologies. You need to leave right now,' he said, pointing at Dad and me. 'Joe stays with us until we sort this out.' I looked at Dad, waiting for him to protest. But he didn't even glance at Joe. He simply got up and walked out of the Spirit House. I hesitated for a moment. The community circled around Joe.

'Go!' Piper yelled at me. I had no choice but to leave too.

27

Now

There's the lightest dusting of snow later that night but almost no wind. I keep myself warm by dressing in every bit of clothing Aida has given me: two pairs of trousers, three jumpers, three pairs of socks and an extra jacket. This roly-poly version of me climbs into my sleeping-bag and wraps the tarp around it tightly. I turn on Joe's phone. Another message lands. *Eyes right. You'll see me.* I hold out for as long as I can. I'm sure Mo is fucking with my head. But my paranoia about where he is gets the better of me. I stand up, scan the darkness below and spot a light flashing in an area to my right just north of the growers' settlement. It flashes on and off ten times. He's trying to draw me out. It's what all good hunters do when their prey goes to ground.

Minutes later another message pings in. *Knew u wouldn't be able to resist, Cassia.* I shudder and blame the cold night air. It's not possible he's figured out where I am. But he's freaking me out all the same. After this, it takes all my will-power to stay in the same place. He's banking on me giving myself away by moving on. But as long as I don't shift from the granite escarpment I'm not visible. Besides, I'll hear him coming even if I can't see him. I hold steady and drift in and out of sleep, sheltered in the overhang between the giant granite rocks with only the black-throated bats for company. It's the coldest night yet and it feels like a triumph when dawn breaks and I can still feel my feet.

At first light, I pack up, then scramble down the snarly rockface. My resolve is absolute. I need to find Mo. Before he finds me. Almost right away I come across fresh tracks leading away from the escarpment into the oldest part of the forest. But when I bend down to examine them it's obvious to me they don't belong to Mo. Haglöfs boots have a unique zigzag sole and the only person with a pair of Haglöfs at the Haven is Dad. I wait to feel relieved but instead my body hums with fear. I haven't allowed myself to think about Dad. I haven't worried about him. And I don't want him to invade my thoughts now. He churns up too many confused shadow-side emotions. Finding his footprints unnerves me for different reasons too. It's unlike Dad to be so careless. He was always good at covering his tracks.

Half wondering if he'll lead me to Mo, I start trailing him. His right print is deeper than his left and I guess he's got the Remington over his shoulder. He makes a ton of errors. Not bothering to dig a cat hole for his shit is basic; throwing the ends of his roll-ups onto the ground is dumb; choosing the snowiest route is plain stupid, especially when the print of his boots is so distinct. I focus on hiding my own tracks, finding the iciest route, doubling back a couple of times to throw off anyone trying to follow me, and when the snow gets deeper, I put on the snowshoes Aida gave me. Judging from the frantic barking, I guess the police must be on the lakeshore close to the growers' settlement.

At first, I feel smug. I imagine humiliating Dad for his mistakes in the same way he used to humiliate us. But when I pause to eat a can of tomatoes for breakfast it occurs to me as I down the last dregs of juice that I'm the idiot because in my arrogance I'm only focusing on how Dad is behaving, rather than why. My mind races. His carelessness isn't because he doesn't know how to avoid being followed. It's because he doesn't care. I keep moving. As the terrain gets rockier, the tracks veer sharply to the right. He's heading deep into the ancient forest towards the far eastern limit of the Haven, where Juan kept his rarest bees. Of course! He's after Juan. I remember Wass mentioning something about red scratches and bumps on Mum's arms. Panicky thoughts collide. What if the marks are bee stings rather than scratches and Mum and Maudie are hiding out with Juan? The idea that Dad might find them together is terrifying. There are still some gaping holes in my memory, but Dad's corrosive jealousy of Juan isn't one of them.

I pick up pace until I'm running at a half-jog and cut back down the slope away from Dad's tracks into the narrow gully that meanders up the hillside to the glade where Juan kept his European bees apart from the rest. It's a tougher route because the slope is steeper and the ground more uneven. But I need to get to the hives before Dad does to warn Juan he's on his way.

From a distance the hives look like cosy little chalets in a miniature alpine village. Each one is identical to its neighbour. Hidden behind them among the trees is a small wooden hut where Juan keeps his equipment. I lean against a tree to catch my breath and cock my head to listen for any suspicious noises. It's so eerily quiet that all I can hear is the sound of my heart beating. I scan the clearing and, to my total shock, I spot Mum, then Juan

339

and Maudie. Drifting between the hives, ghostly figures in the early-morning mist. My chest feels as if it's going to implode. Juan and Mum work in serene purposeful silence, carefully lining up the hives in a sheltered area close to the treeline on the south side of the glade, probably to protect them from the storm that's rolling in. And then a moment of grace. I see Maudie, walking around, fixing surrounds to the door of each hive to make the entrance smaller, so the bees don't get cold. She's only using one hand, but otherwise she looks good. Judging by their dirty faces and grubby layers of coats, scarves and trousers, I guess they've been hiding out for a while too. Lightheaded with excitement, I surge forwards and call out to them in a low whisper.

Mum spins round. Her face crumples. She puts a gloved finger to her lips and burns towards me, arms outstretched, and holds me tight. When I pull away my cheek feels wet.

Maudie burrows into my side and gives me a one-armed hug. 'Where have you been? We thought you were dead.'

'We looked for you everywhere, Cass. It's like you disappeared into thin air,' says Mum. She takes a step back and her smile slips as she spots the blood on the hood of my jacket.

'What's that?'

'It's not as bad as it looks.' I quickly reassure her.

She pulls down the hood and inhales sharply when she sees the deep gash across my head.

'Oh, my God! Who did this to you?'

'I don't know. I think I was in a fight. I can't remember . . .'

We cling to each other. Juan approaches and leans over to take a closer look.

'Who stitched you up?'

'The first time I did it myself. But it got infected so I went to Aida and she healed it with pine resin and stitched me up again.'

'Is Aida okay?' Juan's tone is urgent.

'She's back in her container.'

'*Que alivio.*' He sighs with relief.

'And Joe?' I ask.

'He was with us at first after we fled the cabin but he was too worried about River so he went to look for her,' says Mum, quietly. 'We haven't seen him since.'

'What happened to Joe, it's all my fault, Mum,' I blurt out. 'I was the one who told Mo it was Joe who made River pregnant.'

'That's for later,' whispers Mum.

'How did you find us?' asks Maudie.

'I came across Dad's tracks. I've been trailing him since dawn. I think he might be on his way here.'

'Is he alone?' asks Juan. I nod.

'If Rick knows where we are, we need to get out of here right now. Go and fetch your stuff, Maudie.' Mum's voice is tight. She's already moved into a different gear.

But we're all out of time. There's a commotion in the bushes behind us. A sort of scuffling sound. We turn towards the noise. Dad pushes through the brambles, oblivious to the way they claw at his trousers and lacerate his legs. We see him before he sees us. He looks ravaged. His hair is a tangled mass of muddy knots; his beard has eclipsed most of the features on his face, apart from his wild eyes and the angry crevasses on his forehead. His clothes are stiff with mud and dirt. He breathes unevenly. Despite the chill he's only wearing a T-shirt. I remember his final superpower was being immune to the cold. My stomach snarls up.

'Hello, Rick,' says Juan, calmly, as if we've all been expecting him.

'Get away from my wife, you cunt,' Dad hisses feverishly. His jaw is granite hard. Maudie presses herself into Mum's side until she's fused to her, like the two beech trees by our cabin. I glance over at Juan. His face remains impassive, even when Dad removes the rifle from his shoulder. Mum pushes forward.

'No!' screams Maudie, wrapping herself around Mum, like a vine, so she can't get closer to Dad.

'How about I fix you something to eat, Rick?' Mum asks, as if we're back in the kitchen of our old home. She takes Dad by the arm and attempts to steer him towards the shed. Amazingly he doesn't resist.

'I've finally reached a higher plane, Eve,' he says, suddenly expansive. 'I feel no hunger. No cold. No tiredness. I've escaped the boundaries of my limited existence. My potential is infinite.'

'That's great news, Rick,' says Mum. It's a while since I've seen her doing balm for the soul and I hate it because it reminds me of all the energy she's wasted in trying to appease him over the years. 'Why don't you sit down and tell me all about it?' I notice Juan slowly backing away towards the trees with Maudie. Crack! A twig breaks. We all jump. Dad's focus instantly swivels from Mum to Juan and Maudie. It's like he can only focus on one person at a time. T-shirt billowing in the breeze, he strides towards Juan, who steps away from Maudie. I don't understand how he can't feel the cold.

'You've been sniffing around my wife from the moment

you met her,' rages Dad. He spits out the words as if they're rotten. But it's him that's rotten.

'I found them in the woods. Maudie was in a bad way. She could hardly walk,' Juan explains.

'Juan saved my life, Dad,' says Maudie. 'He put honey from these bees on my burnt arm and it got rid of the infection.'

It's such an innocent comment, but Dad takes it all the wrong way.

'You've turned my own daughter against me!' he yells. He lunges at Juan and punches him square in the face. When Juan doesn't react, it infuriates him even more and he hits him again. This time Juan falls onto his knees, blood streaming from his nose onto the snowy ground. Dad kicks him in the stomach. Juan groans. Mum and I try to drag Dad off him, but he seems to possess superhuman strength. He shoves Mum and she stumbles over. Sobbing, Maudie tries to help her up.

'Mo told me everything.' Dad steps towards Juan and jabs him in the chest with the barrel of the gun.

'What's everything?' asks Juan.

'He told me about you and Eve using the bees as cover to spend every minute of the day together. I know how you fuck her in that shed and while you fuck you wish me dead. I saw it in a vision.'

'Stop it, Rick,' says Mum, sharply. 'You've got it all wrong.'

Dad turns to her. 'You disgust me.' His eyes are cold. 'You've been fucking around with him behind my back all the time you've been here.'

'Mo is using you to get rid of anyone who stands in his way. Can't you see?' She's shouting at him and her voice echoes through the forest.

343

I don't think I'd realized how much I hate Mo until that moment. He'd manipulated Dad, like he'd manipulated me. He knew all our weaknesses. People like to preach peace, love and forgiveness but there's purity in hatred that gives clarity of thought.

'There's nothing going on with me and Juan. We're friends. Nothing more. I promise.'

Dad grabs Mum around the waist and starts trying to half pull her towards the beehives. 'It's time to go, Eve,' he says. 'I know what's going on and you're coming with me.'

Juan walks towards them. 'That's not happening, Rick.'

Dad lets go of Mum and points the rifle at Juan. Mum places herself in front of Juan, like a human shield. Dad holds the Remington at waist height, like they do in the movies, rather than nestling the stock in his shoulder, like Mo taught me. I hear the safety click off so he's now pointing the gun at Mum. I scream. Maudie runs at Mum.

'No!' I yell. I grab my little sister and hold her back. Everything is happening at super-speed. There's no time for any of us to react. Dad's eyes glaze. He pulls the trigger. There's a huge blast. Maudie cries. Juan yells. Mum and I are screaming. Anyone within a ten-mile radius must be able to hear. I look round in confusion. All of us are still standing apart from Dad. There's no blood. And then I see that Dad has toppled backwards onto one of the hives. Because he wasn't holding the gun properly the kickback has thrown him off balance. The loaded Remington lies on the ground just in front of him. I kick it out of his reach.

'Help me, Cass!' he whispers. 'Help me!' He stretches an arm towards me. It's covered with sleepy-looking bees. They're already crawling over his neck, his face and in his hair. He feels one on his cheek and swats it away. 'Ouch!' he cries. 'It's got me!' I frantically pick them off. But Dad is engaged in full-scale warfare against the lethargic little drones.

'Don't make them angrier, Dad, or they'll sting you even more,' I plead. 'The reaction will be worse this time.' More bees appear. He aggressively tries to slap them away and slides to the ground writhing in agony as they sting him. The more infuriated he gets, the angrier the bees become.

'Stop, Rick,' begs Mum, as she tries to grab at his arms.

'Stay still,' Juan instructs him. 'They sting worse in winter.' Dad ignores him. Maudie attempts to sweep away the bees with her good hand. But as fast as she picks them off, others arrive to take their place.

'They won't hurt if you stay calm,' Juan appeals. 'They only act in self-defence.'

'Can't see,' mutters Dad. His eyelids and lips are horribly swollen.

'Dad!' I catch his left arm mid-windmill and interlace my fingers with his. 'I'm begging you, please let us help you.'

A terrible sound, like a giant sob, comes out of his mouth. 'I'm sorry,' he whispers. His mouth is swelling. He seems to relax slightly. He's still thrashing around but his movements are becoming less violent and more sluggish. After a few minutes, he's still enough for Mum to take his pulse. 'We're losing him!' She's crying. I can see he's struggling to breathe. His arms are a pincushion of red raised bumps with tiny black stingers. Juan starts pumping Dad's chest. Mum leans over his mouth to see if she can feel his breath.

'Dad! Dad!' I yell. His breathing becomes more laboured and slower. Juan keeps pumping his heart.

'Don't leave us!' Maudie cries. Dad's lips are turning blue. I touch them with my hand and already they feel cold. Mum rests her cheek on Dad's chest. He's no longer moving.

'He's gone.' Mum breaks down. Maudie throws herself onto Dad. We all hug him. Finally, he belongs to us again. We're all crying. There are no words.

28

Then

I waited up for Joe to come back from the Spirit House all that night, trapped in a state of chest-crushing anxiety at the thought of what Mo might be doing to him, as well as the growing realization of my role in his undoing. But Joe didn't show up that night. Or the next morning. Mum refused to discuss his absence. I guessed she thought that drawing attention to it might create bad karma and somehow make it more real. Dad had gone walkabout. It still wasn't clear if he was planning to leave with us. But we didn't talk about that either.

Instead, Mum packed Joe's bags and put them by the door to underline the fact that his return was inevitable and non-negotiable. She insisted I got Maudie ready, even though Juan hadn't arrived with Gaia, and there was no way she'd make it to the road on foot. To keep Mum happy I bundled up Maudie in blankets and helped her to the bench in the porch. The hours dragged by. Still Joe never appeared.

'I can't believe we're finally going home,' wheezed Maudie, her old lady's chest barrelling up and down like an accordion. 'When exactly are we leaving?'

'As soon as Joe gets back.' I tried to reassure her, even though I was getting more and more concerned about why he hadn't appeared.

'Will I get to say goodbye to Skylar?'

'No,' said Mum, abruptly. There was no comeback from Maudie. I couldn't remember the last time she'd thrown a strop. The accident had taken all the fight out of her.

After a couple of hours of waiting around, Mum got out the sandwiches she'd made for the journey and the three of us sat outside on the bench and ate them in silence. By then I was properly on edge.

'It's going to be too late if Joe doesn't get here soon,' I muttered. After what had happened last night, I was desperate for us all to get away from Mo. The panicked bird started to agitate in my head again. I was his prisoner without anyone realizing that he held me captive. I almost wished I had some visible physical injury, like Maudie's arm, that would make people ask if I was okay and feel sorry for me. The worst part wasn't the way he didn't care about how he'd hurt me or the trauma he'd caused. It was that he didn't even think about me. I meant nothing to him. Dad was his ultimate prize. I was just a bonus.

'I don't care if we end up walking through the forest at night, we're leaving today,' pronounced Mum. She restlessly flitted about, zipping and unzipping bags, endlessly checking everything was packed.

'I'm with you, Mum,' I said.

'Why did you tell him?' she blurted out. 'It shows such bad judgement, Cass.'

She had her back to me, but she couldn't disguise the bitter chill of disappointment in her voice. I opened my mouth to try to explain but couldn't find the words. It was like I'd regressed to being a small child who lacked sufficient vocabulary to describe what had happened to me. But I took on board her criticism because it so closely mirrored how I felt about myself. I constantly beat myself up for getting into the situation with him, endlessly replaying what had happened, imagining how different choices could have led to different outcomes. I focused on the split-second decision to climb up the ladder to his tree-house and how I'd ignored my feelings because I wanted to please him. Even if I'd managed to explain to Mum that I only told Mo about River's pregnancy to save myself, there was nothing that could justify me exposing Joe as the father. That was 110 per cent my fault. Mum was right. My judgement was terrible.

'It was a mistake,' I whispered.

There was the occasional glimmer of self-forgiveness as it dawned on me that my relationship with Mo wasn't a fantasy I'd spun in my head. He'd dedicated the best part of six months to reeling me in, picking me up and dropping me to keep me in a constant state of needy confusion. I could see that now. No one had ever paid me that much attention or made me feel my opinions and feelings were special, so it wasn't surprising he'd dazzled me. But the moments when I blamed Mo for what had happened were tiny compared to the moments when I blamed myself.

'I'm sorry. This isn't your fault.' Mum sighed. She gave me a quick hug. 'It's the madness of this place. Mo has got to us all. We need to get out of here before something really bad happens.' I didn't have the heart to tell her that too many bad things had already happened.

Shortly after this, the wind picked up. The trees responded with creaks and groans of bossy disapproval. But it was the banks of cloud marching across the sky that really grabbed my attention. They hovered menacingly above the highest peaks of the mountains on the other side of the lake until eventually the whole sky turned dark.

'There's a storm coming,' said Mum, getting up to scan the forest for Joe and Juan.

Maudie was shivering, so I ended up taking her back inside. Dad finally emerged from his hole. 'The wind keeps blowing crap into my well,' he grumbled, as he hung his coat on the empty pegs. 'But I've hit the water table.' He triumphantly slammed a bottle filled with a brackish yellow liquid onto the table. 'What do you think?' he asked.

'Looks like piss,' I said unthinkingly. To my surprise he burst out laughing. Nothing seemed to touch him. River's pregnancy. Joe's absence. Maudie's fever. The wind picked up and the windows trembled in their frames.

'Will you give me a hand to close the shutters, please, Cass?' he asked.

His words were swallowed by a loud bang as a bedroom window blew against the outside wall of the cabin.

'Please close it,' begged Maudie, from Mum and Dad's bedroom. 'I'm so cold.' I followed Dad outside. There was something exhilarating about the weather. The wind was already fierce enough that it was a struggle to close the front door behind me and it needed both of us to secure the wooden shutters. Dad leant against them with his shoulder while I slotted a piece of wood across the top and bottom. I dragged the box containing Juniper and Jason back inside the cabin.

'Why are you doing that when we're about to leave?' Mum was at the door.

'It's a bit rough for rabbits out here,' I replied.

I couldn't bring myself to tell her it was obvious we weren't going anywhere. We stood in the porch. The wind whipped up more ferociously. Stuff flew by us. Leaves. Twigs. Wood chip from the composting toilet. In the distance, there were stampedes of thunder followed by volleys of lightning that illuminated the forest, showcasing my favourite landmarks. After Dad was hit in the face by a bird's nest we took refuge inside and piled our bags against the door to stop it blowing open. And then the rain started. It fell in straight lines, not drops, pounding the cabin with such ferocity we could barely hear each other speak.

'Everyone in our bedroom,' instructed Mum. We hunkered down together on the mattress beside Maudie. The shutters shuddered against the window and something smashed onto the roof.

'It's all fine,' bellowed Dad. Which meant it wasn't. 'All you have to fear is fear itself.'

Not true. I thought of Mo's hands squeezing my neck, and how my windpipe crumpled like a paper straw.

'What do you think is happening?' asked Mum.

'It's Nature taking her revenge!' I shouted back over the noise of the rain bulleting frantically onto the roof. That's what River would have said. If we were still friends. Thinking about her made me feel so mournful. Once River had understood how I'd betrayed her to Mo, she hadn't addressed a single word to me.

The wind roared louder. By this time, it was clear we were living through an extreme weather experience. There was a flash of light by the sink. A flame shot out of the gas pipe. It had been hit by lightning. I ran outside to turn off the valve on the canister. The wind tried to blow me off course in a barrage of furious gusts while the rain beat down on my back. I sealed the valve and rolled the canister indoors. There was another flash, and the lights blew.

'You're so brave,' whispered Maudie, when I came back inside.

Dad barricaded the door again and Mum put an arm around me. 'A true warrior!' she agreed. She was trying to make up for what she'd said to me earlier and I was trying to make up for betraying Joe. Her favourite child.

That was only the start. Over the next twenty-four hours the wind blew, and the rain came down relentlessly. With the shutters permanently closed, no light inside the cabin and the dark clouds outside, it was difficult to tell if it was day or night. All we could do was sit it out. Joe's absence loomed large. I couldn't stop thinking about the way Mo had disembowelled the deer and just hoped that Joe was safe and had managed to shelter in the settlement area with the rest of the community until the storm passed.

The following morning, we woke to an eerie silence. I ventured outside and saw the garden had turned into a watery brown bog, littered with twigs and leaves. A branch had struck the composting toilet and sliced off the roof. The shower enclosure had blown away, so we had to wash ourselves in buckets of water in the porch. Nothing fazed Dad. 'All adversity is opportunity,' he declared. 'This is a chance for us to discover our authentic selves.' It suddenly hit me that, in spite of all the destruction, Dad was happy because it meant we couldn't leave.

He instructed me to check the vegetable field behind the cabin to salvage anything that could be turned into a meal. It was a relief to be outside and feel the cool air on my face. When I reached the waterlogged field, I saw the topsoil had been washed away, unearthing a good amount of gnawed but edible vegetables, including carrots, onions and leeks. I collected them up. They were caked in mud, so I decided to rinse them in the stream that ran behind the field. As I got closer, I saw our once docile little stream had broken its banks and transformed into an angry torrent bullying its way through the forest. Trees and bushes that were once rooted to land had become aquatic. I examined the newly formed bank of this waterway and spotted a small blue mound just ahead to my right. I walked towards it, and as I got closer, I saw that it was a figure, lying on their side in the mud, wearing a blue sweatshirt and jeans. I knew right away it was Joe. Lightheaded with fear, I called Mum. She ran out of the cabin and scrambled across the muddy field towards us.

He was lying on his front with his eyes closed, his head turned towards the river. He didn't move or make any noise. His lip was bleeding and swollen. Mum and I knelt in the mud. We each looped an arm under his shoulders and between us somehow managed to haul him up the bank and into the field. We clumsily rolled him onto his side. I thumped him on his back while Mum furiously rubbed his chest.

'Come on, Joe, wake up!' I screamed in his ear.

'Tilt his head back, Cass, to keep his airway open!' yelled Mum. I saw that his nostrils and mouth were caked with mud. I put my finger on the inside of his cheeks and prised out small lumps of soil and tiny stones. I must have aggravated his gag reflex, because his chest heaved, and giant slugs of disgusting brown water and slime poured out of his nose and mouth. He started shaking uncontrollably. We pulled him up into a sitting position and threw our arms around him to warm him up. His skin was waxy and grey and he was thinner than I could ever remember.

'Cold,' whispered Joe. Mum and I sobbed, as all the pent-up stress poured out. It started to drizzle again. 'Cold,' Joe kept murmuring. 'So cold.'

'We need to get him indoors,' urged Mum.

I wrapped my coat around his shoulders and between us we helped him back across the field into the cabin. Maudie got out of bed when she saw Joe and helped us cover him with blankets until he stopped shivering. Mum tenderly kissed the scratches and cuts on his face while I made him lukewarm tea, which he drank in tiny sips, like a bird. For the first hour, he could hardly speak and then it was difficult to stop him. He kept repeating himself but the essence of what he said remained constant. They'd kept him in the Spirit House the first night, endlessly questioning him about River. Mo had taken control of everything.

'What did you tell them?' I asked.

'I told them River and I had never had a sexual relationship, that I knew nothing about her being pregnant and that I was as shocked as they were. None of them believed me, so Mo suggested they lock me up in the root cellar until I was ready to tell the truth. There was a huge row. They couldn't reach consensus. Juan insisted the Haven was all about compassion and forgiveness and that if there was no conclusive evidence I should be given the benefit of the doubt. Not everyone else agreed.

'Mo won the argument and locked me in the root cellar. He beat me up.' Joe slowly lifted his shirt. His torso was covered with horrible welts and bruises. It was too awful. I felt almost nauseous. It was my fault this had happened to him.

'If it wasn't for Juan, I wouldn't have made it. He helped me escape. Everyone else had disappeared. Juan said they'd probably fled to higher ground. He took me to the lake and gave me a canoe to come and fetch you. But the river was raging and I capsized. I've lost the canoe. Juan was so good to me.'

'Where is Juan?' asked Mum, her voice taut with emotion.

'He went to look for River on the other side of the lake,' said Joe. 'He thinks Mo has her.' This was the point where Joe started crying. 'She was there at the beginning,' he wept. 'Before the storm. Mo promised Piper and Sylvie he would find a way to get her to town. River didn't believe him and refused to go. But there was consensus, and because she'd broken the rules, she wasn't entitled to vote. It was awful. Piper and Sylvie decided Mo was her best chance. No one wants her to have the baby. She had no choice but to go with him.' His voice broke again. 'Why did you tell that psychopath it was my baby?'

'Because that's what River said. I'm so sorry.' I couldn't tell him the truth.

'Why is this happening to me?'

When Joe was able to put some weight on his ankle again, we returned to the river to search for the canoe. As we trudged along the bank, we realized, with growing disbelief, that we were surrounded by water. The river had encircled the field, the cabin, the outhouses and the surrounding woodland so we were now living on an island. Dad was ecstatic because it meant we were trapped.

'If you believe, the universe will make it happen!' he told us joyously. Joe and I looped around the river a second time. We finally found the canoe almost fully submerged in the water between a ragged clump of half-drowned bushes. The oars were missing and it had a hole in the stern. It looked like the same canoe Mo had used when we crossed the lake the morning after he had assaulted me.

'We'll have to fix the hole and wait until the water calms,' said Joe. 'Otherwise, we'll capsize or sink.'

'Maybe we can make oars from a couple of planks,' I suggested.

Joe agreed. 'The current will help carry us downstream to where the river feeds into the lake. If we're lucky, it'll take us all the way to that village where we saw the old lady. We're going to get out of here, Cass.' He gripped my hand.

Mum and Maudie backed the plan. We didn't include Dad and none of us interrogated this decision. The truth was he no longer belonged to us. He belonged to Mo. Maybe that sounds harsh but at the time it didn't make any of us sad in the way it should have. It was like we couldn't afford to waste energy on anything apart from working out how we were going to escape this nightmare.

Dad was galvanized by the flood. The rain had loosened the soil in his well and it had filled with water. As soon as he left with his spade in the morning we ran through our strategy. We agreed that once the river calmed, we would slip out of the cabin, while Dad was asleep, and take our chances in the canoe.

Joe and I would go in the bow and Mum and Maudie at the stern to even out our weight. This was the only part of the plan that Maudie disagreed with.

'I want to go in front,' she insisted.

'We need someone heavy to give us ballast,' I tried to explain. She wasn't convinced. Mum calculated we'd need enough food and water for four days. Since our supplies were dwindling, and Dad monitored every last grain of rice, this proved to be our biggest challenge. Mum prepared small plastic bags of anything from a skeletal first-aid kit to equipment we might need in an emergency and kept them hidden in the wooden panel behind the bed that Maudie now occupied.

In the end waiting for the river level to drop proved a big mistake. During one of the fever dreams caused by the infection in her arm Maudie fell asleep on the sofa and started to toss and turn and mutter in her sleep about the canoe.

'What's she talking about?' asked Dad.

'She's hallucinating,' said Mum.

'Hallucinations always have some basis in reality,' replied Dad. 'The diviner's sage highlights the pathway already chosen.'

Joe and I sat rigid with anxiety at the kitchen table, listening to this exchange.

'Where is this canoe?' Dad suddenly asked Maudie.

'Joe hid it.'

'She's having a nightmare. It's not fair to keep questioning her,' Mum interrupted.

'Where did this canoe come from?' Dad persisted.

'Juan gave it to Joe,' Maudie murmured. 'That's how he got here.'

I tried to breathe but it was as if the oxygen had been sucked out of the cabin. Dad abruptly got up. He started searching the kitchen, rifling through cupboards, clearing shelves and examining the boxes we kept under the sink. When he found nothing, he turned his attention to the bedrooms. He went from room to room, overturning furniture, dragging mattresses across the floor and ripping open the plastic bags where we kept our clothes. It was carnage. Every sound made me hum with anxiety and fear.

'She's just dreaming.' Mum tugged at his arm, but Dad

pushed her out of his way, like the angry river. He was manic. Maudie started crying. He went into their bedroom again and started banging and tapping the wooden wall panels. There was the sound of wood splitting as he ripped them off. Seconds later he raged back into the kitchen holding a plastic bag in each hand.

'What's all this?' He shook the bags in our faces. One contained the food Mum had managed to sneak out of the store cupboard, the other the first-aid kit.

'We want to go home, Dad,' I said calmly.

'This is our home,' he said with impassive stoniness. 'We're not going back.'

He steamed round the cabin, grabbing seemingly random items, a hammer, nails, a piece of tarp, then sped outside, slamming the door behind him. Before we could grasp what was happening, we heard Dad flick the bolt across and attach a padlock.

'You leave me no choice!' he bellowed.

'You can't do this, Rick,' cried Mum.

'You were going to leave without telling me,' wailed Dad. 'Only Maudie's on my side.' He started hammering and within minutes he'd boarded up all three windows from the outside.

'You've got to let us go!' yelled Mum. 'Maudie isn't well.'

'We're not going anywhere. It's not part of my plan for us.' His voice was calm, but it had a steely edge.

'What is your plan?' demanded Mum.

'To be rid of the bad energy in this family.'

He'd fully lost it. I thumped on the door. It was hopeless. There was no one to hear us.

Mum tried to calm Maudie, who now realized she'd

plunged us into a whole new crisis by unwittingly giving away our plans to Dad.

'Now what?' asked Joe, defeatedly.

That was when I knew we were screwed because Joe usually had all the answers.

Over the next few days a routine emerged. Dad let us out in the morning so we could go to the composting toilet and wash in what was left of the outhouse. He always carried Maudie. She was too weak to walk on her own and he still displayed sudden bursts of tenderness towards her, maybe because she was always his favourite, or he felt less betrayed by her because she'd let slip about the canoe. That was the only normal element of his behaviour. The rest was pure undiluted insanity.

'What's the end game here, Rick?' Mum repeatedly asked him.

'The spirit guide will show us the way.' Dad always gave the same response. He kept a bottle of water from his well with him at all times. He called it his elixir and said it had given him second sight that had helped direct him to the canoe.

'Now we can stay here together for ever,' he said feverishly.

We had no idea if he'd really found the canoe or was bluffing, but it crushed my spirit all the same. After we got back from our morning wash, he locked us in the cabin again and went to dig his well until dusk, when he came back to cook the only meal of the day, either vegetables he'd scavenged from the field or the pasta and tomato sauce that Mum had stockpiled. Dad always made something for Maudie, but not the rest of us. They say you can go for three weeks without food, but I can tell you that by day four it's really painful. My stomach cramped as if I was getting my period and a lot of the time I felt sick and lightheaded.

'Hunger is a state of mind,' Dad insisted, when Mum explained we were starving. His own face was gaunt and pinched, and his eyes were vacant, like he'd disappeared. She must have got to him because the next day he came back with a dead muntjac. It smelt rancid, and I guessed he'd contaminated the flesh during the gralloch.

'I can't eat it,' said Joe, even as his tummy rumbled.

'If you don't eat it, you don't eat.' Dad shrugged.

Joe tentatively cut a tiny slice of meat, closed his eyes, and put it into his mouth but almost immediately spat it onto the floor. Maudie didn't touch it.

'We can't go on like this,' Mum remonstrated with him. He didn't argue. He just stared at her with his empty eyes.

One day he made us a delicious stew with chopped carrots and onion. It was the biggest meal we'd had in days and even Maudie ate two platefuls. On our next trip to the composting toilet, I saw that Jason and Juniper were missing from their cage. I opened the cage door and although Maudie cried because she thought her beloved rabbits had escaped, at least she never realized she'd eaten them.

Like Dad, the rain didn't let up, although it was more of a constant cold drizzle. The damp seemed to seep out of every pore of the cabin. Maudie coughed her way through the night and kept us all awake so Dad slept in the forest and she became terrified that he might not come back.

'What happens if he disappears?' Maudie asked. 'Do we all die here?' I imagined us starving to death and someone finding our bodies years later. We had some crazy conversations during those long hours we were locked up in that cabin.

'As soon as the river goes down, someone will come and look for us and this will just be a bad memory,' said Mum.

'Everyone fled the day of the flood, apart from Mo,' pointed out Joe.

'How are we going to get out of here?' Almost all our conversations were circular and ended up with us asking the same question. Refusing to give up was what kept us going.

We tried digging under the floor by the outside walls of the cabin but there were too many tree roots. We used kitchen knives to scour the wood around the boarded-up windows. We even tried to batter down the door with a piece of wood.

Ten days or so after Dad had first locked us in the cabin I was in the kitchen when I noticed he'd dropped the flint and steel he used for lighting fires on the floor by the door. I showed it to Mum and Joe. 'If we create a spark, maybe we can light a fire inside and try to burn our way through the outside wall.'

'That's a crazy scheme,' declared Joe.

'You'll burn down the whole cabin!' said Mum.

'Has anyone got a better idea?' I managed a quick smile.

'You know it only takes a couple of minutes for a fire to spread,' Mum pointed out.

'We could fill all the pans with water and put it out if it gets out of hand,' suggested Joe.

The plan lifted our spirits because it gave us something new to focus on. The following morning, when Dad locked us in and left after breakfast to dig his well, we tried to figure out which was the thinnest section of the wooden walls and how we could create a big enough fire to burn a hole without suffocating ourselves in the process. These discussions helped pass the time. Our survival depended on our ingenuity. But our ingenuity depended on having enough food and water, and both were increasingly in short supply.

We lived like that for another couple of days, with the winter darkness closing in. By my calculation it was almost mid-November. The rains eased and we guessed that the river level must have dropped. We had no idea if Dad was lying about finding the canoe. But we were all in agreement. We couldn't wait any longer. We had to get out, even if it meant swimming across with Maudie. The stars had aligned. This was the moment.

As the stakes grew higher our nerves frayed. The night before we put our plan into action, Mum, Joe and I were still wrangling over crucial details. Our biggest worry was when to light the fire. It was obvious we couldn't navigate the fast-flowing river in the dead of night. But we needed to give ourselves enough time to locate the canoe and climb on board before Dad arrived to unlock the padlock in the morning. Joe was still limping badly and Maudie was too weak to walk on her own. So crossing the field and hiking through the strip of woodland until we reached the river would take much longer than it should. In the end we decided to make our escape just before dawn to give ourselves the best part of an hour of daylight to get ahead of Dad.

'How will we know the time?' worried Mum.

'The robin always sings then,' I said.

We hardly slept that night. We carefully built the fire at the bottom of the outside wall to the right of the door, where some helpful rodents had already gnawed a small hole. We used anything we could find, from bits of dry wood hacked from the kitchen table, to fluff and bird feathers. I tore the lace from Maudie's flamenco dress into strips, while she created a small bundle of tinder with hair from Hilda, her favourite plastic dog.

As soon as the robin started up, we all got dressed and wound damp T-shirts around our faces. Joe lined up the containers of water. Mum and Maudie crouched by the kitchen table. Mum gave the nod. I rhythmically struck the flint with the steel. Small sparks like tiny miracles fell onto the tinder. There was a gratifying hiss as it began to smoulder. I carefully placed the tinder at the base of the fire and gently blew on it.

It caught light faster than I could ever have imagined. In less than a minute the flames were licking up the bottom quarter of the wall. The smoke was overwhelming. It stung our eyes and filled the room until we could hardly see. Maudie coughed and spluttered. I was terrified Dad would wake up and see the orange glow from wherever he was hiding out at night.

Once the smoke became unbearable, Joe and I grabbed the saucepans of water and doused the burning wall. The fire hissed and spat in soggy protest as it was snuffed out. The wood was black and charred and still scorching when I began kicking at it with my leather boots, grunting and swearing under my breath, filled with rage and righteous anger. The rotting wooden cladding gradually began to splinter and a ragged hole to the outside world slowly opened up.

'Let's get out of here!' Joe barrelled through the hole and limped into the cold, shadowy landscape beyond. I went next and waited for Mum and Maudie to emerge. I closed my eyes for a moment and breathed the fresh air deep into my lungs.

I scanned the area around the damaged outhouse and toilet in case Dad had heard us. But I guessed he'd used the tarp to build a shelter further in the denser woodland beyond. I clumsily hoisted Maudie onto Mum's back, and the four of us edged along the narrow gully that ran around the outside perimeter of the cabin until we reached the field. We were almost in the middle when Maudie realized she'd dropped her plastic dog.

'I've lost Hilda,' she wailed.

'Quiet, Maudie,' urged Joe. It was now getting properly light and I was painfully aware how conspicuous we were.

'I can't leave Hilda,' sobbed Maudie. 'She's always with me.'

'We can't go back,' said Mum, gently, heaving her higher up her back. But Maudie was inconsolable. Her cries echoed through the still morning air.

'He's going to hear us,' warned Joe.

'Please find her, Cass,' begged Maudie. 'Please.' I glanced back across my shoulder. It would take me less than five minutes to retrace our steps to search for Hilda. Maudie's cries got louder. They were so soulful that it felt like she was crying for the sins of the world.

'I'm going back,' I impulsively decided. Maudie had been through so much and asked for so little. Perhaps I felt this was a way I could atone for the terrible things that had happened since I'd told Mo about River being pregnant. All this was my fault.

Mum tried to hold me back. 'I'll catch up with you,' I promised.

'Thanks, Cass,' snuffled Maudie.

I slowly went back across the field, scouring the ground for the plastic dog. But I couldn't find it. I headed up the narrow gully at the side of the cabin. *Nada.* I'd just reached the corner when I heard the sound of footsteps. I quickly pressed myself against the side wall of the cabin, rigid with fear.

'What the fuck!' yelled Dad. He must have spotted the smouldering hole in the front of the cabin. His anger filled the still morning air like a toxic vapour. My heart hammered in my head as I heard him unlock the padlock. The noise of furniture being kicked over came from inside.

'Maudie's gone,' he wailed pitifully. I almost felt sorry for him. *None of that, Cass*, I told myself sternly. *No more people-pleasing.* I needed to go back to the others to warn them we needed to get out of here right now. It took me a few seconds to realize Dad wasn't talking to himself.

'They've all gone!' said a different voice from the back of the cabin. I recognized it right away. *Lick, suck, swallow, bitch.* The words roared louder and louder in my head. I felt a hand grasp my shoulder. I turned round.

'Where are they?' Mo snarled, waving the plastic dog in my face. My whole body began to shake. I looked up at him and saw the sad watery eyes of the disembowelled deer staring back at me. I remembered his threat. If I said anything, that was what he'd do to me. My tongue felt thick in my mouth. I couldn't form words.

'You're coming with us,' said Mo, yanking me painfully by my arm. He dragged me into the vegetable field, eyes down, searching for our tracks.

'Come over here, Rick!' he called to Dad.

I glanced ahead scanning the field for the others, but they'd disappeared.

'Go!' I yelled, to alert them, in case they'd heard the commotion but were still waiting for me. 'Leave while you can!' Mo grabbed me, slapped his hand over my mouth and shook me so hard that I could feel my brain shudder and jolt inside my skull.

He dragged me through the strip of woodland towards the river. I saw the branches we'd used to camouflage the canoe scattered on the ground and a muddy furrow where it had been hauled into the water. They'd managed to get away. I felt a small surge of joy. Dad caught up with us.

'You go first with Cassia,' Mo instructed him.

Dad waded into the water, holding firmly onto my arm. It was deeper than I'd expected and quickly lapped at our thighs. I tried to reason with him.

'The others have gone. Please let me go. I'm scared of Mo. He hurt me.' He didn't respond or ask any questions. I changed tack, trying to appeal to him by reminding him of our life before the Haven. None of it landed. Instead he gave me a pitying look.

'You have to see beyond the distortions of the material world, Cass,' he said, almost sorrowfully. 'Look outside yourself and attune your consciousness to the infinite cosmic boundaries of our beautiful planet.'

'What's beautiful about helping Mo destroy the forest to grow weed?' I asked. This threw him. 'Or letting him destroy your relationship with Mum?' There was still some residual melting softness in his face when I mentioned Mum. He stopped for a moment in the middle of the river.

Mo glanced at us and frowned when he saw Dad's expression. 'Hurry up, Rick!'

'We all know he's working with the growers. I saw you with him,' I told Dad. 'He's using you to do his dirty work. There is no higher spiritual calling.' Dad put up his hand and struck me across the face. But the force of the blow sent him off balance and he fell into the water. He floundered on his back for a moment. The current started to carry him downstream. He tried to stand but the water was too deep. I felt Mo grip my arm. He dragged me out of the river.

'It's just you and me now, Cassia.'

I scratched and clawed at his arms with my nails. Then I bit him as hard as I could on the hand.

'You fucking bitch!' His fingers unfurled and I slipped out of his grasp and staggered back towards the river. I had no plan beyond throwing myself into the water and letting the current take me downstream.

'You don't truly believe you're going to get out of here alive?' He laughed, as he chased me down. I felt something hit my head. Thud. Then the same sensation again but this time with more force. It was a dull sound, but the pain was excruciating. I put up my arm to protect my head. I stumbled. Suddenly I was in the air. Except I wasn't flying, I was falling.

When I looked up the sky was lit with thousands of tiny gold stars that flickered and shimmered. It would almost have been beautiful if it wasn't for the pain. That part was like razor wire being knotted around my head. I felt something damp drip down my face and guessed it was blood. And then the light faded, and I was sucked into a black hole.

Somewhere in this liminal state, I felt something pulling at my feet. I tried to protest but I couldn't even form the words in my head, let alone open my mouth. The pulling got more insistent and I felt myself being dragged across the cold snowy ground. It was a horrible stop-start of snarling limbs. Each time my body jerked, the razor wire tightened around my head. But the pain was good because it gave me a purity of focus that obliterated all other thought. Eventually I felt someone lay me out on a softer, springier piece of ground. I felt tugging at the zip of my jeans. I tried to twist away from the rummaging hands, but I couldn't move. They pulled off my waterlogged trousers as if they were skinning a dead rabbit, then stretched my arms above my head to remove my T-shirt. I tried to shout. I couldn't fight. *Just get it over with. I'm done here.*

My eyes flickered . . .

When I opened them again everything was red. The sky above. The branches of the trees. A girl held my gaze for an instant, then began tenderly dressing me again. 'Lila?' She nodded.

29

Now

The helicopter is back doing its thing and the dogs are closing in. The gunshot and the noisy chaos that followed have left us exposed. It won't be long now before Wass and Kovac get here. I glance down at Dad, struggling to absorb what has happened. He's lying on the same patch of snow where he fell. His body is covered with dead and dying bees. His puffy blue eyes stare up at the milky sky and his swollen mouth is open as if he's about to make one of his pronouncements. I half expect him to sit up and declare that coming back from the dead is his new super-power. But he's more peaceful than I've seen him in ages. I hug him to me. He's warm but his raging heart is finally still. Everything changes in that moment.

'Bye, Dad,' I whisper. Juan closes his eyelids.

'He was going to kill Mum,' sobs Maudie, in disbelief. She's shaking uncontrollably and refuses to turn round to look at him.

'He was no longer himself.' Mum wraps her arms around Maudie. 'He'd become someone else.' Even in my grief I know this is only partially true. Late Dad was an iteration of early Dad. But the catalyst for change was Mo. It was Mo who saw the darkness in him and turned him into something truly dangerous to his own family. When I think of Mo now, I no longer feel afraid. Instead, it's like I have ice in my heart.

I watch as Mum tenderly covers Dad with a filthy blanket. She tucks it in carefully as if he's just fallen asleep and kneels beside him, head bowed, then gently kisses his forehead. 'I walked as far as I could with you,' she says, weeping.

I put my arm around her. 'You did everything you could, Mum. No one could have tried harder.'

Juan hacks off low-hanging branches from the surrounding pines and lays them over Dad's body. I get out my knife and do the same. I'm not sure why, but it feels like the right thing to do. The voices in the distance are getting closer. The dogs are hysterical with excitement. Juan explains that he must leave before the police arrive. They will want to interview him, and he doesn't want that exposure. Instead, he'll join the rest of the community in the northern sector of the forest.

'We've gone into hiding there before. Sometimes for months at a time,' he reassures us. There's no suggestion we go with him. He embraces each of us one last time and slips into the trees. He leaves no trace. It's as if he never existed.

I need to get going too. I'm terrified of what Mo could do to Joe. I put on my backpack and sling Dad's rifle over my shoulder.

'Please don't leave us.' Maudie clings to me.

'Let the police track him down,' pleads Mum. 'That's their job.'

'And even if they find him, what will they do?' I ask. 'They'll let him go because no one will be able to prove he's done anything wrong. He'll lie and try to pin everything on Dad. You don't know what he's capable of. No one knows how he works like I do . . .'

My voice trails off.

Mum puts her hands on my shoulders and traps me in her gaze. 'Did he hurt you, Cass? Tell me, did he hurt you?' I look away. I can't bear to tell her the truth because it would be like I'm allowing him to hurt Mum too. The voices get louder. I cock my head and cup my ear to listen. Someone calls our names.

'Isn't that Cara?' asks Mum in confusion. There's been no time to explain anything to her. Different voices call us. Wass and Kovac are with her too. I take advantage of her distraction to leave: it's time to split.

I'm not just doing this for Dad, I'm doing it for everyone Mo has ever hurt. For Joe. For Aida. For Morden Spilid. For me. I edge back into the trees and start to run. The Remington lies across my back and my feet seem to glide across the snowy landscape. When I glance over my shoulder, there are no tracks. I'm content to be alone again. That's my superpower. My movements are instinctive, my breath steady. I belong to the forest. My plan is to head upstream onto higher ground where the oak and beech give way to the sheltered gloom of the pine forest. I'm guessing Mo will be looking for somewhere to sit out the blizzard brewing in the sky above. Thick clouds with a pink tint hang low in the sky and soon it's snowing again. Big fat flakes that muffle sound and turn everything still and silent. As I get to the bottom of the slope, I listen out for the hyperactive gurgle of the river, but there's not even a whisper. When I reach the bank and peer over the edge I see why. It's frozen solid like the lake.

I trudge uphill along the bank of the icy riverbed, stopping once to rehydrate. I'm too filled with nervous energy to eat. The higher I climb, the lower the temperature dips.

The voices and the noise of the dogs get quieter. I'm completely focused on what lies ahead. I look for signs of carelessness. Snapped branches. Cat holes. Broken ice. And then I find it. The bloody pelt of a dead rabbit lying in the snow. I can tell from the single perfectly clean cut through the stomach that it's been expertly skinned. There are prints in the snow leading away from it. Evenly spaced, oval, in a perfectly straight line. I follow them up the bank and into the dense woodland.

I'm closing in on him. I look around and see a small but obvious gap in the undergrowth. The branches and twigs have been snapped and there's a small track that looks as if something heavy has recently been dragged along it. I remove the rifle from my shoulder and hold it across my body, barrel pointing down, finger resting on the safety.

I slowly edge through the forest, hyper-aware of my surroundings. I can feel that he's close. The snow falls heavier and covers my tracks within seconds. Through the trees, about ten metres in front of me, I see a figure dressed in layers of clothes, trying to light a fire. It's him. And then it happens again. The sensation of the hands around my neck, the gold ring, the feeling that I'm drowning. But this time when I look up at the circle of light, those flashes of memory don't atomize: they merge together, and I see Mo's face. I step forward, away from the fear, away from the sensation of not being able to breathe.

Just behind him is a small shelter, hidden among the trees, constructed from branches, deadfall and logs with a tarp on top. It's almost an exact replica of the one he built at Maudie's birthday party. I see myself at that party and realize I am no longer the same person, but I don't dislike who I have become. I crouch and watch Mo attempt to balance a pan of water on the fire.

'We've been expecting you, Cass,' he says, without turning round. 'You did well to find us.'

We. Us. He immediately throws me off balance. Keeping my head completely still so I hold him in my sightline, I scrutinize the area around him to check he's alone and step forward a couple of paces to show him I'm not scared.

'I know who you are.'

'Why so serious?' He laughs.

'You go by the name of Morden Spilid.'

'And what of it?'

'He's a Danish man you killed in Spain . . . You stole his identity.' It's a shot in the dark.

'He left me no choice,' says Mo. 'He threatened to report me to the police. He accused me of raping a woman.' There's no pleasure in being right. He points back towards the shelter. In the corner of the hide, I see a small figure crouched on the ground.

'Come here, River,' he orders. River crawls out and stands up with her hand protectively folded across her stomach. Apart from the soft roundness of her belly, she's gaunt and frail.

'I couldn't let anything happen to our baby,' Mo rasps. He puts his arm around River. He's done it. He's managed to disarm me. He's enjoying my discomfort. I look at River in confusion.

'It's not Joe's baby,' she says. 'Your brother was trying to help me escape from the Haven. But he never knew I was pregnant. You were the only person I told.'

'You said that Joe told you to get the pregnancy test!'

'It was a lie. So you wouldn't guess the truth.'

The saucepan lurches precariously on the fire and Mo scrambles away from us to right it. River steps towards me. 'Mudder threatened to kill me if I told anyone about our relationship,' she whispers. 'It was safer for me if you thought Joe was the father.'

My throat jams at the truth of what she's saying and there's a roar inside my head. I'm not the only one. I choke my emotions back down because I have to be strong for River. 'Did he hurt other girls at the Haven?' I know the answer already. She nods and stares down at the ground. I feel her shame because it mirrors my own.

'Did anyone else know?'

'Lila sensed he was a shadow-side person,' says River. 'That's why she started making the dolls, to protect other girls from him. But she couldn't. He gets into everyone's head. He's stronger than all of us.'

She explains how Lila put together the dolls in the van using real hair and clothes that belonged to girls she thought were at risk from Mo. She drilled a small hole to represent their vagina and knotted a red thread coated in blood through the hole. If Mo had raped one of these girls, she undid the knot. There were four dolls without a thread in the van.

Mo grips her arm again and River falls silent.

'We're building a tribe out here, Cassia, and now you can be part of it too,' says Mo. 'You can live with River and me.'

'The police will be here any minute,' I tell him.

'No, they won't.' He laughs again. 'You'll have made sure that no one can follow you. You're a natural. One of us. I told you that at the beginning.'

'Shoot him, Cass,' orders River.

374

This unnerves him. He grabs River around the neck and pulls her tight against him.

'Here's what's going to happen,' I say coolly. 'You're going to let go of River and she's going to come and stand behind me. Then you're going to kneel on the ground with your hands behind your head.'

'Here's what's going to happen,' he mocks me. 'You're going to drop that rifle and give it to me.'

I point the Remington at Mo, but he's holding River right in front of him like a human shield. He laughs scornfully again, 'You won't hurt River. You're not a killer, Cassia. You lack that killer instinct. I saw it the day we went hunting.' He tightens his grip around River's neck.

'Walk into your fear, Cassia,' he mocks me.

'Kill him,' River orders. She's completely calm.

'I can't get him without hurting you.'

'If you let him go, we'll never be rid of him. We'll always be scared.' She stares at me and nods. 'Do it for all the other girls he'll hurt.'

He pushes towards me.

'He won't ever stop, Cass.'

I push the stock into my shoulder and squint through the front sight to gauge if I can get a clean shot of Mo, but it's impossible.

'Just shoot,' says River.

I know there's four rounds in the chamber because I did the checks. I try not to think about the baby in her belly. I wish I could close my eyes so that later, when I look back on what I've done, I can't see it.

'I love you, River.'

'I love you too.'

I click off the safety and use my index finger to pressure

the trigger. Mo looks me in the eye. There's a strange noise. A whooshing sound and then a thud. River stumbles into me but Mo falls sideways onto the snowy ground. A red stain seeps into the snow and I see the bolt from a cross-bow lodged in his spine.

My brother steps out of the trees with Lila.

'It's over,' he says. 'It's over.'

Acknowledgements

I owe a big debt of gratitude to my amazing editor, Clio Cornish. Every draft of this novel has benefitted from her impeccable advice and insights. Thanks also to all the other Penguin people who have helped so much along the way: Ciara Berry, Clare Bowron, Jennifer Breslin, Emma Henderson, Hazel Orme, and Phillipa Walker. To Jonny Geller and Viola Hayden and the wonderful team at Curtis Brown, who make the long journey from concept to publication feel possible, I am truly grateful. And, finally, to my first readers: Maia Simpson-Orlebar, Gabby Turner, Sally Bruce-Lockhart and Louise Carpenter, no thanks are big enough for the ruthless edits.

Loved **The Haven**?

Read on for an extract of **The Betrayals**

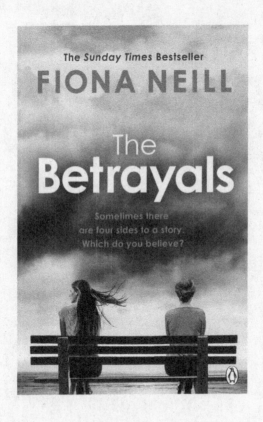

The *Sunday Times* Bestseller

FIONA NEILL

The
Betrayals

Sometimes there
are four sides to a story.
Which do you believe?

WHICH BOOK WILL YOU READ NEXT?

I

Daisy

Three is a good and safe number. I close my eyes and whisper the words three times so no one can hear. They sound like a sweet sigh. If Mum notices she might worry and *the days of worry are over.* I say this three times too, just to make triple sure, remembering how the words have to be spoken on the outbreath.

As I exhale, cold air blows in through the letter box into the hallway, making it flap against the front door. *An ill wind, ill wind, ill wind.* I look round to check Mum is still in the kitchen and bend down to examine the letter on the doormat, even though I recognized the large attention-seeking scrawl the instant it landed. Why, why, why is she writing to Mum after all these years? I don't touch it. Yet.

I hear Mum giggling. It's always a great sound. I can tell she's on the phone to my brother, Max, because he's so good at making her laugh. Much better than me. Even when I tell her entertaining stories about the Russian boy I'm tutoring or something that's happened at uni, there's caution in her response – as if she still doesn't dare trust in my happiness. Parents are the worst for holding you prisoner to the person you used to be. Or rather Mum is. Dad stopped being the resident jailer a long time ago.

I used to accuse Mum of being neurotic but now I understand that Dad's cool was a way of avoiding responsibility. Besides, it's in his interests to believe in happy endings and new beginnings because he got his.

Mum has an uncanny ability to notice tiny changes in me. She's like a meteorologist for my moods, collating and crunching information to predict subtle shifts in patterns. And she rarely makes mistakes. But, as she used to tell me back in the days when nothing was solid and reliable, you learn more by the things you get wrong than the things you get right.

I'm not sure I agree. If you are in Paris, for example, and you look the wrong way when you step out into the road you could get run over and even if you aren't killed you might end up quadriplegic. Generally death and disability don't provide good life lessons. If Max said that, Mum would fall around laughing. If I said it she would want to swab my soul for signs of impending darkness.

A big part of my mother's job is to observe people. She's a doctor, a breast cancer specialist, and she has spent years making sure that her emotions don't leach into her face. She's always trying to explain why empathy trumps sympathy. Patients need their doctor to appear under control, she says, especially when the news is bad. Any other response is self-indulgent. But I can tell when she's emotional because she chews the inside of her right cheek.

My attention returns to the letter. The inside of her cheek would be savaged if she saw this.

My mind is made up: it can't be ignored. I pick up the padded manila envelope and turn it in my hands, noting the following: 1) it is postmarked Norfolk, 2) she has written in baby-blue ink, 3) *truly, truly, truly a good and safe number*, she has included something heavy that feels like a small spoon. And 4) it is sealed with Sellotape. People only do that when they have given a lot of consideration to the contents. I also note that I make four observations rather than three. *Good work, Daisy*, I congratulate myself, although almost immediately I'm aware that counting is a retrograde step.

I head towards the shelf in the hall and randomly grab a hardback book that is big enough to conceal the envelope. Dust flies everywhere because Mum isn't the kind of woman who cleans to relax. It falls open on a well-thumbed page. 'Anxiety Disorders in Teenagers', reads the chapter heading.

Since Dad walked out on us when I was fourteen, Mum has become our responsibility. 'Look after your mother,' Dad always used to say when he dropped us back home from a weekend at his house after they split up seven years ago. Note I never called his house 'home'. The first time he said this, Max – who was only eleven at the time – told him to fuck off. He didn't like the implication that we didn't look after Mum, or the fact that the person saying it was responsible for causing the pain that meant she needed looking after. Dad told Max not to be so rude but it sounded half-hearted. And besides, Max had started crying as soon as the words were out of his mouth. Sometimes back then Dad cried too and I had to comfort him. Things have been calmer over the past four years. Or at least I thought they were. Until this letter.

I head into the toilet and lock the door behind me. It's designed so you can open it from the outside if necessary.

There are four holes above the lock where the old bolt used to be. I peer through one of these to check Mum is still in the kitchen. It's an old habit because I used to spend a lot of time in here: it was the one place no one could disturb me. At least I no longer check the lock three times. Reviewing myself in the mirror I see my face reflect the gravity of the situation back to me. When I'm emotional my lips always go cartoon rubbery. I run my finger across the hole at the bottom right-hand corner of the mirror where there is a tiny slice of glass missing. My fault. But let's not go into that now. The mirror came from the house in Norfolk where we used to go on holiday when we were children. 'Back in the day,' as Mum says breezily. She is all about living in the present. Even though she has spent the best part of a decade involved in the same clinical trial.

I turn my face from side to side to let the light fall on it at different angles and tousle my fringe and short dark hair in an effort to appear effortless in a French sort of way. Kit likes it like this. In fact, I think it's fair, if miraculous, to say that Kit likes pretty much everything about me. The timing of this parcel isn't great because he is about to arrive to meet Mum for the first time. She's been angling for an introduction since I first started going out with him eight months ago, but I wanted to wait until I was completely sure about him.

I close the loo seat and sit down. I'm not proud of what I do next. But who hasn't done the wrong thing for the right reasons at least once in their life? I honestly thought this would be the end of something, not the beginning. I carefully peel off the Sellotape and the padded manila envelope flaps open. I just knew Lisa wouldn't have licked it. She's as careless with things as she is with people. I breathe in and out, as deep as I can, one hand holding the envelope, the other resting on my diaphragm as it rises to make sure that my abdominal muscles are contracting properly on the inbreath. I know more about breathing than any yoga teacher.

In my defence I should say that at this moment I did try to reseal it with the same piece of Sellotape that I had peeled off a second ago. Privacy is a big issue for me. And there was no doubting who was meant to be opening it: *Rosie Foss*. It still surprised me to see Mum's surname because until my parents got divorced we all shared the same one. At the beginning Max and I made a big thing of this. We wanted to become Foss so she wasn't alone with her new name like she was alone with everything else. It felt strange to no longer have the same surname as my closest living relative but Mum argued, quite convincingly, that she had been Rosie Foss for most of her life before she married Dad and that at work she had always kept her maiden name. Max politely pointed out that just for the record, at thirty-nine years old, with two children, Mum most definitely wasn't a maiden. Mum had cracked up at this. Max doesn't have to try to be a light person. He was built that way.

I think about all this as I keep trying to stick the envelope back down. But of course Lisa has used cheap Sellotape. She's always dropping hints about how she and Dad don't have enough money, which annoys me so much because Mum has always worked so hard and Lisa hasn't had a job since she moved in with Dad. Part-time yoga teacher doesn't really cut it. Irritation makes me clumsy and the letter emerges tantalizingly from the top of the envelope so that I can see the uneven line of huge kisses beneath Lisa's signature.

I pull it out, taking care not to crease the flimsy paper. It's two pages long when it could have been one but Lisa's scrawl is big and confident, which is probably why I am even more surprised by what follows.

My dear Rosie,

I am writing to let you know that I have recently been diagnosed with Stage 4 breast cancer. (You know better than anyone that there is no Stage 5.) I thought the lump was a cyst or something left over from breastfeeding all those years ago. Do you remember those lovely, lazy days on the beach in Norfolk? But a recent biopsy proved otherwise and unfortunately the cancer has spread. I do not expect your sympathy. The reason for contacting you is simple: I want to see you one last time. I want to ask your forgiveness for the pain I caused you and tell you something that you need to know before it is too late. I am enclosing the key to the house so that you can let yourself in. I haven't told Nick about this letter and am increasingly too tired to get out of bed to answer the door. I have decided to keep my illness private for the moment and would be grateful if you could respect this final wish.

With fondest love, as always,

Lisa
XXXX

My emotions with regard to Lisa used to be pretty three-dimensional. Variations on the theme of animosity, angst and anger. Pretty textbook stuff. Since I met Kit, I have let go of the anger without even trying. As it pumps through my body again I realize that I haven't missed it. I can't stand the way Lisa assumes Mum will go running to her and cave in to her demands after everything that has happened. I even feel annoyed she has got breast cancer because that territory belongs to Mum. And then a further wave of rage that she has turned me into someone whose first response to a dying person isn't sympathy.

Why is she doing this after all this time? As far as I can see in my dealings with Lisa, she has never shown any signs of remorse for stealing Dad. But mostly I see this emotionally manipulative letter as a big threat to Mum's hard-won equilibrium. It will make her rake up the past and relive all the sadness and disappointment just so Lisa can feel better about herself. And I will do anything to protect Mum from harm. She is one of the most genuinely caring people that I have ever come across. She'll probably even try to help Lisa. Not that I want her to die, because then Max and I might end up having to look after Dad.

But just as quickly a new emotion takes hold. This is one I haven't felt for years. My skin feels clammy and my ribs no longer rise when I breathe. I'm properly anxious. Because I am as sure as shit that I know what Lisa is going to tell Mum.

I try to distract myself with the things that I don't feel: 1) sympathy for Dad, 2) sadness for Lisa, 3) regret at having opened the letter.

I try some breathing techniques but I can't focus, so I

allow myself a bit of tapping. Just three times on the bone below each shoulder. Repetitions in multiples of three. I stop at 21 because 24 is a multiple of a number I don't like. It helps. I don't need to do my toes, heel or the side of my foot. You have probably noticed a lot of my life now revolves around what I don't do rather than what I do. My ribcage settles.

'Daisy,' I hear Mum shouting. 'Can you get the door?'

Kit must have arrived. I look through the hole. Mum's halfway into the hall. With a wooden spoon in one hand and a packet of butter in the other, she looks uncharacteristically domestic. She doesn't notice when a sweaty lump of butter drops on the floor. For someone so well versed in infection control she is surprisingly slovenly around the house. Her bedroom floor is always littered with clothes and her toothpaste never has a lid. Max says she lives like a student. But I love her for it. 'Just coming,' I call back. She turns round and frowns at the toilet door, and I guiltily realize it spooks her because it reminds her of times past.

Judging by the black grains of rice that cover the spoon, she has reached what Max and I call 'the resuscitation of rice' stage of lunch. The smell of charred rice burning at the bottom of a pan that has run dry of water is to my childhood what the madeleine was to Marcel Proust. Actually, Dad said that. When they were still together and did funny banter. They split up in January 2008, almost exactly seven years ago, although according to Dad the marriage was over long before. I once asked Dad when it finished for him, and how come Mum didn't realize when she was living under the same roof. He said he couldn't recall the exact instant, which struck me as strange coming from a scientist who specializes in the nature of memory formation. I wish I were as good at forgetting as Dad. I remember everything.

I put the two sheets of paper face up on the toilet seat and take a couple of shots of the letter with my phone. I make a song and dance of flushing the loo and running water in the basin and put it all back exactly as I found it, except for one thing. I take out the key and slide it into the back pocket of my jeans. I'm not sure why I do this. Later Max pointed out that I had a thing about locking doors when I was ill. But I promise this is an impulsive rather than compulsive act.

Then I notice something else at the bottom of the envelope. It's an old photo of us all, taken in Norfolk, during the last holiday we spent together before the upheaval. When Mum and Lisa were still best friends. We are in the garden of the house where Mum grew up. 'My second home,' Lisa used to call it. Until it became her first home. Dad's part of the divorce settlement. There are fistfuls of irony in this story.

I have never seen the photo before. Lisa must have been running out of printer ink because it's sickly yellow. But it's not the colour that makes me feel queasy. I recognize the liverish lawn of my grandparents' house, dried out by the sun, and the garden shed in the background. It must have been taken on a timer because somehow all eight of us are in it. Mum and Lisa are centre stage, arms carelessly flung around each other, as though they are the married couple. Mum was fatter then. Lisa has always been thin. Mum is squinting at Lisa, whose eyes are shut, which is unfortunate because eyes are the windows of the soul and perhaps Mum would have known what she was up against if she could have seen into them at that moment.

Dad stands beside Mum but no part of his body is touching her. His right arm is around Max, who was probably ten when the photo was taken. His dark curly hair rests comfortably against Dad's thigh. Back then he loved Dad unconditionally. I am standing stiffly between Lisa's son, Rex, and his dad, Barney. I look tense because I was tense. Barney's hands are behind his back and his chest is puffed out so it appears as though he's standing to attention but he's probably hiding a beer can. His lopsided grin confirms my theory. Lisa's daughter, Ava, is on the edge of the frame. We used to be friends but not any more. After everything that happened, we were never going to make a model blended family. I touch Lisa's face with my finger and find myself scratching at it with my nail. Let it go, Daisy, Kit would say if he saw me. *Let it go.* But I can't. I keep scraping until she disappears. If I told him what happened he might understand. Because that was the summer my childhood stopped.

I come out of the toilet. Mum is offering Kit the hand that holds the spoon. He has the self-possession not to look alarmed. He's very calm, my man. Instead he deftly takes the spoon so they can shake hands.

'I'm Rosie,' says Mum, giving Kit the same reassuring but professional smile she uses on patients.

'It's so nice to meet you,' says Kit. His blond hair flops over his face, surfer style. He glances over to me and does that thing where he raises one eyebrow. That's all it takes. I realize this is meant to be one of those awkward moments but it really isn't. The good thing about having a super dysfunctional family is that there isn't a lot to live up to.

He just wanted a decent book to read ...

Not too much to ask, is it? It was in 1935 when Allen Lane, Managing Director of Bodley Head Publishers, stood on a platform at Exeter railway station looking for something good to read on his journey back to London. His choice was limited to popular magazines and poor-quality paperbacks – the same choice faced every day by the vast majority of readers, few of whom could afford hardbacks. Lane's disappointment and subsequent anger at the range of books generally available led him to found a company – and change the world.

'We believed in the existence in this country of a vast reading public for intelligent books at a low price, and staked everything on it'
Sir Allen Lane, 1902–1970, founder of Penguin Books

The quality paperback had arrived – and not just in bookshops. Lane was adamant that his Penguins should appear in chain stores and tobacconists, and should cost no more than a packet of cigarettes.

Reading habits (and cigarette prices) have changed since 1935, but Penguin still believes in publishing the best books for everybody to enjoy. We still believe that good design costs no more than bad design, and we still believe that quality books published passionately and responsibly make the world a better place.

So wherever you see the little bird – whether it's on a piece of prize-winning literary fiction or a celebrity autobiography, political tour de force or historical masterpiece, a serial-killer thriller, reference book, world classic or a piece of pure escapism – you can bet that it represents the very best that the genre has to offer.

Whatever you like to read – trust Penguin.